Polaris: Empress of Ning

Book Two of the Series

Han Bei   Shu Jin

寒備   屬金

ISBN-13: 978-0-9966338-1-9

Titles in the Series:
Polaris: Emperor of Nan Rong
Polaris: Empress of Ning
Polaris: The Demon General and the General Practitioner
Polaris Special: Dui's True Ending
Polaris: The Curse of Ice Blue Eyes

Polaris: Empress of Ning

By Lenne Penry

Polaris: Empress of Ning

Notice to Readers

If you've previously read *Polaris: Emperor of Nan Rong* and would like to skip ahead to the path divergence for Jin and Han Bei, please go to page 183.

Chapter 1: A Missing Monarch

"To the east, the elder star lies." A familiar tune bursts as I walk down the dirt road. It is late afternoon and the sun's vigor isn't as oppressive as it had been earlier so, I decided to return home. What a great day it was for fishing! I caught three large catfish! This should last for the rest of the week.

"The younger's name is Bao Lai! Pft! Ha-ha! What was that? That was way too shrill!"

Singing at the top of my lungs to test my terrible skills for the sheer fun has become a habit of sort, to stave off silence. It's a good thing no one's around to witness my embarrassment, or so I thought.

Without warning, the ground begins shaking and a few stones beside my feet jump as though scattered on a beating drum. When I look up, two horses are galloping hither at full speed. The men atop are clad in heavy armors decorated with unmistakable colors of the imperial army. What could soldiers possibly be doing in this secluded little area? Every succeeding, rapid thump of horses' hoofs peppering the road gives evidence that the fleeting thought is inconsequential. The men see me, I know they do, but there is no sign of them yielding. This little road is barely enough for them to ride side-by-side as they are. There is no room for me, too. They are going to run over me!

Every second they near, panic escalates. Without thinking, I dart for a gully to be out of their way. As luck would have it, my foot slips and I fall onto a thick thornbush. My precious fish are covered in dirt and my clothes and flesh are cut by the jagged thorns. Small amounts of blood begin trickling from my arms and back. Such as it is, I at least had my life.

The horses fly by where I previously stood on the road. Those men undoubtedly would have trampled me without a second thought. There is no remorse from them; not even a slight apology. But then, what could anyone expect from imperial soldiers? They cower before their lords and treat everyone else their doormats.

Naturally, temper gives into fury. Climbing out from the gully, words begin gushing without discretion. "I'm so sorry to be in your ways, my lords! I just thought men wearing imperial colors are supposed to protect the people, not run them over!"

The horse on the right comes to a halt, followed by the one on the left. The men whip around their steeds. I can feel blood draining from my face. I never speak when I should and always do when I shouldn't, I realize that, but it is too late. Retreat seems an obvious choice. Yet, they have horses, how can I outrun them? Then again, why should I run? I've done nothing wrong.

The two mumble a few words to one another and then advance. The one on the right, the man who stopped after having heard my charges, dismounts and approaches first. He is tall and his eyes are sharp and cold. Even so, I can't help but notice the hazel colors of his irises and the long majestic silver hair. What an unnatural combination! He appears more of a demon from an old silk scroll than a man; and maybe, he is. That scowl on his face is sending chills down my spine. I'm not inclined to believe myself a coward. Still, it takes clenching both hands just to keep from shaking.

The odd man scans me over, every inch from the top of my head down to my toes. Then, like a beast, sniffs the air around me as if searching for something. His strange actions fill me with dread, but also restlessness. The sun is on the verge of setting. I need to go home. Whatever fear overtaking me is pushed back by sheer obstinacy. My lips part; yet, I do not have the chance. The galloping of another horse down the dirt road startles me to turn as another armored man rides forthwith. Unlike the others, his light suit is common and bland, without their intricate, expensive embellishments. I assume he must be of lower ranking. The brown mare stops abruptly and the rider jumps off.

"I'm sorry, Generals! I got lost! You both were riding so fast, I couldn't keep up!" The young man gasps for air, though I wonder why, since the mare had been sprinting and not him.

"If you can't keep up, then you shouldn't have come." The sinister, demon-like man replies. "And, if you are going to be a burden, I will kill you."

17

The young man winces, before embarrassment sweeps over. I don't think that was an empty threat considering the feral expression crossing the older man.

"I'm sorry, General Hu. I'll try harder." The young man mutters through a low bow.

Since his arrival, I've been gawking at the newcomer. He appears particularly childish. I didn't think the army is so desperate that it needed such young recruits. Then again, what do I know about warfare? When the young man finally notices my silent intrusion, he flusters, kneels down, and then bows deeply onto the ground.

"Your Highness! I didn't see you there! I'm so sorry! Generals, you've found our lord at last! Thank goodness!"

"He is? Where?" I spin around, only to meet my shadow. The phantom he addressed isn't there, but a demon suddenly flies past me.

"Get up, you idiot!" General Hu growls furiously.

"I don't under—" The young man is forcibly pulled to his feet before he can finish.

"Do you have any idea what you've just done? Give me a reason not to kill you right here and now!" Immediately upon his outburst, Hu unsheathes the sword latched to his hip. Gold engravings on the blade reflect the setting sun, turning the fearsome thing blood red.

"Hold on there! What's your problem?" Jerking the young man back, I step in between the confrontation. "He didn't do anything. What's wrong with you?"

"Stay out of this!"

"How is anyone supposed to stand idle when you threaten a boy for no reason? Bully someone your own size!"

"You've got a big mouth for a little girl."

"And you've got a pretty big skull for someone with no brain."

Where did that come from? Insulting strangers isn't a habit of mine. That slipped out naturally as if I were bickering with an old friend. My master often said trouble followed my temper.

"Why you—!"

Resentment boils within his gaze. I have no doubt that if he were inclined, would cut through me to slay the young man. General Hu's grip around the sword tightens and the surrounding heavy feeling heightens. I really thought he would strike. Just as the end seems near, a hard voice terminates the scene.

"That's enough, Bai Hu. Qing Hai meant no harm. Anyone could have made such an easy mistake. Had you let insults go, we wouldn't be in this mess." The man who rode on the left horse had watched the event without interest, but now he thinks it's necessary to intervene.

As he comes closer, his tall figure and broad shoulders tower over me. Black raven-colored hair, encompassing the strong face and stern jaw, flutters in the gentle wind. Kind eyes, as blue as night skies, though distant as they are, seem to study me with great care. Never in my life have I met men such as these. The capital must be another world comprised of fantastic people so very different from commoners elsewhere.

"Qing Hai, don't be so impulsive," continues he.

Qing Hai smiles weakly and bows to both men. By the by, he glances at me from the corners of his eyes, though I don't understand why.

"You, girl. Why are you dressed as a man?" The one with blue eyes inquires.

"What do you mean, *'girl*?!'" Qing Hai flusters terribly while turning completely to face me.

"Answer!" General Hu pushes on.

Well, that's a silly question. "It's none of your business," is how I want to rebut. Actually, there are a number of reasons, but I won't be bullied into admission.

"Because men's clothes are more comfortable," is my indolent reply.

"Sarcasm, is it? Or, do you think you're funny, girl?" General Hu growls. "Maybe, you are. I see a complete fool standing before me and the only usefulness for a fool is to die and make room for others."

"I expected as much from imperial soldiers. You want to harass the common—to boast whatever little power you have? Go for it, but do it in your own time! I've got places to go and things to do."

Turning around, I start away when Hu grabs my collar. "Where do you think you're going? Do you think we'd let you leave after this?"

"She's a woman, General! You can't just manhandle her that way!"

"A woman who knows too damn much! We have to kill her! There is no choice! Don't you agree, Yue?" Hu turns to the other man, but the one with blue eyes I thought to be kind, simply shrugs.

"I don't know anything!"

As I attempt to pull away, Hu's grip tightens. A hefty jerk from his meaty paw slams me against the heavy armor. It feels nothing short of hitting a wall. My back is now bruised and bloodied.

"Leave her alone!" Hai reaches for me but Hu knocks him to the ground.

"I told you, I don't know what you're talking about!" Turning around for one final effort, a fist slams across

Hu's face with every bit of strength I can muster. Slowly, the hold on my collar loosens. The General rubs his face absently.

"That really hurts," Hu remarks flatly.

I can't tell whether he is mocking me. That doesn't matter. I've backed far enough from him that another escape could be attempted. Should I fail, he'll kill me for sure. Then again, could I reason with him instead? Maybe an act of faith by not running would be more prudent. My mind races but I only have seconds to decide.

Before resolve can form, my feet decide for me. Hu reaches out and misses by a hair's breadth. Wind whips across my cheek and tousles unkempt hair, drowning Hu's incessant cursing and the surge of voices trailing behind. After an indeterminable span of time, I stumble and fall to the ground. My chest and legs are burning in tandem. Quickly, I crawl over to a nearby bush and lie still to recover.

Soon as the thought of escape resumes, Hai suddenly picks me up from the shrub. I never heard him approached.

"Ack! C-Calm down! Please, Miss! Stop flailing!"

"Let go!"

Despite my voice and body trembling erratically, his pleading, apologetic stare hold more anxiety. The rounded eyes and boyish face peering down remind me that he's just a child. Hai has no interest in my death. He's in as much trouble as I am, if not more. My reply is a short nod and then, he puts me down.

"Are you going to let me go?"

"I-I can't do that. I'm good at tracking. He'll know I'm lying if I say otherwise. Listen, I won't let him harm you. You have to believe in me. General Yue won't allow him to kill you in cold blood."

Hope rising in my chest is dashed away sorely; replaced by exasperation. "Are you kidding me? General Yue couldn't care less what happens to me! He just shrugged when Hu said he'd kill me! And you... Hu would have killed you if it hadn't been for him! You can't even protect yourself. How can you protect me?"

Hai's gaze lowers. Though I didn't mean to, it's obvious I wounded his pride. A short pause ensues and then Hai looks up and gives a brief smile.

"General Hu's not all that bad. It's just... it was my fault. I said something I shouldn't have and he's only trying to protect the country."

"How is killing me going to protect the country? I'm not the emperor of Ning!"

"There's no time to explain. You'll just have to believe me. I won't let him hurt you." Hai extends a friendly hand. By the ardent expression of kindness in his eyes, it's palpable that he will do everything to protect me; though, his ambitions may be too much for his skills.

Running is pointless. He's found me after all and he can do so again. Even if Hai were to let me go, General Hu might slay him for failing and I don't want that on my conscience.

Chapter 1 – 2

"Took you long enough, kid." General Hu mutters gruffly as he sees us emerging from the woods. As we come near the two men, Qing Hai moves in front of me whilst keeping the right hand cradling mine behind his back. He squeezes tightly to reassure everything is well. When he speaks, the hardened tone is completely unexpected.

"She is willing to cooperate. There is no need for violence. I will not stand by and allow you to harm a civilian when no crimes have been committed."

"You dare speak to me like that, Recruit? Pass basic training and you think you're tough? You're lucky you're Minister San An's nephew or I'd take your head."

Qing Hai does not respond. Even though his back is to me, I can feel strong defiance in his stance. Following a long pause, Hu lets out a sarcastic laugh. "All this for a woman you thought was a man a moment ago? Fine. Whatever. Yue and I decided not to kill her after all. She could be useful to us; at least, she better be if she wants to live."

"Useful how?!" Hai's grip tautens.

"Don't be such a pervert. I wasn't implying anything depraved. I like my women to look like women and I definitely don't need to coerce anyone. Bring her along. We'll let San An deal with her."

"My-My uncle? What does he have to do with this?"

"The sun is setting. Don't waste any more time." Hu turns around and remounts the ironclad steed. Yue does the same. They start for the road ahead at a slow trot. Hai gradually lets out a heavy sigh. It's obvious he was more frightened than I was during the exchange.

"Let's go. My uncle won't let anything happen to you. I promise." Hai throws a smile over his shoulder. I'm inclined to believe him, simply because I don't have a choice.

Chapter 1 – 3

Well into the dark night, hoofs steadily pound against the ground, stopping only a time shortly before daybreak, and then continue again. My body and mind are exhausted; mostly, I'm anxious of what lies ahead. Why must I meet Minister San An in the capital and how can I be a threat to our country's security for dressing as a man? I want to ask, but Hai had said nothing of import for both of us to be in trouble. If he does tell me something useful, I am certain General Hu will end us.

In the late afternoon, we finally reach An's massive gates. The bustling capital is beyond anything my imaginations can dream. Beautiful buildings, beautiful people, and beautiful things all crowd together in this magnificent place of commerce. Each wondrous sight, exotic scent, and cheerful tone sends my heart fluttering from elation. At the same time, fatigue wreaks havoc and all I want to do is collapse.

"Just a little farther," Qing Hai whispers encouragingly. If it weren't for him sitting behind keeping me upright, I would have fallen off the horse long ago. His amiability is greatly appreciated. All the same, I hate these imperial soldiers. They brought me into this chaos, of which I don't want any part.

Eventually, we near the massive palace jutting above every surrounding structure. The wealth of a nation is clearly displayed for all to see. The breathtaking scene seems surreal. Charmed by magnificence, a smile begins curling over my lips, which then abruptly dissipates when General Hu turns about.

"We're going through the back entrance," he snaps. His eyes are as sharp as knives. For whatever reason, he is vexed again.

After a while, the back entrance comes into view. General Yue goes inside to fetch the Minister while the remaining two stand guard. I don't know why they bother. I have nowhere to go. At least, I have no way of returning home. I don't even know which way home is. My sense of direction has always been terrible.

Feet shuffle and sway to keep awake while stress and lack of sleep are slowly pulling away consciousness. Qing Hai pats my shoulder and smiles. I do my best to return the gesture. All the same, my vision is reeling. I can barely see straight. In time, another man dressed in beautiful silk exits with General Yue. As he sees me, charming brown eyes grow wide. His face is the last thing I remember before losing all consciousness.

Chapter 1 – 4

A large decorated room finely furnished with polished, dark-colored wood furniture. Windowpanes, wall panels, and arched doorways are exquisitely embellished by unmatched intricate patterns. Surrounding me on this massive bed are silk sheets the color of honey so luxuriously soft that by comparison, rose petals are no less than jagged thorns.

Sitting up, I rub my head absently but fatigue suddenly surges, and then I fall back, caught by two large, fluffy feather pillows. For a moment, I thought I must be dreaming, until *his* voice shakes me to be on alert.

"Boo!" He's glaring at me from the sofa by the closed windows. What madness is this? His hair is no longer silver. It is dark brown. The long locks hang loosely toward his waist. Upon construing my confusion, Hu laughs.

"I'm not a hundred years old. There's no reason why my hair should all be grey. Makes me look like a demon though, doesn't it?" He grins and his fangs can clearly be seen.

"You are a demon." I roll my eyes.

He returns another laugh. "Glad you liked my costume. It makes people in battle so very afraid of me. Anyway, after all I did to frighten you, it was the

Minister who made you faint? That's a big insult to the Demon General."

He sounds like he's joking around but that seems out of character for him. If he had held a sword over the bed and tried to stab me, it would be more believable.

"Is that why you're here? Do you want an apology?"

He smirks, though there is something strange in the response I can't quite understand.

"Our guest needs sustenance and rest after the previous ordeal. Would you mind sending Jin in here for me, Demon General?"

The voice that abruptly enters our conversation belongs to Minister San An. For a quick moment, he turns to me with a slight smile, before refocusing attention to Hu. The younger man grumbles incoherently; though, ultimately complies and leaves the room.

Wasting no time, Minister San An sits on the edge of the bed and raises the back of his hand to examine my forehead. He is in his thirties, I surmise, rather too young and handsome than I had imagined a minister would be. Dark coal black hair draping down his shoulders swing gently when he reaches for my wrist. "Remain still and let me check your pulse."

I figure, I have no choice. Since the Demon General takes orders from him, then Minister San An is not a man to be reckoned with. After a minute or so, he frowns.

"I'm afraid your pulse is rather weak. Please, allow Jin to tend to you. Inform him should you need anything. I know you must be very confused but I—no, your country—needs a great favor from you. Later, I will explain everything and I hope you will consider the matter. For now, I must return to court for the assembly. Please, excuse me."

I haven't the chance to say anything when he parts from the room as swiftly as he had entered. I will not lie, I am enjoying the pampering and attention of such handsome men; the Demon General included. Whatever it is the Minister will ask of me, I don't think I will deny him, especially since I am, after all, being held hostage. Going against the wishes of the imperial court could easily be viewed as treason.

As I ponder San An's unspoken request, a young man in his twenties enters the room with a tray of food and tea.

"Oh, hello."

He ignores me until the tray is on the side table. The young man, knitting his brows, carefully studies my face. "I can't believe it. You look just like him."

"Just like who?"

"His Highness," he replies.

The answer to the ordeal is so obvious, I can't believe how slow I am. Qing Hai mistook me for our emperor when he thought the Generals had found him. It must be that His Highness is missing. This is not something known throughout the land. Why should it? Once Ning become aware of the situation, war would come to our borders immediately. This is the reason Hu wanted my demise and also the reason I was brought to the capital.

"Do you understand now?"

I bite my lip and nod.

"Good. I advise that you agree to this, but I also want you to know that this is not something to be taken lightly. This is not a chance to be pampered. This is an opportunity to protect your country. If you do not play the part wholeheartedly and are exposed, you will be executed for impersonating His Highness. Even though the idea was not yours, no one will stand behind you. The council will deny all connections to this plot. Worse, if it is discovered that His Highness is missing, our land will suffer not only from external political strife, but internal. The vast number of nobles vying for his authority is endless. They will stop at nothing until one is left to claim the throne. I know this is a lot of pressure. That is why I am here to assist you in any way I can. My name is Shu Jin. I go by Jin. I am His Highness's personal attendant."

"I am... Bao Lai. I-It's nice to meet you."

This is not news I want to hear. I need to flawlessly impersonate the most important person in the country or everyone could die? What nonsense! Aggravation surges but it only makes me lightheaded. I fall back onto the bed.

"Are you all right?" Jin rushes over and puts his arms around me. This is a little friendlier than expected from someone I'd just met. I decide to say

"Isn't it inappropriate for you to touch His Highness this way?" (Continue to page 34)

Nothing (Continue to page 35)

Chapter 1 – 5

"Isn't it inappropriate for you to touch His Highness this way?"

A startled expression bursts in exchange for my weak laughter. Then, he smiles. "Yes. I'm sorry, Your Highness."

Jin moves away, fetches the tray of food, and places it in front of me. Before exiting, he turns around once more. "Oh, I had forgotten. General Bai Hu and Qing Hai asked for permission to visit you. I advise only speaking to one of them since you need rest and they tend to draw out conversations whenever they are together."

"What would His Highness do?"

"He would not meet with either. His Highness He Pi is selective of his acquaintances. Should I send them both away?"

"Yes, send them both away." If I am to play my role as I should, I cannot do anything His Highness, He Pi, wouldn't. Even if it means offending a few people, I will have to get used to it.

Continue to page 36

Chapter 1 – 6

I'm too embarrassed, words won't come. The warmth of his sweet demeanor only tempts silence to remain. Disappointedly, Jin realizes his folly. Colors rush to his cheeks while Jin attempts an apology.

"I'm not offended," I assure him.

"A man doesn't need to offend a lady for her to feel uncomfortable. I'm sorry."

No one's ever considered me a lady before; due understandable reasons. Still, it's nice meet such a gentleman after the assault of the ungentle Bai Hu.

Jin moves away, fetches the tray of food, and places it in front of me. Before exiting, he turns around once more. "Oh, I had forgotten. General Bai Hu and Qing Hai asked for permission to visit you. I advise only speaking to one of them since you need rest and they tend to draw out conversations whenever they are together."

"What would His Highness do?"

"He would not meet with either. His Highness He Pi is selective of his acquaintances. Should I send them both away?"

"Yes, send them both away." If I am to play my role as I should, I cannot do anything His Highness, He Pi, wouldn't. Even if it means offending a few people, I will have to get used to it.

Chapter 2: Someone Special

When the moon is high overhead, the door creaks open and Minister San An enters. He smiles sweetly whilst giving an amiable glance. Unintentionally, slight color creeps over my face.

"I did not mean to disturb at such late hours, but I've received word that you've considered the task."

"I don't truly have a choice."

"Perhaps, not *truly*, but there are other choices. By that, I mean if you appear a fool at court, the truth will be known and you will not have to pretend very long."

"Of course not, I would just be executed." My sardonic answer is accompanied by a tepid wave into the air.

The Minister smiles again and then I become embarrassed for my brash response.

"I know you feel trapped but I am not cruel. I cannot permit you to leave because you know the truth and yet, I don't think an unwilling person would be of use to us. We can always continue the ruse we have been using for some time now, while our men search for His Majesty. After careful deliberation, I've come to a single conclusion that will relieve you from this deception and also preserve your life."

My posture stiffens. The Minister draws close and leans down to face level. "The only way is to have you watched over by one of us."

"I don't understand. You're all watching me."

"Yes, well, perhaps at a closer level." He looks away for a quick moment. A delicate hint of uncertainty enters the expression; dissipating as quickly as it comes. Turning back, he smiles. "You may enter the Circle at the Peony Palace or you can simply wed one of us and become the responsibility of whomever you choose."

He has to be joking. Become a consort to the missing emperor or marry a random person? Either path would certainly keep me from having to impersonate His Highness and allow my life to be spared, but they are far from what I'd expected. I stand frozen in place; my face as crimson as the sash around San An's waist. The reaction must amuse him, because the Minister laughs.

"Was that too sudden? I will permit you some time to think things over. There's no need for an immediate answer. One is required come sunrise. I hope you will consider these alternatives if truly, you do not wish to take part in our political ploy."

"I don't understand. Why must these be the alternatives? I could stay as a servant to one of you or just tend to the gardens. I am not very bad at tending to gardens."

"I'm afraid these boys won't take their duties seriously were they to watch over a servant. But a wife... a man will be inclined to give all his attention to his wife and therefore, will ensure both your safety and honesty from allowing another soul to know our secret."

So, it is all a matter of trust and I am not viewed as trustworthy, is that it?

"It's not that I do not trust you," San An answers my mental inquiry. "I cannot say the same of the others. Once you leave these grounds, one or more might attempt to take your life."

There's truth to his reasonings—bizarre as they are. I have no idea which path to take. As I contemplate the choices, he continues.

"And, should you choose me, I will ensure for you a life without hardship. You will never be in want of anything. I am not your first choice, perhaps. I am not young and handsome, but as I am not as young as these boys, I am also not as foolhardy. They can love and hate on a whim. I will undoubtedly love you with every part of me until I draw my last breath. So please, do consider things carefully."

If I flush any deeper, my head would turn into a tomato! What is he talking about? He's gorgeous! And yes, he is older than the others, but there is something dignified and mature with this age. Ack! What am I saying? I have no interest in this! I just want to go home and eat my fish and water my garden.

I turn elsewhere and try to think of anything and everything to distract from the moment. When San An places a hand on my shoulder, I jump back.

"Do I frighten you?" Slight pain crosses within the tone.

"N-No! I... just... I don't understand! Yesterday, your boys thought I was a man and I know I'm not half as pretty compared to the women I saw strolling around the markets. I can't even imagine how beautiful the women in the Circle are! You, sir, can do a lot better!" I fold my arms and keep my head down, embarrassed by my own outburst.

"Conceivably, you are not the most beautiful woman, but beauty is only part of the equation. You have all of our attentions and that makes you special. Everyone wants to claim someone special."

Inexplicable resentment begins creeping over my psyche. My eyes dart to his face. "A prize, is that it? Because I resemble His Highness, that makes me special? You want to win me because it inflates your ego? If that's the case, then I'm sorry to say you don't understand what love is, Minister!"

Taking a seat near the window, I scratch my head irritably. I thought he would be angry. Instead, San An laughs. A smile reappears.

"No, I'm afraid you don't understand what love is." He replies. "To find someone special is ordinary inclination. It is natural to be able to discern between beauty and ugliness, intelligence and stupidity, and yes, even common and rare. Love simply means to care for, so how can caring for someone I find special means that my love is less than any man who loves for beauty, intellect, or even money? Love is love, no matter the reason. If love needs to be based on any particular reason, then I think that is too mechanical."

My head tilts due confusion. I don't know how to argue with that and my own ignorance just draws me deeper into a void. I want to reply but nothing will come. Following the painful ensuing silence, San An relieves a sigh.

"Forgive me, I did not mean to grieve you. I only wanted to speak my mind, for I fear regret will consume me if I did not at least try. You are entitled to your opinions. I merely hope you will not think too poorly of me for having caused your anxiety."

"N-No. I don't think poorly of you at all! It's just that you don't even know me. I could very well drive you mad." My attempt to chuckle off the tension is met with his simple smile.

"What if I say that you already have?" The sheepish tone comes forth and then, he quickly glances away.

"I don't understand."

"That you don't understand makes me admire you even more."

San An reaches out; though, before his fingers graze my cheek, he withdraws. My heart immediately flutters and my face feels warm. Following a span of silent contemplation, a soft chuckle breaks from his pale rose lips.

"It's late and you need rest. Let us end here for now. I look forward to speaking with you again. Please, don't hesitate to call for me should you require anything. It is my desire to fulfill all your wishes." The Minister bows gracefully before taking his leave.

My eyes widened during our exchange and even now that he's left, I can't seem to force them back to the original position. I'm so confused! What was all that about? Did he just seriously propose to me? The image of his smiling face is engraved into my mind. The more I struggle to push it away, the more it comes flooding back.

Around him, I feel inferior in every way, and for some reason, it makes my heart race. The intellect and guidance of an older man, is that what I need most? What am I thinking?!

Vigorously shaking my head, I stuff my face in my hands. Sometime later, I fall asleep in distress and before I know it, Jin comes into the room and wakes me to prepare for the dreadful event.

Chapter 3: The Path to my Future

Around noon, the men assemble in the chamber and after a brief conversation, my decision is requested. Before me stand the Generals Zhen Yue and Bai Hu, Qing Hai, and Minister San An. Yue is indifferent, so he looks off elsewhere, while Hai is terribly embarrassed with his eyes to the ground. Hu smirks at me but I don't understand why. Finally, San An smiles sweetly with hopes in his eyes.

The idea of imposing upon uninterested parties bothers me. I'm certain Zhen Yue, Bai Hu, and Qing Hai would object even if I were so bold. As for joining the Circle, it's unthinkable. Not only have I no desire to become a courtesan, the thought of being a prisoner in painted cells brings angst. I don't know the right answer, but as I glance from one to the next, the choice is obvious after all.

"I want to become He Pi. I want to help maintain peace for Nan Rong until His Highness is found."

"You are willing to risk your life and the lives of the people? Are you certain you can play the part?"

"Yes, Minister. I will become He Pi no matter what."

"Very well." San An replies. "Jin, she is your charge. Amongst current parties, you are most acquainted with His Highness. Teach Bao Lai his mannerisms, his speech, and aspects of his mind. Should she fail, the country may fall with her."

He is not determined to scare me. San An is merely reinforcing the risk. Despite having made my choice, I'm still nervous.

Jin bows deeply while the others exit the room. Aside from the Minister, I doubt I can associate very much with them from now on. For some reason, that makes me a little sad even though our encounter in prior days had caused much distress.

Once we are alone, Jin nears and leans down to face level.

"What are you doing?"

Jin grabs my arm when my feet toggle back.

"Hold still. You look like him, but not perfectly. He spends most of his time inside and I can tell that you do not. No, this won't do. Stay here."

Jin abruptly parts from the room, leaving me to shuffle irritably, until curiosity gets the better of me, and then I'm left perusing the room for clues of the man I must become. Ah, who am I kidding? I have no idea where to begin. Thankfully, Jin walks through the door and throws a set of clothes on the bed along with a box made from redwood. It's beautifully carved with images of lotuses and water lilies on every panel.

"First, you must mirror his image. Then, you must walk and sit as he does to at least endure the assemblies. Lastly, and only when compelled, should you speak and make decrees on the council's behalf. Come, sit here for me." Jin points to a chair in front of the vanity while opening the redwood box to remove a set of powders. Once I settle, he begins painting. The unfamiliar scent of powder is making my nose twitch.

"Tell me about him." The quick attempt to distract Jin is more so in part, to distract myself. "What should I know about He Pi?"

"His Highness speaks very little during assemblies. He finds them boring. That will be to your advantage. However, he sits with great posture, which you do not have. Control your breathing to remain still. Later, I will teach you the proper pose. He is also a very intelligent man despite masking his talents through childishness."

"He is childish?"

"Ostensibly. He shirks going to assemblies whenever he can, teases every woman in the Circle, and inveterately vexes his ministers through sarcasms. He'd sleep until noon, if I would let him, and tends to sneak out of the palace at night to wander about."

I can't believe this. Who knew our country was led by a man so... "Irresponsible! How irresponsible! How could *he* have taken the throne over anyone else? Why even bother searching for someone that irresponsible?"

Jin frowns at the uncouth outburst. I withdraw. Sighing deeply, he slowly resumes the task and applies another layer of powder to my face.

"Irresponsible, yes, but he is a good leader. He is brilliant even if he is lazy. He is powerful even if he is small in stature. He is always aware even if he seems absentminded. I was not worried at first, but when he did not return after two days, the Prime Minister sent men to search for him. He's never gone for more than a day at most."

"How long has it been since he's left?"

"Over a month. The ministers told the court that he is away at the Summer Palace. More and more, they can see through the ruse. His Highness tends to stay solely in the capital now. The Summer Palace has been sitting bare for years. The plan is to next tell the court that His Highness is unwell to buy additional time, but that excuse will just bring more questions with his prolonged absence. You are our only hope, you see. However, you must remember that this position may not be temporary. If he is never found, you must live his life for the rest of your days, but without his freedom. The ministers will direct you to carry out their will. You will simply be a puppet. Do you understand?"

I nod. Since stepping foot into the capital, I have been a puppet without freewill. I can accept that if it means peace. However, should war come and the people look to me for He Pi's intellect and guidance, then all will be lost. Not to mention that although the ministers are one for now, who can say they will not eventually struggle for control over me? I need for everyone to believe I am He Pi, so that should anyone challenges my authority, I will have the support of the court.

"Tell me more. How does he normally speak? What does he like or dislike?"

"He rarely speaks to most people aside from me. I have been his servant since we were both children. To me, he is always cheerful and sometimes, even playful. To others—except to women, I suppose—when he does speak, does so with little fervor. You can even say his speech is somewhat indolent. He likes women and wearing disguises when he leaves the palace. He dislikes... pretty much everything else."

"So, he's a lecher? Great! A sarcastic, indolent lecher who likes to play dress up!"

Jin laughs when I roll my eyes. "Well, a lecher in performance. He actually never does a lecherous thing."

"What do you mean? He... pretends to be a lecher?"

"He doesn't trust women; hence, His Highness flirts with any he'd meet. If the woman is disgusted by his advances, then he thinks she is trustworthy."

"How so?"

"Though it's flawed logic, he decided that decent women without ulterior motives would not suffer lecherous men; even when the man is royalty. In any case, since His Highness is interested in every woman, he gives off the sense that he's not interested in anyone at all. Those who can take the hint shy from him. The others, frankly, are wasting their time."

"So, he's not interested in marriage? That is a relief."

"I would not jump to conclusions. He is engaged."

"I don't understand. Didn't you just say he's not interested in anyone?"

"An emperor must marry. That is a duty he must oblige. To keep from civil war, he must provide an heir."

"Then, what am I supposed to do about that?" I shuffle uneasily. Jin signals for me to remain still.

"Don't worry. He's been engaged since he was sixteen and has yet to marry. He's twenty-two now and not a step closer toward anything finite. I understand his dilemma. It's one of the few illogical things he actually ever does."

"And what is his dilemma? Maybe, I should not pry into a stranger's business, but since I must become him, then I need to know how he thinks."

Perhaps Jin doesn't want to tell me for fear of betraying his master, because he pauses for a long moment before complying.

"He was not first in line for the throne. His mother was not empress. She was a consort. She fought hard to secure his position and it was upon the late emperor's deathbed that His Majesty He Pi was declared the new heir. Empress Pai retaliated. This caused great battles at court for many years between all the women whose children had claims to the bloodline. Factions upon factions formed. Everyone thought civil war was near until, finally, things settled when a mystic was called to court and it was proclaimed that divine right belonged to the child with the Mark of Heaven on his shoulder. His Majesty, of course, was the only one."

"Mark of Heaven?"

"He has a red dragon-shaped birthmark on his left shoulder. That is something we will also need to prepare. Now then, I think you finally have his complexion."

The first thought that comes to mind when I look in the mirror is that He Pi needs to go outside more. How ivory his skin must be for this many layers of powder to portray! I think he may have appeared more of a woman than me.

"Now, for his garb. Take off your robe."

The moment those words leave his mouth, we both flush profusely. I may look just like their man but I'm definitely not one. Even though I'm sure he doesn't want to see whatever is under my robe any more than I want to show him, Jin fights with himself and repeats the request.

"I can't do that. Anyway, why can't I just dress myself?"

"His Majesty only appears in court after I dress him and every little detail counts. He likes his clothes a certain way but can never do it himself."

"I'm not half as helpless as His Majesty!"

"You agreed to this: to do whatever is necessary to become His Highness. Have you changed your mind?"

"N-No. But I... Promise me, you won't laugh."

"I would never..." Jin begins glancing over before deciding against imprudence. The awkward gaze averts to the wall.

Oh, thank goodness! I nearly keeled over from embarrassment upon disrobing. Luckily, there are bandages wrapped all over my upper body. Who could have done this? Certainly, it wasn't Jin since he's blushing ear-to-ear just from staring at the wall. The Demon General was in the room when I woke. The thought of this possibility makes me shudder; though, I can't imagine it was Bai Hu either.

"You're hurt! Who did this to you?" Sudden resentment sparks in Jin's voice like that of a provoked mother hen.

"It's a long story. Half of it was my fault. Not as bad as it looks. Whoever bandaged me exaggerated the severity."

Although his brows are still knit tightly, the subject subsides. Jin then drapes the gold robe around my body. Immediately, he frowns. His Majesty has a flat chest, as he should. I do not.

"This is not possible," he mutters. "Can't just... No, that won't do."

"Well, if you tie the robe loosely, maybe they won't show."

"We can't give the notion that anything's changed. Would you be willing to possibly... remove... No, what am I saying?!"

Jin turns away again. As much as I want to help, is he seriously suggesting that I remove my breasts? That is not what I agreed to! But, I did say I would help and I always strive to keep my words. I mean, if I am to impersonate He Pi, possibly, for the rest of my days, I have no need for such things. On the other hand, if he returns tomorrow, then all would be for naught.

No, I don't want to! Shaking my head, I start to tell Jin that I can't do that but he's already formed another idea. Taking a large sash off the bed, he binds my chest.

"Allow me to try this alternative. It will hurt you. I'm sorry. Bear with me."

"Ngh!"

Though it would not flatten, the sash compressing my chest is enough to hide the majority of the area that needs to be hidden. The compression is painful; more so, it is difficult to breathe. I'm becoming lightheaded.

"You're wobbling. What's wrong?"

"I... *Oomph!*" One misstep from my staggering legs sends me stumbling headfirst into Jin's arms.

"Hey, are you okay? Stay awake!" Jin places me on the bed and removes the sash as consciousness begins seeping away. I hear him call my name but I can't comply.

Chapter 4: Second Proposal

"What's the meaning of this?!"

"Awake already? How do you feel?"

Is he joking? When I opened my eyes, Jin's face was inches away. I immediately darted off the bed and woke him in the process. Through it all, he still has the gall to answer casually against my shaking finger.

Slowly rising, Jin runs fingers through his dark, let down hair. The long strands hang loosely around the handsome features of his face. Naturally exuding grace and charming airs, Jin is more deserving of playing the emperor than the servant.

"Come back to bed. You're obviously still tired. Rest for today and we'll try again tomorrow."

"Try what exactly?!"

"Try preparing for your role. Look, I'm not that type of person, okay? You fell unconscious. I stayed to ensure you were safe and then I fell asleep, too. I'm sorry. I shouldn't have been so rough with the execution. I'll be gentler next time."

"What *are* you talking about?!"

"I am talking about binding your... particular area. Do you have such poor views of me that you interpret everything I say and do to be dishonorable?"

I have no idea what happened. I was unconscious after all. Then again, he is so exquisite and I am nothing to be desired. There is no reason he would ever...

"No, I'm sorry."

"Come back to bed and rest." He pats the area adjacent. I don't want to continuously offend him so, I hesitantly comply. Jin moves off and starts for the door just as I lie down.

"I'll bring your breakfast in a bit. Don't overdo things or you'll start bleeding again."

What does he mean by, "*again*?" I was merely punctured by thorns and those small wounds should have sealed by now. After disrobing, I examine the fabric to find small specks of blood scattered over the fine silk. When he had tightened that sash around me, the cuts must have reopened. What a shame. This robe is probably worth more money than I'll ever have.

A few moments later, Jin returns with a silver tray and after placing it on the table, moves toward a dresser and retrieves a small box.

"Turn around. Let's change your bandages."

"It's not that bad. I think I'm better off without it."

"Then, at least let me apply this balm on your wounds. Save your stubbornness for the ministers, Your Highness." His tone is somewhat teasing. I don't want to argue either way.

Jin removes the bandages and applies the balm once my back is turned to him. The cold sensation makes me jump and suddenly, soft chuckles erupt from behind.

"You're quite the sadist," I scoff.

"Yes, I know." He replies coolly.

What an answer! I twist around to return a quip, but words can't form in the midst of Jin's burning cheeks provoking my own. His expression is one of fright.

Something is definitely off. Jin's looked away and the room is suddenly becoming chillier. I reach to pull the robe tighter and instead, clutch at nothing. Oh, dear heavens! There are no more bandages covering what should be covered, and the robe is on the other side of the bed.

"I'm sorry!" Nearly slamming my head against the bed frame, I dive under the sheets. All I hear in response are retreating footsteps.

Obviously, there is nothing about me that deserves to be viewed fondly, but his reaction is a little harsher than expected. A teasing remark here or there; even a snide one would have been better than to have simply fled. What else could I expect? I was mistaken for His Highness. I was mistaken for a man.

Chapter 4 – 2

San An comes around noon and brings a new tray of food. It is unlike the Minister to serve anyone. He must have come on Jin's behalf. I wonder whether anything was exchanged between them regarding my shameful display. As usual, San An smiles tenderly.

He sits on a side of bed and touches my forehead. "I hope you don't mind. I heard you are not well. This is my fault. I should have personally taken you into my care instead of leaving you in the hands of a boy."

"I'm not sick. Please, don't worry about me."

"Perhaps, physically, you are well. Something inside troubles you, am I wrong?"

His tone is so friendly and calming; I want to tell him everything.

"Well, it's just... I don't know if I can do this. I want to, but wanting to do something and being able to do it, are two very different aspects."

"It is still early. You can change your mind. No one will be angry. I just hope you'll consider my offer, if you do."

The touch of San An's fingers gently stroking my hair makes me impulsively recoil. Why is he acting this way? No one as wonderfully handsome and sweet as the Minister should think so much of me; even if his reason is not one I find flattering. Though, I could do a lot worse than be married to him. More like, even in my wildest dreams I couldn't imagine marriage to someone this incredible! Who am I kidding? If I had any other face, he would not look at me twice. I feel as though I'm cheating to win his attention through means I cannot control and therefore, I don't deserve his affection.

"Thank you for your support and kindness, Minister. I will stay the course."

"I see. I am glad you have convictions, even though it means I will be denied my ambitions."

Through dejection, San An smiles cordially. My conscience is writhing from tumult. He's been so thoughtful. However, without the right words to ease glumness, the room defaults to awkward silence. A warm sensation unexpectedly touches my hand. Instinctually, I jump.

"Do I make you uncomfortable?"

His soft, but firm hand is covering mine. Self-consciousness is billowing from realization that my skin is rough and worn. I want to pull away for this reason, but if it means he'll take it as a slight, I probably shouldn't. Without my reply, his thumb begins smoothing over the coarse skin. Immediately, my hand jerks back.

"S-Sorry!" So much for not wanting to slight him. My face is burning from embarrassment.

"Why must you apologize? I am the one who has offended you. Forgive me."

The Minister stands up and I feel terrible for being so uncouth. How it happened is unbeknownst to me; my hands are holding onto his sleeve. I don't know which of us is more surprised by my brazenness.

"You did not offend me. Please, I'm sorry. I'm just not used to..."

An incoherent mumble veils the last words of excuse. Taking no offense, San An resumes my side. The Minister gently picks up my coarse hand and flips it over to survey my palm.

"Would you like me to tell your fortune?"

"You can do that?"

"Are you surprised? Not every man who becomes a minister is all noses."

"I didn't mean *that.*"

"I know," he chuckles. "Shall I begin?"

"Please."

"To be fair, someone taught this to me very long ago. I can't vouch for my memory after all this time. In any case, here is your life line." His finger slowly traces along a crevice on my palm. The ticklish sensation sends my heart shooting like a rocket.

"This one represents wealth and this one represents intellect." His finger runs over the two lines. Each time, my breathing shifts.

"Now, give me your other hand."

"What's different about this hand?" I put out my left palm.

"These are the same lines, but for your soul mate."

"So, the person with these matching lines on his right hand is my soul mate?"

"That is what I was told," San An laughs. "I've yet to meet anyone successful in finding their counterpart through this method. In my opinion, hands should be held, not examined, and fingers should be used to feel, not just touch." His fingers run from my palm to my wrist and then, flipping my hand over, he brings it toward his pretty lips.

"Minister!"

He pauses. "You need not be so formal. San An is just fine."

"San An..."

"Yes, Your Highness?"

"Don't take this the wrong way, but I'm very embarrassed right now." My hand withdraws.

"For what reasons could you be embarrassed?"

"Don't tell me that you didn't notice how rough my hands are."

"Is that the only reason?" San An chuckles mirthfully. "I favor your hands because they belong to you. How they appear matter little to me."

"Well, I'd rather keep them hidden all the same." Folding both arms across my waist to keep the rough things shielded, the sound of his soft chuckles merely causes further embarrassment. Am I that amusing?

"If you insist, Your Highness. I did manage to read something else off your palm. Would you like me to tell you?"

"Sure."

"Very well. Your fate is intertwined with someone who has a place within this palace."

"And is that person you, San An?"

He takes little notice of my sarcasm or my frown.

"Fortunes are meant to guide. The rest is entirely up to you, Your Highness."

We stare at one another for a short moment. He sounded so serious, I couldn't do else but laugh. Without taking offense, San An returns my sentiment. After a few more pleasantries, he quits the room.

As I unfold my arms, memories of his touch make me blush. Why do I keep feeling so worked up when he's near? Secretly, I enjoy his consideration. I do wonder whether his attention toward me has any connections to his feelings toward His Majesty. However, that is something I have no right to ask. I should relinquish the subject for now.

Chapter 5: A Test of Intuition

In the evening, Jin came to the room and hastily shuffled together the contents of the empty trays. Without acknowledging me, he quietly left the room. I understand the offense he must feel. There was no point to make him face me. In truth, I couldn't look at him either.

Late at night when the moon is overhead, I lie awake and wonder if my convictions, as San An called them, are right. Every stupid mistake I've made has led up to this point. What if, by continuing to make these mistakes, I will cause suffering for others? How could I impersonate an emperor? What was I thinking? I can't even fit his clothes. How am I to fit his shoes? In my heart of hearts, I believe this to be the right course even though the very idea is preposterous.

Argh! I can't take this! I'm so tired but my eyes are wide-open! Vexation torments me and my heart is beating wildly out of my chest. As I sit up and bury my head in my hands, an unsettling feeling suddenly weighs down. I can't stay in this room any longer—this room that doesn't belong to me. I'm wearing clothes that aren't mine, breathing in air from this fine palace that never should enter my peasant lungs, whilst pretending to be someone regal. I can't do it! I have to leave!

Hallways after hallways and nothing's changed. I've been traversing through this endless maze for the past ten minutes. There should be a flight of stairs, an exit to a balcony... anything! Oh, dear heavens. What was I thinking? I'm lost. If someone sees me with His Majesty's face and not his body, the ruse would be for naught.

Where is He Pi's chamber? Logically, I should retrace my steps and return to the same hall from whence I came. Right. That's what I'll do.

Just my luck! Upon arriving at the end of the corridor, the path diverges. Another choice is before me and another chance for mistake. Then again, what if I am doing the right thing even though I do not know it? I want intuition to take over and prove the validity of my resolve. Should I go right or left?

Go right (Continue to page 63)

Go left (Continue to page 66)

Chapter 5 – 2

I decide to go right. Just as I reach the end of the corridor, Jin comes around the corner. At the sight of me, he becomes livid.

"What are you doing out here? Did anyone see you?"

Before I can reply, he grabs my wrist and pulls me down many hallways until we reach His Highness's chamber. Upon opening the door, Jin flings me inside and I stumble to the ground. However harsh is his reaction, I know that he saved my life.

"No one saw me." An answer chokes out. "I couldn't sleep so I... I don't know what I thought. I just wanted some air."

"Do you know what would have happened had someone else caught you?" His voice is as cold as ice. "You cannot leave this room until you appear his exact replica. Otherwise... otherwise, they'll have you executed." Jin kneels down behind me as his voice trails away.

"I know. I shouldn't have been rash. But maybe, I shouldn't be here. Maybe, I should just join the Circle so I don't cause more trouble."

One stupid mistake after another. It's one dumb mistake after another only to accomplish nothing in the end!

I turn back to apologize. However, slight tears misting over Jin's light brown eyes put me off guard.

"I won't leave again without your permission, I promise. Don't be sad. No one saw me. I can still be useful, if you think I should stay."

Jin bites his lips and stares for a long moment. Suddenly, his arms fly around my shoulders. "If they execute you, I don't... I don't want to think about that! I don't want you to die!"

Jin's grip tightens as his arms shake. I don't understand the reason for his reaction. Why is he so protective when he barely knows me? Is it just his disposition to be caring? He'd spent his entire life guarding He Pi, who is now lost. Maybe, he doesn't want to lose me, too, because of this face. I am his He Pi returned. He must be lamenting for his friend through me. Jin doesn't want He Pi to die; neither, do I. I hope that he will come back and free everyone from this bondage of secrets they all have to carry. As I return the embrace, hot tears wet my shoulders.

"It's okay, he'll come back. I know he will. He has to!" In saying so, my own mouth quivers and tears flow down my face.

I don't personally know He Pi, but I understand how important he is to everyone—not just for what he is, but also for who he is as a person. I can't replace him. If I can make Jin happy by being a surrogate friend, I want to at least try.

Jin draws back and places a warm hand on my face. He brushes away a few tears and smiles, though it is rather sad.

"I know he will. All the same, you must not be reckless."

I nod and there is nothing more that needs to be exchanged between us.

Continue to page 67

Chapter 5 – 3

I decide to go left. Just as I near the end of the hall, a guard spots me and believes I am an intruder. My attempt to flee fails. When the ministers are called for, I am sent to gaol. San An and Jin push for leniency but the council would not hear it. No one else defends me, as was expected. The other ministers have long decided that the moment I become a threat to their credibility, the only choice is to dispose of me.

At the next assembly, I am sentenced to death for treason; the charge fitted for anyone who impersonates His Highness. By noon, I am executed before the assembly.

The End.

Chapter 6: His Highness's Shoes

When he comes the next day, Jin is friendlier and more importantly, he appears a little happier, too. Before I can greet him, a small bouquet of three flowers wrapped in colored-paper is presented. The blooms are exceeding large and fragranced.

"I apologize. You must endure living solely in this room for a while longer. Hopefully, these peonies can remind you of the outdoors and bring a little cheer to your day."

No one's ever given me flowers before. Considering all the troubles I've caused him, he's too kind. Slowly, heat rises to my face as the bouquet is cradled close to my chest. An odd elation wells inside while an unruly smile forces its way to my mouth.

"They're beautiful. Thank you, Jin!"

Jin nods. After placing the pile of clothes on the bed, he begins dressing me. The ordeal from prior day that caused tension between us was useful after all. He's already seen underneath my robe. There is no reason to be shy about it now. Well, I say that, but we're both still as red as tomatoes.

Jin loosely binds my chest and states that contrary to the gold robe, a black one would help shade upper curves. I have no sense of fashion, so I have no objection.

"Enter the assembly from behind the throne; never the side. Sit straight but don't puff out your chest. We can practice later. Don't look at anyone directly but still, keep your head up. Don't grab the arms of the seat; do curve your fingers around them." He throws the list of things I must do into the air. Jin had given this much thought. I must not fail him.

When the many pieces of clothing find their places on my body, I turn to the mirror and nearly fall back. I do not recognize my reflection and that is a good thing, I suppose.

"Not bad at all. Besides from your complexion and height, you can easily pass for him now."

"My height? His Majesty can't be that much taller, can he? Especially, since Qing Hai mistook me for him."

"Yes, well, he's only a little bit taller than you. Most people wouldn't notice. I do. I'll have to adjust the shoes. Go on, walk around the room. Let's see your posture."

I nod and step forward. As I do, nearly fall on my face. He catches me, though, I can't erase utter flooding embarrassment.

"I can't fit his shoes," I sigh.

"Don't be so hard on yourself. The first step is always the most difficult."

"No, I mean, I can't fit his shoes!" The shoe slips off when I raise my foot. His feet are almost twice the size of mine.

"Another adjustment. Good. Best we find them now than later. Take the shoes off and try again."

I do as he say and then stroll across the floor. My movement is rigid and slow.

"Why are you walking like that?" Jin chuckles. "Regal doesn't equate to rigidity."

"That's not it at all! His robes are so long, I'm just trying to keep from falling."

Jin surveys me for a moment, then comes close and puts his right arm around my waist. His left hand grabs onto my left hand.

"Come. I'll hold you so you won't fall. Follow my pace. Too fast... too slow... just like that... you're slanting, stand up straight."

Before I know it, we've gone on like this for an hour or two. There's a gentle air about Jin that makes me feel so safe. His arm around me, his hand in mine—I don't want Jin to let go. It's a strange thought; or perhaps, rational. More and more, I will come to depend on Jin for the rest of my days until He Pi returns—if he ever will.

In any case, I'm glad to have his guidance and support.

Chapter 7: Age behind Innocence

In the afternoon, Jin brings my meal and takes away the shoes for modifications. I don't want him to wait on me but he insists keeping his duties. Although he's only giving me attention because of these duties, I enjoy it all the same. Still, I know nothing of Jin and how he came to be an attendant. I only know he has pride in his post and that no one else could do more for He Pi.

As I lean back in the chair, a loud sigh fills the room. What great meals Jin always brings! He Pi and I must have the same taste or maybe, he has much better taste than me. I ate too much and have nowhere to go. For fear of becoming sluggish, I start from the chair and practice walking. Without Jin to hold me, I stumble about and trip over the loose robe. Then, as expected, fall flat on my face right near the door.

"Ouch." I'm useless without him. Depression takes over and I decide to just lie here for the time.

"The floor is no place for an emperor to sleep." A familiar voice calls for my attention. Minister San An, smiling by the threshold, gazes down. How he comes and goes without me noticing is somewhat frightening.

"S-San An!"

I sit up and attempt to regain what little composure I could. San An kneels down, takes my chin in his hand,

and then slowly closes the distance between our faces. Nerves freeze me in place.

"I cannot believe it. You are his spitting image. For a moment, I thought he had returned." A soft laugh accompanies the smile.

"Everyone thinks we look alike, anyway," I mutter.

"Perhaps, though some of us are not foolish enough to believe you are him. Jin has outdone himself."

"Y-Yes. Yes, he has. Jin is very meticulous and accomplished in all aspects of his duties."

San An chuckles. "That's quite the compliment. I'm sure you've grown fond of him over these past few days?"

A frown falls over my mouth. Suddenly feeling defensive, I want to tell him that it's none of his business; though, I manage to hold my tongue. When I do not respond, he continues. "I hope you realize it would be foolish to pursue a relationship outside of master and servant between you and Jin. Should His Highness be found, Jin will simply resume his usual duties and you will be returned to your home. Jin cannot go with you and you cannot stay with him."

"Jin and I are just friends. At least, I'd like to think we have become friends."

"Just friends? One would reason that after displaying your bare body to Jin day after day, friendship would be the last thing on either of your minds. Were you a child, I would otherwise consider. Though your face is youthful, I see a mature soul through those eyes. You are a woman with a girl's disposition. Nothing is more deceiving than age behind innocence."

A momentarily glance into his gaze sends chills over me. Where has the former gentle expression gone? He sounds so callous and distant; his demeanor is almost unrecognizable.

"What are you accusing me of?"

"Don't misunderstand. I am not accusing you of anything. You seem confused and lost; drowning in thoughts you've yet to comprehend. It is natural for a woman, who's oblivious to the idea of love, to fall deeply for a man who tends to her needs daily; who has seen every part of her and returns for more. I only implore that you will consider the consequences of your actions in jeopardizing the country's safety when you decide to chase after the selfish desire of first love while impersonating His Highness."

It's true that I've never loved anyone and the idea is fascinating, but who is he to charge upon me impure expectations from Jin? I feel unclean just to hear him speak. Doubt disrupts my intention and resolve. My hands are balled into fists.

"Why are you so presumptuous to tell me how I should and shouldn't feel? I'm here for one reason and one reason only. That reason has nothing to do with building relationships with anyone! When this ordeal is over, I will leave. Alone!"

I have a short temper; that much is palpable. I'm also easily offended and easily embarrassed, which always make things worse. I grasp that this is not appropriate behaviors for He Pi, but I am still me for now. Even so, I know he meant no harm. San An never says a mean thing that is baseless. For that reason, his words cut even deeper. Then again, what can I do but just let it go?

"I'm sorry, Minister."

I thought he would lecture further or mock me in some way. Nothing of the sort happens. What does happen next makes me turn cold. My vision reels wildly around the room when San An encircles his arms tightly around my waist and places a warm, passionate kiss on my mouth. All the strength abruptly drains from my body. What on Earth is happening? Did I do something wrong again? I must have but... this hardly feels like punishment.

He must be testing me—to see if I would falter easily from a simple kiss. Yet, this is my first kiss. How can he carelessly steal away this special thing I can never have back! My head jerks away; his lips flutter to my neck.

"Stop testing me, Minister! I don't want to raise my hand against you, but if I must..." The words choke their way out. What's come over me? I can barely breathe.

"You are mistaken. I trust your resolve. It is mine that is dwindling."

His soft, seductive voice is lulling away my soul. The more I try to make sense of the situation, the more confusing everything becomes.

"I confessed my love and yet, you chose to become Jin's charge. He has the pleasure of tending to your needs; to know parts of you from which I am forbidden. Age behind innocence. I knew you would be my bane the first moment we met. I will be the person to jeopardize peace if I cannot find control, but your age behind innocence is robbing me of all composure!"

His lips make their way from my neck to my cheek, and then another kiss presses upon my mouth, taking my breath away. Never in my life has someone pursue me as fervently as San An. In reality... no one has ever pursued me, and I would be lying to say that I want to resist him. I've been strangely attracted to San An since we've met for reasons I cannot fathom. However, this is inappropriate in so many ways!

Pushing away San An, I stumble backward. "You don't know what you're saying, Minister! I'm not as innocent as you think!"

"You're not?"

He raises an eyebrow and heat inexplicably rushes to my face.

"What I mean is I'm not a child who can be easily distracted and swayed by kind words and sweet temptations. I know Jin is only looking after me because of his duties and you're right, I am an adult. I can take care of myself. I'm not hiding age behind anything. This is the real me. I'm childish because I'm ignorant—sometimes, borderline stupid—but that doesn't make me innocent!"

"You have never known a man's touch, have you?"

How can he ask a woman that without any discretion! My whole body is burning from embarrassment. I don't know whether it's more mortifying to tell him the truth or to lie. People my age should already know such things. Besides the fact that no one's ever wanted me, there are multitudes of other reasons why I'm behind. All I can do is look at the floor and hope for him to change the subject or for my heart to just stop and end my misery; whichever comes first.

Suddenly, he chuckles. My breathing ceases.

"That's about the reaction I expected. Age has nothing to do with innocence. It's all a matter of disposition. An experienced woman would become defensive when her claim to virtue is assaulted; an innocent one is embarrassed for still having it."

There's naught I can use to respond. It's not as though I can question his innocence! My eyes dart back and forth across the floor to search for relief. The sudden touch of his hand caressing my cheek throws me into rage.

"How dare you put your hands on me, Minister!"

Darting up, an angry glare directs back. I take my post as He Pi before someone who knows the ruse. "You have assaulted your monarch. We will allow the transgression this time. Next time, we shall not be so kind!"

San An draws back and smiles sweetly. The unaffected attitude turns me immobile. The Minister stands up, makes a low obeisance, and then leaves.

Once he is out of view, strength falters and my knees buckle. Why do I feel terrified of him? The idea is perplexing. In truth, San An has never caused me any harm and I believe he has my safety and best interest in mind. His recent strange behaviors I can only surmise alluded to jealousy. Still, the very idea of him now makes me shudder.

Chapter 8: A Servant Prince

For the past few weeks, endless days were spent with Jin, who tutored me in aspects of He Pi's personality, charms... or lack thereof, mannerisms, speech, and even his political mindset. I know nothing of politics while Jin seems to know as much about court matters as any minister. I can't tell whether progress was made, but he assured that I receive a passing grade. The true test, though, will be tomorrow when I must attend the assembly.

"Don't be afraid. Do exactly as you've just showed me and everything will be fine." Jin pats my shoulder while I slump down on the bed. "Just remember, posture is everything. The ministers have warned the court that His Highness has been ill. You won't be expected to sit very long or address them. And also, remember to remain seated until Minister San An approaches to assist you off the dais. He will shield your... particular area. Turn your back to the court immediately and then retreat slowly. Don't rush. Understood?"

I nod sharply. "I feel like an actor rehearsing for a stage performance."

"Yes, that is very accurate."

"I can do it," a soft mutter falls to reassure convictions.

Though I didn't think he heard me, Jin places a hand on my back. "Yes, you can, Bao Lai."

For a split second, I'm slightly confused as to whom he had addressed. I've almost forgotten that is my name. While returning a smile, I look up at his gentle face and sudden confidence overflows.

"Thank you, Jin."

"Are you hungry, yet? Should I fetch your dinner?"

"No. Please, sit with me a little longer. If you don't mind, Jin, could you tell me about yourself? Maybe it's too early to make presumptions but I feel we will be together for a very long time." I said something stupid again. My face turns crimson and I fluster like an idiot. "I-I meant we as in y-you and me—He Pi! Not... not the other me. I—"

"I knew what you meant," he replies. "You want to know how I came to be a servant? The simple answer is that my mother lost the fight against Consort Yi and Empress Pai."

"Your mother?"

"Yes, Consort En."

"What are you saying, He Pi is your... your brother?"

Jin nods as sadness creeps over his countenance. I'd always thought there was a regal air about him. Nothing suggests to me that he is a servant except for his claims. Jin looks away for a short moment to sort his thoughts and then continues.

"After Emperor Jin passed, the consorts and Empress Pai waged wars against one another. All of us children of the court were pushed and pulled like puppets on strings to carry out ambitions we could hardly grasp. Empress Pai staged a mass poisoning and was successful against all the consorts' remaining children, except for His Highness He Pi and me. My mother, then feared for my life, withdrew from the competition. However, Consort Yi retaliated with greater force. The enraged women, who lost their children, joined her faction. In the end, it was the mystic Wu Ling who resolved the conflict. To assuage the tension at court that would not subside, His Highness gave Prince San An the title of Prime Minister."

"S-S-San An? You mean he's... he was the crown prince?"

Jin nods. "Yes. Not only are they half brothers, they are also cousins. I imagine that was one of the reasons His Highness did not perish during Empress Pai's scheme. She spared her nephew believing her sister would step down, but Consort Yi was an ambitious woman."

"You are not a minister even though you should be a prince?" I ask because that seems a little unfair. Jin simply laughs.

"I have no desire to be minister or hold any political office. My mother grew ill near the end of the conflict. A short time later, I was left an orphan at court. With no one to back my political claims, His Highness did not see me as a threat, so he proposed that I become his personal advisor. I was sick of politics, sick of court, sick of people killing each other for something so meaningless, that I asked to be his personal attendant instead. So, don't feel sorry for me, Bao Lai. I'm not a servant by force. This is what I want: to be near my brothers, the only families I have left."

Sadness deepened when he spoke of his mother. There is no doubt that he loved her dearly and the memories of youth spent not in happiness, but in political wars, have taken its toll. I want to comfort Jin but what could I possibly say?

Eventually, Jin glances over and smiles. "I'm sorry. I didn't mean to be so depressing."

"What? No! It's not that at all! I was just thinking how wonderful of a brother you are to take such good care of He Pi. He sounds like a handful. You're older than him, aren't you? If I had younger siblings who are that unruly, I would beat their butts red!"

"I can't very well beat the emperor's butt red," Jin laughs.

"No, I guess you can't."

"What about you, Bao Lai? Tell me about you." He smiles charmingly as though burdened sadness was released. I think he is merely suppressing it.

"About me? Well, I... It's a little complicated."

"More complicated than being a servant prince?"

"Maybe not that complicated," I nudge him. "The truth is I don't really know who I am or where I came from. Ever since I was an infant, I've been living at a temple in the south. The old man—well, the priest—said I was dropped in front of the place without so much as a note. The old man—sorry, I kept calling him that because he hated it. The priest raised me because the nearby villages were poor and no one wanted another mouth to feed. I grew up as a student of the temple. Mostly, I just did meager chores.

I guess you can say I was a servant, too. They dressed me as a boy, so the other young men wouldn't feel awkward. Eventually, I came of age and the old man passed. The temple didn't want a female to interrupt their path to enlightenment. I left and well, wandered for a long time until I found an abandoned house near the village of Kou and made it my own. That was maybe a year ago? I'm bad with dates."

I glance over to see what Jin thinks. His brows are furrowing from outrage. Did I say something wrong again? My posture stiffens and my fingers twirl together nervously. Finally, he breaks the awkwardness by beating a fist against one of the bedposts.

"Path of enlightenment!" He scowls. "They want to reach enlightenment to end the sufferings of humanity, when right before them, a young woman in need is thrown out to fend for herself? Hypocrites!"

"It's—It's okay, Jin! I'm glad they threw me out. I would never have left if they hadn't. I wanted to but I lacked the nerves. Worked out in the end. Here I am a year later living in the palace as emperor and all, huh?"

He returns my humor with a glare.

"This life is not as grand as you think. You are in constant danger, not just from the court realizing the truth, but also from numerous political adversaries wishing to end your life. You cannot trust anyone. On top of that, you'll never be able to live as a normal woman with someone to care for you."

"I've never really been a woman to expect all those things."

"What do you mean?"

"I was raised as a boy and told to behave as a man so my presence didn't disturb the monks. I've never worn women's clothing and no one's ever truly treated me as such. I don't know what a normal woman's life is and for a long time, didn't know anything about life outside of temple. So, it's no big deal."

He doesn't know what to say to that. Everyone here sees me as a woman. I certainly don't think of myself as a man, but I don't ever think I am as a woman should be either. After leaving the temple, I shied from everyone my gender because I felt inferior. It is strange for me to actually pretend to be a man now, and yet, no one close to the situation views me as such.

In any case, I would be content to live the rest of my days here with Jin. San An's warnings abruptly shoot across my mind. A sharp pain wells in my chest. What am I saying? That's completely selfish! Who cares what I covet! I shouldn't be coveting anything! What about Jin? After all, he stayed at court to be near his brothers. If He Pi never returns, then why should he waste his life here?

A phantom itch is suddenly crawling over my arms; I can't keep from shuffling. "What about you, Jin? Don't you want to marry and have a family of your own?"

The question startles him. Eyes widen and his lips become half-parted. Following a moment of hesitation, he thoughtfully replies, "I've never considered the option. I've decided to devote my life to His Highness. I see no other path for me."

"But I'm... not him. I want for him to return as much as you do, but if he doesn't, you should at least think of the alternative."

Scoffing, long fingers run through his hair. "Yes, I'm sure women are very interested in a servant with nothing to his name. Realistically, I'm not fit to be anyone's husband."

Enraged by his self-degradation, I'm suddenly in front of him. "Are you kidding me? You're gorgeous, smart, and sweet! Any woman would be lucky to have you! How can you think that way?"

There is no response. He simply looks off elsewhere. I wonder whether there is more to his story. He hated court and thus, denied his birthrights and became a servant. And... he doesn't want to marry because he hates himself? No, that doesn't sound logical. Even if that were the case, would he deny any woman who pursues him? He keeps himself secluded, but why?

"You don't trust women, do you?" The accusation indiscreetly projects without comprehending how the thought formed.

Jin directs back a bewildered stare. His cheeks are burning from embarrassment, whilst frighten eyes broaden. He tries to deny but can't bring himself to rebuff. In the end, he says nothing at all.

"I understand. You were a puppet in others' ambitions. Women made your childhood a torment. You saw your siblings perished and attempts were made on your life. You are afraid history will repeat itself should another woman have control over you and use your claim to the throne against He Pi."

Maybe I sounded preachy, because his soft gaze suddenly becomes as sharp as knives.

"Don't presume to know me or how I feel! My mother was a good woman! She didn't deserve her titles stripped from her or the pain she had to endure during the conflict. Yes, she was a part of it, but she did it for me! No matter the heinous acts other women have accomplished, my mother was a good and virtuous woman who was pulled into a travesty that never should have happened!"

"I-I didn't mean to say anything poorly of your mother."

"Why wouldn't you? She took part and lost. For her failure, she was subjected to unbearable humiliation. Even after her death, they still shamed her! Women! The only things on your minds are power and pamper. Aside from my mother, I doubt anyone of you truly know what love is!"

His views finally brought to light; the resentment he feels toward all women is clear to me. I know he can discern the idea to be illogical, despite anger clouding his mind for reasons that are logical. It was because of this face that he had allowed me to come close, but since he hates the idea of me for being what I am, the best thing I can do for Jin is to keep distance. However, he is suffering. Retreat would be an act of cowardice. He's always been there to comfort me when I was unsure of myself.

Moving closer, my arms wrap around him. Surprised, Jin leans away. I draw him back.

"I am a woman. I am not your mother nor am I the women from court during your childhood. I have not proven myself to be worthy or vile; at least, I don't think I have. If I do cause you pain, chastise me. If I make you sad, then scold me. For the first time in my life, I feel happy and safe. It's all because of you, so I don't want you to hate me just because of my gender. I have no right to ask but I'm asking anyway. I don't know what love is; if ever I do, I promise I'll love you. I'll love you however you want me to; as a friend, a sister, a confidant. Maybe, I'll even make a good brother for you."

A weak smile forces its way over my lips. His expression is empty. Perhaps, it was too much to ask. He is merely my instructor. I've overstepped our boundaries and caused him more grief. Just as my hands leave his shoulders, Jin's arms encircle my body. I'm suddenly looking up from the bed into glistening unshed tears peering down. My heart is racing uncontrollably.

"Jin..."

"You can't just say something like that to me!" Such pain exerts to the surface. He speaks through gritted teeth in attempt to hold back the tumults.

"I don't understand."

"You can't just tell me you'll love me and expect me to keep composure!"

"I... won't do anything you don't want me to."

I didn't think my promise was inappropriate. Knowing me, I must have done something wrong. Bewildered and confused, the crimson face peering down fully reflects my sentiment. For a drawn moment, the room is silent except for the sounds of our hearts furiously beating in tandem.

Slowly, little by little, he leans down until our lips barely graze. Something keeps him and Jin withdraws.

"I'm sorry, Your Highness."

Jin abruptly leaves the room. I'm frozen in place.

He certainly behaves erratically. One moment, I think he hates me, and then the next, the opposite. At times, his moods shift on a whim. I wonder whether my actions confounded him or this is the true Jin. Regardless, my opinion of him will not change. In my eyes, he's one of the best people I've ever known. I respect and care for him deeply.

As I close my eyes to reflect his image, my heart begins racing once more. What's wrong with me? This is hardly turmoil I need on the day before appearing in front of the assembly. With San An there, it will take everything to retain control. This tension with Jin might really break my concentration.

Chapter 9: The Assembly

Jin was sterner than usual this morning when he came to dress me for the performance. I thought it best to leave conversations for later. At the moment, it's taking every last bit of composure to ignore San An's smiling face. The more he smiles, the more unsettling everything feels.

Arriving at the position, I wait for my cue. The orator calls out, "His Majesty, the Great He Pi, arrives at court!"

"His Majesty, the Great He Pi, may he reign for eternity!" The court responds in a reverberating echo while every member bows low to the ground.

Taking a deep breath, I walk from behind the large gold seat placed before the court. My back is straight and my hands are together. I march to the front of the throne and sit with posture. My gaze is directed ahead but not at anyone in particular. My hands circle the armrests but I do not grasp at them.

Below the dais is a sea of noblemen and others of import in their respective seats. Contrary to expectations, the assembly is held in open-air instead of an enclosure. Wouldn't they want to keep out prying eyes? I suppose this is simply a show. The council, comprising of He Pi, the ministers, and Prime Minister San An, actually creates policies and formulates decrees.

This assembly is to illustrate goodwill and resolve those issues not of great impacts to the country.

Jin instructed me to remain silent. No one else is speaking either. Awkwardness is making me want to shuffle. I almost did. Thankfully, Jin's preparations helped me catch foolishness in time.

After fifteen minutes of utterly deafening silence, San An steps forward. "His Highness has been ill and is still recovering. The court should allow his return to rest."

"His Majesty, the Great He Pi, may he reign for eternity!" The court repeats the previous display.

San An moves into position and I quickly turn my back to the assembly. After he escorts me from the stage, I sigh heavily knowing the performance is over.

"Very convincing, indeed." San An smiles amiably once we are inside.

"Thank you."

As I turn to leave, he calls out. "A moment of your time, Your Majesty. If you will escort me to the gardens."

I want to see the gardens, of course. I just don't want to see them with him. After knowing who he really is and after considering the perturbed behaviors he exhibited toward me, I lost all trust in him. When I hesitate, he pushes again.

"Please, I insist, Your Majesty."

I don't want to, but the cold tone that suddenly takes over his calm voice turns me into a coward. Heavy feet grudgingly swing around and follow him. The path we take is void of guards, which is to my benefit, since I can't help but shuffle uneasily. My eyes are everywhere except San An.

Finally, we reach the doorway that leads outside. Lost in amazement of this wondrously beautiful place, I didn't notice he had stopped and inadvertently, slam right into his back.

"I'm sorry!"

"You don't have to apologize, Your Majesty. Go on, enjoy the view. The gardens are not far away. I'm sure you need a bit of fresh air after being cooped up in that little room."

Little room? That room is bigger than my old house! He's right, though. I do enjoy the fresh air. Although, I don't want to drag out this encounter more than needed.

"No, please go on to the gardens. I will follow you."

San An slightly bows and continues. We pass several more picturesque archways until finely carved doors painted red and gold appears. The surrounding walls are a mixture of white and sand-colored stones arranged in impressive mosaics. Jutting from the enclosure are dense leaves I'd recognized anywhere. The peach garden is beautiful and it is massive!

Despite the impressive foreign sight, I'm suddenly stricken by nostalgia. When the old priest was alive and before age weakened his body and kept him bedridden, we used to venture up the nearby mountains during late summers to pick wild peaches. I spent those days climbing up and down tall trees, and then ran wildly beneath the shade; after which, the priest would call me over and flogged me for being too rowdy. In front of the other temple members, he never scolded my unladylike conduct since the subject of my gender was laboriously avoided by everyone. When we were alone, he made a point to teach me proper behaviors. I was annoyed by his lectures back then. Now, I understand the reason. He knew I could not live at the temple forever, and with all his efforts, tried to civilize me. If only I'd listened.

Stopping beneath the shade of a particular tree, San An searches the branches and picks one of the small fruits above. The presented token is nervously received. After which, I merely fumble the rounded fruit between my hands.

"These peach trees were specially sown by the request of my mother, Empress Pai." San An gazes lovingly at the charming flora above.

I look up. Why does he suddenly want to speak of this subject?

"Yes, I know Jin has told you of our past, that I am his brother and the former crown prince. Do you find it fair, Your Highness?"

"I don't know what you mean. Do I find it fair that Jin told me of your past?"

San An swiftly turns about. "Do you find it fair that the crown prince is not emperor when his brother has gone missing? I am the rightful heir. You have no claim to this throne; I hope you understand that."

Of course, I know that! However, I didn't know the Minister wanted the throne. I thought he was satisfied with his post. More so, wasn't it San An who suggested for me to become He Pi? Why didn't he just send me to the gallows in the first place? Actually, there's something else unsettling that just occurred to me.

"Is that why you wanted to marry me? To remove me from this ruse, so you claim authority?" Rage overtakes prudence and the peach in my hand is harshly thrown to the ground. San An's eyes glide toward the object and follow as it rolls away. He is offended.

"Pity. You do not appreciate the hard work of others. You only know how to throw away what isn't yours."

"Did you... Did you do something to He Pi?" Both hands clenched, I step forward.

"Don't be absurd," he glares back angrily. "He is my brother and I am his prime minister. I have almost every authority he has without the fear of others aspiring to take my life. His Highness has left me in the best possible position."

"Then why do you want to know whether it is fair that you are not emperor?"

"If He Pi never returns, then the country should not be in the hands of a stranger with no blood ties to the throne. Had you accepted my proposal, I would have made you empress; a true title, not one you pretend to hold."

"You want to marry a woman who resembles your brother? I think the throne is not the only thing you are aspiring for."

"And what is that supposed to mean?" He frowns.

"I wouldn't know," is my airy reply.

He tried to use me, to seduce me, and made me questioned my decency. He attempted to drive a wedge between Jin and me. Anger is enough to clear my mind of fear. Without allowing a response, I turn to leave. He rushes forward and seizes my wrist.

"I have not spoken all my thoughts, Your Highness. Please, stay!" With one swift motion of his hand, I slam hard against the ground. I sit there obediently not knowing why; the fear of him now winning over my rage.

"Do not think for a moment that my intentions toward you are anything but a man's desires for a woman. You resemble him, yes, but you are not him. I can tell the difference, if that's what you're asking. I am the eldest and yet, I must serve my younger brother. Titles mean nothing. Respect is everything. He will never in his life respect me. You must, once you are mine."

What kind of sick twisted logic is that? He must have lost his mind! I don't know else to do except look away. Immediately, he pulls me closer.

"Everyone respects him—respects you—because his whore of a mother manipulated my father! My mother, the empress, lost to a harlot! She died in shame, for how could a woman feel any less to have scorned the affections of her husband? The things they said—the pain she endured—and all for what? That birthmark on his shoulder? That red blot of nothing!

Everyone knows the mystic was a fraud. Master Wu Ling died years prior to this man's arrival at court. To deter a civil war, they turned a blind eye to the truth and robbed my mother of her pride and respect! My pride and respect! And you, another fraud to claim what isn't yours. The other ministers would have it no other way. I am but one man in a position without absolute respect. There is naught I can do. And yet, if I didn't care for the country to break into war, would simply expose you for what you really are!"

San An grabs the collars of my robe and forcibly draws them open. My secret would have been revealed if not for Jin's sash. Frustration is eating at my core. I can't tolerate his madness any longer!

"Don't blame me for your wretched misery!"

In an attempt to pull free, my strength works against me and I fall flat on my back. Before I can fathom what had transpired, I look up and all I can see are his long fluttering lashes. What is happening? Something isn't right. I'm too numb to notice what had come to pass. Then, I feel it. His lips are firmly pressed against mine. I had inadvertently taken him down with me.

Pushing off San An, I struggle to my feet. However, he promptly gives reminder of my rumpled state. As I stop to fix the robe, San An moves in front.

"You needn't be in such a hurry to leave," he smiles sweetly. I shiver at the sight of that smile.

"What exactly do you want from me, Minister?! Respect? I respected you from the moment we met, but your actions have robbed every drop of it from me! I'm sorry that you are not emperor. That is not my fault! In the end, the title belonged to your father. Whomever he chose to give that right has the true claim. Your mother poisoned your brothers and sisters for the sake of respect! I do not know her, but I know that cruelty is! If you have done anything against your own brother for the sake of respect, then you don't deserve to rule!"

"You would talk about my mother!" San An grabs my arm and jerks me forward. His grip is so severe, I feel as if my bone is breaking. "Did you think no one tried to take my life? That Consort Yi and Consort En were without faults? Those two were the worst of the lot! One tried to burn me alive by setting fire to my residence. The other sent guards to slay me after the attempt at poison failed! My mother did what was necessary to protect me and ended the fighting. If it hadn't been for her, the wars at court would have lasted much longer with even more casualties, I assure you!"

I had no idea. I guess in political wars, no one is innocent. While they shared similar childhoods, San An is much different from Jin. His ambitions and hatred twisted everything about him to search for power and validation, while Jin turned into a recluse.

I still don't fully understand what he wants from me. At the moment, all I can think of is for Jin to retrieve me. I want to feel safe again. I don't know how to deal with this madness or if I can even break free from San An. One thing is true. Should I somehow manage to leave, I won't be able to do else except cower at the sight of him; more so than I already do. With whatever courage is left, I grab San An by the collar and draw his face closer. His eyes broaden for a moment and then resume their usual expression.

"Since I am the only thing standing in the way of your ambitions, then I give you every right to remove me. You're right! I have no blood ties to the throne and

I am a fraud! Do whatever you must. I know you are a careful man. There's no reason you would walk about unarmed. No one is around. Kill He Pi and take what's yours!"

His eyes narrow and his lips purse. Maybe, he doesn't quite know what he wants after all. The long, excruciating moment seems to span eternity. Suddenly, the empty gaze arches upward and terror floods his countenance. San An embraces me while swinging around for us to exchange positions. Instantaneously, an arrow pierces through his shoulder. He lets out a pained groan.

"San An!" From behind his slumped shoulders, the assailant's blurred figure runs away. Panic takes hold and my body turns to ice.

"Run," he whispers. San An falls unconscious in my arms.

I don't want to leave him but his advice is best. Running back across the path, I scream for the guards. In moments, a horde of soldiers comes forthwith, including the three I met in prior days.

Generals Yue and Hu search for the attacker while Qing Hai and I rush to retrieve the Minister. Once we are inside, Jin comes with us to find the court physician.

Sharp phantom pains shoot through my chest when I glance at his face. This can't be happening. Why would he do that? Why would San An protect me? I'm nobody! It should have been me! I would trade anything for him to just wake up!

The physician forbids us from entering the infirmary, but I feel dread flows, the same dread I felt that day when the old man passed away. I don't care what San An did. I don't want him to die! He saved me—had attempted to save me so many times through his own coarse methods by having offered succeeding chances to leave this post. Whatever he said or did, I thought deep down he genuinely cares for me. He doesn't deserve such an end; an end meant for me.

Jin tries to calm my guilt but there is no way I can sit out here while who knows what is happening in there! Yet, I can't just storm in and make a scene. I still have this role to play. I don't know what to do but I need to decide now. I fight with myself and then decide to

Go inside (Continue to page 99)

Let the doctor do his work (Continue to page 106)

Chapter 9 – 2

I run inside and Jin follows suit.

"How is he? It's just an arrow wound! He should be fine, shouldn't he?!"

The court physician is startled. "Your Majesty! Please, forgive me. I don't know what more I can do."

"What is that supposed to mean?" The sight of San An lying still makes my heart drop. "Is he..."

"No, Your Majesty. He will soon unless an antidote can be found."

"Antidote? He was poisoned?" Strength leaves all of me in the instant that inconceivable idea takes form. Jin manages to catch me in his arms.

This can't be. San An had escaped all the terrors of his youth, all the claims made on his life, just to die now because of me. I refuse to allow that!

"No, you must save him! What are you sitting around for? I don't care what you do, you have to save him!" My fist slams against a nearby table; bitter tears can't be restrained.

"That won't solve anything, Your Majesty! Please, let the good doctor do his work."

Jin tries to pull me from the room. I push him away and rush toward San An. The physician is just going to watch him die. This should have been my death, not his! If he has to walk into the other world, I won't let him do it alone. The arrow is still on the tray nearby, dripping with his blood.

"Your Majesty, what have you done?!" Jin cries out as the tip punctures my palm.

The physician frantically approaches. I order him to desist.

"If he dies, I die. Get it? So, unless you want the death of an emperor on your hands, you will save him!"

My heart is racing. Pain is shooting up my arm. The poison is quickly taking effect. Breathing is becoming a chore. I've no choice but to lie down beside San An.

I can hear Jin telling me to stay, but I don't know how long I can keep from falling unconscious. Maybe, the end is nigh and thoughts are flying toward home. I suddenly recall following the old priest up the mountains when I was a child. An unbearable pain touched me when I ran off and climbed one of the tall trees. Even though the old man told me to stay close, I never listened. A strange plant nested up in the branches pricked my leg and then this same pain had taken over me then. The old man called it... what did he call it after he treated me... he called it...

"Sleeping nettle... Sleeping... nettle!"

Chapter 9 – 3

Perhaps I died; I am not certain. How can anyone be sure of reality when dreams sometimes feel more real than life? I was floating somewhere and speaking to someone. I think it was the old man. I miss him dearly. He was the only person in the world who truly cared for me; at least, before I came to this palace. Everyone here only wants me because of my resemblance to He Pi. Wherever he is, I hope he comes back. He never would have placed his brother in danger. I don't want anyone's life in my hands. I thought I could handle it but I was wrong. San An, please live. Please, San An, live!

Someone nudges my arm and impulsively, I sit up. A surge of pain ripples across my body. A groan escapes.

"I'm sorry. I didn't mean to... You were talking in your sleep. Are you all right?" Jin smiles wide through fatigue covering his brows.

"Where's San An?"

"He's fine. He's resting. You gave the court physician quite a scare." Jin's laughing; though, the expression is sad. "Lie down."

"No, I won't until I see San An!" Pushing off the bed, I try to walk. My lungs burn and then I fall back.

"I assure you, he's safe. Do you not trust me?"

"I trust you but I don't trust me. Am I awake?"

"San An means that much to you, does he?" Jin looks away. There lies a hint of jealousy in the tone.

"He saved me. How can I ignore that? He's your family! I don't want anyone to be sad because of me! That assassin... did they catch him?"

"No. He disappeared by the time the guards gave chase."

"He must have overheard... everything! He knows! He knows I'm not He Pi!" I failed on my debut. I put San An and the country in danger. How could I have been so reckless! A fist slams against a bedpost as tears stream down in torrents.

"We'll deal with things as they come," Jin reassures.

How can he still be so optimistic when nothing is certain? He makes me feel safe when I don't deserve it for this failure. San An was right. This pretense authority is nothing. Without He Pi, he should reign. He could save this country.

"Where are you going?"

Jin reaches out while I start from the bed. I shake him off but my legs give away and I fall to the floor.

"I'm going to give the former crown prince back his title. You don't want authority and He Pi is missing. San An had to suffer a monarch's tribulations; he should be rewarded as such. He can protect this land. I can't do it! I don't want anyone's death on my hands!"

The idea of crying is despicable. More and more, tears fall endlessly. I shove my head into my palms to hide the shame. Jin says nothing because there is nothing he can say. My weakness is clearly displayed to the man I wish to hide it from most.

Just when nerves are on the verge of consuming all of me, faintly, a familiar voice draws my soul from despair. San An, leaning against the doorway, is riddled with fatigue.

"That you don't want blood on your hands is a sign you are fit to wear He Pi's crown."

"San An! You shouldn't be up."

"She's right, Prime Minister. Please return to bed."

Though Jin addresses him by title, I can see he is worried for his brother. The older man gives a small smile. Then, stumbling through the door, he collapses in front of me.

"I'm alive. That is enough at the moment. Go fetch our dinners, Jin."

Even in this state, he is barking orders. I do not think it's very nice to treat his brother with such little regards. Perhaps, this is just their ways. Jin is not offended and seems glad to be useful. When only we remain, San An faces me.

"I heard of everything you did for me, Your Highness. You refuse to marry me, but you are willing to die for me? Quite the enigma." He chuckles, but pain soon puts an end to the endeavor.

"You're one to talk! You want to be emperor but you saved me. Why? I don't deserve kindness from you. Your ambitions would have been fulfilled through my death."

"I never had any intention of causing you harm," his brows furrow.

I offended him again and can't do else except blush in embarrassment at my own misguided accusations.

"Then, what do you want from me? If you want this throne, I will find some way to give it to you." I owe San An a great debt that can never be cleared.

"You know what I want," he replies airily. A crooked smile follows.

The insinuation makes my entirety bursts into flames. I can't believe he's willing to tease me at a time like this!

Embarrassment keeps me from responding. In due time, San An places a hand on my head.

"Don't do anything obtuse like that again... Your Highness."

"Same to you!"

Finally, I think we've come to an understanding. He sees me for who I am; not for the person I resemble. I understand him to be as confused and conflicted as Jin. He is not a bad person. Whatever it was that clouded his mind and caused his assaults against me in prior days dispersed. San An returned to his old self. Every notion that he had part in He Pi's disappearance is relinquished. This is enough to make me trust him; just not enough for me to desire being in his attention more than needed.

Continue to page 108

Chapter 9 – 4

Despite my guilt, the country's safety is more important. I must retain composure and keep this pose. Thus, instead of intruding, I fall to silent prayers for his safety.

In the end, San An lives and I couldn't be gladder. After several days in the infirmary, the Minister finally calls for me.

"San An, how do you feel?" I sit on the chair beside his bed.

"My state of affairs should not concern you."

His eyes are cold and distant and his demeanor is completely indifferent. Against my protest, San An slowly sits up.

"I shall make this quick. The assassin undoubtedly heard our conversation and realized you are an imposter. Therefore, your role as He Pi is rendered moot. I've instructed Jin to prepare a sum of gold for your services. Qing Hai will return you to your home."

"You're letting me go?" My heart aches for reasons I cannot construe. He's right, I'm not needed anymore. This is what I wanted, isn't it?

"I won't take anything from you, San An. You saved my life. I'm forever grateful."

"Don't be ridiculous. The arrow wasn't meant for you. Regardless, we are done here. Leave me."

San An returns to rest. Hesitantly, I part from the room. My mind and body are stricken by phantom pains. Why do I feel this way? Intuition tells me that I made a terrible mistake, but what was it?

"Bao Lai, are you ready?"

I look up to find Jin holding a small parcel. Though dejected, he continues.

"The Prime Minister—"

"I know, Jin. I can't accept any gifts. But, thank you, for everything. I hope someday we can meet again."

There's more Jin wants to say that can't take form. I leave the palace and return home.

For the rest of my days, I live as a recluse. I never amount to anything and I never serve any purpose. Each day, I feel utter regret but I don't know why. What mistake did I make? Was there another path I should have taken in life? I'll never know.

The End.

Chapter 10: Mu Dan

A few nights later, Jin and I are called to San An's quarters. When we arrive, Zhen Yue, Bai Hu, and Qing Hai are also present.

"Why have you summoned us, Prime Minister?"

My body hasn't fully recovered from the poison's effects. Making for a chair, I collapse in a thud. To my surprise, San An appears as though he was never injured. Of course, it's not like him to show weaknesses in front of others.

"Patience, Your Highness. Now that we have all gathered, General Yue has some good news to report."

Zhen Yue nods. Taking a step forward, he begins. "Qing Hai was able to trace the assailant's retreat for a short distance. We believe he headed east to Mount Fei Yang."

"That's great! Let's go capture him!"

I'm on my feet, excited by the prospect of bringing the person who'd injured San An to justice. Had the Minister perished, I could never forgive myself. However, the Minister shakes his head to signal that I shouldn't get my hopes up.

"We cannot enter Mount Fei Yang, Your Highness," San An explains. "Sending our soldiers there could be viewed as an act of aggression against Ning."

"They sent an assassin after us! Is that not an act of aggression?"

"We cannot prove that the assassin belongs to Ning or that he came on Emperor Yuan's orders. They will turn about and say Bei Ling instigated the offense or that we staged the ordeal to march on them."

"Then, what? Do we just let them get away with it?"

"No. We will send an emissary to speak with their representatives and ask permission to search Mount Fei Yang."

"Are you kidding me? We need to ask permission? Even should they agree, there's no way we'll find him! Unless..."

"Unless what? Spit it out already!" Bai Hu snaps crossly. No matter how I appear, he will never accept me as He Pi. In some ways, I appreciate that.

"Unless, the target joins the expedition to search for the assailant. Whoever wants He Pi dead won't waste the chance to correct his error. Let me go, too."

"Don't be stupid! You said the attacker knew you aren't His Highness. Why bother?"

"If our enemies knew, then why not just attack Nan Rong already?" This conversation feels out of my league. However, I'd already inserted myself, so I might as well continue.

Hu does not reply. The Demon General's grimace is so severe, I can feel it burning a hole through my head. San An smiles shortly and places a hand on Hu's shoulder. The younger man desists.

"You both have good points. It was through my carelessness that our secret was revealed. I will travel to Ning with General Yue and sort this out. If they truly know our ruse, then it will be obvious. Until then, remain calm on the matter. There's no reason for us to instigate a war over what ifs."

The last time San An protected me, he barely managed to survive, and now he wants to walk straight into Ning? Something is severely wrong with him! At the end of the day, he is the former crown prince and the prime minister while I am nobody. There's no reason for him to be placed in danger instead of me.

"No, I will go." Standing up, I slowly approach the group.

"You? You couldn't charm your way out of a wet paper bag!" Bai Hu smirks. "Let someone who doesn't appear a fool get this done. Besides, if they don't know you're a fake, then you'll really be in danger."

"Can't you be a little nicer to her?" Qing Hai interjects. I don't know why he feels compelled to defend me. I don't care what Hu says because I don't disagree. It was nice of Hai, anyway.

"When she is dressed as a woman, I'll treat her like one." Hu responds gruffly.

Hai protests and they go on for a few minutes about nothing. I now understand what Jin meant when he mentioned they always draw out conversations when they are together. This doesn't concern me at the moment. Ignoring the squabble, my attention refocuses on San An.

"Prime Minister, I will go with you."

"That is not possible."

Maybe he's forgotten I'm as stubborn as he is.

"I'm going with you."

"Please, don't argue with the Minister." Jin reaches for my arm. I shake him off.

"You are the former crown prince. My first decree as He Pi is to restore your title. So, if you want to let this country fall to chaos by being reckless, then I hope you can live with yourself."

San An raises an eyebrow. I know I'm being an imbecile. I have no idea where this is going. From the corners of my eyes, I see Yue thinning his lips. He's disapproved of me from the very beginning. Strange enough, Hu is more than amused.

"That so? It was my idea to bring you to court. Don't I get a fancy title, too? Want to make me the Duke of Zhou?" Hu nudges my arm while laughing boisterously.

"I'm demoting you!"

For my reply, I receive a grin.

"That's enough, Bao Lai."

By using my real name, Jin gives reminder that I have no authority. The bitter frown on his mouth makes me withdraw. I suppose there is no point arguing about this now. To persuade San An, it is better to be frank with him; alone and without all these interruptions. I'll visit him later when no one else is around.

Once things settle, Jin and I leave. He seems tense as we traverse the halls together. However, the tension is short-lived.

"Darling!" Someone cries out from behind. Suddenly, a pair of arms flings around my neck and the noxious scent of blooms envelopes me.

"Who the hell...?"

My attempt to request for his assistance is thwarted; Jin is stricken by embarrassment. I turn back to face the assailant and the extremely beautiful woman before me appears vexed. Dressed in luxurious royal garbs, her face is flawlessly painted, her lashes are long and curly, and her brown hair sways airily, making the woven jewel and flower headdress tinkles with delight.

"Where have you been?" She scolds me. "Everyone said you left for the Summer Palace and then they said you were ill. I say that's impossible! You wouldn't go to the Summer Palace without me, would you?"

"Uh..." I stare at Jin but he's looked away. Is he blushing because of her? She's ten times the woman I could hope to be; all the same, I am always nervous around females. The feeling of inferiority is taking over me by the second and it's beginning to show on my face.

"What's wrong? Cat got your tongue?" She leans closer.

I step back. Nervousness is chipping away at composure; my voice suddenly increases in pitch. "Who-Who are you, again?"

"Excuse me?" She puts both hands on her hips and pouts. "Have you been consorting with other women again to have forgotten me? It's Mu Dan, your fiancée."

"My what?"

My eyes grow wide from terror, until I remember Jin's account. This is the woman to whom He Pi is engaged. Suddenly, I feel sorry for her. Should He Pi never return, she will be cheated of her nuptial. I am in no position to do anything about that. Anyhow, I have other things to worry about. Taking a step toward Jin, I feign fatigue.

"I'm sorry... dear. I'm not well. Can we talk later? Jin, please help me back to my room."

Jin complies and assists me down the hall. The stubborn woman can't take the hint. She starts after us and then walks beside me.

"Your voice sounds different. My poor darling, you really are sick! Let me tend to you."

When she puts out both hands, I press hard against Jin to escape her grasp. "No, no! I'll make you sick, too. Go back to the, the... wherever you just came from. Jin will take care of me."

"Where I came from? You're delirious! Jin, let me help you care for my beloved."

Jin doesn't reply. I don't understand why he refuses to help me! He just keeps on blushing. Clearly, she's beautiful, but to make Jin speechless is not something I expected. Is he nervous around women? He obviously doesn't trust them. Maybe, he is terrified of them, too. What am I saying? I'm a woman! He doesn't behave this way around me!

We arrive at my chamber. As soon as Jin and I slip inside, I immediately turn and lock the door before she has the chance to enter.

"What are you doing? Let me in!" She beats the door furiously.

"I'm tired! I'll talk to you later!"

My body still hurts. The encounter with this madwoman made it worse. A deep sigh escapes as I fall onto the bed. She is yelling something through the door. Whatever it is, I don't hear it. It's becoming difficult to stave off slumber.

Hours later when night descends, my eyes finally open. I think Jin must have already gone to bed. Usually, he'd wake me when I sleep too long. Today, he didn't. Was it because of her? It's pointless to feel jealousy, especially when she has no interest in him. Still, to have seen him behaved that way makes me uneasy. In my mind, Jin is claimed. He is mine! Perhaps, not in that way, but I see him belonging to me solely until He Pi returns. Then, I'd have to give him back. I don't know why I feel this way. I just do.

After an hour of feeling infuriated for no reason, I start from the room for San An's quarters. Crossing hall after hall, a familiar dread suddenly surges. I'm lost again. Where are San An's quarters? I thought Jin and I turned left here earlier or was that on the way back? Recalling our path, the memory of her previous intrusion suddenly enrages me. The nerve of that woman! I blame her for having been a distraction. This is the reason I can't remember where San An's quarters are located. That's not true; I'm naturally bad with directions. I still blame her!

Yet, standing still and being angry won't solve my dilemma. I just need to walk around until I find his quarters. First, I need to pick a path.

Chapter 10 – 2

I turn right and scuttle down the hall. Whilst peering around the corner at the next turn, an unsightly creature emerges a short distance away. Of all the luck! It's He Pi's fiancée. I hastily swing around to run back from whence I came before she can see me. Of course, it is too late. In mere seconds, her arms fling around my neck. As I stumble forward, she immediately pulls me into an embrace.

"Darling! Did you come looking for me?" She chirps happily.

"No, I did not!" My attempt to pull free is futile. Her grip is like iron shackles.

"What do you mean? Why are you avoiding me?" Mu Dan is wounded by my carelessness. I know I must feign He Pi's persona, but this is insufferable. Everything about her irritates me and I wonder what it was His Majesty saw in her.

"I'm... sorry." I mutter under my breath.

"I forgive you!" She hugs me again.

Well, that was easy! Obviously, the lecher and this crazy woman are perfect for one another.

"Listen... dear, I'm a little delirious right now. I need to speak to Minister San An. Do you know where his room is?"

"I thought you didn't like San An," she pouts. "Anyway, wouldn't you rather spend the night with me?"

All my nerves suddenly fire at once. Why my heart suddenly race because of this woman, I'll never know. "Well, it's important. Do me this favor just once."

"Why are you blushing?" She glares accusingly.

"I-I'm not. I'm sick. High, high fever... delirious!" A fake cough erupts. Using the excuse, I manage to pull free.

"My poor dear. Why don't you return to bed?"

"No, I need to do this. Please, help me."

Mu Dan stares directly into my eyes. Something in my words or expression startled her. I understand I am not behaving as she expects, but I don't think anyone really knows what He Pi would do in this situation except for He Pi. Slowly, a smile flows across painted lips. Linking our arms together, she drags me down the hall.

"You've never been so adorable, Your Highness!" She laughs happily.

"What is that supposed to mean?"

"Blushing and asking me for help. It's so unlike you!"

"Well, I am sick, you know. If I wasn't, I wouldn't."

"Liar," she frets.

We walk down several more corridors and then I realize that this is not right. We are nowhere near San An. Where is this crazy woman taking me? My arm withdraws but she holds on steadfast. I haven't felt strength like this since General Hu accosted me on the road.

"Where are we going?"

Disregarding my panic, Mu Dan continues. I think she enjoys this. Turn after turn, and then we are outside. In the dark of night, I can barely see her in front of me. Yet, Mu Dan walks as quickly and precisely within the path as though the sun is right above. I thought women of the Circle had to stay in the Peony Palace. She apparently knows every single inch of this massive place.

Intuition swiftly signals danger; more so, I'm irritated for too many other reasons. Agitated, I cry out, "Will you stop already?!"

Mu Dan abruptly complies and I lean down to catch my breath. My chest is heaving while she is unfazed. Turning around, her hands squeeze my arm. The grip feels like boulders crushing my bone.

"What are you doing? Let go, damn it!"

"You don't sound like you at all, Your Highness." Her blithe response is also somehow menacing. I can't see her face but perceptibly, a grimace is present.

"You dare disobey your lord? I said let go!" The authoritative approach backlashes. Air drains from my lungs when Mu Dan slams me ferociously against a nearby wall.

"What is my name, Your Highness?" She comes closer and speaks in a low tone.

"What? M-Mu Dan, obviously. What's the meaning of this?"

"My real name," the voice draws deeper. Is a completely different person standing there? She was my height moments ago; yet, I now feel someone tower over me. What does she mean by real name? I had no idea she existed until earlier today.

Obviously, she saw through my disguise. This is quite an overreaction. Should I just admit the entire thing? However, I can't trust her. She's standing here threatening me. How can I be sure she will keep my secret? Better for her to turn me in to the ministers and accept my fate than to imply the ministers and have them all, including San An, answer to the court for conspiracy. Mu Dan pushes the question again. Her grip is so severe, my arm is turning numb. I need to say something.

Lie (Continue to page 120)

Tell her the truth (Continue to page 122)

Chapter 10 – 3

"I told you, I'm sick. I can't remember anything! Let me rest and I'll tell you tomorrow!"

"Tell me my name or I'll break your arm," the tone draws even deeper.

"I don't... I don't know!"

"Why don't you know?"

Pain is slowly spreading. If she isn't going to break my arm, it wouldn't take much more for her to dislocate my shoulder. Who does she think she is, trying to pry an answer from me when she is hiding a secret of her own? My other hand is forming into a fist. I don't want to hit a woman but this may be my last choice. When her grip tightens, my decision is made.

"I don't care what your name is. If you're going to accuse me of something, then do it already!" My left arm swings across where her face should be; instead, my fist hits something more solid. I was right! She did grow taller. Reaching out into the darkness, I realize my fist connected with her chest. However, this is not a woman's chest to be sure.

"You're a man?!" The strident cry projects much louder than intended. From afar, the sound of shuffling footsteps nears us. The guards are making their rounds. My immediate reaction is to call out to them, but I can't. This man shoves his mouth over mine while pressing his body against me, choking all the air from my lungs. I struggle to push him off to no avail. He feels like a brick wall. And yet, if this person is really a man, should have the same weakness they all share.

My knee swiftly rams into his most sensitive area. Mu Dan groans and withdraws. His grip around my arm loosens. A hard fist slams against his face just for good measure and then I run toward the footsteps. They have long retreated. In the dark of night, the path is obscured. Honestly, I probably couldn't traverse this place in broad daylight.

My heart races and my lungs constrict. I haven't felt this fearful for my life since that day on the road. Why can't any of them, even the Demon General, be here now? I should call for help but if that madman catches me first, I'll be done for. Stumbling forward, I hit trees and pillars along the way and eventually slam into a wall. This is good. It is something to go by. Following the stone structure, I hope a door will soon appear.

However, time chisels at hope in the midst of the unending path. My breathing is growing more ragged. How much longer will it take for me to recover from the poison's damage? What a frivolous question! Unless I find help soon, I may not live long enough to worry about that. My body is shaking and I'm turning cold. Suddenly, footing is lost and the hard ground connects to my slumped body. This is it. I can't move a muscle. Consciousness is seeping away.

Continue to page 123

Chapter 10 – 4

I should tell Mu Dan the truth. She is He Pi's fiancée after all. Taking a deep breath, I admit to being a fake and carefully explain the situation.

"I see. This is a dangerous game you play." Mu Dan strokes my cheek and leans in closer. "It's too bad you're not trustworthy. If this is all it takes for you to reveal the Minister's ruse, you'll only end up causing trouble for Nan Rong."

"But, you're His Highness's fiancée! That's why I'm telling you!"

"It's a good thing I am his fiancée. Anyone else would sell this secret to many, many interested parties. His Highness needs a country to return to and you only serve to mitigate that certainty."

Without allowing a response, firm hands grasp at my throat. I can't breathe! All my attempts to retaliate are futile. The hold increases as time passes and eventually, life disperses before my eyes.

The End.

Chapter 11: That Bastard!

Waking up in my quarters, logic reasoned that the whole ordeal must have been a sordid dream. At least, I thought as such, until I push off the bed and shooting pain freezes me in place. Beneath the right sleeve is a large bruise running up and down almost the entire length of my arm. I poke at it and the pain makes me wince. It is completely swollen.

"That bastard!"

"Yes, I am a bastard. I apologize."

Oh, god. Who just said that? I turn about frantically and then notice someone by the window. There she sits. He appears the same as before, the same height as me, but I can't trust anything anymore.

"Who let you in here? Jin! Jin, where are you?!"

Mu Dan moves to the corner of the bed, all the while, glaring amusedly as I inch back, clutching at my arm.

"Don't bother. I told Jin to leave us be. We need to talk."

"Excuse me if I disagree! The last time we talked, you tried to break my arm! What did you say to him?"

"I said nothing and he told me the truth anyway. It's that simple. Frankly, had I wanted to break your arm, I would have. There's no need to try."

"You arrogant prick! Get out of my room!"

"Quite the mouth on you! I don't take orders from commoners. Besides, this is not your room. We can talk like civilized ladies or we can repeat last night's affair. That's up to you."

"Are you threatening me?   Do they know your secret? You're no lady!"

"Neither are you," he smirks. "I liked you better last night when you were shy and adorable. Believe me, you'll want to be in my favor."

The nerve of this man! I've never met anyone so insufferable! If only the chair by the vanity were closer, I'd throw it at his head! I don't care what he wants to say. I don't want to be anywhere near him!

Quickly darting off the opposite side of the bed, I make for the door. He stands up and blocks the path. "Get out of my way!"

"I told you, I don't take orders from commoners." He grins. "Sit down and hear everything I have to say."

"I don't take orders from people who've injured me!"

"You should take orders from people who've injured you and who have no hesitation in doing so again."

The grin widens and I so badly want to hit him. However, upon raising my right arm, the pain becomes unbearable. I have to let it drop again. I'm in no state to fight him. Even at full recovery, he'd probably win.

Chapter 11: That Bastard!

"Jin! Jin! Shu Jin, where are you?"

There is no response from beyond the door.

"Are you deaf? I said he's not there. Sit down and listen."

That authoritative tone is intolerable! I can't do else at the moment but it isn't like me not to retaliate. Moving to the window, I stand still and ignore him.

"Well, that's very cute. Are you waiting for big brother to come save you? Jin will not return until after I leave, Your Highness. Don't believe me? We can be here all day."

He doesn't deserve a response. My eyes are locked on the closed panels. He can talk himself to sleep. I don't care. Time passes by in mind-numbing silence. Luckily, it seems he's grown tired of bothering me because Mu Dan hasn't said another word for the past thirty minutes. Good. I just need to find Jin and sort out this madness.

"What are you doing?!" Just as I turn, Mu Dan is at my heels. Putting out both arms, he locks my body into a tight embrace.

"Will you listen to me now?"

"No!"

"Well, that's too bad because I'm going to start talking and you're going to hear everything I have to say whether you want to or not." With that, his arms constrict, pressing our bodies into a single line. Mu Dan leans closer to my ear and begins. "Don't struggle. You're irritating me. I told Jin this is a conjugal visit. He's not coming back until I leave, understood?"

"You told him what?! D-D-Does he know you're—"

"No. He thinks I'm so pretty, he would do whatever I tell him. Men are easy to manipulate once you know how to hit the right spot. Women on the other hand, women like you, are too unpredictable."

"How long did it take for you to realize..."

"The first moment my arms flung around you, I knew. I spend all my time in the company of beautiful women at the Peony Palace. You think I can't tell an ugly one just because she's wearing men's clothes?"

My fidgeting ceases at the word, "ugly." I know I'm not pretty but I didn't think... and that must be the reason Jin does not behave so childishly near me. Still, it begs the question: he knows I am a woman, so why did Jin agree to this conjugal visit from He Pi's fiancée? More importantly, this man is He Pi's fiancée. Does His Majesty know?

"Yes, His Majesty knows my gender." Mu Dan answers my direct mental inquiry.

How did he do that? Only one other person has done that to me thus far and I want him to be here instead. I would gladly trade this man for San An in a heartbeat.

"I thought you were usurping his throne. Is he actually missing?" Mu Dan whispers.

"Yes. Did he say anything to you? Do you know where he went?"

"Don't ask silly questions. If I know where he is, I would fetch him. There was something he mentioned to me, though at the time, I did not think it relevant."

"What did he tell you?" Hope dash high; I jump a little.

"Calm down. I'll tell you in a minute. First, is there anything else you'd like to ask?"

"What? No! Tell me what he said!"

"You're being embraced by a beautiful man. Are you sure you don't have at least ten more questions for me? You may never be in a position like this again."

"Arrogant bastard! Just tell me already!"

Mu Dan chuckles softly while his warm breath tickles my ear. "All those years engaged to His Highness and I never had the chance to embrace him like this. Mainly, because we both prefer women. To have you in my arms now is quite a treat."

Damn it. Why am I blushing again? I hate Mu Dan! I hate that everybody keeps using me to exact whatever secret feelings they have for He Pi!

"I'm not him!"

"No. That is precisely the reason I can hold you this way. Be still for a moment and let me relish the thought."

"Are you crazy?"

"A little. Now, are you sure there's nothing you want to ask me? I'm willing to answer anything."

Honestly, I have a million questions but I don't want to drag this out. I decide to ask him one question and one question only so we can move on. What should I ask?

"Why are you engaged to He Pi?" (Continue to page 129)

"Why do you cross-dress?" (Continue to page 130)

"Who are you, really?" (Continue to page 131)

Chapter 11 – 2

"Why are you engaged to He Pi?"

This bothers me severely. Jin knows almost everything about his brother. This Mu Dan holds secrets no one can fathom.

He sighs softly and then leans closer. "Because he trusts me."

That is not what I wanted to hear. I need more details. He purposefully answered in such a manner that could easily lead to nine questions more. Not wanting to give him the satisfaction, I accept the incomplete answer.

Continue to page 132

Chapter 11 – 3

"Why do you cross-dress?"

He said he's interested in women, so it doesn't make sense for him to pretend being one.

He sighs softly and then leans closer. "It's easier this way to get close to women."

I don't even want to know what that means. I accept the befuddling answer.

Continue to page 132

Chapter 11 – 4

"Who are you, really?"

He sighs softly and then leans closer. "I'm the prettiest girl in your harem, Your Highness."

He giggles in my ear and I become enraged. Anyway, he's not going to tell me the truth and I don't want to give him the satisfaction by asking another question. I accept the impertinent answer.

Chapter 11 – 5

"Tell me everything he told you," I insist.

"That's all? Are you sure there's nothing else you want to know?"

"No!"

"Disappointing. Ah, I am a man of my word." He sighs again with a heavier air and holds me even tighter. "Here goes. His Highness questioned whether he is truly best for the country."

"That's it? That's your secret? Who doesn't feel that way when they're in charge? Even I've had my doubts and I'm not the real thing!"

"You don't understand He Pi. He's not a man with low self-esteem. That is to say, he never portrays himself as being pathetic to anyone. We were in his study drinking and well, liquor loosens tongues."

"He drinks?"

"Oh! I thought you didn't have any more questions for me! Liar!" Mu Dan laughs childishly.

"I don't. That was a question for me. Now, I've listened to what you had to say; so... get out of here."

"Just for that, I'll stay a while longer." The embrace sharpens and pain becomes unbearable.

"My arm hurts! Let go!"

My forehead rams against his painted face. He backs away, holds onto his nose, and then runs to the vanity. Over and over, Mu Dan continues surveying his reflection in the mirror.

"Look what you did!   You almost injured my beautiful face!"   Still holding onto his nose, Mu Dan turns to me wrathfully.

Shrugging, my body slumps to the ground. When I lift up the sleeve, it's apparent the color has deepened. Every touch feels like needles jabbing deep into my arm.

"I didn't think it was that bad." Mu Dan suddenly kneels in front and lifts up my injury.

"Stop! You're making it worse!"

"Be quiet for a moment," he waves a free hand at my face. "When Jin sees this, you'll tell him that you fell, right?"

"Why? Isn't he in love with you? Can't you just brush it off or tell him it's my fault?!"

Mu Dan smirks. Without another word, his long, bony index finger runs over the purple skin. The sensation is of a knife cutting through my flesh. I wince and draw back. He holds on steadfast.

"Don't be such a baby." He frowns. "Let me test something. Try not to scream."

"I think you've done enough! It'll heal if you'll leave me alone!"

"I wasn't really asking for permission."

With that crude response, he pushes my shoulder back with one hand and yanks my arm straight with the other. It feels as though he's ripped my arm completely off! Even if I wanted to scream, nothing could come out.

Pain puts me into shock and I fall over. For once, I want to lose consciousness, to be free from the torment, but it won't come. Every inch of me is paralyzed aside from my racing mind. Mu Dan is doing something to my arm. The feeling is nothing short of repetitious stabbing. I think he is talking to me, but I don't hear a thing. Eventually, I just fall asleep from boredom.

Chapter 12: An Innocent Mistake

When sunlight pierces through the window, Jin wakes me from slumber. I lost an entire day all thanks to that woman. It's my ambition that should I ever see him again, to order his execution.

"Did you have fun with Mu Dan yesterday?" Jin smiles while placing a tray in front of me.

Immediately, sarcasm comes to mind but when I look up, see that he is genuine. I want to respond but my throat is sore. Instead, my head shakes violently.

"Oh? She said she had a very pleasant time with you."

I nearly spit out all the water I'd just drink. If by a pleasant time, he meant ripping my arm off, then sure! Speaking of my arm, I'm somehow using it freely. When I lift up the sleeve, only a slight discoloration near the elbow is present. It no longer hurts.

"Is something wrong with your arm?"

"Not anymore." There goes my evidence to hang him. "What exactly did she say to you, anyway? What did we do yesterday?"

"What do you mean? Weren't you there? She said you two spent the day discussing His Highness... something else about how soft he was to cuddle... I don't... I don't know." Jin flushes thoroughly.

Poor Jin. I don't have the heart to tell him the truth about Mu Dan. "Jin, did He Pi ever question his ability to rule over Nan Rong?"

"No, why?"

"Mu Dan said His Highness told him—her—that shortly before he left."

"You think he left because of doubt?" Jin settles beside me on the bed.

"I don't know. What if he did?"

"Then he will see how wrong he is and come back."

His words of optimism put me at ease. Yet, when I glance at his face, perceive that he is distant. As usual, Jin hides everything he feels.

"You don't have to lie to me, you know."

He looks over and smiles. "I'm not."

"You're doing it again. I'd rather you tell me that he won't come back; not because he can't, but because he doesn't want to. Then, at least, I think San An should be the one to restore stability."

Jin bites his lip and throws a hard gaze to the floor. "It's not that simple. Prime Minister San An can't take the throne."

"Why?"

"Because the country will erupt in civil war."

"That doesn't make sense. He has a legitimate claim."

"That may be, but old wounds haven't healed. Did you notice Master Yu's lack of effort in finding an antidote for him? If it hadn't been for you, he would have let the Prime Minister die."

I saw the court physician sat idle, but would he truly have just let San An die? How could he! I don't have a chance to ask when Jin continues.

"The court physician's sister was a consort to Emperor Jin. Both her son and daughter were poisoned by Empress Pai. You can see why he thought the end would be just for the Minister. I realized it when you barged in the room. And then, to see you lying there dying with him, I..." Jin's fists clench. Unshed tears glisten in his eyes.

"I'm fine." My hand moves to pat his arm. "Good thing I remembered sleeping nettle."

"What is sleeping nettle?" He returns curiously.

"The poison was sleeping nettle, wasn't it? I thought I screamed the answer to you."

"No," Jin replies through the blank expression. "After you fell down next to the Prime Minister, you were completely unconscious."

"Then, how did you find the antidote?"

The simple question is met with unexpected reactions. Jin looks at the ceiling, the door, and then the floor. He tries to ignore the subject. I can't let it go.

"Tell me!" Grabbing his arm, I give a light shake. He hesitates.

After a long moment, slowly and indecisively, Jin lets out a stifled sigh. "I... did something I'm not proud of."

"You know if you don't tell me, I'll just ask San An."

"Well, since that's the case, then I don't have a choice." A sad smile surfaces. "I threatened Master Yu. I said that if my brothers die, I would take the throne and well, it was a threat, you get the gist."

"Oh. Don't feel too bad. I sort of threatened him, too."

Jin neither notices my nervous chuckles nor shares my sentiment.

"I swore to myself to never covet power. At the time, power was the only thing to save you both. I was weak and foolish."

"But, it saved us. You didn't do anything wrong. I thought my actions saved San An when it was you all along."

Jin's head shakes. "I was willing to put my brother's life fully in Master Yu's care. He would have undoubtedly perished. Your impulsiveness forced my hand. Without it, I would have been alone again. Thank you."

The sweet smile on his face makes me smile, too. It's just like him to be so modest!

"You don't have to thank me, Jin. So long as you're happy, that's all I want."

Picking up the crystal cup, I drain the remaining liquid. My throat is as dry as sandpaper from lack of sustenance in the previous day; all because of a certain woman. After setting down the cup, I push away the tray and lie down behind Jin.

"I'm still tired, sorry. Do we have assembly today?"

He doesn't respond, so the question is repeated. When he appears to be ignoring me, I nudge his back. "Hey, are you awake?"

What childish behaviors! Since he's chosen to snub me, I'm going back to sleep.

"Ahh," a quiet exhale escapes while my eyes close. Soon after, he stirs, and then they prop open in search of his figure. I don't have to look far. He's leaned over me. Our faces are inches apart. The unexpected sight throws my heart into furious palpitations, and then just as quickly, calms at the realization that this must be another instance of his erratic moods. I shouldn't take this seriously.

"Are you okay, Jin?"

"Do you... really care about my happiness?" His voice quakes. Jin is utterly apprehensive.

"Obviously."

"Don't joke!"

I shouldn't have rolled my eyes. He didn't take the blithe response in good stride. Color is creeping over his face and deepening as time passes.

"I'm not joking. Truly, I do. Why do you ask?"

"No reason. I'm just glad." A hint of delight sparkles within the gaze and then he smiles happily.

This is rather odd. After the encounter with Mu Dan, I realized I'm ugly. I am better off as a man, I suppose, and I thought Jin saw me as such. Or maybe, I'm overreaching in my assessment of his reaction and it doesn't really mean anything at all.

Reaching up, I pat his head and grin. He takes my hand between his own. His palm is warm and slightly trembling.

"I want to make you happy, too." He continues softly.

"What..."

Jin closes in and presses a warm kiss on my mouth. It isn't vulgar like Mu Dan's or seductive like San An's. It is loving and passionate. My heart throbs a new sensation that overwhelms from head to toe. Never in my life have I felt such a thing!

His hand slowly reaches for my face, but as his fingers touch my cheek, I remember whose visage I carry. Perplexity causes my momentary withdrawal. It's enough to inadvertently force him away.

"I'm sorry, I thought..." He stammers. Jin is hurt and confused.

"N-No! Don't apologize! It's just..."

I peer over at the mirror and see He Pi's face. With a sleeve of the long robe, I rub off some of the powder, and then hastily untie my hair and throw the crown on the side table. Maybe, Jin realized his folly or maybe, he realized my stupidity. Either way, when I reach out for his arm, Jin abruptly quits the room.

Chapter 13: Vainglorious

Jin doesn't return and I resolved that while he is sorting through his thoughts, it would be counterproductive to interfere. Hence, in the afternoon, I make another attempt to find San An's quarters. Surely, once I turn left at the junction this time, all will be well.

Of course, I should have known not to get my hopes up. Another impasse is presented after the turn. My choices have been terrible thus far. I can't decide which route to take. While leaning against a wall to contemplate the consequences, someone disrupts my thoughts.

"Are you lost, Your Highness?"

Believing it's her, panic strikes my nerve. I twist around, prepared to retaliate, yet before me is a gorgeous young man with emerald eyes and light brown hair. He's dressed in dark green clothes and holding a silk fan. Such noble airs float about him; I assume he must be someone of ranking.

"I-I-I... y-y-yes."

The young man is so utterly charming, I can't keep from stammering. For my ridiculous response, the stranger graces a boyish smile.

"You'll want to take a right here. His quarters are down that hall."

"Whose?"

"Prime Minister San An's," he answers casually.

"How did you..."

I can't finish the question since the answer is so obvious. Recollection of the pain he's caused me rushes in torrents. Quickly rounding the corner, I attempt to escape. What madness is this? He's already moved in front. It's as though he teleported, but that's impossible.

"How is your arm?" He taps the fan to my shoulder.

"Do you expect me to thank you after everything you've done?!"

"I do."

The smug response makes my blood boil. My anger must bring him happiness because he's grinning triumphantly.

"I don't have time for this! Get out of my way!"

Shoving Mu Dan aside, my objective is resumed, though he promptly calls out a warning. "There's no need for that. The Prime Minister has already left with the caravan. He left yesterday whilst you were busy sleeping in my embrace. And yes, we did cuddle after I fixed your arm. A woman doesn't work for free."

I can't believe it! San An put himself in danger to find the assailant who attacked me, and I didn't even have a chance to at least thank him before he left, all because of this person who seems to like tormenting me. The angrier I become, the happier he smiles.

How could He Pi be engaged to this jerk? Everyone spoke highly of His Highness. I'm beginning to question his sanity. Had he run away because of doubt just to leave the country on the verge of war, then I hate him for it. I want that if he doesn't return now, for him to never come back!

"What's the matter? Are you sad?" Mu Dan leans down until we're face level while making no attempts to hide his sarcasms.

My jaw grinds furiously. Ultimately, I decide to hurt him where he'd hurt most. Grabbing his cheeks with both hands, I yank them every which way. He flusters and hastily withdraws but my revenge had already been exacted. His cheeks are red and slightly bruised. Mu Dan drops the fan and holds onto his face.

"You evil, evil woman! What did you do?!" He screeches.

I shrug and wander back down the hall.

"Come back here! You have ruined a work of art! Do you hear me? A work of art! I will make you pay for this!" He keeps muttering something under his breath while running to find a mirror. I can't make out what it is.

Chapter 14: Kang Lang

The court grew restless in the passing weeks. I only attended the assemblies once since my arrival and that is not enough. They were told He Pi was ill and then were informed that he was injured. Naturally, the ministers pushed for another appearance lest the court believe His Highness had perished. Jin was against it but his words made little difference. Without Minister San An present to speak on my behalf, I panic at the prospect of needing to address the court.

Decidedly, the assembly will be today in the afternoon. Jin is dressing me for my role while I frantically play scenarios after scenarios in my mind. If anyone says this... then I should do that, and if not that... then this.

As usual, I look to Jin for reassurance. However, he's preoccupied and doesn't notice my pleading gaze. At the moment, his younger brother is missing and his older brother is off somewhere in Ning. We haven't heard any news since the caravan left. If I were in his position, I couldn't keep half of his composure.

When I finally give up the notion of binding his attention, ironically, Jin starts to speak. "Don't worry too much. Just do the exact same as last time and everything will be fine."

Why is he trying to bolster my confidence when he is obviously more troubled? It's what I wanted, but when he does reassure me, I only feel annoyed.

"You know that's not possible. San An is not here and the other ministers won't take part in my performance because they fear being tied to the ruse. Besides, everyone is aware of the recent assassination attempt and the measures Nan Rong has taken. They'll want answers."

Jin frowns. I'm making his attempt to calm me futile. More so, I've actually just stressed him further.

"I'm sorry, Jin. I'll do my best, I promise. I won't speak unless necessary and if I must, then I'll..."

I can't finish the thought. What am I supposed to do? I don't sound like He Pi. I can't attempt to copy his voice since we've never met. Not only that, I've yet managed to learn how to speak in the manner to which he was accustomed.

"Ah..." I said I would try my best to become His Highness. Instead, I've spent most of my time caught up in the chaos of his personal life. I feel like a failure.

Just when I think this will be my last day on Earth since the court will undoubtedly charge me for being a fraud, a familiar voice comes through the door. That woman returned.

"Darling!" He bursts into the room and embraces me. His arms feel no less than iron beams crushing my ribs. Jin flusters and turns away.

"I don't have time for this!"

Upon my outburst, Mu Dan releases his hold and tells Jin to leave. Once more, the latter complies without question. I take a few steps away from this crazy person. He glances over and smiles.

"Don't look so frightened. I'm not here to torment you. Not yet, anyway." The voice is his real voice—a complete mismatch from the disguise.

Twitching nervously, I retreat a little more. "What do you want?"

Mu Dan folds his arms and stands at a slight angle. "You're very rude! I came all this way to help you and this is how you speak to me?"

"Help me how?" Mirroring his stance, I frown.

"Get on with it. I don't have all day. You'll make me late for my chess games." Mu Dan replies languidly. The voice that came from him is different from any I've ever heard. A sudden smile covers his painted lips; his expression is one of victory.

"I-Is that He Pi's voice?"

"A perfect match, I assure you. I also know his personality well enough to pass for him. So, what do you say? Will you be my puppet?"

With Mu Dan providing He Pi's voice coupled with my physique, we'd be able to fool the court for another day. Soon as elation comes, hope is suddenly dampened by an uneasy thought. Could I really trust this person? Should he purposefully say something to propel his agenda forward—whatever that agenda's objective may be—I could not stop him without exposing my secret.

While I'm desperate at the moment, he's not the type of man who does anything without expecting payment. Maybe, it is better to rely on myself than to constantly seek help from others. Once more, he reads my thoughts.

"You're awful!" He scolds in the female voice. "I just want to help Your Highness however I can. You're my fiancé after all."

The word "fiancé" provokes another twitch from me. Once I rely on him, there will surely be a price. Nevertheless, he could guarantee the stability of this political structure until San An returns. On the other hand, this task is mine and I don't trust him. I don't want to be so pathetic that I need Mu Dan to save me from my own incompetence.

"Thank you for your offer. I will do this alone." A short bow and then I start for the door.

Mu Dan frowns. His arms fly around me. As I begin to protest, he sweetly interjects, "Good luck, darling!"

Giving a swift peck on my cheek, he then disappears down the hall.

What a strange and annoying person. Is he mocking me because I'm a woman or because I'm a commoner? I doubt he behaves this way toward He Pi. I just wonder whether is it due their gender or because he knows the consequences for expressing his feelings? Hmm. I suppose that curiosity is more suited for another day.

It's time for the assembly.

Chapter 14 – 2

The moment I lay eyes on him, I'm thoroughly stunned. I'd always thought he was handsome. In clothes befitting a prince, Jin is utterly sublime. However, he fidgets terribly upon noticing my silent intrusion. I guess he really hates the idea of being a court official after all. It just can't be helped. Without San An present, Jin must take his previous position. To appear before the court means he can't dress as a servant.

"His Majesty, the Great He Pi, may he reign for eternity!" The crowd responds to the orator's call while I enter the assembly in the previous rehearsed manner.

The familiar deafening silence returns and all eyes are on me. I'd hoped this display is enough to suffice the court's suspicions. Of course, that is hardly the case. An older man steps forthwith and the orator calls out, "Lord Po Sui of Hong Ran has the floor."

Breathing suddenly constricts, causing my arms to shake. Despite all my efforts to subdue the reaction, it is noticeable.

"Is His Majesty unwell?" Lord Po Sui gawks curiously.

My mind frantically weighs the outcomes of possible options. I can't form a resolve. This was a bad idea! I should have asked Mu Dan for help!

At the thought of Mu Dan, my mouth reflexively moves on its own. "Get on with it. I don't have all day. You'll make me late for my chess games."

The voice that bursts forth is not my own, nor is it He Pi's. It's a mixture of something strange. The attitude, however, is nearly a perfect match.

Lord Po Sui is taken aback. A crooked smile quickly follows. "Yes, Your Majesty. The court wishes you a speedy recovery. We know you are still recuperating from your previous injuries. Please accept our apologies for having pushed this appearance."

Lord Po Sui retreats following my nod of acknowledgement. Jin then crosses the dais to assist me while the orator and court calls out the usual phrases. Once we are alone behind closed doors, Jin bursts into laughter.

"What's so funny?"

"You," he answers coolly. "You'll make me late for my chess games?"

I rub my head shyly when he raises an eyebrow.

"Oh, Mu Dan taught me that."

"She's a good influence for you."

"The hell she is!" I should learn to control my temper. Jin is unaware of Mu Dan's sadistic side after all. "Never mind. It's better that we don't speak here."

Though he's thoroughly confused by my outburst, Jin nods and then follows me to He Pi's quarters.

When we enter the room, my agitation returns. Mu Dan is sitting on my bed, smiling as usual. At the sight of him, Jin abruptly leaves. I didn't even have the chance to fully gawk at my wonderfully handsome Jin yet! Once more, it is because of this woman.

Mu Dan claps his hands together and grins. "So, you owe me, don't you?"

"Owe you what? I don't owe you anything."

"You used my line. I told you, a woman doesn't work for free."

"You-You were at the assembly?"

"Of course! I wouldn't miss your performance for the world."

"Are you stalking me?"

"Obviously," he scoffs.

"Why?"

"Why else? I can't forget how adorable you were that night I nearly broke your arm."

At the mention of my arm, the pain momentarily returns. I look away while he starts from the bed.

"You can't imagine how cute you were; standing there with his face behaving so femininely. It's straight out of my fantasy!"

"You've been engaged for six years. I can't imagine you don't have the nerves to be forward with him."

"He and I are engaged because of a mutual agreement. Regardless of your opinion, I have no interests in men. Often though, I dreamt that one of us could switch gender. Alas, reality is disappointing. And then, you came along and won me over." Mu Dan draws nearer and I step back farther.

"Won you over? You harassed me! You think I want anything to do with you?!"

"And you harassed me. I guess we're even."

"I did no such thing!"

"No? You practically abused me; kicked me, punched me, and even bruised my beautiful face."

He keeps coming closer and like a fool, I keep moving back.

"That's because you started it!"

I don't know why I thought arguing with this crazy person would render merit. His face is purely delighted by amusement. Retreat continues until I suddenly trip on the hem of the long robe and tumble back onto the wall. Immediately, he is standing close, towering over me. How he keeps changing height is completely befuddling! Reaching out both arms, Mu Dan pushes against the wall and encloses me in between. I feel trapped inside a cell.

"Jin! Jin, come in here!"

"Why do you always ask for his help? I'm right here. Why not ask me?"

"I need his help to get away from you!"

"You can't just ask me?" He frowns.

What kind of nonsense is that? His impertinence makes me shake with rage but I know that any act of aggression would merely excite Mu Dan to continue. All because of this face! Memories of Jin's retreat haven't left me. This man must be just as confused. I quickly rub the powder off my face and remove His Majesty's crown. Long hair flows down my shoulders and I appear my gender.

"There! Do you see? I'm not He Pi! Your fantasy didn't come true, so leave me out of it!"

Mu Dan's expression grows severe. His eyes narrow and his lips thin into a line. I keep gawking at the door hoping for Jin to return. Of course, he doesn't. Mu Dan's right. All I do is rely on Jin for everything. I've never done anything for him. When he needed comfort, I thought letting him sort through this thoughts alone was best. I see now that it was selfish. Every time I feel troubled, including now, I keep expecting from him that which I've never given.

Slowly, my eyes meet Mu Dan's. He momentarily withdraws.

"What's wrong? Why are you sad?"

"I need to find Jin. Please, just leave me alone."

Pausing, he seemingly appears wounded.

"Do you really not like me?"

"I think it is you who do not like me. If you did, you would do as I ask."

A sudden burst of laughter erupts. His fingers forcibly run down my cheek. "You want me to be obedient to prove my affections? I didn't think you were that type of person!"

I don't know what type of person he is referring to but it couldn't be good. An angry glare is my single response.

"Tell you what, Your Highness. I'll be obedient from now on if you will fulfill your promise to marry me. After all, an empress can't disobey her lord."

"Quit mocking me!" I grab his fingers and throw them from my face.

"I'm not mocking you."

"Then, what the hell do you want?! I told you, I'm not He Pi! Why do you keep harassing me?"

Like a child being bullied, tears are welling. I know they're bound to fall in torrents and I don't want to give him the satisfaction. In a state of bewilderment, I do another foolish thing: I shove my face in his chest and sob. He initially falls back. Slowly, Mu Dan returns an embrace but it isn't the bone-crushing feeling I expected. His body is warm and his arms, comforting. I begin to forget why I'm even crying.

Coyly lifting my head to meet his gaze, I notice he's flushing more so than me.

"You're cheating," he chuckles nervously. "I can't bully a woman when she cries."

"I wasn't crying!"

"You are such a liar."

"So, you admit it! You're bullying me!"

"Obviously," he scoffs.

"Why?"

"Are you really that innocent at your age? It's because I'm in love with you."

His answer is so casual, it's as if he hadn't said anything at all. My cheeks are on fire and my heart skips a beat. What foolish reactions! By now, I should have learned not to take him seriously. I'm embarrassed for having believed him and even feeling a little excited by the prospect; however brief was the moment.

Rolling my eyes, I shove Mu Dan away.

"You're hilarious." As I start for the door, a heavy hand grabs my wrist.

"That's it? I told you I love you and this is how you treat me? Are you brushing me off? Are you rejecting me?" Pain crosses his expression; though mostly, he's just agitated.

"Do you think I'm stupid? You don't know who I am and I don't even know your real name! There's nothing about me to love except for the fact that I resemble your fiancé! That's hardly enough of a basis to place true affection!"

Mu Dan bites down on the lower lip while contemplating my frustration. Still, he is a stubborn sadist whose pride was challenged and thus, refuses to yield. The grip around my wrist tightens with his usual brute force. Pulling me into an embrace, his other arm chains around my back.

"I'm not lying!" He protests.

"I don't care!" I scream back.

Heat from his body rises tremendously and imprints onto my skin as though seeking to burn me. His rage is frightening. Still, I won't be intimidated. I don't know what love is but I don't love this person; this much I am certain. Despite his protest, whatever it is he feels must be misguided lust for He Pi. Every moment that passes, his grip becomes noticeably tighter while intense heat spreads to burn another part of me. Although I don't want to show more of my weaknesses, pain causes me to involuntarily wince.

"You're hurting me."

"Good! Then you know how I feel!"

A fervent kiss presses against my mouth. I try to turn away but his grip shackles me in place. A strange sensation of pain and pleasure passes through and then my body falls limp in his arms.

I hate him so much, but for whatever reason, I don't want him to release me. Confusion and frustration rise in tandem and threaten to drown me under their weights.

Chapter 14 – 3

"What is the meaning of this?!" A voice erupting with fury pierces the silent room, carrying a force which is only comparable to that of roaring thunder. Mu Dan quickly relinquishes his grip while I, pulling myself together from shock, stumble to regain control of my body.

Prime Minister San An steps inside and surveys the younger man. When he briefly glances at me, both displeasure and anguish cross the furrowed brows.

"I always knew something was insincere about you. I never would have guessed it was your gender. And here you are in His Highness's chamber assaulting my charge! I won't tolerate such a thing! Not even from his fiancée. You will be executed!" With that, San An prepares to retrieve the guards. Before he can move more than a few steps, I rush forward and grab onto his robe.

"Please, San An! He didn't mean any harm!"

San An's livid glare gradually fades to disgust. "Did you want him here, Your Highness?"

The Minister's tone is so bitter and cold that chills run down my spine. I don't want Mu Dan to be executed but I also fear his impulsive nature. I can't keep composure when he's near. How then, can I expect to maintain the ruse? This may be my only chance to be rid of Mu Dan. Yet, I cannot bring conscience to accept that.

"I asked him to tutor me. He knows His Highness as well as anyone. I made it through assembly today, didn't you hear? It was because of Mu Dan."

"And I suppose you were repaying him for his kindness?"

"No!"

"Then he accosted you!" The tone hardens. San An peers wrathfully in Mu Dan's direction.

"He was... It was my idea for us to role-play! We went a little far, I'm sorry!"

"You don't have to lie, Bao Lai." Mu Dan suddenly steps forth. I never told him my name. All the same, it's not surprising he knows more than he should.

"I was taking advantage of her, Minister." A sweet smile accompanies his admittance. "She's so tempting when she's angry, isn't she? You should know. I'm not the first man here who has forcibly put his hands on her."

Mu Dan grimaces. San An returns the gesture in full fervor. Just how much does Mu Dan know?

Leisurely, the younger man's expression relaxes. Both hands rise to signal surrender. "Well, do what you have to do, Minister. I am fully guilty of all charges."

Still scowling, San An carefully examines my expression and then shortly after, parts from the room. In believing that he is going to retrieve the guards, I give chase. Just as I do, Mu Dan grabs at my collar.

"I thought you didn't love me. Why do you care?" The tone is teasing but he's staring blankly at the wall.

"You idiot! Do you want to die?"

"Might as well, if it means I can't have you." He grins.

"Stop joking! Look, even if you do l-l-lo... meant what you said, that's no reason to be reckless! You only live once! Don't waste your life on something so useless!"

"You think love is useless? Typical idea from someone who has never been in love." Mu Dan scoffs while ruffling my hair. "If I weren't going to be executed, I'd teach you a thing or two about being a woman. You look like a kid!"

"Then, that makes you a pedophile!" I knock his hand away.

"Well, I can't be a pedophile since you're older than me."

How does he know my age? I've never told anyone outside of temple. Laughing at my dismay, he moves to the door.

"Where are you going?"

"To find the Minister. I'll save him the trip. Besides, I don't want you to shed tears for me. I'd rather walk to my death with fonder memories than you crying."

He smiles shortly then continues out the door. My chest tightens. I hated this idiot! I still do! Whether he lives or dies is not my business! I tell myself that but my body instinctively moves forward and reaches for his hair. Immediately, he shrieks and whips around.

"Don't mess with my hair! I don't want to meet the lord of the underworld looking unkempt!" Darting back inside the room, he makes for the vanity. "You evil woman! I think you pulled out a few strands! My beautiful hair!"

Mu Dan removes every pin and begins reassembling his locks. He's muttering something under his breath. Expletives, I imagine.

Strange, he is such a brute but when it comes to appearances, Mu Dan is as high-maintenance as a princess. The way he flusters amuses me. I inadvertently laugh.

"You think I'm funny, Your Highness?"

"Hilarious." I wonder how a man who cannot stand the sight of a few strands of hair falling is fine with the prospect of losing his head. "Listen, Mu Dan... or whoever you are, just leave the palace. I'll talk to San An once he returns."

"Leave the palace? Me? I'm too beautiful to be thrown into the filthy world of the common. I'd rather die!"

"You are really something, you know that!"

His attitude is vexing. I've never met anyone so disagreeable! At this point, I don't care anymore. Frankly, there were a few times I wanted to kill him myself. Shuffling angrily to the bed, my fingers reach up to rub my forehead. He's giving me a headache.

Following a short pause, I let out a heavy sigh and glance up. He's standing right in front of me. How did he move so fast? I never heard him stirred.

"What now? If you want to die, then go!"

"You're so cold," he pouts.

Damn it! I forgot to contain my frustration. With little effort, Mu Dan pushes me down and hovers atop.

"I'm going to die because of my love for you. Can't you at least reward me before I go?"

My first thought—a counterproductive one—is to yell his ears off. However, he likes it when I erupt with rage and he likes it when I'm shy. He wants that I am anything but neutral. The more I look into his eyes, the more I realize he can't feel satisfaction unless he holds power over another, or that he is incapable of feeling anything without going to the extremities. He mocks me because I am weak. He teases Jin to validate his narcissism. He couldn't overpower San An, so he challenged his authority the only way he knew how: by being impertinent.

My last resolve is to ignore him. Both eyes shut tightly.

"You've tried this before. Ignoring me doesn't work, remember?" His index finger taps my forehead sharply. For his effort, Mu Dan receives no reaction. He kisses me fervently but I manage to keep still. His hand then brushes against my face and then slowly, fingertips glide over my skin and descend toward my chest. I want to kill him but unless I'm actually going to do it, would solve nothing.

He doesn't really desire me, I know that. Mu Dan conveyed that I'm ugly. There's no reason for him to behave this way. The word "ugly" keeps echoing in my mind; spawning other thoughts that run in a repetitious loop. "I'm ugly. I might as well be a man. I am a man. I am He Pi."

Abruptly, his fingers stop their descent. Mu Dan whispers in my ear. "Who said you're ugly?"

"What?"

My eyes reopen to his perturbed expression. How does he keep reading my thoughts?

Mu Dan repeats the question while resentment manifests into a scowl over his painted mouth.

"You did."

"When?" He's taken aback. In moments, the memory comes to him and a small crooked smile appears. "Why don't you ever take me seriously when I'm actually being serious? I was just teasing you. You're such an imbecile."

"Yes, I know." My tone is flat and my expression is indolent; mirroring the true He Pi. Mu Dan pouts and then moves away. He lies down beside me for some time before a long sigh erupts.

"Kang Lang."

I glance over from the corners of my eyes. "What?"

"That's my real name. Don't ever call me that around other people. When we are alone, call me, 'Kang Lang.'"

"I thought you were going to die for the sake of my love. When will we ever be alone together again after this? Unless... you had no intentions of dying."

"Don't be sarcastic. I'm too beautiful to perish in such an ugly manner!"

"You knew San An wasn't going to fetch the guards?"

"I knew the Prime Minister would not do anything to upset you. I'm a little jealous. He is a fine gentleman."

"Are you... jealous of him or are you jealous of me?"

"Both," he laughs wryly. "I thought if I could persuade you to feel guilty enough, you'd give yourself to me, but you're so cold." He moves off the bed and starts for the vanity.

"You're a real bastard, Kang Lang."

"I like it when you say my name. I'll have to make sure we are alone together more often from now on, Your Highness."

"I can only tolerate you in small doses."

"If you were any other woman, I'd punish you for that." He replies curtly. "I don't find you amusing anymore. Although, I'll tell you a secret, if you want."

"Do I want to hear this secret?"

He turns around and grins. "I should hope so. I know the identity of your elusive assailant."

Does he really? Before I even consider believing him, I'd already flown off the bed.

"Who?!"

A teasing smile and then he turns away. I shake his arm severely. "This is not a joke! Do you have any idea what San An and the others have been through? Whatever secrets you hold, you will tell me now!"

"So demanding! I know just about everything that goes on around here," he smirks proudly. "Collecting information, infiltrating bases, impersonations, assassinations, and so forth. That assassin and I used to serve the same lord."

While Kang Lang is genuinely beautiful, there hides something utterly dark underneath, that for a moment, he let slip across his eyes. It is eerily frightening. My breathing stalls just as I catch a glimpse. He quickly represses it. Finally, everything makes sense. This is the reason he's so strong, manipulative, and outright talented at his craft.

"Tell me!" I shake his arm again.

"A woman doesn't work for free!" He giggles in Mu Dan's voice.

"Is that what Kang Lang would say?"

Placing both hands squarely on my shoulders, he replies, "No, darling. Kang Lang would not answer anyone for anything. Mu Dan will answer to her lord under every circumstance."

"I don't understand. Would He Pi not eventually fulfill his engagement?"

"He Pi is not here, my dear. Besides, His Highness never had any intention of taking Mu Dan as his empress. Haven't you figured out by now the nature of our relationship?"

No, I haven't. Admitting that I don't understand anything is an understatement. "What must I do for Mu Dan to answer me without becoming her lord?"

"Don't ask to buy the merchandise when you're not willing to pay the price." He shakes his arm free. "I won't tell you a thing until I'm empress."

"Why is that title so important to you?"

"You have the emotional intelligence of a child! You'd never understand! Speak to me again when you've changed your mind."

Kang Lang frets and starts for the door. I yank him back.

"You're very forward tonight, Your Highness." Although his reply is playful, his voice is taut and cold. He's lost all interests.

"Please, just tell me. I don't have the authority to make you empress. You know that! I'm barely able to fool the court into believing my authority. How can I instill yours?"

"That is your problem, Your Highness, not mine."

I need to confirm whether Ning is preparing for war if indeed they know my secret. San An surely has news but I doubt he'd found anything at Mount Fei Yang. This is my chance to be useful. Yet, Mu Dan's proposal is preposterous! San An knows his secret. He would never allow it! Should I just promise Mu Dan whatever he wants?

Don't lie (Continue to page 169)

Make a false promise (Continue to page 170)

Chapter 14 – 4

I can't do it. I can't lie and make a false promise. He would see through it anyway. I'm the fool here, not him.

"I'll give you anything else but I can't promise you that."

Mu Dan jerks back his arm and leaves. I'm disappointed. However, it was presumptuous of me to think the Minister's efforts were for naught. San An would probably not want to receive me after that shameful display. I should search for his generals instead.

__Continue to page 172__

Chapter 14 – 5

"Fine! Help me! Once everything is settled and if He Pi does not return, I will marry you."

"That's a big if, isn't it? Should His Highness return, then I'd get nothing. If he doesn't, then I'd still lose him. Doesn't feel like a win."

"Should he return, how can I make you empress?"

"Don't be dense. Declare me empress now and secure my title. He Pi won't make a fuss to strip it from me."

"I can't do that."

"Of course not. You know full well there are no time constraints. He may return in a day or in ten years. Until there is proof he's perished, you are free from the arrangement. Given the lack of constraints, you're willing to agree to anything. How despicably deceptive of you!"

As expected, he saw through my ruse. I'm the fool here, not him. I cast down my gaze to hide my shame.

"I really like this side of you," Kang Lang whispers as an arm slips around my waist.

"Are you serious? My being deceptive excites you?"

"It's only because you're so transparent. What would you really do if I had agreed and there is proof

His Highness will never return? Would you really marry me?"

"I..." can't finish the sentence. I suppose a promise is a promise.

"You would, huh?"

How does he keep doing that! Maybe he's right. I am transparent.

"Tell you what, Your Highness. I'll take that deal. All you have to do is be willing to have our honeymoon tonight, after which, I'll tell you everything I know."

"What happens when he does return? I would be cheated in that case!"

"I suppose. Should he come back, I'll marry you anyway. See? No harm done." He grins sweetly. The boyish tone is exasperating.

"That's the stupidest thing I've ever heard!"

"Why? Your proposal isn't any better for me. One of us will be cheated either way. I hold what you need. Speak to me again when you're serious about making a deal."

Kang Lang darts from the room so swiftly, I can't catch him. I'm disappointed but it was presumptuous of me to think the Minister's efforts were for naught. San An would probably not want to receive me after that shameful display. I should search for his generals instead.

Chapter 15: An Emperor's Privilege

In the barracks, Qing Hai and Bai Hu are fussing near the archery range. They really fooled me before. From afar, they seem really close, almost like brothers.

"Oh, it's you!" Hai waves as I approach.

Hu smacks the younger man's arm and then stomps forward.

"What are you doing out here, Your Majesty?" Hu glares at Qing Hai as a mean of chiding him for being too informal toward He Pi.

"General. Hai. Have you any news from Ning?"

"Isn't that something to ask the Minister, sire?" Bai Hu folds his arms and puffs out his chest.

"I didn't want to disturb him. He's had a long trip."

The elder of the two knows I'm lying. Due to the other soldiers nearby, he has to feign respect for my authority. Though, he's not happy about it. Hai, on the other hand, is as innocent as ever.

"We weren't allowed to accompany the caravan," he begins. "Maybe you should talk to General Yue. Oh, never mind. He's already left for his rounds."

"Or maybe, you should talk to the Minister!"

Hu's tone is as sharp as his tongue. Obviously, should Bai Hu know anything, he'd never tell me. With a short nervous nod, I leave the barracks.

More than anything, I want to see San An. At the same time, I don't think I can face him. Have I done something wrong? Was it my fault Mu Dan tormented me? My mind keeps replaying Kang Lang's embraces and kisses. It is the same unsettling thing that occurred to me after San An's previous advances.

How it happened is unbeknownst to me. I'm suddenly in front of San An's quarters. I don't remember walking here, yet here I am. Why then, am I afraid to call for him? While I struggle to decide whether he should be disturbed, the door abruptly opens and San An signals for me to enter. I drag my feet and keep my head down; just waiting for him to scold me. I want that he would instead of looking so disappointed.

"I've been expecting you, Your Highness."

At the table, the Minister pours fragranced white peony tea into a pretty cup and carefully hands it to me.

"Thank you."

"No need to thank me. Although, I suppose I should apologize for having interrupted your affairs earlier."

My eyes lock onto his face but San An won't give acknowledgement. He's hurt and betrayed when there's no reason for him to feel this way. I thought after the ordeal in the garden, he came to his senses and saw me for what I really am: a stranger of little import.

"Prime Minister... San An.   Have you brought favorable news from Ning?"

By trying to brush off the uncomfortable subject, I thought we can move forward. If there was more to say, he decided against it. San An nods slightly and places his cup on the table.

"Yes, I'm glad to report it doesn't appear Ning is aware of our ruse.   Furthermore, when we entered Mount Fei Yang, we were able to capture some ruffians who revealed that the culprit did in fact impeded on their territories and killed several of their men. The assassin then fled and returned in the direction of Nan Rong. Specifically, toward An."

"He's here in this city?!" In shock, I spill tea on the pristine table. San An pulls a kerchief from his jacket and clears the mess before I can apologize.

"It's no trouble, Your Highness. You do not have to worry while I'm here. In any case, I've thought about the subject for some time on the return trip. It is practically unheard of for anyone to attack our grand fortress during the day. The peach garden is one of the safest areas in the palace. My thought is that whoever attacked us did not have to put much effort into infiltration. That is to say, I think the traitor is amongst us. Not only that, he could have easily poisoned us through other means. There was no need for such a direct method. He wanted to be followed to Ning."

"Why now and why implicate Ning?"

"I am sorry to say I do not know."

Logic points at Kang Lang. He said he knows the assassin. I wonder if he is the assassin. Yet, he had so many chances to be rid of me. All he's done was toyed with my emotions. Still, he's the manipulative type and I can't even begin to postulate his final objective. My mind drifts away as I contemplate the matter. In due time, San An places a comforting hand on my shoulder. The unexpected sensation causes me to jolt.

"You do not need to fear me," he remarks sadly.

"No... I was lost in thought. You surprised me."

"What were you thinking?"

Should I tell San An? I have no proof whether Kang Lang is the assassin or not, and bringing him into conversation might just push San An to send him to the gallows. I don't want innocent blood on my hands. Yet, should Kang Lang be guilty, he needs to pay for his crimes.

"Nothing. I've troubled you long enough, Prime Minister. Thank you for all your help."

After a short bow, I start for the door.

"Are you going back to him?"

The bitter words cut through me. A mixture of tumultuous emotions overwhelms my heart, causing my entirety to freeze in place.

"As I've conveyed before, in your role as He Pi, you cannot pursue a romantic relationship. Then, you had a choice. It is far too late for that now. The court has acknowledged you. An attempt was made on your life. You must take this seriously; if not for your country, then for yourself."

I would be lying to the Minister by saying I'm not leaving to find Kang Lang. Neither can I confirm his suspicions. He would misunderstand my actions. Instead, I leave without responding. However San An interprets that is entirely up to him.

Chapter 15 – 2

The Peony Palace was easier to find than expected. The edifice is directly to the right of the main palace. Yet, as strikingly beautiful as the structure may be, it brings great offense to the sense of smell. Heavy scents of blooms engulfed the area to such extremities that I immediately shoved a sleeve over my nose to filter the air. When I approached, two guards at the front bowed low and then exchanged meaningful looks. I didn't understand the reason until stepping inside.

There must be a thousand women in this place! Each lovelier than the next! The sight throws my heartbeat into variations. I feel like a brute standing in a field of flowers and inferiority is overtaking me once again.

"Wh-Whoa!" It doesn't take long until I grasp that jealousy is moot. Like a stampede, they all rush at once. Realizing my folly, I attempt to flee but many pairs of hands tug at my robe. Almost in unison, the women chatter in maddening shrill voices. My arms fly over my chest to protect from groping hands. The more I fight to leave, the farther I'm dragged away from the door.

"Why are you so shy, Your Majesty?" A woman shrieks in my ear.

"He's nervous like a little boy, it's so cute!" Another cry out.

"Stay a little longer. Don't you want to spend the night with me?"

"No, he's mine!"

"You already promised tonight to Minister Leung, he's mine!"

On and on this goes. My head is aching from the nonsense while my body is tugged back and forth like a leaf stuck in a typhoon. Hands instinctively ball into fists, but I can't just swing at any of them. Right before breaching my breaking point, the crowd around parts as an infuriated woman bursts through the lines.

"He's mine! Keep your hands off my fiancé!"

I've never been so glad to see Mu Dan in my life! He throws the other women aside like ragdolls and after wrapping our arms together, pulls me to his chamber. Once we are finally free, I breathe deeply and collapse onto the floor.

"How in the world did He Pi manage to survive these crazy women?"

"By becoming my fiancé." Mu Dan moves in front of his vanity and gasps. "Those harpies messed my hair out of place!"

While combing the tangles out of his long locks, he mumbles incoherently. The only word I catch repeatedly is, "harpies." His reaction amuses me, so I watch him for a time. The line between his genders blurs. I can't tell whether Mu Dan or Kang Lang is his real self.

Eventually, boredom sets in, and then my attention is captured by each expensive thing in the massive room. It's inconceivable that there are identical luxuries for each courtesan.

"It's such a waste."

"What is?" Mu Dan calls back.

"I'm glad he's not actually consorting with these women. All the same, it's taxpayers' money he's using to keep them here; well-clothed and well-fed."

"Well, that's an emperor's privilege. Your privilege. Marry Mu Dan and rid yourself of these harpies. You'll make the taxpayers very happy."

"You don't give up, do you?"

"Never!" Mu Dan leaves the vanity and sits before me. He pokes my face and then laughs. "Look at you, all afraid of those harpies! You make such a cute He Pi!"

"I took the trouble of coming here. Hear me out."

"Well, I'm listening, Your Highness. If you want answers, that's a different matter."

"Fine. Then, listen. I don't know who you are, Kang Lang, so I don't trust you, but I must rely on you because you hold the truth. The assassin who attacked me fled to Mount Fei Yang in order to implicate Ning. He then returned to Nan Rong. The council thinks he is amongst us. Since you are the only assassin I know, I naturally think it's you. Honestly, did you try to kill me? Maybe the better question is, did you kill He Pi?"

Contrary to expectation, Mu Dan is not offended. A steady smile stays on his face throughout my charges. He stares for a long moment and then pokes my face again.

"You're so silly! If I wanted to kill you, you'd be dead by now! San An was shot in the shoulder. My aim is not that bad. I would have pierced the arrow through his throat just to watch him choke on his own blood." He relishes the violent words as though recalling fond memories. "As for your last question—No, I did not kill my fiancé. He is precious to me. Not in any manner you would ever understand but I do cherish him."

"Then who is trying to implicate Ning? Tell me!" My fist inadvertently flies against the wall.

"For that answer, you will have to pay the price."

"Or I could just have San An torture the answer out of you!"

"Don't make me excited. I won't be able to sleep!" He laughs happily. An eager smile curls over the petal lips which then widens from my disgust. "It's getting dark, Your Highness. If you're not going to hand me over to be tortured, then we should go to bed."

He isn't going to cooperate after all. Still, I am satisfied with his response.

"Fine!"

Upon reaching for the door, I freeze when his firm hands squeeze my shoulders.

"You misunderstood me, Your Highness. I meant, we should go to bed."

"I know you're mocking me, Kang Lang, and it's hardly charming."

"Why did you come all the way here just to flaunt yourself in front of me and tempt me with the notions of torture and murder? Why not summoned me to the main palace?"

I had forgotten that in front of everyone apart from the council, I do have some authority. What a waste of time this was.

"That... was not my intent. I didn't want anyone to be suspicious."

"You mean, you didn't want the Prime Minister to be suspicious. I thought you desired Jin. Increasingly, I think you favor San An. Although, since you've come all this way for me, I must have won you over."

His tone suddenly makes me shiver from dread. While I shrink back, he sends a sultry and seductive whisper into my ear. "It'll be fun. I promise to make you feel so much pain that you can't ever forget me."

My response of twisting away is met with vociferous giggles. I want to pound his face in but that would just excite him. Instead, I take the friendly approach. Turning around, I clutch at his arm.

"Escort me back to the entrance. I'll send flowers to Mu Dan and make the harpies jealous."

He contemplates for a short moment and then smiles smugly. "You finally understand this barter system. Don't send me lilies. I want roses, orchids, and peonies."

"Yes, yes! Any flower you want!"

The door opens and my fiancée parades me through the crowd of women. Regardless of Kang Lang's sentiment, Mu Dan is happy.

Chapter 16: First Love

"It's not safe to wander here, Your Highness."

Almost a week has passed since Jin's spoken to me. We've been in each other's company from time to time while he fulfilled usual duties; not much has been exchanged. After our previous awkward encounter, he withdrew emotionally. Perhaps, he's still not forgiven my foolishness. There were so many things I could have done to better our relationship but I fell short.

"Jin. I didn't know there's assembly today."

"There isn't. Why are you in the peach garden? Have you forgotten everything that transpired? "

"I'm just looking for clues. The assassin won't likely return here."

"The generals have combed through this area. Anything of import has been taken into account. Please, go back inside. It's not safe for you to be in the open like this."

"Jin... What if I told you I may have a way to find the assassin?"

"We're not using you as bait." Jin reaches for my hand.

I refuse to move. "You misunderstand me."

Pausing, his full attention thrusts upon me. I'm unsure whether this burden should be placed on his shoulders. Whatever I tell him will undoubtedly be transferred to San An and I can only guess *his* reactions. Doubts cease my convictions. As always, Jin is reassuring.

"You don't have to hide anything from me. I'll keep your secrets. My duties are to look after you. I can't execute them fully unless you trust me."

"You're the one person I never want to keep secrets from, Jin. I don't want this to trouble you, so try not to overreact. Mu Dan is actually Kang Lang, a former assassin."

I expected for Jin to become alarmed. He doesn't bat an eye.

"I know," is his calm reply.

"You know? How do you know?"

"Despite Mu Dan's opinions, I am the closest person to His Highness. Mu Dan did not do this."

"May I ask why you always retreat when he's near? Are you enamored with him?"

"Don't be ridiculous." Although he denies the attraction, his attention is forced away. Colors ever so lightly appear over his cheeks. "I shy from him because he is a man. It's unnerving to see another man look so..."

"So... beautiful? I thought I was the only one unnerved. Wait, you knew Mu Dan is a man. Why did you leave me alone with him?"

"He said you wanted to learn more about His Highness and he would teach you how to be a woman. You mentioned that you didn't know what it meant to be one since you've never worn women's clothing. I thought since he's experienced, Mu Dan could be a good influence for you. Why are you frowning, is something the matter?"

"If by teaching me to be a woman, you mean he can put his hands all over me, then sure!" I don't know what brought me to confess. Or, am I only complaining?

Jin becomes startled and then another indescribable expression takes over. I hate the idea of keeping secrets from him. I want him to know my lips *have* been stained by the kiss of another man, despite having been repulsed by the grotesque act. Why this matters to me is perplexing.

Jin's eyes gradually darken. The expression turns to pure outrage. His hands clench tightly into fists and his entirety trembles. What have I done? I didn't intend for him to become upset.

"Jin—"

"Don't worry, Your Highness. He will pay for this. Kang Lang will never bother you again!"

"What? N-No, Jin, that's not important."

"How is it not important?! Am I supposed to be complacent knowing another man's put his hands on you?!"

I've never heard his voice raised this way. I don't know what he's implying or whether he is implying anything at all. Shock turns me immobile.

Immediately, the countenance on his crimson face turns wrathful. I lunge forward when he turns to leave and grasp at whatever I can; only to fall on my face.

"Jin, stop! He knows the assassin's identity!"

Pausing, Jin tilts his head in my direction. A brief moment of contemplation ensues and then without hesitation, he continues on the path.

I have to stop him. Once he removes Kang Lang, our only source of information will be relinquished. I have to do something. Anything!

Chapter 17: A Dream Realized

"Jin! Wait! I'm marrying Kang Lang!"

He stops and everything feels frozen in place. For a long moment, I can hardly breathe from hearing the outlandish words that escaped from my mouth. I don't want this, but if it's the only way to protect Nan Rong and Jin, then the price is just.

Slowly, he turns and stares incredulously, giving no response.

"Once I marry Kang Lang, he'll reveal the assassin's identity. I am He Pi and Mu Dan is his fiancée, so it only makes sense."

My attempt to force a weak smile is thwarted by his disdainful glare, which eventually fades into indifference. I don't know what I expected but anything is better than this unnerving silence. Jin's shoulders drop. Just as tension seemingly subsides, Jin rushes forward without warning and pulls me from the ground. Both arms encircle my body with great force; our foreheads are pressed together. Embarrassment burns his face and I feel flames burst into my own. My heart is pounding furiously.

"How dare you?" The deep tone of his whisper is filled with both anguish and elation. "How dare you consider another man after promising you'd love me?"

"But—"

187

"Don't argue. I won't let anyone else have you. Whether you want me or not, I won't let you go!"

What is happening? Since when does Jin love me? Ah, except he didn't say anything about love. Why did reason jump to *that* conclusion? After our last kiss, he's avoided me like the plague. I can't imagine this reaction is due to else but his desire to protect me from Kang Lang. Certainly, I do need to be protected from that insane person.

"Jin, just because I marry Kang Lang doesn't mean we can't still be friends. I'm not going anywhere."

"Friends... I can't be your friend. Do you truly not understand my intention?"

Maybe it's not that I don't understand; I just can't believe it. This is everything I've been hoping for, yet now when my deepest desires have come true, doubts taunt me. This doesn't make sense. I haven't done anything for Jin. Why would he feel this way? Then again, how does he really feel? By expecting too much, I'll just end up with mud on my face. I know Jin doesn't desire me. He couldn't. Someone of his disposition and caliber deserves a lady of eminence. I'm far from anything special and not even dressed in the clothes of my gender.

Even so, elation overwhelms me to such an extent, I feel as though I could fly. This is too surreal, too shocking! It feels nothing short of a dream. And therefore... it must be. It's the only logical explanation!

And, since this is a dream, should have no consequences once I wake. The warmth of his arms and gentleness of his touch tempt me to exploit every emotion and sensation which reality would never dare entertain. Sadly, this delusion won't last forever. I might as well hasten.

Both arms reach around Jin's shoulders. My lips press a heavy kiss against his mouth. With all my strength, I lean forward and push Jin to the ground, planting countless kisses over his soft lips until my chest heaves.

When I pull away, Jin is blushing furiously. Beyond bashfulness, confusion fully covers his expression while a hint of fright and amazement reflect from brown eyes.

"You're... not a very good girl, are you?" He mutters with a nervous chuckle.

"Aren't you supposed to say something more romantic? Well, if you won't, then I will. I love you. I love you so much, I can't stand it! Maybe it's brash since we haven't known each other very long, but this is how I feel. Yet, every time we grow close, you run from me. I may often say and do the wrong things but I would never hurt you. I'm not perfect and I haven't done anything for you. If you'd only give me the chance, I'll try harder. Then maybe, you can come to love me, too. Do you think the real Jin would appreciate that or would he just laugh at me?"

"Real Jin?"

"Never mind. Thanks for humoring me. I'd never have the nerves to say this to you while I'm awake. It's good to get it off my chest. So, what do you think? Should we go a little further while there's still time?"

Without permitting a reply, I reach for the collar of his shirt and pry it open. Jin darts up. I've never seen him fluster so terribly.

"You're awfully shy for a phantom."

"This is not a dream!" Jin yells crossly, pinching both my cheeks in the process.

"Cut it out! That hurts!"

Wait, that *hurts*? This is real?

Blood is draining from my face. My eyes nearly fall out of my head.

"What made you think you were dreaming?"

There goes that same hard tone from the last time I vexed him. If he temporarily withdrew before, he'll definitely avoid me permanently now.

"I..." feel like a complete idiot! What have I done? I can't answer him. More so, I don't want to!

Taking to my feet, I flee from the scene.

Chapter 17 – 2

So embarrassing! Why did I do something that irrational? I want to crawl into a hole and die! These bed sheets were the closest things I could find. How long have I been lying here replaying the horrendous mistake over and over again? My head feels as though it will split open.

Just as the mental scene replays for the thousandth time, light footsteps suddenly trickle down the hall. Undoubtedly, he's coming to bring my dinner. I can't face him!

Pulling the covers tighter, I lie still and pretend to be asleep. Thumping footsteps increase and then cease once Jin enters the room. For a long moment, the silence is so deafening that I can hear my own heartbeat. I continue holding my breath until his pace resumes and then gradually dissipates. When I feel certain that the room is empty, slowly, a heavy sigh falls as do the covers. I should have known better. He's standing beside the bed looking down.

"J-Jin!"

"We need to talk."

"N-No, we don't! I know what you'll say, so let me just apologize and then we can move past this."

He sits on the edge of the bed and gives his full attention. Usual gentleness is wholly replaced by austerity.

"I'm sorry," Jin mutters.

Isn't that my line? He beat me to it! Why is he apologizing? Is he sorry for not returning my affections or sorry that we can't ever speak again because I've made things irreparable? In the end, it doesn't matter. I hate to see him unhappy. Maybe, it's best that we don't associate anymore.

"I understand. It's okay. Please forgive me, too. I wish you all the best in finding your happiness."

"What are you talking about?" Jin's eyebrows rise to arches.

"What are *you* talking about?"

"Quit jumping to conclusions and listen to me. It's as you've said. I keep running away every time something awkward comes between us. I must stop being a coward. So, I'm sorry. Anyway, we need to talk because your impetuousness is driving me crazy."

"I'm sorry."

"You misunderstand me. *You're* driving me crazy."

"Uh... wha—?"

Not fully grasping the intent, I glance up. A sudden, fervent kiss presses against my mouth, pushing waves of coursing heat over my entirety. Once more, I'm so elated that there's a good chance I might float off the face of the earth. As his body moves closer, his hands grasp for mine. Passion turns thoughts blank; leaving a repeating wish. I wish time would stand still so that we can remain this way forever; lost so deep in each other's embrace that the world around simply fades away.

When our lips finally part, I find myself on top of him again. How did this happen?!

"You're really not a nice girl, are you?"

"I guess not."

The nervous reply receives a sweet, genuine laugh. My ears perk to catch every delightful note that, until now, was a rarity.

Jin wraps both arms around my shoulders and then rolls over for us to exchange positions. His fingers then thread through mine.

"I know I've confused you to no end, so allow me to express my thoughts.   You promised to love me however I choose. Will you keep your word?"

Though his voice is calm, Jin's body is tremulous. His cheeks are lit crimson.

"Of course I will."

"Then love me as the only man for you; as your first and last. I don't want to hear you mention anyone else. I love you, so don't you dare refuse me."

"I do not dare," is my factual reply.

Jin exchanges a sharp laugh for my grin. To hear him finally say those words makes me indescribably happy. An unrestrained smile won't leave my face. Truthfully, I don't know why he loves me but I don't care. Even though I've done nothing to earn his favor, I will do whatever it takes to make him happy.

His palms lift from mine. His fingers caress my cheeks. Jin removes He Pi's crown and presses a warm kiss on my forehead as his fingers run through my hair. He's being so contrary to his usual self, I find him utterly charming. My lips arch to request another kiss and Jin immediately complies.

"How long have you pined after me, Shu Jin?" The whisper is more playful than I imagined myself capable.

"Longer than I realized. What about you?"

"It's hard to pinpoint the exact moment. For a while, I haven't been able to stop thinking of you. I kept silent because I thought you saw me as a friend, if even that. Last time we were this way, I was so surprised by your sudden kiss that I withdrew. I didn't mean to. I'm sorry."

"No, it was my fault. I was... unsure of myself. When the powder was wiped off your face, I grasped that this is, as you've said, a stage performance. I was afraid of what may come once the curtains draw."

"Then, what changed?"

"You. Every time I saw you, I felt so conflicted. Considering the precarious position Nan Rong is placed, any emotional attachment between us would make things too complicated. I just thought while you are still He Pi that you're my charge. For you to then consider Kang Lang, I... I'm not afraid anymore, Bao Lai. Nothing would be worse than to see you in the arms of another and know that I can't ever call you my own. I won't fret over what may come. When the curtains draw, we'll begin a new story. That is, if you can accept me as I am."

"I'm the one who attacked you in the garden, Jin. And I would do it again. My answer is perfectly clear, isn't it?"

I send an index finger into his right cheek. Jin chuckles and then leans over to press his lips against my hand.

"Yes, perfectly."

For the remainder of the night, we are by each other's side. I confess every unpleasant thing that's happened between San An, Kang Lang, and me. I want Jin to know the truth; from every unwanted kiss that's ever stained my lips to every touch by another's hands.

I won't ever lie to Jin just as I know he would not lie to me. By the end of our conversation, I feel absolved and renewed. This happiness is unimaginable. I never thought this wondrous feeling could ever be reserved for someone like me. Even if this were a dream, I never want to wake up.

Chapter 18: Understanding Jin

The scent of blooms calls me from slumber. I wake in a field of flowers. There are fragranced blossoms littered on the bed and bouquets on every chair and table. He went a little overboard; still, it was very sweet.

The moment my beloved's reflection comes to mind, Jin enters the room with the familiar silver tray, topped with yet another red and pink blossom whose even petals are frilly lace.

"Did you sleep well?" He asks cheerfully.

"Yes. What's all this? And Jin, don't serve me anymore. It's not right!"

I dart off the bed to steal away the tray. He easily avoids my attempts and navigates by. After placing the items onto the table, he turns to me with a smile beaming with affections.

"For now, you are His Highness—No, that's not it. Even after His Highness returns, I will continue serving you. It is my pleasure to be of service to you, my princess."

He bows and I suddenly feel flushed. It's difficult enough to imagine anyone actually seeing cross-dressing, uncultured me as a woman—but princess! Gracious! Blood gushes to my face in torrents, scorching every inch. Jin laughs at my ridiculous response. I can't do else except turn away to hide embarrassment. His arms immediately slip around my shoulders.

"What's the matter, Princess?" He whispers lovingly. The sensation of his breath on my ear makes me quiver.

"Don't call me that." The false protest falls through a low mutter.

"Would you prefer, 'Goddess?'"

"Now I know you're teasing me! Stop it!"

I gently tap his hands. His arms tighten to a full embrace. Jin's chin rests on my shoulder; soft lips run gently across my cheek while he lets out a soft exhale. Leaning back against the broad chest to fully feel his warmth, excitement begins overtaking my senses. Jin continues light kisses across my burning cheek, chuckling ever so softly whenever the ticklish sensation causes my body to jerk.

When did he become so playful? Did I hit my head in the garden yesterday when I fell and everything that's happened since is a dream even if this phantom claims otherwise?

"I'm not teasing you." He finally replies. "I mean it. You are precious to me. More than anything. So please, wait for me."

The unexpected plea sends a flood of panic. I swiftly swing around and clutch at his shirt. What is he saying? Is he going somewhere?

A knowing smile surfaces. Strong arms deepen the embrace to comfort my angst. "I'm leaving for Xiong. It's ill timed that we are finally together and yet, we must part. I promise I won't be away for long."

"Why are you going to Xiong? May I come with you?"

"When my mother was alive, once a year at this time, we would visit Xiong to pay obeisance and offer prayers to our ancestors. It was her tradition and so, it's also mine."

"Oh, that's so filial of you."

He's such a good son. I, on the other hand, have not burned one incense stick or offered a single prayer for Master Tai Hung—the old priest who raised me—since he passed. Despite my insolence, Master Tai Hung was a grandfather to me. The least I could have done was made the effort to visit his resting place once a year to provide assurance. He was always fussing over my wellbeing. I bet if he were alive, he'd scold me for being thoughtless.

Every time I think of my master, I can't help but feel regret. I could have done more for him and less against him. He died before I could put apology to words.

My melancholy must not be well hidden because Jin is staring anxiously while chewing his lips.

"I suppose I can delay the trip or skip this year altogether. With things as they are, I should stay here."

"Are you just saying that because of me, Jin? If you are... I'll be fine. You should go. I can tell this trip means a lot to you."

"It does, but now that I think more on it, I'm not comfortable leaving you. You're my charge. I would have you come to Xiong but I doubt the Minister will approve. It's fine. At least here, we'll have more time together."

"No, you shouldn't forgo cherished traditions. I'll talk to San An. Without you, I'm useless as He Pi. There's no point for me to stay. Will you give me some time? I'll find the Minister right away."

Jin doesn't have the chance to object. I was afraid he might, so I run from the room posthaste.

Chapter 18 – 2

"Your Highness?"

San An was reviewing a stack of documents neatly piled on the tea table when I stormed in. On the chair adjacent is another large stack and behind him on the sofa are several stacks more.

"Oh, you're busy. I'm sorry, San An."

"That's quite all right. These are the tax reports from May. The majority has been examined and I'm nearly finished with the remainder. What can I do for you?"

I never knew the Minister's job was so exhausting. Beside from dealing with the court and council and ensuring political diplomacy, he's stuck with the tedious task of evaluating ledgers too? Here I am, doing absolutely nothing of value for Nan Rong, and still I want to run off and cavort with Jin in Xiong. I can't do else except stare awkwardly at the floor. Eventually, the Minister leaves his chair, and with a gentle hand, pats my shoulder.

"You may ask anything of me, Your Highness."

"I-I don't know if I should. W-Well, the truth is, Jin is leaving for Xiong and I want to accompany him."

His smile fades. For a moment, San An appears wounded. The gentle hand coyly withdraws from my shoulder and then he simply looks away.

"Even after my warnings, you have chosen to put desire before duty. Does Jin approve of your affections or is this an attempt to draw his attention?"

His tone is unexpectedly cold; the very same from our previous unpleasant encounter when he charged me with having impure expectations from Jin. I guess he wasn't entirely wrong. The recollection makes me shudder and I can't respond. Momentarily, Jin startles me when he comes into the room and replies on my behalf.

"Prime Minister, if you will permit Bao Lai's request, I will escort her to Xiong. She does not have to draw my attention. I've fully given my considerations."

San An turns to his brother, utterly shocked by the change in the younger man. I understand his sentiment. Jin has always been reserved; mostly, he was aloof. The only person who could instill his confidence, I assume, was He Pi. No one else was close to him; be it by their choice or his. Parts of me wonder how Jin was able to break free from his self-made prison while the remaining parts fear he might, at length, withdraw.

"I did not think it was necessary to lecture you, Shu Jin, about avoiding relations with our guest. You have obligations to His Highness. Likewise, Bao Lai cannot resign this task. Once the ruse is found, danger will befall you both."

"I understand. Still, I will not give up Bao Lai. I am prepared to receive any and all consequences and I will protect her with my life."

San An returns Jin's confidence with an exasperated sigh. Obviously, he's not used to disobedience. As far as I know, he's only abided impertinence from two people: His Highness and me.

Following a short pause, the Minister turns to me. "Bao Lai, is this truly your wish?"

To have heard Jin speak with such assurance forces a smile to my face. Despite my elation, his last thought brings unease. Of course I want to accompany Jin but San An also has a point. Jin and I both have our duties and the closer we become, the less we'll likely keep our relationship hidden. It only takes one error to end this dream and put Jin in danger. Knowing me, I'll likely make that error. The thought scares me and resolve begin wavering.

"Jin, maybe... I should stay."

A hard glare immediately directs toward my face. Jin is upset. Though I fear he would retreat, his hand reaches for mine and with adamant determination, Jin turns to San An.

"Prime Minister, wasn't the point to keep Bao Lai a mean to stall the court? If His Highness accompanies me to Xiong, then the ruse can be extended for another month. With everything that's happened, Bao Lai is safer the farther away she is from the capital. That assassin easily evaded our guards. Staying here hardly equates to protection."

"Your opinion is considered, Jin. However, it's Bao Lai's choice. I will not deny her of anything but neither shall I relinquish her to you until I've heard the words."

San An stares intently at the younger man and Jin reflects the gesture. They must be quarreling; though, the true subject of their discord escapes me.

When it becomes apparent that they've reached stalemate, I nervously enter the conversation. "Is it really all right that I go, Jin? What if I cause more trouble for you? If someone sees His Highness in Xiong—"

"You will accompany me as yourself, Bao Lai. There's no need for disguises; not until we return to the capital. Beside, you will always cause trouble. All the more reason I need to look after you. Stay with me."

Jin smiles sweetly. San An scoffs harshly and with gritted jaw, turns to me for a final confirmation.

Although Jin is encouraging, I can't deny the responsibilities San An's entrusted me. The only reason we're in this predicament is because I insisted to leave the capital and Jin was accommodating. Since he initially thought to leave me behind, then he shouldn't mind that I stay. On the other hand, this indomitable side of him is still new. If his moods are shifting again, as they have before, I fear declining this opportunity might make him resent me. I should

__Stay in the capital (Continue to page 205)__

__Go to Xiong (Continue to page 208)__

Chapter 18 – 3

It's irresponsible to put my desires before the nation's welfare. Even though I haven't accomplished anything, being present in the capital keeps the court's stability. Who can tell what might happen after my departure? San An shouldn't have to shoulder this burden alone. Jin will understand that I'll wait for him.

"Jin, I'll stay. Come back to me soon, okay?"

The cheerful tone is accompanied by an encouraging smile. Jin frowns bitterly and then releases my hand.

"Do you lack all faith in me, Bao Lai?"

"Of course not."

"Then you have made your choice."

"What do you mean? Jin? Jin!"

He throws a frustrated glare at his elder brother and then abruptly quits the room. The moment I start to give chase, San An reaches for my wrist.

"Let him go, Your Highness."

"But—"

"Since he is willing to surrender his desires so easily, he doesn't deserve you."

"Surrender? You mean he surrenders *me*? Why would Jin—"

"How do you both claim to be in each other's affections when you hardly know anything of the other's disposition?"

San An is probably right. Still, I refuse to let Jin flee back into his cell. My hand withdraws from the Minister's grasp and then I rush from his quarters. To my terror, Jin's nowhere to be found. Each moment without him, without knowing his whereabouts, is torture.

Why do I keep saying the wrong things? Why didn't I just agree?!

Later in the day, San An calls me to his quarters to confirm my fear. Jin's left. Though I thought the Minister would be gladdened by my choice to stay, San An dismisses me from court.

"San An, what about my role?"

"The council will manage His Highness's absence as best we can."

My chest tightens when I look into his apathetic stare. Once I leave the palace, I'll never see Jin again. Ultimately, that's not my choice. Without San An's approval, I have no place here.

My every attempt to tactfully persuade San An fails; however, for my pervious services, the Minister imparts the reason for my dismissal.

"Jin no longer wishes for your company and although my partiality for you is deep, he was right. So long as you remain in this palace, you are in constant danger. Furthermore, Jin's temperament is fickle. Should he chooses to pursue your attention in the future, I fear our kinship is not enough to deter conflict. I've seen enough brothers fall for want and desire of the unattainable. It grieves me, but you must go."

I don't have the chance to grasp his intention when Bai Hu enters to escort me from the chamber. After returning He Pi's crown and garbs, I adorn my old clothes and then the Demon General sends me back to my old life.

Months later, I make my way to the capital but no one at the palace will receive me. I wander daily near the gate, hoping for a glance of the man for whom my heart yearns. Eventually, time takes from me what I can never have back and I return south to live the rest of my days as a recluse.

The End.

Chapter 18 – 4

I must dispose all reservations to keep Jin from retreat. He's fragile, I see that now. My hand squeezes his tighter. Through a deep breath, my decision is solidified.

"San An, I will go with Jin. I'm sorry if that's irresponsible but Jin has a point. If nothing else, my absence can be used as an excuse. I'm bound to do something foolish at court. It's best that I stay away altogether."

Displeasure overtakes San An and eventually erupts into deep anger. Jin's grip on my hand tautens.

"Prime Minister, Bao Lai made her decision. As you would not *deny her of anything*, please excuse us."

Jin bows low and then pulls me from the room. Though San An remains silent, upon exiting, I look over my shoulder to see torment in his eyes. I can't grasp the reason for his sorrow. At the moment, Jin is my primary concern. When we return from Xiong, I will apologize to the Minister and hopefully he can forgive whatever transgressions I have made.

Chapter 18 – 5

"Why are you wearing that?"

Jin chuckles while coming into my chamber with a bundle of fine silk in his arms. I'm sitting on the bed dressed in my old clothes.

"You said I shouldn't dress as He Pi in Xiong."

"I didn't mean to cross-dress. I am sorry you had to wear His Highness's robes. You are a lady. These are more suitable."

He brought those pretty clothes for me? And he guessed my favorite color, too! In the palace, I don't have a choice but to wear He Pi's garbs. I've been careful not to put holes in them and I've managed so far due to his restricted regimen. The pieces Jin brought are so delicate that I'm afraid to wear them outside. When I hesitate to reach for the clothes, Jin throws the bundle onto the bed and gives an embrace.

"What's wrong? Did you change your mind? Would you rather stay with the Minister?"

"No, it's not that. I... don't know how to wear women's clothes."

I'm sure he'd laugh if he knew my concern. Instead, I choose the more obvious excuse of ignorance. Who knew my ignorance is also amusing. A light chuckle bursts. Jin begins to undo the sash around my shirt.

"Jin! What are you doing?!"

"I've dressed you many times before. Why are you flustering?"

"Because..."

What can I say? Prior, duties bound us to endure discomfiture. Now that we are together, I'm mortified to have him see me. Jin stares at my reddened face for a long moment. Without warning, a severe kiss lands on my mouth. The sudden exploit forces back my feet before his arms draw us closer. A heavy pulse is throbbing in my ears. There's not an inch of me that's not blushing. When he finally moves away, I'm too shocked to even blink. Thus, he continues changing my clothes without further protest.

"Now, let me see. That color really suits you, pretty miss."

The tone may be casual, but Jin too, is blushing profusely. I knew it! I'm not the only one who finds this change in our relationship awkward. That's not to say the change is bad. It's the best thing that has ever happened to me. Only, it's so abrupt that I'm still deciding whether this is real.

"Hmm?!" The unexpected sensation of his fingers touching my face makes me jump. I didn't realize how quiet the room has become. The expression that immediately crosses him is clear: I've offended Jin.

"Bao Lai, do you want this?"

"Yes, the robe is very pretty. Thank you."

"That's not what I meant." Jin chews on his lips.

My blank stare furthers tension in the still room. It takes a moment more to finally understand he's insecure. "Jin. I want to go with you, really."

"Why? Because I forced this relationship between us? I shouldn't have pushed you—"

"Don't be ridiculous! I professed my love first."

"Only because I refused to let you marry Kang Lang."

"Jin, had I known you'd ever consider me, I would never have thought to marry Kang Lang. Marrying him would be a last resort. I didn't think I had anything to lose and at least, we'd learn the assassin's identity. I wanted you—I still do. The truth is, I dreamt of this— us—but I never expected for it to come true. Now I wonder whether this *is* a dream. I don't know what to do."

Despite my earnest confession, Jin leans down to fully convey an impish smile. "You dreamt of me, did you?"

Why did I tell him something so embarrassing! My bulging eyes drift to the floor as a light chuckle flutters from his pretty lips. Unwilling to spare me, Jin pushes on.

"Yesterday in the garden, was your shameless display of affections for me, typical of these dreams?"

I know he's joking; nevertheless, I can't find the right defense. Words are stuck in my throat. Before I know it, an angry groan bursts while my feet make for the exit. Right before my fingers touch the door, my body is swept off the ground.

"J-Jin! What are you doing?"

"It's obvious what I'm doing," he whispers smoothly.

Jin walks to the bed and then gently lays me down. His lips cover mine with longing kisses which then slowly descend toward my neck. Strong hands pry open the collar of my robe. I'm too confused to move. Even if I could, what exactly is expected here?

The abrupt touch of his hands running over my body makes me quake. On impulse, I push him away. Why did I do that? He's staring at me with wounded eyes. I must stop slighting him but there should be some limit to entertaining his whims, shouldn't there?

Following a pause, offense turns to apathy. He speaks in an almost hollow tone, resembling his ever-increasing distant stare. "Don't you want me, Bao Lai?"

Didn't he just ask this? Of course I do, but is consummating our bond the only way to prove that?

Truthfully, I'm nervous and also excited by the thought. There's no one else to whom I can imagine entrusting myself. Only, an irrational aspect keeps nagging at me. Just days ago, Jin purposefully avoided me. It doesn't make sense that his perception could alter so much, so soon. He explained that his former detachment was due to uncertainty. I'm not so sure that's all it was. Why he suddenly cares for me as a woman is unimaginable. How have I changed since yesterday morning that he could come to love me, even to desire me, in this way?

My rejection forces his attention to avert toward the door. Once again, there must be more to the story. He's hiding true feelings. Is Jin *that* insecure? He held my hand the entire length of our earlier conversation with the Minister. I thought the act was to reassure me; maybe, it was for him. Jin's said that he's not fit to be anyone's husband because no woman would want a man with nothing to his name. I couldn't care less how little he has. I have nothing to my name either. Does he think that poorly of me?

That can't be. If he thought I was that type of person, then he'd never love me. Maybe, having nothing is the key. He's leaving for Xiong to uphold his mother's tradition. It's his way of keeping memories of her alive. And now, after his quarrel with San An, constantly seeks validations of my affections. Is he afraid? Does he think claiming me will keep me by his side? Is that why he's pushing himself to be so contrary? I'm afraid to ask.

My continuing silence provokes Jin to his feet. In response, I dart up and throw my arms around his waist. "Don't, Jin! Don't leave. I want you. I love you! No matter what happens, I won't leave you. I swear it!"

His body slightly trembles. Knowing that words won't come to him, my grip tightens. A cheek presses against his back.

"Jin, it's okay. You need to stop hiding your emotions; otherwise, they'll surface in torrents and force you to do things you may not intend. If you wish to claim me, I won't deny you. But, the act must stem from affections and not to hold my regards."

A sharp exhale causes his body to jerk. I understand his apprehension. It's also mine. I trust Jin, but I still dread losing his attention. It's happened before. Now that we are this close, I fear his regards, if lost again will be lost forever. He can take as much time as he needs. I'll hold him this way until he comes to his senses.

In time, Jin glances over his shoulder and casts down a crooked smile. "You... You're always finding ways to humiliate me, aren't you?"

"What? No, I'd never—"

"Ah, that's not what I meant. You always want to expose the weaknesses I try to hide. You constantly rip away my bandages and attempt to mend the wounds. I despise you for it but I... love you for caring."

His affirmation sends a surge of newfound elation through my chest. Jin turns around and presses a gentle, sweet kiss on my lips. This is the Jin I remember. Thank goodness.

Once he pulls away a short distance, a soft whisper flows into my ear. "So, were you honest? Are you willing to let me claim you, should I desire?"

Every inch of me is burning up. An incoherent stammer returns neither confirmation nor rejection. Jin laughs teasingly; tapping his fingers to my cheek.

"You blush so easily."

"Look in the mirror! So, do you! And, don't make fun of me!"

"Why? It's endearing when you fluster." Another round of laughter and then his demeanor becomes stern. "Bao Lai? Will you stay with me no matter how foolish I may become?"

"Yes. Until you command me to leave—well, even if you do—I'll stay. I know you don't trust women but please, trust me."

He hesitates. After some time, Jin firmly nods. "I trust you, Bao Lai."

"Good, I'm glad. I trust you too, Jin."

Jin sighs contentedly. "I'm sorry to have burdened you with my doubts. At my age, I should be the one to guide and protect you, but I haven't. I'll be more diligent from now on to deserve your attention."

"Don't say that. You've done more for me than anyone since my arrival. Anyway, we can't be very far apart in age. I'm twenty-six."

Skeptic eyes immediately pierce my face. Did I say something strange?

"I'm twenty-five," he smiles in spite of himself. "I can't believe you're older than me."

"Oh. Then quit teasing me. Respect your elders!"

He takes hold of my wagging index finger and, while grinning sweetly at my frown, pulls me into an embrace. Time seems to span endlessly while wrapped in the warmth of the exchange. Once our bodies part, the sensation lingers, calming all our anxieties.

The remainder of the day is spent making preparations for the trip. All the while, friendly conversations flow. Every now and again, he would glance over and smile. There is something indescribable in those glances, a twinkle of sort, that I've never before experienced. What a wonderful feeling, to be viewed by the loving eyes of the man who sets fires in my heart!

Finally, I know this isn't a dream.

Chapter 19: The Trip to Xiong

Three days later, we arrive in Xiong. The small town to the south is bustling with commerce. The people are genuinely pleasant and hospitable. Their mild-mannered dispositions are semblance to those of country bumpkins. Xiong is nowhere as grand as the capital; though, there are certain charms that remind me of the villages near the temple where I grew up.

Upon entering the town center, several elders come to greet us, along with a handful of young women who are more than disappointed that Jin did not come alone. I wonder whether he is oblivious to his popularity with the fairer gender or that Jin chooses obliviousness as the excuse to overlook their blatant admirations. Either way, I'm not jealous. I don't doubt his loyalty. Not to mention, he is hardly the type to welcome advances from women he doesn't trust. As far as I know, he only trusts me and even that trust was only solidified recently.

Following short pleasantries with a handful of acquaintances, Jin escorts me to an inn at a corner by the market district. The decorated sign above the doorway is old and worn, baring the half-rotted wood below, which juts between flaked dull brownish paint. Along the former glorious plaque, a few words are scribbled in black letters which too, have seen better days. I think the sign once states, *"Shu Fu Xiao Lu Guan."*

"So, where to now?" I stretch my arms into the air once our things are deposited in the room.

The room itself has a simple layout; one bed and one table with two chairs. The idea of sleeping beside each other is hardly uncomfortable. Still, my face wouldn't be on fire if he hadn't told the innkeeper that I am his wife. He said it so casually, even *I* believed him. I thought he was a gentleman. Now I see he merely wishes to tease me every chance he gets. Not that I am against said teasing but still, I must retaliate, somehow.

"You should rest. It's been a tiring trip."

Immediately after saying so, Jin pulls down the collar of my robe a short distance. His firm hands squeeze my shoulders.

"What are you doing?"

"What does it look like I'm doing? Don't you want a massage?"

"No, I'm not tired."

"Oh, well, I am. You should massage me then." Taking to the bed, Jin removes his outer layers before lying face down.

Is he joking? Since when did I agree? He's always been so formal and proper. Is this the real Jin or is he in one of his moods again? The more I stare curiously, the more I realize it doesn't matter. I love this man and all his facets.

Once settled on the edge of the bed, I attempt to unknot the tight muscles on his shoulders and back. He wasn't joking. His body is exceedingly stiff. A servant's job is not easy and Jin is constantly busy.

It's difficult to not take notice of his well-built physique. At the same time, San An's warnings are becoming clearer. Jin has his duties. He joked that I am his wife and for that, the thought is seared into my mind. I wonder what life we could have. If I remain He Pi forever, we can't wed and if His Highness returns, Jin will continue to serve his brother. Will I stay in the palace too, for the rest of my days with Jin? I'm not against the idea. I just worry how much of Jin I can keep for myself when He Pi is his primary concern. It may sound selfish, but that's how I feel.

"Why are you so quiet?" Jin mumbles into the pillow.

"No reason."

Tilting his head to the side, light brown eyes bear into mine. "You told me not to keep my emotions bottled up but isn't that what you're doing?"

"I'm not bottling anything."

"I've goaded you several times since we've arrived. You haven't said a thing and now you look worried. What's wrong?"

"I'm not worried and my method to retaliate against your teasing is to not retaliate at all. So, just rest."

"Should I try harder?"

His arms wrap around my waist. Jin pulls me down onto the bed before moving atop. His lips flutter over mine and then playfully, he kisses my cheek. The sensation tickles. Consequently, he misconstrues my chortles and thus, slowly withdraws. Despite the deep gaze penetrating into my eyes, Jin's demeanor turns shy.

"Bao Lai, do you still love me?"

"Yes, of course."

He's insecure again. I know he must be hiding more secrets to his past. Whatever those secrets are, won't release their hold. In time, Jin may come to share them with me but for now, it's not my place to force the answers from him. My attempt to assuage his disquiet through a kiss has little effects against rising angst. Following the failed endeavor, I reach for his hands to find them trembling. What must I do for him to understand my affections? Perhaps the answer is too obvious; though, I fear it all the same.

"Jin... do you... want to?"

"Want to what?" He smiles gently.

"Don't act so innocent. You know what I mean." Fervent heat rises to my face. Though I try to suppress the embarrassment, it is futile.

He studies my nervous demeanor for a short moment, frowning, and then steadily moves off the bed.

"Don't use your wiles to tempt me from the truth. If you're worried about us, then tell me."

"What are you saying? I'm not pretending anything. I love you, Jin. I thought... I mean... Weren't you the one who wanted this a few days ago?"

"You refused me. Don't silence me now with this offer because you doubt my affections or maybe, are in doubt of yours."

The accusing tone coupled with his implication suddenly irks me. Temper best judgment. Thoughtlessly, words escape without discretion.

"Is that how you think of me?! I would not proffer pleasure to seal your repetitive interrogations! My *offer* is stemmed from my love for you. I'm afraid you'll withdraw again and I can't abide the thought of it!"

His furrowed brows look off elsewhere. Why does he keep doing this? Every time we are too close, he finds a reason to turn away. We've come far, but how far can we go when he keeps retreating two steps for every one he's taken.

"Jin, why must you constantly doubt me? There is no else but you!"

Without his answer, my chest quivers and my eyes mist over. I fear to cry, to show my abhorrent weakness, but I've lost whatever little control I had. As my vision becomes hazy, a dreadful thought forms.

"It's not *my* affections that create your doubt, is it? It's yours."

His shoulders immediately jerk. Jin throws a hard glare in my direction, gritting his jaw tightly, while sudden anguish surges over his countenance. Even so, he can't deny it. Therefore, it must be true.

On impulse, he confessed an uncertain love, but having been impulsive and jealous with passion has put Jin into a position which further pushes his insecurities. He wasn't ready to admit affection; now, I wonder whether he has any for me at all. His recent overexertion of nonexistent adoration merely served to convince conscience that he cared; though ultimately, it accomplished nothing aside from impelling the guilt of that uncertainty to me.

I understand he doesn't trust women and I do love him enough to eventually let this transgression pass. For now, I can hardly breathe from sorrow while every part of me is trembling from anger. My eyes are burning from hot tears. I can't bear for him to see me so pathetic. Without thinking, I dart toward the door and then make for the streets. I have no idea where my feet are taking me. At the moment, I don't really care.

Chapter 19 – 2

I lost track of time. Wandering endlessly led to these massive stone steps, whose long path spirals upward toward a temple that appears at least a few hundred years old.

It's late afternoon and the sun is on the verge of descent. Despite that, I can't return to the inn. My chest is still stricken by pain. I can't believe how stupid I've been. How could I believe anyone would love me? I'm not a real woman, even if I'm finally wearing women's clothes. I spent my life pretending to fit in with the monks and couldn't truly because I wasn't a man. Once I left, pretended to fit into normal society and couldn't adjust because I didn't know how to be a woman. In the end, I became a recluse.

Jin is the only person I've ever loved this way and I had hoped with all my heart that he could accept me as I am. His sweet words, sweet promises, and sweet kisses run rampant in my mind. He's turned into such a vulgar person and it's because of me. The Jin I met, the Jin I've come to know, is a true gentleman. He is kind and loving and he would never injure me so callously.

This man who now waits at the inn doesn't know what to do with me. He's lonely, so he wants my company, but he doesn't really want me. I know it's my fault. I pushed him into this by having said and done foolish things. The single reason I'm anything to him in the first place is because of my resemble to He Pi.

Come to think of it, after our confession, he was still very sweet while I was dressed as His Highness. The moment I changed into women's garb was when dissension erupted between us. Was I wrong? Jin doesn't just love He Pi; he's in love with him! What am I saying?! His Highness is Jin's younger brother! How can I be so cruel to even think that!

Still, it's possible I'm not far from the truth. While I wore He Pi's clothes, Jin saw me as his charge and diligently cared for me. The moment I'm in this garb, he finally sees me for my gender. His distrust and dislike of women must run deeper than I thought. Regardless of his claims, he'll never trust me. And, if he can't trust me, then love is meaningless.

The ache in my chest deepens. Not knowing else to do, I start up the stone steps. It's only been a little over a year since I was at temple, though it's felt an eternity. Life was busy there but it was, for the most part, peaceful. For twenty-five years I lived a single day. Back then, I often thought about leaving to seek a new day and now, I can't do else but think of then. Then, I did not know pleasure, so I was spared pain.

As I near the top, the smell of incense reaches my nose and nostalgia overflows. My eyes close for a short moment to recall fond memories, until a familiar voice assails my nerves when he calls out my name.

Jin is standing at the top of the steps gazing down. He must have come to pay obeisance to his ancestors.

This was the whole point of his trip. Why didn't I know better than to have climbed up these steps?

Once more, on the verge of despicable tears, I whip around and attempt to fly down the stairs. Just as I do, Jin swiftly seizes my arm and forces an embrace. I try to pull free but his grip is too strong. No, that's not true. I don't really want him to release me.

"It's late. I was beginning to lose hope. Don't run off again! I've been worried sick waiting here for you!"

"You don't have to force yourself, Jin. I'm not that much of an idiot. I understand how you feel but you can't just toy with my emotions!"

"I know. I'm sorry."

"You know? Are you saying, you admit it?"

"Don't cry. Just come with me."

Grasping my hand, Jin takes the lead toward a shrine to the right of the main temple. Gold letters are scribbled on a metal plate by the door. Like everything else around, time has stripped away its former beauty. We enter, and upon nearing the altar, Jin kneels down and bows low to the ground. Out of respect for whoever resides here, I do the same.

Following a long pause, he lifts up and begins. The first word out of his mouth throws me into panic.

"Mother," he begins. "Mother, this is Bao Lai. She's from the south of Nan Rong. Recently, she's been living at the palace. I've come to care for her... more than I ever thought myself capable of caring for anyone. I've never forgotten your teachings: to never marry a woman from Nan Rong. Just this once, I will have to disobey."

What did he just say? It's fine to joke in front of strangers but to do that in front of his mother! I know he doesn't love me. How can he say that? Without thinking, my hand flies over his mouth.

"He's kidding, Consort En! Jin is a little confused!"

"What are you doing?" Jin scolds me while lifting my hand off his mouth.

"What are *you* doing? You can't lie to your mother!"

"I'm not. I will marry you."

"Are you out of your mind?! *I am a woman!*"

"Yes... I can see that."

His eyebrows rise while I stammer like an idiot.

"That's... what I mean is, I'm not He Pi. You don't have to look after me. Once he returns, you won't be able to. Don't mistake concern for him as partiality for me. We may have the same face but that's about as far as our similarities go."

"Just what are you accusing me of?"

"N-Nothing."

Embarrassment sends my gaze to the floor. I was ready for him to scold me again; instead, his arms drape around my shoulders.

"Must you keep jumping to conclusions? What did you come up with this time? That I'm in love with His Highness?"

"N-No. Well... are you?"

"No," is his firm response. "He Pi is my brother. I care for him because we are kin and because it is my duty. When the chaos at court ended, members of his faction called for my execution; to ensure that I won't ever claim authority from His Highness. Needless to say, he did not allow a hair on my head to be displaced.

After I became an orphan, I lost my place in this world. My mother was everything to me. I may carry my father's name but since the day of my birth, he's never once looked at me. The other court members made me feel guilty for existing, as though the thought of me living takes something away from them. Without my mother, I was alone and for a long time, only wanted death to reunite us. It was He Pi who reminded me that we are family and casted aside my pointless guilt. At the time, he protected me. What can I do now but to return the favor in kind?"

I can't believe what an incredible fool I've been. I was wrong to think ill of him. Jin withdrew from everyone except His Highness because of loneliness and resentment. I never knew my parents but Master Tai

Hung treated me like family, even though many times, I purposefully vexed him just to be insolent. I was never alone; not like Jin was. He's trying his best to let me into his life. Due to his previous experiences, it must be difficult. I haven't been understanding. All those times he ran from me, I didn't know to follow. Despite everything he's recently said and done, Jin has taken meticulous care of me and I know he is genuinely kind. For his kindness, I've returned vulgar presumptions and hurt him with my judgmental disposition.

Embarrassment keeps a direct gaze from venturing into his eyes. "I-I'm sorry, Jin. I didn't know. So... is this the real you?"

"Real me? The last time you asked that, you tried to take advantage of me. Just in case you intend to make me blush in front of my mother, I can assure you, this is not a dream."

"N-No. But, you've changed. After I donned women's clothing, you treated me differently, and not in a good way. If you don't love me, just say so. I'll wait until you can decide. Before then, don't tease me and don't overcompensate by pushing desires you don't have. I don't expect you to trust me, but you don't have to insult me with pretenses."

He stares back blankly. Impertinence urges me to return the act; however, confidence wavers and then I just stare at the floor. Lost in thought, I nearly fall back when Jin's lips lightly press against mine. As time passes, the sensation grows deeper until every inch of my body flushes.

"J-Jin, your mother—"

"I don't care that she sees. You're right. This is the real me. I can be teasing and I can be mean. I am human, Bao Lai. Can you accept me this way or must I revert to the obedient servant?"

"I'll love you however you are. I just won't tolerate being accused of deceit. What's more, I can't stand to see you miserable because of me. What do you honestly want, Jin? Tell me what you want and I'll do anything you ask."

His calm expression suddenly turns suggestive. Jin leans over to send a sultry whisper into my ear. "*Anything?*"

"Don't tease me in front of your mother!"

A gentle peck lands on my cheek. Still chuckling softly, he continues. "I'm sorry. I do want to be with you but it scares me. And maybe, as you've said, I don't actually love you. At this point, I'm not entirely sure what love is. I only know that I want us to remain together. Is that okay?"

"Yes, that's okay." I'm glad to have his honesty.

"Then, let me confess one more thing. I don't trust you because you are a woman, and the reason is I still resent my mother for her role at court."

"Jin! Don't say that!"

"Why? It's true." Turning to the altar, Jin bows deeply. "I'm sorry, Mother. I know you did everything for me. You were the only woman I trusted. Even so, I knew every vile thing you'd accomplished. Your crimes against He Pi, San An, and the other children are unforgivable. I never wanted authority. I begged you to leave the palace so we could live in peace, but you refused. For most of my life, I thought if the one woman I placed my every trust in—the one woman who I was absolutely certain loved me unconditionally—could not see anything beyond power and authority, how can anyone else? I hated you for it, but I don't hate you.

Your crimes are mine and I will live with them forever. Guilt persuaded me into believing I don't deserve to be happy. For that, I made Bao Lai cried. She doesn't warrant the mistreatment. I'm not justifying my misery by blaming you. In fact, I don't truly blame you. I only wish to convey my thoughts so I may finally let the torment subside. From now on, I'll look to Bao Lai. She'll care for me and in turn, I'll protect her. If I go against any of your teachings, it won't be stemmed from disrespect. Please, give us your blessing and keep Nan Rong and my brothers safe."

I bow low and pray that Jin's words will reach Consort En. If she can hear me, too, I hope she will entrust Shu Jin's happiness to me.

Chapter 20: First Date

By the time we leave the shrine, evening has taken over the horizon. Hand-in-hand, we descend the staircase. I'm glad I chose to climb up these steps.

"Jin, you said you were waiting here for me. Did you know I would come?"

"Yes. I thought you'd find the temple since it would remind you of home. What better place to seek comfort than home? Also, the structure is massive enough that I knew you'd see it."

"Actually, I came upon this path by pure chance. Why did you assume I wouldn't leave Xiong?"

"Subconsciously, you were drawn here despite intent. Your sense of direction is also terrible. I knew you'd walk in circles if you tried to leave Xiong."

My sulking stare is returned by a beaming smile. So, this is how it's going to be from now on. I'm stuck with this teasing man and I couldn't be happier.

As soon as we near the markets, sulking becomes impossible. Bright lanterns glow in the dark night. Unlike the relaxed atmosphere of day, by night, the town is so lively, one would think there is a festival. The air is exciting and robust. Adults are chatting noisily while children run about, shrieking loudly during their games, engulfed in their sheer youthful state of wonder. The noise is slightly deafening. I like it.

231

There are stalls and shops lined on both sides of the streets as far as the eyes can see. Trinkets and baubles clink jovially; now and then, sparkle when catching slivers of light. The scent of food and other delicious aromas are unbearably tempting. Much to my dismay, Jin heard my stomach growled.

"We best subdue that beast before it devours Xiong. What would you like to eat, Princess?" He grins.

"Whatever you'd like, *Prince* Jin."

Jin throws a soft smile while the grip around my hand tightens. "I'm sorry. I'm not good at this. I know a lady must be respected. Beyond that, I'm helpless on the subject. To be honest, I'm not sure how to treat you."

"Then, what made you think calling me, 'Princess,' was a good idea? I prefer, 'Commander!'"

"Yes, I'm sure you do." Jin chuckles. "Once, when I was in the market searching for His Highness, a noisy pair caught my attention. Perhaps there was more to their story, but I merely saw the girl giggled loudly and leapt into the arms of the man who held to her a flower and called her, 'Princess.' She couldn't have been happier. Also, His Highness often said women like to be teased even though they won't admit it. But, you're not enjoying any of this, are you?"

"Is that why you've been acting so strange— amongst the multitude of other reasons? I don't know much about relationships either, Jin. I prefer for you to just be you. Unless you expect me to be the girl you saw in the market or the women He Pi dotes on, don't treat me differently. Anyhow, He Pi, for all his charms, is quite alone. Well... despite being engaged. Don't put too much thought into his recommendations."

"You'll have to lecture His Highness when you have the chance. As for me, it won't be easy to *be myself.* I've shown you too much of my ugliness. Besides, you're not just my charge anymore. You're my... What are we, exactly?"

"I don't know. More than friends and less than lovers. That would make me... your girlfriend?"

"Girlfriend," Jin slowly relishes the word. A hint of delight spreads across his expression.

"Long ago, a boy who trained with the temple's students said I'd never find a man if I kept dressing as one. At the time, the only thing I could do was beat him senseless when we sparred. Too bad I can't rub it in his face now!"

I don't know why I suddenly recall his stupid smirk. He always bore his fangs at me whenever I won our matches. Why can't I remember his name?

Jin chuckles. "My girlfriend has quite the temper."

Although it was my decision for him to consider me his girlfriend, my face is lit crimson. In only a few days, I've worn women's clothes, confessed my ardent affections, and gained a boyfriend. I wonder what other experiences are in store for me. As I glance into his beautiful eyes, I realize that with Jin by my side, I will always welcome the new day.

"Bao Lai, should we stop here?"

Jin points to a small shop on our right. Patrons crowd heavily inside and out while scents wafting from the pots make my stomach growls; two signs to guarantee delicious food. Nevertheless, I hesitate. I don't have any money. At the palace, I didn't mind enjoying the luxuries since in the very least, I could return a service. Here, as Jin's girlfriend, taking from him doesn't sit well with me. In fact, this entire trip hasn't cost me a single coin. That seems rather unfair.

"What's wrong?" Jin nudges me.

"Nothing."

He frowns. After all our troubles due withholding honesty, I'm now being contrary. I want us to be honest with each other and that can't happen when I'm not willing to oblige. So, here goes.

"Well, I mean... I don't have any coins and I feel bad for forcing you to spend your hard-earned money on me. Let's just go back to the inn."

His fingers gently tap against my cheek. "Most girlfriends to noble princes expect pamper. Are you being coy to win my favor?"

"Coyness isn't enough to win your favor, is it? Master Tai Hung, the old priest who looked after me, used to say that nothing's more dangerous than coveting what others have than to take what isn't yours."

"Doesn't that only imply stealing is wrong?"

"Not to me."

"You really must be a monk." Jin playfully taps his fingers to my cheek again. "Bao Lai, you're my girlfriend. As far as I'm concerned, what's mine is yours. So please, don't feel guilty."

"Well... are you really sure?"

"I wouldn't say so if I wasn't."

"Then allow me to give you something in return." I fumble inside my pocket and then produce a smooth marble made from shiny black stone. The fine intricate carvings of a phoenix rising toward a star are detailed into the small stone with slivers of gold.

"The old man gave this to me on my eighth birthday. The phoenix is flying toward Polaris, he said; Polaris is of course, my name. The other symbolisms are lost to me. He promised to explain their significance when the time was appropriate but he passed before having the chance."

My nose is burning. I've shed countless tears for my master and still, I never think they're enough. At the moment, I need to control myself. Jin and the several hundred other patrons around don't need to see my bawling. "Ahem... When held under bright light, the dark stone can sometimes glow like a star. Isn't that amazing?"

Jin, retrieving the marble from my hand, slowly examines the fine details. "I wondered what it was you kept slipping into your pocket every time I dressed you. I thought I must have imagined it. A marble, huh? I envy your innocence, Bao Lai."

"What innocence? It's a pretty marble!"

"Indeed," he smirks. "A fine marble that can mesmerize any child for hours."

"Are you calling me a child?"

"You're certainly pouting like one."

"I know it's nothing compared to the fine jewels of the palace but it's special to me. The sentimental value is worth more than a thousand times its weight in gold. If you don't want it, I'll take it back. You don't have to laugh at my gift."

"Don't take offense. I was laughing at how adorably juvenile you are." He holds the marble toward a lantern, though it doesn't glow in the weak light source. "Since you want me to have this precious thing that is dear to you, I'll gladly accept. Only, do you honestly want to part with this fine gift from your master?"

"Yes. I want you to have it. Aside from the wonderful memories it carries, Master Tai Hung also said the marble was blessed for protection. It's protected me just fine over these years."

"I see. Without your charm, you are asking for my protection, Bao Lai. Very well, then. I shall be the one to protect you." He states matter-of-factly.

"I'll have you know I've trained under the famed General Zhuang Gu of Ji back at the old temple. I don't need your protection."

Whilst I fret, Jin bursts into laughter.

"Only you would take offense over my endeavor at romance!"

"That was supposed to be romantic?"

He responds by tapping his fingers gently against my cheeks while a smile brimming with affections beams down. An offer of protection, that is rather romantic. However, in my past experiences with men from the temple, it's an insult to be viewed so weak. Jin is different. He's seen my weaknesses and is partial toward me for showing them.

"I... I don't mind if you protect me," the admittance comes out as mumbles.

"You don't mean that one bit, *Commander*! Thank you for this gift. I'll treat it with care. Right now, I'm hungry. Why don't you find a table for us? I'll be right out."

Jin goes inside while I search around for empty seats. Three rows down, a pair ready their belongings for departure. I rush to snag the table just as they leave. The moment I sit down, he's back outside. Once I signal for him, Jin comes over with the full tray.

"That was fast!"

"Yes, this restaurant is always busy but their staffs are also efficient. I hope you like this. It's their specialty."

Jin places a bowl of noodle soup along with a plate of herbs and vegetables in front of me. He then takes a smaller bowl and scoops several large spoonfuls of his rice dish for me to sample.

"Well, you have *spoiled* me terribly at the palace. It's not every day a simple girl can eat an emperor's repast. I still like this better, just the two of us having dinner together."

"Me, too. We should make this our ritual once we return."

"I'd like that. Jin, while we're on the subject of our return, San An was angry when we left, wasn't he? Did I do something wrong? I plan to apologize but I don't know the reason."

Jin's head shakes. "No, you didn't do anything wrong. His fury is against me. You could say I stole his beloved."

"I won't pretend that I don't know you're insinuating his beloved to be me, but that's not possible. After the attack in the peach garden, he's come to his senses."

"Don't you see? It was because of the event from the peach garden that he fell for you. I saw the loving way he looked at you in the infirmary and how grieved he was when you chose me. I can't blame him. His reaction was reasonable. If it weren't for you, he would have died."

"No, Jin, it was because of you. Still, if everything you've said is true, then I feel really guilty."

"For what? Risking your life for my brother? Have no regrets. Your impetuousness earned his favor and deepened mine. I'm only sorry that he loves you and I don't—and yet, you're mine." Jin pauses. "Bao Lai, you winced when I said I don't love you. Are you sure you're fine with this?"

"No, it wasn't that. The broth is still boiling. I burned my mouth."

"You're the worst liar ever."

He frowns whilst seemingly on the verge of falling back into insecurity. I reach across the table for his hand, to assure that all is well between us. Jin returns a soft smile and then sheepishly pushes the question. "Bao Lai, why do you love me?"

"Why? Because I think you're sweet, gentle, and kind. You're smart and dependable and on top of everything, you're obviously *gorgeous!*"

"You're so shallow." Following a scoff, he laughs shortly. "It would be unfair for me not to warn you. That Jin from the palace was only meant to serve you. The man sitting here may not be everything you've come to expect."

"If I'm expecting too much then that is my fault. You've told me at least thrice now that you don't love me and I haven't run off yet. So please, don't feel anxious. Anyway, you slighted your own mother for my sake. Even men who are madly in love don't have the gall to do that! We should buy some flowers and visit again to pay our respects."

Jin smiles charmingly while squeezing my hand. "I think she'd like that. Let's go near daybreak. The flowers will be fresher."

I return a quick nod and then dinner is resumed with more pleasant conversations. It's apparent he's still somewhat troubled, though for the most part, I think Jin has calmed.

Chapter 20 – 2

The night air is cool and refreshing. Jin's arm remains tight around my shoulders as we stroll through the town. Above, stars cast a net over clear dark skies, illuminating the heavens to match the lantern lights surrounding us below. I feel so tranquil and warm in his embrace. Though we are practically joined at the hip, I press toward him a little more so we can be closer.

After several turns down nearly empty streets, a small house comes into view. It's evident the abode has long been abandoned; though, it's not in very poor conditions. Jin stares nostalgically at the structure.

"That is my mother's house. When I was little, we often stayed there for months on end. See that tree on the right? My father met my mother under the shade. She said it was pure luck it rained that day and she came home early from the markets to find him shivering beneath the branches. It was love at first sight."

"That's a beautiful story."

This picturesque scene is where a love bloomed, which ultimately brought Jin into the world. I could imagine him as a child sitting beneath the same tree that meant so much to his parents. A chance encounter like that is rare, isn't it? To meet true love at one's door? In some ways, my encounter with Jin was also by chance. For His Majesty and I to have been born with the same face, for him to go missing, and then for Bai Hu to have met me on the road—if all these events did not lined perfectly, I never would have known this happiness which I now share with Jin. There are no words to describe this elation just from being in his arms.

"Only because I'm curious, upon first sight, what did you think of me and our chance meeting, Jin?"

"I thought you resembled His Highness very much and I was glad you agreed to the task. Not very romantic am I? Why do you ask?"

"No reason. Our story is odd, I suppose. I met you as a man and I resemble your brother. It's not something to tell the children."

A sharp laugh ensues but I was the only one who laughed. Jin is quiet. His reaction to my crude observations is to pull me away from the scene.

"Jin, what's wrong?"

"What do you think? I show you my childhood and suddenly, we're expected to have children. It's best we leave before you develop more troubling ideas."

"I was joking!"

"Were you? Now I'm disappointed. I really wanted at least ten. Definitely, an even number. I won't let you refuse me."

At least ten? Five is probably enough to kill me!

Bewildered by his sudden demand, a prying gaze arches up. He's teasing me again, isn't he? Of course he is. A corner of his mouth is curled into a smirk even though all else on his face is quite serious.

I can't find the right rebuttal. Silently, I follow wherever he leads. Jin drops a kiss on my forehead and then we continue strolling down several more lighted streets. He stops once or twice to point out other significant places from his childhood. Each new piece reveals another part of him. Someday, I hope we can visit the temple south so I can share with him pieces of me.

Chapter 21: He Pi

Upon entering our room at the inn, someone darts up from the bed. Running forward, the grinning stranger draws me into his arms and presses a kiss to my cheek. Jin quickly tugs me away, moving in between to guard me from the assailant.

"Your Highness, I won't tell you a second time. Bao Lai is mine."

I thought he looked familiar. Well, of course he should, he's standing there with my face!

"He Pi? Where have you been?!" Relief flows and likewise, rage begins to engulf my temperament. I was afraid His Highness had perished or was held captive somewhere. Here he is, healthy as a horse and smiling, even after all the troubles he's caused.

"What a coincidence! Jin, did you say her name is Bao Lai? Not long ago, I was at Tian Mao Yi Temple, going by the same name. So much for being men of the cloth! A cute smile here, a bat of eyelashes there, and all the monks fell for my seduction. Boy, were their faces red when they discovered my gender!"

His grin widens while my breathing stops. What did he just say?

"You-you-you did what?!"

"Bao Lai. Your Highness. We should continue this conversation with more discretion."

"You're always such a worrywart, Jin." Despite the careless declaration, He Pi goes to survey the perimeter. A moment later, he comes back and then carefully locks the door. After taking the seat opposing Jin at the table, he continues in a low and serious tone.

"Master Lo Han mistook me for you in the market. I couldn't help curiosity. I took your place at the temple, Miss Liang. You'll have to forgive me. Anyhow, after San An was attacked, I tracked down the assailant's connections to Bei Ling. At this time, I'm still not definite who ordered the assault. However, there are a group of people who may be able to help. I've been waiting here to relay the message to Jin but since you've come, I must ask a favor of you, too."

"Me? Wait. Why did you call me, 'Miss Liang?'"

He Pi grins. The moment I stand up to confront him, to ask how he could know my family name which I did not know myself, His Highness promptly presents a letter from his breast pocket.

"This is for you. I think Master Tai Hung meant to return this before he passed."

"What is it?"

He replies by nodding encouragingly.

Does that document contain my past? I'm elated to know and yet, I fear that knowledge. My parents abandoned me. Why should I care to find out who they are? Since they didn't want me, I shouldn't claim to be part of their lines now. Every bit of me that wants to know is held back by an equal measure of indecision. My eyes waver while I stand frozen in place. In my stead, Jin reaches for the letter. When he attempts to open the note, His Highness immediately drops both hands on top of Jin's.

"Hey, now! Don't read that in front of me or I'll be forced to propose to your lover!"

"Why would you do that, Your Highness?"

"Why else? A beneficial marriage to ensure Nan Rong's safety. So long as we're all seemingly oblivious here, let's keep it that way. Anyhow, I really must return to Bei Ling. Something tells me the instigators will likely move soon. I don't have a lot of time. Miss Liang, about that favor. My request is for you to take the letter to Lord Han Bei in Ning. If he won't entertain an audience, then go there as me. Whatever you do, be sure to show him that letter. It's vital. You should be able to figure out the rest."

"Wait! Who is Lord Han Bei? Why Ning? And, you can't go to Bei Ling! What about Nan Rong?" I move toward the table at the same time He Pi rises to his feet.

"I'm doing this for Nan Rong. Trust me." His gentle smile then shifts to a wide grin when attention returns to his brother. "Shu Jin, if in a year's time you haven't married Miss Liang, I'll make her my woman."

His brusque announcement is followed by boyish laughter. Needless to say, my blood is boiling.

"If you have the nerves for it, I'll make you regret it! And if I don't, Mu Dan will!"

"Oh, you met Mu Dan, did you?" He Pi chuckles nervously. "I hope she didn't give you too much trouble."

I was ready to blurt out complaints but managed to clamp my mouth shut. Mu Dan loves He Pi. I shouldn't badmouth another "woman" in front of her fiancé.

"Hmm. It's late and you're more of a brute than everyone at the temple suggested, so I'll take my leave." He Pi sighs. "Jin, when everything is settled with Ning, come find me in Bei Ling's capital. Send a letter to the White Crane Inn's owner, Zhang Tang, before starting out. Remember to sign your name. He'll direct you to my location."

"Yes, Your Highness." Jin replies.

He Pi pats Jin's shoulder and then casually stretches his arms into the air. As he walks by, His Highness plants a kiss on my lips and then immediately darts out of the door, guffawing like a moron. He moved so fast, I did not have a chance to swing at him. Rage is building in torrents. I need to hit something! Thoughts suddenly recall Kang Lang's image. Why didn't I see it before? They are two peas in a pod!

Chapter 21 – 2

"What is it, Jin?"

While I've been sitting here contemplating my revenge against He Pi, Jin's been reading the letter. Actually, it's been a long while. Every time his eyes fall on the last line, they shift back to the top. It's possible I'm imagining it; I think he's grown pale.

Jin doesn't respond. I step behind him to catch a glimpse of the message. Barely do my eyes fall on the faded ink, he folds the paper and then shuffles it away with our luggage.

"Jin, what's wrong?"

Still no answer. I make for the luggage. He bars the path and then pulls me into his arms. Is he defaulting to insecurities again? What could possibly be written on that paper? I was undecided at first but his reaction just now causes curiosity to swell. I need to know.

"Jin! Say something!"

Quivering arms force a stronger embrace; growing ever tighter. He's pleading for me to give up the endeavor. Though it means I'll disappoint He Pi, I need to respect Jin's choice. My arms fly around his back to return the fervor in full.

"Don't look so glum, Jin. Remember what I said? I won't do anything you don't want me to, so I won't read the letter since you're against it."

"I'm sorry, Your Highness." He mutters pitiably.

"Highness? He Pi left. Who are you—"

"*You*, my princess."

"I told you to quit calling me that!"

"I'm sorry I did," he smiles sadly. "Ironically, now I fear the idea of it and yet, you are."

"You're not making any sense, Jin. Does this have something to do with the letter?"

"It's not a letter. It's an edict from the late Empress Piao of Ning to confirm the birthrights of her second daughter, Bao Lai, half-sister of Dong Xing and Princess of Fan Fa."

"I told you to quit making fun of me."

He's not serious, is he? Either he's joking or that note is a prank. Despite my unwillingness to believe the nonsense, everything in me wants a past, something to which I can bind my existence, to know I truly lived. Jin must understand my frustration. Though reluctant, he fetches the edict. My eyes run over the page several times, believing that somehow the words will change, but they don't. The Eastern seal is still firm on the page.

As averse as I was to accept the idea, once my fingers glide over the raised lines, certain happiness erupts in my heart and I want more than anything for this to be real. This seal—my mother's seal. This is the only thing of hers that I have. I finally know my mother's name. And, Dong Xing is my sister. I am from Ning. As crazy as it is, this is my past and I'm glad to know it.

"Jin, who is Han Bei? What will he do once we present the edict?"

"Based on old records and recent intelligence report from the Minister's trip, Lord Han Bei of Ren Liu is the Grand General of Ning and only council to Emperor Yuan. His Highness expects you to claim kinship to the royal bloodline and earn Ning's alliance for Nan Rong."

"And who is Emperor Yuan to me? Is he my brother?"

"No. He's your nephew."

"Nephew. I have a nephew!" The images of rosy cheeks, chubby fingers, plump gait, and a wide smile of a toddler come to mind. My eyes can't keep from lighting up. Another relative! The knowledge is so excruciatingly exciting that I can't help but jump a little. "I bet he's cute! What about my sister? Where is she? Is she in Ning's capital, too?"

"Bao Lai, your nephew is not a child. He's fourteen years old. Empress Dong Xing passed shortly after his birth."

"What? My-My sister passed? She must have been so young!"

"She was. I'm sorry. First thing tomorrow, we'll return to An and then prepare a caravan for Ning."

"We can't leave tomorrow. You still have to offer prayers to your ancestors and bring flowers to your mother. Let's leave the day after."

"No. You have family waiting, Bao Lai. I'll return you to them, I promise. My ancestors can no longer speak, so if they're angry, I can't hear their complaints."

What is he doing? A moment ago, he didn't want me to read the letter. After everything he just said, this feels like goodbye. I don't covet power or authority. They're meaningless without him. Is he worried that I'll give him up or does he aim to give me up?

Suddenly drawn into a panic, I toss the letter onto the table and wrap my arms around him. He withdraws. I hold steadfast and bury my face in his chest.

"I'll meet with Han Bei for Nan Rong's sake but the South will always be my home and you are my family now, Jin. I care more for you than anyone. Don't run from me again."

"That wasn't my intention. Your happiness is important to me. From your excitement, I know you've been hoping for family all your life, haven't you? Now is your chance."

"Yes, I have, but that was foolish. I had family. Master Tai Hung was my grandfather and the other students at the temple were my brothers. And you Jin, I can't even begin to describe what you are to me. Boyfriend will have to suffice. So, I'm happy."

"When you put it that way, I'm happy, too. I have my brothers and I also have you. Anyway, don't worry. We'll return next year to apologize. Nan Rong is our priority right now."

So, there will be a next year for us. Good. I'm glad.

Slowly, I release him. Jin carefully places the letter into our luggage. We lie down beside each other and lulled by the comfort of warmth, fall into deep slumber.

Chapter 22: My Very Sweet Boyfriend

San An was surprised we returned so quickly, and stunned silent when He Pi's plan and the edict were relayed. Jin urged the Minister to prepare a caravan but the request was denied. Evidently, Ning's emissary, Lord Han Bei, will come to Nan Rong next week to discuss matters regarding Mount Fei Yang. It is convenient; though, I really wanted to meet my nephew.

Currently, Jin and I are in He Pi's quarters deciding how to approach Han Bei with the edict. The emissary wishes to discuss relations between our two countries. If I push the decree and declare myself Ning's princess in order to force an alliance, he might just take offense and tear it apart. That will absolutely destroy every chance to form a bond with the East.

"He'll expect to meet He Pi, but appearing as His Highness won't convince him that I'm honest. Meeting him as Bao Lai will likely make Lord Han Bei suspect the document to be forgery."

"Right. We need to be tactful. Emperor Yuan looks to Lord Han Bei for guidance. Unless we can earn favor from the latter, the former won't have anything to do with us. Han Bei has little opinion of every nation but Ning. It won't be easy to win him over."

Jin sighs heavily. He hasn't slept much since we came back. The bags under his eyes are too apparent and with more stress building daily, he'll wear himself out. I've come to depend on Jin for too much, I know that. I still want to be useful. While searching for resort, the same thought which entered my mind earlier comes back: I want to meet my nephew.

"Jin, what if I venture to Ning? You mentioned that Yuan look to Han Bei for guidance. If Han Bei disapproves of me, then so will Yuan. But, if I meet Yuan and earn his favor without Han Bei's influence, then we can at least force Han Bei to entertain the edict."

"You're quite devious," Jin smiles. "One problem though, we can't enter the East uninvited and likewise, can't ask for permission without raising suspicions. Ning's emissary already plans to visit Nan Rong."

"Then I will go there as Bao Lai and not as He Pi."

The moment I jump up, Jin seizes my wrist.

"Bao Lai, I'm not against your plan but this is dangerous. Not to mention, the Prime Minister won't approve. Why don't you let me take that letter to Ning while you stay here and wait for Han Bei?"

"He Pi asked me for this favor, Jin. Don't put yourself in danger for my sake."

An arm immediate wraps around my waist, drawing me onto his lap. Softly, his breath trickles into my ear. "I am your boyfriend. You should let me protect you."

"Shu Jin! Are you trying to seduce me with your sweet words? I refuse to listen!"

My hands fly over my ears. Jin laughs sharply. Leaning back onto the bed, he takes me down with him and attempts to move atop. I retaliate and eventually, we simply wrestle until a victor is apparent: me.

"You can't win, Jin! The boys at the temple gave me a hard time. Until I proved my worth, they didn't accept me. This is not my first match."

Frowning, Jin gently brushes a hand against my cheek. "I told you not to mention other men."

"They weren't men at the time," I return his frown. "By the way, I know you let me win. This long robe is hard to move in. When I'm back in my old clothes, I expect a rematch."

"You're still this impetuous at your age. I wonder how reckless you were as a child."

"Entirely too reckless."

"I see. So, you've never been proper then."

Blood suddenly drains from my face. What did he mean by that? Was this inappropriate? Am I still the same, at age twenty-six, as when I was age six? Wrestling with other children my age was fine; I'm too old for this now. When adults wrestle, it usually implies something more. In short, it's unbecoming. Jin deserves a lady. I don't even know how to feign being one.

"Bao Lai, what's wrong? You've grown pale. Did I offend you?"

"No, you didn't." Moving off Jin, I take a more serious pose on the edge of the bed. "I'll attempt to be more of a lady from now on."

"I really hope you won't. You're still pretending to be His Highness and he's no lady." Jin nudges my arm teasingly.

"You know what I mean. I want to become someone respectable; someone who can earn your ardent affections. I will become a lady, for you."

"I like you as you are." Following the bashful response, his hand reaches over and squeezes mine. "I've seen what ladies are capable of behind their façades. I prefer the capricious brute that you are."

"I am not capricious!" My hand jerks away and I take to my feet.

"You're offended by capricious and not brute?"

Behind the incredulous stare, he's laughing at me again. I don't know how to rebut. I stand still, dumfounded. In one swift movement, his arms pull me onto the bed. Without my retaliation, this time he's atop.

"See? It's not fun unless you vie for this position." He smiles sweetly while running his lips over my cheek.

I was still searching for a quip when the doors swing open and deep gasps fill the room. Jin and I turn toward the source just as Mu Dan runs over. Pouting, both hands fly to his hips.

"Jin! What are you doing to my fiancé and *your brother*?!"

"Knock it off, Kang Lang. Jin knows your secret."

As the troubling thought comes, my eyes dart to Jin's face. I was afraid he might flee and leave me with this madwoman again. This time, however, there's nothing in his expression that suggests he's still intimidated by Mu Dan's beauty.

His brows furrow into a knot. Jin moves to his feet and then faces Kang Lang. A serious, almost resentful impertinence builds into tempestuous rage which then plasters over his face.

"I'm telling you once and once only. Keep your hands off Bao Lai. If you ever make her uncomfortable again, you will regret it."

Kang Lang stares back wide-eyed. A drawn moment passes and then he breaks into boisterous laughter. "Are *you* threatening *me?* That's a joke! What would you do if I were to *kiss* and *caress* your dear Bao Lai again, as I've done *so many* times before?"

A derisive smile accompanies Kang Lang's taunts. Fearing Jin's reaction, I reach for his hand. He shakes off the attempt.

"Lord Han Bei is coming to Nan Rong. I can't think of a better way to greet our guest of honor than by presenting the traitor, Kang Lang. Hopefully he'll be lenient, as you are his only brother after all, and instead of execution, just let you rot in a cell for the rest of your life."

Kang Lang turns pale and so do I. Is that true? This crazy person is an assassin nobleman from Ning and brother to the famous Lord Han Bei no less? What other secret is he hiding behind that perfect marble mask?

A bitter smile sweeps his painted lips. Kang Lang, wholly dejected, glances at the floor. "My fiancé told you, did he? So much for loyalty."

"Do not dismiss His Highness's loyalty, Kang Lang. He's provided your protection and you have lived as a prince these last six years. You've seduced almost every woman in the Circle. Life has not been bad, has it? Out of respect for His Highness and due a great deal to Bao Lai's forgiveness, I will turn a blind eye to your previous transgressions. My kindness is limited. Don't expect this benefit a second time."

Kang Lang, still defiant, stares back boldly without a single notion of alarm. In the end, his hands are thrown into the air. "I didn't think the pup had any bark in him without his master around. Whatever. You two are so boring, you deserve one another. I merely came to torment Bao Lai but since she must endure your *dull* company, that's punishment enough."

Pouting, Kang Lang turns to leave. As he does, I rush forward to seize his arm.

"Kang Lang, since Lord Han Bei is your brother, you must help us! Could you convince him to grant me an audience with Emperor Yuan or at least, consider a certain letter?"

"Bao Lai, we don't need this help." Jin's protest is less against my request and more against my friendliness toward Kang Lang.

"He's our best option, Jin."

Kang Lang scoffs. "My brother couldn't care less what I have to say. More importantly, why should I do anything after your lover insulted me?"

"If you do as I ask, Emperor Yuan will pardon whatever crimes you've committed."

"Really? And how do you plan to pull that off?"

"Empress Dong Xing was my sister and Emperor Yuan is my nephew. He won't deny his aunt's request for a simple pardon."

From the corners of his eyes, Kang Lang peers cautiously in my direction. He's questioning my honesty. I was still contemplating how to secure his compliance when he breaks into guffaws.

"You think Han Bei will believe your baseless claims? I hope you have proof. In any case, your lover is right. I am no less than a prince in Nan Rong, so I don't care to be pardoned."

"By those claims, Nan Rong has treated you well. Why not do this small favor? I need Han Bei's alliance to protect the Southland."

"Hmph! I will protect Nan Rong should peril befall the South. Convincing Ning's Grand General to accept you as empress is to your benefit and a dangerous game to play at that. If you will bribe me, make the offer worth the risk."

What could I possibly offer someone in the league of a prince? He's mentioned coveting the title of empress but I still can't grant the preposterous request. I best avoid that subject altogether.

"Tell me what you want that's reasonable and I'll find a way to give it to you."

"Oh, so accommodating, Your Highness? If you want my help, then kiss me here and now. I don't promise to be gentle."

"*Bastard!*" Jin and I mutter in unison.

"Oh! You even share the same mind! How *adorable!*" Kang Lang gives a sarcastic frown. His index finger jabs against my cheek. "Bastard or not, I'm your only hope. Are you taking my offer?"

"Not on your life!" is Jin's response.

Shrugging, the younger man resumes his path toward the door. I can't let him leave. What he's asking for is a small price to pay in the grander scheme.

"Wait, Kang Lang! I'll do it."

Kang Lang turns around, wearing a victorious grin. His proud stare serves to frustrate Jin, whose wrathful glare in my direction signals that his insecurities are mounting. I know this must pain him but it can't be helped.

"Jin, it's okay. You can scold me as much as you'd like afterwards. For now, please wait in the hall."

"You sly girl!" Kang Lang interjects. "Surely, you knew I want your guard dog to watch. What would be the point otherwise? He's not going anywhere."

"But you didn't say—"

"My request. My choice."

Why is he such a jerk? I don't want to hurt Jin, but I need Kang Lang's help. What do I do?

Kiss Kang Lang (Continue to page 263)

Don't kiss him (Continue to page 266)

Chapter 22 – 2

"I-I'll do it." The pathetic whisper chokes its way out. Without acknowledging Jin, my feet drag forward toward Kang Lang's open arms. For this distasteful act, I hope Jin won't run from me again. Even if he does, this time, I'm determined to follow.

Before Kang Lang's hands touch me, Jin rushes past. Instantaneously, an unbelievable sight occurs which forces red blooms to my face. My heart is beating out of my chest and I can't stop staring. Jin's grabbed Kang Lang's arms and pressed his lips against the courtesan's. The latter stumbles back while Jin's hold fastens. I don't know whose eyes have grown wider, Kang Lang's or mine.

Secretly, I'm disappointed that the incredible moment was short-lived. I'm not sure why.

Jin pulls away and brings up a sleeve to cover his mouth. His eyes are twitching from utter disgust. Those same reactions are mirrored by Kang Lang.

The younger man is stricken mute, and so am I. Our attentions thrust upon Jin, who finally breaks the silence over the room.

"You only wanted a kiss from her to torment me and *that* was torture, believe me! You will keep your promise to Bao Lai!"

His tongue clicks sharply. Kang Lang directs an angry stare at Jin and then an agitated glare at me. In time, a forced smile forms over his nervous demeanor. "How foolish. Since your lover kissed me, for every special moment you both share, my lips will vicariously imprint onto yours, Your Highness. For that, I'll see what I can do."

With reddened face, Mu Dan leaves the room. I'm still in shock and can't do much else except stare at a flustering Jin, who's busy rubbing a sleeve furiously over his mouth. I can't believe he did that to protect me.

"What are you staring at?" Jin's mutter carries both agitation and embarrassment.

"My very sweet boyfriend."

"There was no other choice," he mumbles bashfully.

"No? Well, that must have been some kiss for Kang Lang to have changed his mind. He usually doesn't quit until he gets exactly what he wants. Unless, he knew you would... and he coveted you all along!"

"Instead of mocking me, why don't you comfort my humiliation?"

"I-I'm sorry. Do you want a towel?"

"Yes," is the succinct response. Jin kneels in front of me and then rubs his mouth onto the collar of my robe.

"That's not a towel!"

"Obviously," he scoffs. A fervent kiss follows to seal my protest or maybe, as a mean to cleanse his lips.

With our plan to approach Han Bei decided, Jin's tension gradually dissolve. More so, he's become playful again. I'm glad that even after all the discomfiture, he stayed by my side.

Continue to page 269

Chapter 22 – 3

I won't do it. I can't hurt Jin! And yet, I can't bring myself to send away our best option. Kang Lang, irritated by my stalling, lets out a scoff and then promptly starts for the door.

Panicking, I foolishly follow. As I do, Jin immediately rushes past me. He grabs Kang Lang's arms and pushes the latter against the door. Instantaneously, an unbelievable sight occurs which forces red blooms to my face. My heart is beating out of my chest and I can't stop staring. Jin's pressed his lips against the courtesan's! I don't know whose eyes have grown wider, Kang Lang's or mine.

Following the short, exciting, and awkward moment, Jin pulls away and brings up a sleeve to cover his mouth. His eyes are twitching from utter disgust. Those same reactions are mirrored by Kang Lang.

The younger man is stricken mute, and so am I. Our attentions thrust upon Jin, who finally breaks the silence over the room.

"You only wanted a kiss from her to torment me and *that* was torture, believe me! You will keep your promise to Bao Lai!"

His tongue clicks sharply. Kang Lang directs an angry stare at Jin and then an agitated glare at me. In time, a forced smile forms over his nervous demeanor.

"How foolish. Since your lover kissed me, for every special moment you both share, my lips will vicariously imprint onto yours, Your Highness. For that, I'll see what I can do."

With reddened face, Mu Dan leaves the room. I'm still in shock and can't do much else except stare at a flustering Jin, who's busy rubbing a sleeve furiously over his mouth. I can't believe he did that to protect me.

"What are you staring at?" Jin's mutter carries both agitation and embarrassment.

"My very sweet boyfriend."

"There was no other choice," he mumbles bashfully.

"No? Well, that must have been some kiss for Kang Lang to have changed his mind. He usually doesn't quit until he gets exactly what he wants. Unless, he knew you would... and he coveted you all along!"

"Instead of mocking me, why don't you comfort my humiliation?"

"I-I'm sorry. Do you want a towel?"

"Yes," is the succinct response. Jin kneels in front of me and then rubs his mouth onto the collar of my robe.

"That's not a towel!"

"Obviously," he scoffs. A fervent kiss follows to seal my protest or maybe, as a mean to cleanse his lips.

With our plan to approach Han Bei decided, Jin's tension gradually dissolve. More so, he's become playful again. I'm glad that even after all the discomfiture, he stayed by my side.

Chapter 23: San An's Proposal

"Oh, it's you. Long time no see."

Qing Hai smiles kindly when he sees me coming forthwith to San An's quarters. Usually, he accompanies Bai Hu, whose rude, obnoxious, and overbearing manners overshadow the former's sweet nature. For that reason, I haven't had the chance to truly distinguish Qing Hai until now. He must be in his late teens, I surmise, though there's a definite innocent air about him not common in young men these days. He's quite handsome and rather tall. His most noticeable trait is still that endearing smile.

When Bai Hu accosted me on the road that fateful day, Qing Hai intervened and protected me despite the fact that I was a complete stranger. I haven't forgotten that. If it weren't for him, I don't know if I would be here now, happy with Jin. I've never even thanked him.

"Qing Hai. It's good to see you again. How's your training? Is the Demon General giving you a hard time?"

"Likewise. General Hu is not making things easy for me." He chuckles nervously while also slightly wincing from the recollection. "But, he's preparing me for the real deal. So, I'm learning."

"That's great! I know you'll make a fine soldier. Were you just visiting with the Minister?"

"Yes. He's waiting for you, I think. Must be something important. He was still pacing when I left."

"That's unlike him. Say, you mentioned that San An is your uncle. That makes you Jin's nephew, too, right?"

"Um... not quite." Qing Hai looks away and smiles timidly. "I'm not the Minister's nephew by blood. We're in the same household but... ah, I have to get going. If General Hu finds me dawdling, he'll double my duties in the barracks. Take care. I hope we'll meet again."

That's odd. Contrary to the young man on that road who had little reservations calling the Minister, 'Uncle,' this Qing Hai is absolutely nervous and somewhat embarrassed for their relationship. San An doesn't particularly seem close to his brothers, which makes me wonder the unique circumstances that could have allowed him to take an outsider into his family. I thought I knew the Minister, but he's an enigma. In any case, since Qing Hai is against discussing his past, I'd better let things be.

"Yes, me too. And Qing Hai, thank you, for protecting me that day we met. I'm sorry it took so long to express my gratitude. I don't know what would have happened if it hadn't been for you."

"Oh, don't mention it." He looks down and blushes. "I, uh... didn't do much. The General pretends to be a demon but he... though sometimes he is. What I mean is, General Hu is—"

"Not happy! What do you think you're doing slacking off? I thought I told you to come back the moment your business with the Minister was over."

Speak of the devil! Bai Hu's curt interruption is followed by his usual brutish etiquette. Stomping toward Qing Hai, he grabs the younger man by the ear and then starts down the hall.

I reach for Hu's arm and then pluck his heavy fingers off Qing Hai's ear. "Hey! Leave him alone! What is your problem? Why are you such a jerk?"

"Stay out of this! It's none of your business!"

"You barged in our conversation just to harass Qing Hai, so of course it's my business!"

"Your conversation never should have happened if Qing Hai didn't dilly-dally in the halls! Why'd you keep him, anyway? Don't you already have enough men to keep you company?"

"What is that supposed to mean?"

"Just that," he replies matter-of-factly. Hu withdraws his hand, which I didn't realize I was still holding onto. Letting out a quiet sigh, he mutters, "I can't believe after all these years, you're still oblivious."

"W-What—"

Before I could utter another word, Hu swiftly returns down the hall. Qing Hai gives an apologetic smile and then rushes after his trainer.

What was that about? What did he mean by *all these years?* Have we met before? Considering how much he seems to dislike me, if we had, I must have slighted him or we were never on good terms. Whatever is the case, I don't have the chance to muse the possibilities since the commotion brought San An to fetch me.

Chapter 23 – 2

From the moment I entered his quarters, San An began pacing with both hands cupped behind his back. Every once in a while, he'd glance over near the door and then resume pacing again. I should say something, though my mind's drawing a blank. San An is usually composed, too composed at times, that seeing him anxious brings about my apprehension.

After fifteen minutes of the uncomfortable silence, I suddenly realize dinnertime is near, which means Jin will be coming to my quarters with our meals. He's been more resolute about our relationship lately but that doesn't mean I should give him a reason to falter back to his old ways. The easiest mean to create doubt is to break a promise and we promised to spend this part of each evening together.

"San—"

"Marry me. That is... if you would do me the honor... that is, if you could..."

His eyes drift to the floor. San An sighs sharply while shaking his head as though chastising his own clumsiness. In time, he heaves a sharp exhale and with upturned eyes, musters greater determination. Moving toward the door, with great care, the Minister reaches for my hands.

Contrary to his confidence, I've held my breath since those shocking words came from his mouth and haven't been able to move an inch. He can't be serious.

"Please, don't look so frightened." San An smiles sadly. "I... have loved you for some time now. That's hardly surprising, is it? So long as you were He Pi, I couldn't... but you won't be anymore, Empress of Ning."

"San An, there's no guarantee Lord Han Bei will accept me or the edict. If by some miracle he will, I'll do whatever I can to ensure an alliance for Nan Rong."

"Is that all you think marriage means for me, an alliance?"

His grips on my hands tighten. San An looks so pained that my heart is writhing. Every time I think I've found the right words to ease his troubles, they disappear before taking form so that in the end, I couldn't do anything for San An.

Following a long silence, he manages to repress the apparent overwhelming emotions surging in tempest. When he continues, his breathing is noticeably strained. "There is validity to your concern and possibly, an inherent truth. Marriage between our royal bloodlines will greatly strengthen Nan Rong's stability and my authority. However, please don't take my offer too lightly. I have not been a gentleman or shown myself to you in a worthy light, but I can assure you that no man will ever love you more ardently or passionately than I. I know this confession can only make you think worse of me because I am fully aware of your considerations for my brother, but it had to be said. There would be no greater torture for me than to call you, 'Sister,' and no greater pleasure than to call you, 'Wife.' By your expression, the answer is clear, though I need you to understand that wherever fate or life may take you, I will be here and the offer to my heart will never change."

His hands slightly tremble. San An smiles dejectedly while bringing up long sleeves to wipe my eyes. I can't believe I have the gall to cry when he's the one who's hurt. Is this what Bai Hu meant by having enough men to keep me company? Did I do this to San An? The worst part is that I don't know what I must do to erase his pain.

"San... San An," It's so hard to speak through this lump in my throat. "You are a gentleman and I think very highly of you."

"But you can't love me because your heart belongs to Shu Jin, isn't that right? This entire ordeal was my fault. Had I just taken you into my care from the beginning—another of life's mistake I have come to regret."

"Please don't say that. Fate has someone more deserving of you in mind. I know you are destined for happiness, San An! By chance, I was brought to your door, but that doesn't mean I am the one. The person you're meant for, perhaps you may find yourself at her door soon."

"While I am glad for your optimism, what type of man would I be if my heart were that fickle? You have been the only one allowed inside in a very long time and there you shall remain for the rest of my days. Should fate have another planned for me, then I must be her punishment, for she is destined to marry a man who will always cast an eye wherever you may reside. Aside from you, I would not wish that fate on any woman."

Never in my life have I ever thought such sincere and loving words would reach my ears. My heart won't stop aching. At the same time, I feel my blood boiling. He doesn't have a real reason to love me and yet, he's throwing away his life before giving life a chance. He is a wonderful person who deserves happiness and he could have it if his views of me weren't so misguided.

"Minister... you are... the most stubborn man I've ever met in my life! I didn't save you and even if I had, that's not a good reason to fall for me! As I remember it, you saved me and Jin in turn, saved you. *He* threatened Master Yu!"

"What... do you mean by that? Why would Shu Jin threaten the physician?"

"He didn't tell you? From what I saw, Master—"

"Bao Lai, you're late for dinner."

The door opens right after the chiding tone enters the room. Jin tugs me away from San An and then moves in between to divide us. His actions are far from impromptu which means he must have been listening from outside. Just how much did he hear?

"Did you suddenly forget your manners, Shu Jin? Should eavesdropping be forgiven, you should know better than to barge into others' conversation uninvited." San An's tone is hard. In mere seconds, all his previous warmth is completely wiped away.

"With all due respect, Prime Minister, it's hardly polite to propose to another man's girlfriend when he is still alive and well."

Scoffing, San An returns a deadly stare. "Life only lasts so long. A woman should enjoy as much of it as possible. I am not afraid to offer her everything nor would I deny her anything. Her boyfriend may be alive and well but the only thing he can offer her is a living death saturated with unfulfilled promises."

"Minister! That is uncalled for! Jin—"

"Don't mind the Prime Minister, Bao Lai." Jin interrupts my defense with a smile. "For once, everything he has to offer still isn't enough."

Before I can get another word out, Jin bows to the Minister and then drags me from the room by the wrist. San An grimaces during our retreat; his anger gradually fades to pain. Once again, I feel terrible for leaving him this way, though I see now that an apology will not suffice. I just can't imagine what will free San An from his delusions of me.

Chapter 23 – 3

Immediately upon entering He Pi's chamber, Jin pins my wrists against the door, planting kiss after kiss until feeling reassured. It's a terrible thought, but my heart warms from his blatant envy. Barely do I yield to the moment, he moves away and starts for the table where our meals are now cold. His demeanor is stiff and distant. More and more, I feel the former barrier between us slowly erect.

"Jin, I'm sorry. I didn't mean to break our promise. I should have waited until after dinner to return San An's summon."

"Why? So I wouldn't discover the Minister's secret proposal? It was *exaggeratedly* romantic! Being the amorous man that he is, I'm sure he could make you very happy."

"Since you were eavesdropping, you must know I rejected his proposal."

"Did you? Because I never heard you said so. If anything, your replies only served to drag him farther along. He's more determined to have you now than ever. Ten more minutes of that and I have very little doubts he'd have advanced on you."

"I was trying not to injure him more than he's already been wounded. Since you noticed my tactlessness, why didn't you stop me sooner?"

His eyes glance in my direction and then look away again. More bottled up emotions. More secrets. He's angry but he won't say it. I start for Jin; wrapping my arms around his waist while pushing for the truth. If he could just reveal more of himself to me, then at the very least, we can move forward.

Once he grasps that the subject won't subside, Jin finally admits, "Maybe I thought... you'd agree. And, maybe a part of me wanted that you had."

"Why?"

"Because he loves you and because he's right. I'm not willing to offer you everything now, and it's possible, I may never be able to. I want to, but if I can't... having you both decide in my stead makes things easier."

I knew Jin wasn't fully committed to me, but I can't say I'm not hurt by how effortlessly he speaks about ending our bond. He wanted me to accept San An, so he doesn't have to face the eventual guilt of breaking my heart, which means Jin doesn't intend for us to last. He's already distancing himself. I've held him since coming over while he's kept both hands flat at his sides. It's apparent the more I cling to him, the more he aims to pull away. Since that is the case, I release him and then take to the bed.

Unable to cope with his implicit rejection, I can't help but become flippant. "If that was the easy answer you wanted, then why did you barge in? Maybe ten more minutes and I could have agreed."

"I don't know. Nothing is ever easy for me when you're involved."

"You pulled me from San An's quarters the moment I mentioned your role in saving him. Are you sure you weren't just being modest?"

Sighing softly, his eyes fall to the floor.

"That would make sense, wouldn't it? Had the Minister realized the truth, he wouldn't have hesitated to order the physician's execution. What Master Yu did was borderline treason. Still, now that I've had time to think things over, I doubt he would have allowed you both to perish, with or without my involvement."

"So, you're saying the only reason you retrieved me was to protect Master Yu? Why did you kiss me just now?"

"The Minister's audacity was agitating. Permit me a fraction of pride!"

"Now that you have your pride, if I march back to his quarters and take his offer, would you stop me?"

"You want me to say that I would, but the honest answer is I don't know. It's doubtful."

"I see."

At least he's honest; I have to keep reminding myself that. It's what I wanted. I'm not certain why I'm even surprised by his indifference. Despite how happy and loving he is one moment, his mood could change the very next. I told myself I'd follow if he'd run again and this occasion isn't any different. Be that as it may, at the moment, we seem to be at stalemate. I'd like to think he was actually jealous or that his interference was an allusion to unexpressed affections, but pushing the idea will only further his agitation; forcing my affections upon Jin might just hasten the retreat. I best give him space, for his sake and mine.

"Thank you for your honesty. And thank you for bringing dinner. I'm not hungry. I just need some fresh air. Good night, Jin."

I part from the room and as expected, he makes no acknowledgement.

Chapter 23 – 4

Of all the places to come! Why did instincts bring me here? I wandered aimlessly in the night only to find myself at the gates to the peach garden. This is where San An was attacked, which led him to foolishly fall for me, and where I foolishly confessed to Jin, which led him to believe he fell in love.

I can't change the past and I don't feel any control over the present. All the while, I should be more worried about the future. Lord Han Bei will come to Nan Rong and I still don't know what to say. The worst and best case scenario will be for him to accept me as Ning's missing princess. Nan Rong will be safe but I also can't imagine having a future here. Jin won't leave his services to He Pi, thus our relationship can only result in separation. Maybe I should have just married Kang Lang. At least that would have accomplished a means to an end.

During my pensive march, his voice—as light as wispy, translucent clouds in the night sky—flows gently through the wind in a whisper. Up the path a distance away, Mu Dan is having friendly conversations with a tree... so it seems. I'd barely taken notice when he quickly turns to me. At the same time, from atop the large tree trunk, a shadow shoots across toward another branch, disappearing into the night. It happened so speedily that my mind can't discern what I actually thought I saw. Whilst I try to piece things together, Mu Dan promptly marches forward and with his usual brute force, seizes my arm.

"Nosy, aren't you?" Scowling, his fingers dig into my clothes.

"I didn't see anything."

"That's right. You didn't. What are you doing out here, Your Highness? Were you looking for me?"

"No. I didn't know you were here. Now let me go."

The scowl slowly fades, and in its place, a derisive smile forms. "You're breaking my heart, darling! The same way you broke San An's. What's it like to hold that much power over someone, especially someone as unruffled as the Minister? I can easily take a life but to make someone suffer a lifetime without lifting a finger, now that takes talent!"

"San An isn't—! I know what you're trying to do and it won't work, you sadistic bastard."

"Whoa! That mouth on you! How ladylike! If you weren't my fiancé, Your Highness, I'd teach you some manners. Hmm, I hope you know your indiscretion is also the reason Jin is having second thoughts. Isn't that why you're outside? Big brother finally became bored of playing house, hasn't he?"

My eyes grow as round as the moon above. Kang Lang smiles victoriously for having caused my distress through his accurate deduction. He can always read my mind, sometimes even before I realize the thoughts. I wonder what it is he's thinking or better yet, what he's trying to hide.

"Why so quiet, Your Highness? Shall I comfort you?" Mu Dan releases his grip and then swings an arm around my waist, pulling our bodies close.

"Who were you talking to?"

"I thought you didn't see anything," he replies sarcastically. "I've killed plenty of nosy people for having seen far less than nothing. Are you sure you wish to continue this interrogation?"

"If you were determined to kill me, I wouldn't have the chance to ask. Since you won't, why not drop the act? Who was that person? The one nestled in the tree."

"Hmph. My arms are around your waist, our hips are practically joined, and you're not making a fuss. Does this mean what I think?"

"That you can avoid my questions through lewd comments? No, I won't let it go. Was that person another assassin?"

"A woman doesn't work for free!" He giggles.

"I see. I assume you want another kiss from Jin."

The moon isn't particularly bright and still, it's apparent his cheeks are ablaze. His jaw grits and then his lips pucker from displeasure. That scene is still fresh in my mind. Each time it plays again, my heart flutters a bit faster. I can't keep a smile contained.

Annoyed, Mu Dan moves away while clicking his tongue. "He kissed me with more fervor than he's ever kissed you, darling. Doesn't that tell you anything?"

"Undoubtedly, he finds you a more desirable woman than me. I can't blame any man for thinking that."

"I don't need your sarcasm. You're very unattractive in that way. Anyhow, I'm not in the mood to share any secret so, good-night."

Waving a hand at my face, he then starts for the garden gates.

"H-Hey! Wait! That person was your informant, right? What did he say?"

"You're so certain that person's gender and their role, why even ask me?"

"I can reason only so much from what I thought I saw. When we met, you pretended not to know He Pi was missing but nothing ever gets by you. You're very good at discreetly controlling information, which leads me to think if you already knew the assassin's identity, that informant wouldn't risk coming here. Which is it? Did you finally ascertain his identity or has something more important been discovered?"

"You give me too much credit. Flatterer! I'm not against it but I also won't hand anything over without payment. Lucky for you, my offer hasn't expired."

"Offer? What offer?"

For a moment, he stares back incredulously and then sharpened eyes lower seductively. Mu Dan comes near. Placing a hand on my cheek, burning fingertips begin tracing over my skin and slowly descend toward my neck, playfully tickling all the while; sending shivers over me. His rose lips, smiling mischievously, come closer.

I see. This is what he wants. Kang Lang's never been shy about his affections. After having suffered Jin's indifference, I'm tempted to accept this mounting passion. Please, show me what it means to feel desired, Kang Lang. I'm aching for your touch.

My own lips pucker while my hands gently reach for his beautiful face. Kang Lang nods as though accepting my mental request; his smile widens. In an instant, I pinch both his cheeks severely.

"Let go! What are you doing?"

Kang Lang flusters and tries to draw back. I move to keep my position, tumbling forward and slamming onto his chest.

"This is what you get for invading my thoughts! Now, unless you want your pretty face stretched flat, tell me everything your informant said!"

He attempts to pry off my hands which merely cause his cheeks to further stretch. Still, unwilling to surrender, his evil mind concocts another devious plan. The next moment, shrill laughter involuntarily escapes as I fall into his arms, releasing his cheeks. He's tickling my sides, somehow finding the most sensitive areas along the curves to make my body violently writhe.

"S-S-Stop! Kang Lang! That's cheating!"

"So? You cheated first. I thought I was clear. My beautiful face is off-limits."

By some miracle, I manage to grab onto his traveling fingers and pull them off my body. Without hesitation, his hands aggressively latch onto mine, drawing them around my back while pulling our bodies close. Every inch, from my chest to my toes, is pressed against him. With bulging eyes and stifled breath, I look up to find the same expression reflected back. Streaks of crimson run rampant across his face.

"You... you're a violent woman. I like it." He grins.

"Tell me everything your informant said!"

"Don't you remember my offer, Your Highness? Marry me and I'll tell you everything. When you think about it, there isn't a good reason to say no. Did you hear how you laughed just now? I'm much more fun than your *dull* boyfriend."

Two marriage proposals in one night and neither came from the man I love. I couldn't joke this way in my wildest dreams. That day, when I shamelessly attacked Jin in this garden, I'd decided to take Kang Lang's deal despite its folly. Due to jealousy, Jin stopped me. Now that his envy has been replaced by apathy, Kang Lang's providing another opportunity. I'm back to where I started weeks ago, only with another chance to correct things should I choose. With a word, I can erase Jin's misery.

"What's the matter, darling? Conflicted? It's clear why you're stalling, so just accept it. There's no shame in putting yourself first. The only shameless people are the ones who guilt others into enduring their abuse."

"You don't know what you're talking about."

"Don't I? Who's always pointing fingers at whom and who always end up performing the chase? When was the last time he came after you?"

I haven't told him a thing about my relationship with Jin and somehow, Kang Lang can see through me. The only time Jin remotely came close to running after me was when we met on the steps of that spiral staircase in Xiong. Even then, he didn't actually run after me, we basically ran into each other. Kang Lang may have a point, but I love Jin. I promised to stay with him even should he tell me to leave.

"That's a sordid promise." Kang Lang scoffs, having miraculously read my mind as usual. "He knew he'd hurt you, so he made you promised to endure the mistreatment? Doesn't that just prove my point?"

Jin's misery can cease once I find constancy in San An or Kang Lang. That looming thought in the back of my mind is running in repetition. In the end, this makeshift relationship can't last unless both Jin and I are unyielding in our love for each other. Love, the idea is a joke. He doesn't love me, I know that, but my own selfish desires are keeping me from setting him free. Kang Lang may believe Jin's keeping me hostage; I'm not so sure that the reverse isn't true.

"I... I'm sorry. I can't marry you. I'll put my faith in Nan Rong's council and His Highness to find the assassin."

"He Pi and the Minister, possibly. You'll die of old age before the rest of the council can find their own asses."

"Then I'll rely on He Pi, San An, and Lord Han Bei."

I jerk away from Kang Lang and start for the gate, stopping in my tracks when his brother's name escapes through a barely audible sigh.

"What?"

"Han Bei." He mutters again; his teeth sinking into the painted lower lip. "You're depending on him?"

"I hear Lord Han Bei's a competent man; not any deficient to San An. If he'll help, I don't see why not."

"You're overly optimistic. I know my brother. Han Bei won't let Ning fall in with the South's troubles."

"Against their volition, Ning's been dragged into this circumstance. There's no helping it."

"Han Bei will pursue the assassin himself before allying with the South."

"Then I'll just have to convince him."

"Obviously, you don't know anything about Ning's history if you think Ning's champion will be *that* accommodating."

"At least I'll try! What are you good for except lecturing me?!" I didn't mean to shout. I just couldn't control frustration. Jin's indifference was enough to wreak havoc on my nerves; I don't need Kang Lang's stubborn secrecy. A name is all I ask and he can't comply. Considering how well he's lived these past six years through He Pi's good grace, this is the least he could do for Nan Rong.

Embarrassed for my outburst, I stomp away. Kang Lang jerks back my wrist. Falling into his arms, my body grows limp the moment smoldering lips sear unrestrained passion onto me. The more I push back, the stronger his hold becomes. His kiss grows ever deeper until my lungs are drained and my mind turns dizzy.

Once he finally withdraws, his chest heaves ragged breaths while I gasp for air in his trembling arms. Though I contemplate swinging at him, my blatant retaliation might just provoke him to continue. Instead, I settle for silent rage.

"I can feel your fury, Your Highness." His stifled whisper flows into my ear. "You know how much I love it."

"I'm not angry."

"No? Then you won't mind that I carry on."

The instant his seductive stare and puckered lips lean closer, my composure is lost.

"You caught me off guard. Do that again and I'll break your nose with my forehead!"

"And... there you are, my enraged fiancé." He giggles.

"You... incorrigible... so and so!" Slapping away his hands, I start for the gates again. This time, something stranger happens: he's chosen to be helpful.

"Ying." Kang Lang calls out. "That's his name. A former Ning assassin who defected to Feng Jia."

I veer about posthaste to find the courtesan pouting for having given up his advantage.

"I appreciate it but why are you telling me now?"

With his eyes averted, Kang Lang mockingly replies, "The exchange wasn't free, was it? Deny it all you want but your body pulsated and arched from my touch, undoubtedly asking for more. Be sure to tell your boyfriend that he isn't the only man who's excited you. Maybe, I'm the only one who ever has."

His derisive smile grows into a grin; though, he refuses to look at me. I'm just thankful Jin wasn't here to witness my embarrassment. Despite the awkwardness, this was a small price to pay.

"Thank you. I'll relay the message to San An. Is there anything else I should know?"

"You're still as boring as ever," he sighs at my bland response. "Ying has heterochromia. One eye is blue, the other is brown."

"And he's with Feng Jia?"

Feng Jia is to the northwest of Nan Rong and borders Bei Ling and Ye. Ye is to the west of Nan Rong while Bei Ling is to the north.

"He *was*, which was the reason my informant thought to look there. Since you mentioned He Pi decided Bei Ling is involved, I made contact and had my informant switched routes. That's what you saw just now."

"I see. Thank you, Kang Lang!"

"Yeah, whatever. If you're really thankful then ma..."

His voice trails away into inaudible mumbles. Frowning, he rushes past me out of the peach garden. The long sleeves of his pink Hanfu dress flutter by like wings of a butterfly. I can't help but stare after him, lost in awe by the elegant gliding gait. If he weren't such a brute, I could never imagine under that graceful stature is truly a man.

Chapter 23 – 5

A few steps away from San An's quarters and then my feet turn to lead. I know I shouldn't face him after the egregious event earlier. It's one thing to decline his proposal; it's another to be the reason for his quarrel with Jin. They're brothers and family shouldn't fight, especially over me. Then again, the only person who truly fought for me was San An; another reason I shouldn't face him. However, I can't keep Kang Lang's revelation to myself. Whatever awkwardness may transpire will be forgotten with time.

Swallowing a lump in my throat, I muster remaining nerves and then raise a hand, prepared to knock. Suddenly, the familiar sandalwood scent envelops my senses. A firm hand wraps around my waist and another around my wrist. Startled, I turn toward him just as a soft kiss lands on my cheek. Before I can utter his name, he's wrapped me completely in his embrace.

"Don't marry San An." The hoarse, pained whisper filled with passion pleads with me so tenderly that my heart wrenches. He repeats the words as though they were a prayer while resting his chin feebly on my shoulder. His breathing is heavy and worn.

"Jin, I-I won't. What are you doing here?"

"You didn't come back. I was afraid so I... and now you're here. Don't marry him. I didn't mean what I said. I won't let you go."

"It's not what you think. Kang Lang revealed the assassin's identity. I have to tell San An. Maybe he knows who Ying serves."

"Ying?"

"Yes, are you familiar with the name? Kang Lang said he originally defected from Ning to Feng Jia. Now he's with Bei Ling. He has heterochromia; one blue and one brown eye."

"No, I don't believe I've heard of him. Why did Kang Lang suddenly choose to help?"

"Oh! I, uh, caught him with his informant and after... a... he was in a sharing mood."

"A... what? What did he do? Did he put his hands on you again?"

There's temper in his voice; ardent jealousy coupled with the slight panic of an overprotective mother hen. This side of him is rather endearing. I'm happy he proved Kang Lang wrong. Jin came after me. How could I not be flattered?

"Why are you smiling?"

"Because I love how sweet you are. The truth is, he kissed me but it meant nothing, and therefore, it was a better trade on my part. At least we've somewhere to start."

"Ying can wait. I thought I told that idiot to keep his hands off you. So, he didn't take me seriously."

"Jin, that's a very scary face you're making. Kang Lang putting his hands on me isn't a dire concern. We're standing in the open and you're holding *your brother* a bit too close."

"Considering our other brother proposed to you, a harmless embrace pales in comparison." Jin chuckles softly, planting another kiss against my cheek before moving away. "It's been a long night. Why don't you retire to your quarters? I'll talk to San An."

"Are you still worried that I'll accept the Minister's proposal?"

A wide grin breaks across my face. I nudge his arm. Jin's initial frown slowly morphs into a warm smile and then his fingers tap against my cheek.

"I'll come to your room shortly to express my qualms and cleanse every part of you that Kang Lang touched. Wait for me." Pausing, he chuckles. "You blush so easily."

"So do you!"

Another tap of his fingers against my cheek and then Jin slips inside the door. Every time he smiles, my heart skips a beat and my downtrodden soul feels renewed. While I'm not pleased with the precariousness of our relationship, I am ecstatic to know that we've become a bit closer. He unexpectedly came after me. I can't do else but smile at the thought. I only hope with continued perseverance, a future for us is more certain.

Chapter 24: Like Father Like Son

Jin enters the room, freezing in place when he sees my hand down my shirt. Without even asking for an explanation, his face turns crimson.

"It's not what it looks like," I let out a short embarrassed sigh. "I loosened the itchy collar and accidentally dropped a piece of food inside. It's lodged beneath the sash around my chest, I can't reach it! By the way, did San An know anything about Ying? I'm sorry I fell asleep last night before you came."

"It's fine. I was too tired to have been good company anyhow. The Minister didn't have additional insights. He's hoping that since the assassin originated from Ning, you'll have more success."

"Oh, that's right. Maybe Lord Han Bei knows. I'll be sure to ask. Actually, Jin, I've been wondering. How is everything at court? Isn't it time for me to make another appearance at the assembly?"

Jin sits on the edge of the bed and runs a heavy hand over his tired face. "That is exactly why I've been away since this morning. The council's in uproar. Everyone except the Minister doesn't support your plan to ascend Ning's throne. They're too myopic. The immediate fear of a country without a leader is their greatest concern when, sensibly, having Ning's alliance and support will create the greatest stability we can hope for."

"They're getting ahead of themselves. We don't have any guarantee that I'll be able to persuade Lord Han Bei. Either way, I'm not meant to stay here forever. He Pi is alive. The council should find solace in that."

As I continue rummaging for the elusive radish, Jin glances over and chuckles.

"Is this funny to you?"

"Yes, it is. Wouldn't it be easier to take off your shirt?"

"Ah! You're right!"

Darting up, I remove my belt and outer layer. To my surprise, the man who suggested the act stops me when I loosen the collar of my undershirt.

"Did you forget I am a man, Bao Lai? Show a little more discretion."

"Why? You dressed me this morning. What haven't you already seen?"

"Yes, well, *undressing* in front me so casually is…"

He can't finish the sentence. The averted gaze is accompanied by flushing cheeks. For all his teasing, he's as shy as ever. The more I stare at his endearing bashfulness, the more an impish desire to taunt him rises to my chest.

Grinning mischievously, I approach my flustered boyfriend. "Jin, surely you would do anything for me.

Would you mind reaching inside and finding that rogue piece of radish?"

I don't know how it's possible but his face turned a few shades redder. While I giggle obnoxiously, Jin pulls me onto the bed, planting countless kisses over my face and lips in retaliation. Whether he intended to be playful or otherwise, his body grows exceedingly warm, spreading fires to my own. The exhilaration of his touch is enough to set my heart thumping; coupled with his fiery lips of ever-growing burning kisses, I begin to lose myself in his embrace. However, the moment I allow his heat to envelop me, Jin abruptly stops. The severe expression on his face then reclaims my senses.

"Why are you angry?"

"I'm not. I just wonder how much more of your caprice I can endure."

"O-Oh. I'm sorry. I'll stop being so inappropriate."

"Don't." His eyes soften. "I like how improper and impetuous you are. When I'm with you, I feel a lost part of me return. There's a carefree innocence about you, a sort of childishness that is endearing. You are the embodiment of a youth I could not have. You make me want to shed away this stiff shell, so that I may share with you more of me. My one regret is our late encounter in life. If only we could have met a decade ago, I wouldn't be so dull now. So please, don't change."

"You're not dull, Jin! Ignore Kang Lang! I love you as you are and however you choose to be. Never in my life have I ever met someone who could capture my heart and soul as you have. You make me feel safe, happy, desired, and protected. I may be in men's clothes but for the first time in my life, I finally see myself as a woman. Mu Dan couldn't do that. It's you who has accomplished this for me. For that, I'll forever be grateful. To me, you're wonderful in every way!"

My face bursts with red roses while exclaiming my admirations. For my embarrassment, he smiles.

"Only you would think that."

"So? It may be selfish, but I don't want anyone else to see how amazing you are. If any other woman does, I... don't think I'd stand a chance to gain your love."

"Are you worried?" A corner of his mouth lifts into a smirk. From the smug expression, it's clear my jealousy pleases him.

"Obviously," I roll my eyes.

"Why? Don't you trust me?"

"Well, y-yes, I do, but..."

"But what? Bao Lai, you've already seen the ugliness in me. If you can accept that, then I can accept anything."

"Nothing is ugly about you. I adore you in every way. During our stay in Xiong, I saw a filial son and a loyal brother. Those are two sides of you that I've learned, neither of which deserves disdain. And, you were honest enough to admit that you don't love me. I am grateful for your honesty, really! However, that doesn't stop the unpleasant thought from crossing my mind. Maybe, the reason that you don't is because you can't. This relationship between us is comfortable. I only worry that should you ever meet her, the woman of your dreams who can stir your every passion, what chance do I have? It would hurt me to let you go; it would hurt much worse to keep you from happiness. In some ways, I fear I may have already taken you hostage."

Every anxiety escaped in a single breath. Though his eyes are on me, I can't engage him. Admitting my irrational fear was embarrassing. All I can do is avert my gaze toward the wall. In time, a hand lands on my cheek to draw back my attention.

"Why is it when I come to trust you, you learn to doubt me? I have already met the woman who stirs my every passion; that woman is you. You cannot fathom the dangerous thoughts that cross my mind when I'm in your company. I merely kiss and embrace you to assuage my desires, but I want more. I'm horrified by my dishonorable yearnings. Yet, I know fulfilling my passion won't equate to love."

"Then, am I horrible too, for wanting you?"

Jin's eyes grow wide and so do mine. I can't believe I said that! Although, why is Jin surprised? Did I not express that he can claim me as long as the action is not stemmed from insecurity? Maybe he didn't think I was serious. To remind him of my absolute adoration, slowly, my lips approach his. Barely do they meet, he withdraws.

"I am not my father!" He spits the words through gritted teeth. It's unclear whether the declaration is to him or to me. "I won't claim any woman until she is my wife and then only her for the rest of my life. And you, Bao Lai, should not urge the dishonorable act from me, or any man for that matter, to gain affections. You'll only be disappointed in the end."

"Jin, I wasn't! How many more times must I say it? I love you! That is why I—"

"I don't doubt you," he replies succinctly while moving off the bed. "Many women loved my father; for their loyalty and adulation, suffered greatly. My mother included. I am not my father but I am still his son. Of all the children, I am his spitting image and I carry his name. It was his defect, his inability to control unending desires, which caused a great deal of misery for everyone.

I removed myself from power so I wouldn't be tempted, but with my growing desires for you, I wonder what else can tempt me to stray from decency. Should I demand it, He Pi would not deny me the throne. With that title, the women of the Circle would flock to me. I'm only a hair's breadth away from becoming my father and the first step to fall down that path is to indulge my lust for you."

Where is this coming from? Are we on the verge of another argument only because we care too much for want of the other's touch? He came after me last night. I finally thought our relationship took a step forward and still, we are on the precipice on falling back onto this seesaw between eternity and parting.

"J-Jin, that's irrational! I don't know your father but you can't possibly be like him. You are a gentleman and you are kind and loyal! Simply because you resemble his image doesn't mean you will become him! I love you, and if you desire me in the manner that I, too, desire you, then doesn't that mean you love me?"

"You don't believe that." He scoffs. "If you did, then you wouldn't be worried. Deep down, you think I'm fickle and unfaithful, just like my father. And, you're probably right. Since our return, I've been asking myself what love is. The single idea I've formulated that even comes close to any truth points to one thought: if I cannot live without you, then that is love. As it stands, I can."

He's admitted several times that he doesn't love me. Acknowledging that fact doesn't dampen sharp pains shooting through my heart. This is how it must feel to be struck by lightning. Every fiber of my being is coursing with unrelenting pain. Stunned silent, I can hardly breathe.

"Bao Lai," he continues; the tone drawing ever deeper into apathy. "I tried, but you're right. Despite how I've struggled to love you, I still don't, because I can't. I'm sorry."

What cruel parting words! He pushed for this relationship and then insulted me for being false when it's obvious the commitment dilemmas are solely his. He distrusted me for my gender and now he's chosen to withdraw again because he's afraid I'll tempt him to become his father? Of all the nonsense! The heartbroken tears that were streaming down my face turn to angry stains on burning cheeks. My chest heaves from vexation and words rush to my mouth in torrents. Without discretion, I blurt them out as they come.

"You... You won't admit you love me because you're too much of a coward! Say whatever you want! You haven't changed one bit! Every time you're happy or sad; practically, anytime you feel anything at all, you run away! Don't use your mother or your father as excuses for your weaknesses. Whatever they've done, however miserable they've made you, has nothing to do with me!

You're scared and alone but when I reach out to you, you brush me off through idiotic justifications! Instead of companionship, someone to take you from the darkness, you'd prefer to pull me into the same pit. To sit in the same endless obscurity! You don't want me to be in the arms of another but you also don't want me.

Frankly, I'm certain you only want one thing: for me to be as miserable as you!"

My shaking body and wrathful expression mirror Jin's in every way. A short moment passes and then I notice distress crossing his eyes. My resentment is not baseless, but I know there are more secret torments he's hiding inside which Jin won't willingly share. I told myself to follow when he runs; once more, I failed my convictions.

"Jin, I'm sorry! I didn't mean it!" The pathetic apology falls on deaf ears. He leaves the room without rebuffing my accusations.

Why do we keep arguing over nothing? Just moments ago, we were happy in each other's arms. I can't imagine we are anything to each other after this. Why did I have to bring up the subject of love when I knew the answer? Even though he doesn't love me, he needs someone to stand firm by his side. Yet, I keep faltering.

Chapter 24 – 2

Storming out of the room, I run down the hall. Without announcement, I clamber into Jin's chamber, the sight of which puts me to silent shock.

There's no bed inside; only a simple spread on the floor. The single blanket is worn and thin while the pillow is worse. No wonder his body is always so stiff! Besides from the lack of bedding, the small table and chair look as old as the ones from my house. The other items in the room are a shoddy lantern and a parcel of clothing laid on the low table.

Not far from his chamber, guest rooms a thousand times more furnished sit bare. His Highness would undoubtedly give Jin anything he asks. There's no reason for him to live this way unless it was by choice. Just how much does Jin loathe himself?

Upon my intrusion, he turns around. His temper erupts into bitterness.

"J-Jin. We should talk." I must avoid the subject of his living space. It is a projection of his emptiness and self-degradation; therefore, to critique any part of it would mean to critique Jin and he's been injured enough by my carelessness for one day. My attention keeps directly to his face which, for some reason, further provokes his resentment.

Bitterness becomes anger and then simply outrage. Not only are his eyes without affection, they propel pure hatred toward me.

"We've both said all we had to say. I won't contend with you, so leave."

"Jin, I'm sorry! I shouldn't have said all those terrible things. I was angry, I didn't mean it!"

"How tiresome," he sighs exasperatedly. "Wasn't it obvious I only used you because I was lonely? Other women aren't stupid enough to let me take advantage of them in exchange for pretense partiality."

"Will you stop putting yourself down?! You're not that type of person! I'm not leaving until you stop running from me, so you might as well tell me what's really bothering you!"

"Then stay. After I've packed my things, I'm going to Bei Ling. Don't even think to follow, Your Highness. You have important duties here."

He turns his back to me and continues folding a few belongings into a parcel. The distant manners are unrecognizable and his tone is so cold. I can't believe this is the same man who, only days ago, kissed Kang Lang to save me. I said the wrong things to lose his regards and I don't know the right words to win them back. Should the right words come, I know he doesn't care to listen. I might as well stop talking.

Rushing to his side, my arms wrap around his waist. He attempts to shirk my hold, which grows tighter the more he retaliates.

"Don't you have any shame at all? Wasn't it perfectly clear that I don't love you? What do you hope to accomplish by troubling me?"

My rebuttal is to bury my face in his back. Letting out an exhale, Jin turns sharply on his heels and loosens my arms. His hand tersely grabs my jaw, forcing it upward while he peers down.

"What do you want from me? Are you deaf or dim-witted? Which part of my rejection is too difficult for you to grasp?"

As he speaks, the grip tautens until my cheeks turn numb. The more stupid things I say, the more reasons I give him to withdraw. Thus, my enduring silence is the response. For a drawn moment, he waits with abated breath, and then finally, Jin lets out an aggravated groan. His arms swiftly sweep my body off the floor.

Moving to the thin bedspread, he lays me down and then imprints a heavy kiss on my mouth. I hurriedly return every stroke of his lips to project my constant affections, though there's nothing sweet in his actions. His kiss lacks the usual warmth. I don't know whether he's pushing false passion to drive me away or simply using the occasion to release his frustration. It matters little. Perhaps, he was right about me. I am stupid enough to give him everything for the chance that he may offer a fraction of his love.

In the end, we succumbed to our every desire. Though he kissed me on pretense, everything that came after was genuinely fervent. A hidden part of him, the part concealed behind his usual teasing and distant self comprised purely of feverish yearnings, was released. I've never seen him so free, so wholly taken away by indiscretion, that his temperament became both frightening and thrilling. I gave him all of me and he took every part without hesitation, imprinting the full force of his everlasting impression to my soul.

Despite the ardent passion, throughout the wondrous event and after, he never spoke a word. Similarly, I was so utterly lost in the new sensation that all words felt meaningless. While he held me tightly in his arms, I fell asleep with hopes that on the morrow we could begin anew.

To my disappointment, I open my eyes to loneliness.

Chapter 24 – 3

After our night together, Jin dressed and laid me in He Pi's chamber before leaving for Bei Ling. The black marble, my treasured gift to him, was set on the side table. I wonder whether he meant to leave it for my protection since he'll be away for a while or because he's resigned from the task of playing my protector. Then again, the most palpable reason is likely the truth. This was his way of saying good-bye forever.

Misery takes me but for unknown reasons, I can't shed a single tear. Perhaps it's because I never expected for him to stay. No matter how I covet the role, I am not the woman to make Jin happy.

Once I exit to the balcony for fresh air, find the skies darkened by storm clouds. Not long after, rain begins pouring. I retreat into Jin's chamber and lie on the bedspread to recall the warmth of his arms. His scent still lingers on the thin sheets. I inhale as much of the comforting nostalgia as possible before they fade.

A dreary cold then causes me to shiver from head to toe. How chilly this room is! His light blanket serves no protection against the draft that casually enters through the poorly sealed windows. How he endured the winter months all these years is beyond me. More so, how much has he suffered? I'd always expected for him to find me whenever I sought company, so I never once bothered to enter his room before last night. If I had, would things have turned out differently?

Nothing in the room hints the reason for his self-punishment. He doesn't enjoy this, I know that. Jin forced on himself this repentance for guilt hidden deep within that I can't fathom. His resentment wasn't only against women, but also his mother and his father. Just how many people have injured him? Why didn't I do more to heal his wounds! If anything, I injured him worse. I doubted him, and in turn, Jin doubted himself. I'm such a child! I let insecurities and temper reign, only to shatter his confidence and trust.

All my life, I thought love equated to happiness. This love I now feel, tears at my heart. Is it supposed to hurt this way or was I wrong? Maybe... I'm not in love with him either. That can't be true. He doesn't want anything to do with me while I can't do else but think of him, and I will for the rest of my life.

For all I know, Jin and I may never meet again. Deep inside, I fear that every passing moment apart erases another piece of his already limited partiality for me. Though I can't make Jin happy, I'm unable to find the courage to relinquish our attachment.

At the moment, I hope he's safe. I wonder whether he had any trouble on the route to Bei Ling. Just what exactly does His Highness plan to do and why must Jin be involved? With Han Bei's upcoming arrival and Nan Rong's safety at stake, I can't venture north. Jin still needs a country to return to; I have to secure that for him.

Despite my opinion, it is painfully evident that alone, I can't do anything for Jin. Aggravated by my own uselessness, an angry groan escapes and then I rush from the room. Upon exiting, the person I almost slammed into is the same one I'd hoped to find.

"Kang Lang!"

My sudden ambush startles the courtesan, who returns a sulky frown while studying me from head to toe. His jewel headdress sways when the perfect marble face tilts every which way, seemingly searching me for something. The moment I begin to speak, his index finger lands on my lips and then gradually, a grin forms over petal lips as he giggles incessantly.

"Well, well! Could it be? I knew it! You naughty girl! Or, should I say, naughty woman? Do you deny it, Your Highness?"

Slapping his finger away, I force back a hard stare. "Stop giggling and listen! I changed my mind. Instead of persuading Lord Han Bei for an audience, would you escort me to Ning's capital? That assassin slipped across the East's borders easily and since you're in his league, you could do the same, right?"

"Don't insult me," he pouts. "Ying's nowhere near my league! In any case, a deal's a deal, even if your lover cheated the deal. I'll keep my end of the bargain as is."

"What I'm asking for takes less effort on your part than our original deal. You won't have to face Lord Han Bei."

"True, but returning to Ning is also a pain. Besides that, I'm just not really in the mood to be helpful; not when my fiancé prefers his brother's advances over mine."

"You don't have to be so vulgar."

"No? There's nothing more vulgar than lies and nothing as uncouth as denial of the truth. So, which part isn't true? Aren't you even a little curious why these Nan Rong princes don't hesitate to lust after you when your face so painfully reminds them of His Highness?"

"They see me as I am."

"Are you telling me that in their entire lives, they've been waiting for a cross-dressing, temperamental, unladylike, inept woman with the emotional intelligence of a child?"

"What do you hope to accomplish by tearing me down? You are the better woman! I concede!"

"I'm not tearing you down. These are mere observations any fool can make. If you couldn't see that, then you don't stand a chance against Han Bei. He has little patience for most people and a worse opinion of those who can't maintain dignified composure. If you take his insults, he'll think you're a coward, and if you become defensive, he'll consider it a challenge. Believe me when I say that as you are, he'll think you're a joke."

"I... I see. Thank you for your warning. If he's as arrogant as you say, then it won't matter whether I meet him as He Pi or Bao Lai. He'll still disapprove. That doesn't mean I shouldn't try. I'm asking you again. Please, help me reach Ning's capital."

"Tsk! Didn't you hear a word I said? You really are stubborn. The answer is still no. A deal's a deal."

"Fine. Then I'll do it alone."

Disappointed as I am by his refusal, maybe it wasn't proper to drag him into this conflict in the first place. In any case, it's raining heavily outside; the first rainstorm since my arrival. Even with my poor infiltration skills, perhaps the rain will provide enough cover to pass the borders undetected. As I stumble by, Kang Lang tugs at my collar.

"Imbecile! First of all, what makes you think it's raining anywhere near the borders? Second, by the time you do arrive, I'm certain the rain will have subsided. You'll accomplish nothing except catch a cold and die! Lastly, Ning is far from incompetent. Should you manage to pass the borders, there's no chance you'll pass the gates and once past the gates, enter the palace. It is futile!"

"Since you can read my mind, you must know I don't care! I won't sit around and do nothing!"

Knocking his hand away, my path is resumed. Kang Lang grunts angrily before moving abreast.

"What's the matter? Did your boyfriend break up with you? Why so quick to die?"

"I have to do this. The longer I wait, the longer Jin is in danger."

"So, after taking your only good quality, Jin left, did he? I should have given him more credit. Who knew under that sheep disguise was such a beast!"

"It's none of your business."

"Sure, it is. You're my fiancé! Stop frowning and slow down, I have an idea."

Pausing, I give him my full attention. "What idea?"

Although he sounded confident, Kang Lang hesitates. After exhaling sharply, his deep stare burrows into my eyes. When he speaks, the tone is more serious than I thought him capable. "Are you absolutely certain you're the real thing? Can you guarantee my pardon?"

"I don't know. He Pi said that I am; the edict states the same. As for your pardon, if I am the real thing, I'll do whatever it takes. Why?"

His tongue clicks. A moment more of thoughtful contemplation and then he sighs. "Your lover was correct. I am a wanted man in Ning. If you take me to the palace and claim the reward, I'm sure Han Bei will give you an audience. Whether he believes your document or not is entirely out of my hands. Should you fail, we'll both be executed. Understood?"

"Are you willing to risk your life for me? Why?"

"You're my fiancé!" Kang Lang chirrups sweetly while pinching both my cheeks.

"Stop that! I'll gladly risk my life, Kang Lang, but I can't die peacefully if anything happens to you."

"Save your senseless worries for your boyfriend. His Highness tasked you with this dangerous chore because he intended for me to help. Of course, it would be easier to just wait for Han Bei. Since you'd rather run off and get killed, I don't have a choice."

He's all smiles, though I can clearly see a hint of fear and despair lingers whenever he mentions Ning. It may be my homeland but I don't know the first thing about the East. Since Kang Lang is certain of their ways—is certain of his brother's ruthlessness—then who am I to contend? I can't expect to be treated kindly by Han Bei as I've come to expect from the men in Nan Rong.

Kang Lang is probably right. Should I fail, I will die. And, if I die, I can't secure Ning's alliance for Nan Rong in order to protect Jin and everyone else. Moreover, San An's injury from having saved me is still fresh in my mind. I can't stand the idea of others pained for my sake. Taking Kang Lang to Ning is nothing short of walking him to the gallows.

"I'll wait for Han Bei."

"Too late! I've already made up my mind!" Linking our arms together, Kang Lang drags me down the hall.

"Wait! Stop joking! This is dangerous, Kang Lang! "

"Oh! You're anxious because you love me, don't you, Your Highness? I can see it! Big brother left and now you realize the handsome assassin is a much better catch, huh? Well, I won't be swayed that easily!"

"I'm being serious! I don't want you to die!"

His quick pace snaps to a halt. Kang Lang sends over an awkward glare from the corners of his eyes. Using the opportunity, I try to break free but can't. His thin fingers seize my wrist, holding on steadfast through an iron grip. For someone with this much strength in just one hand to be so fearful of entering the East, I finally realize how daunting the task really is.

Slowly, he lets out a short scoff. "Don't insult me. I won't go down without a fight."

"That's not the point! Besides, I have a stake in this. You shouldn't risk your life unnecessarily."

"Despite how you think of me, I've come to see Nan Rong as my home. And, as crazy as it sounds, I agree with your plan. If Han Bei comes to find He Pi and instead meets Bao Lai, well, let's just put it this way, he doesn't tolerate deception."

"Isn't pretending to hand you over for the bounty also deceptive?"

"Hmm. You have a point but sometimes, it can't be helped." He shrugs. "Show me that you care, Your Highness. Don't fail."

Without allowing further protest, he continues pulling me down the hall.

Chapter 25: Girl Talk

Near sunrise, Kang Lang came to fetch me and then together on one horse, we rode east. We're both dressed as men. Needless to say that as a woman, he's much more beautiful than I am, and as a man, he's still more charming. When we first met, instead of having been jealous of his greatest attributes, I should have asked for his advice. Perhaps if I'd passed for a lady, could have bound Jin's attention longer and kept him in Nan Rong. A part of me hopes Jin will find happiness in Bei Ling while the rest of me shudder at the thought. Well, despite everything that's happened between us, I don't regret having met Jin and for a time, as short as it was, lived happily by his side. Even if I never feel such happiness again, I'm grateful for the memories.

"Do you want to talk about it?" Kang Lang suddenly calls over his shoulders.

"Talk about what?"

"Girl talk! What happened between you and the pup?"

"We're hardly dressed as girls and one of us isn't even though he's very good at the pretense."

"How tedious! It's a long ride to Ning. Unless you want me to die from boredom, in which case your plan won't succeed, then let me hear some gossips!"

"There's nothing I want to discuss."

319

"Don't be so cold! I'm only trying to help. For the last six years, I've lived at the palace, and during that time, saw a dead man pretended to be alive. Imagine my surprise when that shell of a man had the nerves to threaten me. How is it that a simple temperamental girl was able to bring the dead back to life?"

"You won't let this go, will you?"

"Never!"

"There's not much to explain. I resemble His Highness, so Jin allowed me to come close. Maybe my gender is the reason he emerged from his shell and also the reason for his retreat. In short, I couldn't do anything for Jin."

"Oh! I think you did *plenty* for Jin!" Kang Lang cackles boisterously.

"What do you mean?"

Kang Lang looks back and winks. The suggestive smile needs no explanation.

"Why are you so damn vulgar?"

"Me? I'm only calling it as I see it. And you're wrong. His Highness tried to do for Jin as you have; without success. Obviously, he didn't use any of your feminine wiles but you get the idea. Try not to take offense; your boyfriend has a lot of mommy issues."

"I'll ignore that last comment."

"If you ask me, He Pi was merely wasting his breath. No matter how he tried to convince the stupid boy, he's just too stubborn to forgive himself."

"Jin said He Pi cleared his pointless guilt."

"Not all of it, apparently."

"Why does Jin think the wars at court were his fault anyway? He was only a child, wasn't he? And, what about his father—what did Emperor Jin do?"

"Oh? He has daddy issues, too?" Kang Lang giggles while stiffening his posture as if readying for interesting gossips.

Not one part of me wants to betray Jin's secrets; however, Kang Lang's known him much longer and seems to have hidden knowledge of most happenings at the palace. Instead of assuming Jin's past, I should rely on someone who is better versed in the conflict.

"Jin said he isn't his father. That is to say, he's afraid of becoming his father. Does that mean anything to you?"

"Don't you know? Aside from their differences in disposition, he is his father in every way. The late Emperor Jin was a handsome man, worshipped by many, without a trace of loyalty to anyone. Or maybe, he was too loyal to everyone since he never denied any woman his company."

"Fickleness was his father's flaw. What does that have to do with Jin? He's loyal like no other!"

"Who are you trying to convince? He's not here. Listen, I don't know any more than that about his actual life history. On the other hand, most of my life has been spent understanding women so I can infiltrate Circles. Using my experiences, I have formulated a plausible deduction."

"Which is?"

"Pfff! You should know me better by now."

I can't believe he's right. I can hear his insinuation as clear as day. *A woman doesn't work for free.*

"I can't make you empress."

"No? Two empresses too progressive for you?" He giggles.

"You're the one who initiated this girl talk."

"And? There's girl talk and then there's therapy. My valuable skills don't come cheap." Pausing, his tongue clicks. "I know you're frowning back there and I don't like it."

"There must be something else you want. Aside from your pardon, I could grant you more power and property than your heart's desire."

"It's a long road to Ning's palace and suicidal to enter uninvited. The only reason to make extravagant promises is if you plan to die. I hope that's not the case. Anyway, property and power are useless. Don't insult me by offering things I can simply take by force."

"Says the man who wants to become Nan Rong's empress. You're one contradiction after another. If not wealth and power, I don't know what else to offer."

"Oh! So sassy today, Your Highness! You listen to my words but you can't grasp the motive behind them. *Disappointing!* Actually, I'd like to hear more about this reckless night of yours. How was it?"

"Do you really think I'd tell you?"

"Certainly! If you won't, then it must have been terrible."

"I know what you're trying to do and I'm not falling for it. You won't hear a thing from me."

"Then you won't hear a thing from me either, darling."

Though his back is to me, I know there's a stupid grin on his face. Just when I thought he's become helpful, Kang Lang is still the jerk he's always been. I must be an imbecile to feel surprised.

"Why do you even care? Haven't you ever...?"

"More times than you can count! What can I say? I was looking forward to taking your only good quality and Jin beat me to it."

"This is your revenge? Aren't you being a little petty? I would never give my only good quality to anyone except Jin."

"No? The way I remember it, you had decided to marry me when big brother became jealous and advanced on you... or did you advance on him? It seemed both ways from where I stood. Under different circumstances, I would have claimed your good quality long before he had the nerve."

"Wh-What were you doing spying on us?!" As if my shameless advance on Jin in the peach garden wasn't embarrassing enough, knowing that Kang Lang saw the entire ordeal is mortifying.

"Us? Not at all. I was spying on *you*, Your Highness. What a fool he was! Had you advanced on me, I would have gladly made you *submit*."

His tone draws deeper, almost maniacal, and he relishes the word '*submit*' as though it evoked a latent, unsettling fantasy. Usually, his crassness irks me but today, I just feel so detached.

"Stay on topic."

"Not until you tell me what I want to know. Undoubtedly, he was a clumsy fool who couldn't tell heads from tails. Am I right?"

"Here I thought you were interested in my experience, Kang Lang. Are you obsessed with Jin because he stole a kiss from you?"

"You'll have your turn, my dear. First, tell me how much of a fool he was, so I can tell you how a real man would have carried on. Then, tell me how painful it was for you and I'll explain the greater pain of pleasure which you were cheated. Oh, and spare no details."

Jin was fantastic (Continue to page 326)

Jin was a fool (Continue to page 328)

Chapter 25 – 2

"Jin was fantastic, you'll never come close," is my dry reply.

"How would you know?" Kang Lang scoffs in a manner which vaguely hints offense. "Hmm, is it just me or have you changed? The old you couldn't have answered that casually, joking or not. Was one night all it took? Had I known you'd become this drab after losing your only good quality, Your Highness, I'd never have wasted my time pursuing you. Without your innocent charms, you really are nothing special. No wonder Jin left."

He keeps pushing the idea and like a fool, I wonder if maybe he's right. Maybe Jin left because he took all I had to offer. I don't know which is worse, to be rejected for being undesirable or to be casted aside for having lost my use. Then again, what does it matter? If he's happier without me, then I can't object.

"Insult me however you want. I've told you all I had to say. Unless you really want the specifics, which I will embellish in the most romantic manner, so sweet that you'll feel your teeth rot just from hearing the words, then get on with it."

Kang Lang sulks during the following long pause, after which, a deep sigh casts out in an exasperated breath. "I don't like this sullen, depressed side of you.

You're as boring as your boyfriend! Fine, I'll tell you my theory, only so you'll appreciate how profound I am."

"Any insight you offer can always best my ignorance. Please, go on."

Continue to page 330

Chapter 25 – 3

"Jin was a fool."

"Do tell!"

"Had he not kissed you, your awkward fixation on his *performance* wouldn't burden you so much that you'd interrogate his girlfriend for a glimpse of the experience."

"Hmph! His *performance* is guessable. He kissed a man too eagerly. What does that tell his girlfriend?"

"That if he can make an experienced man blush, then he is a better lover than He Pi's fiancée."

"Hmph!" Kang Lang repeats his dissatisfaction. His ears turn slightly red. "Your Highness has only tasted the fruit from one tree. Don't presume to know them all. At best, your boyfriend is a common apple, while my exotic taste rivals the Buddha pears."

"I would never dare savor the fruit rivaling Buddha, Your Divine. Celibate fruits are too bland a taste for those who've had the pleasure of experiencing the common apple."

Kang Lang sulks during the following long pause, after which, a deep sigh casts out in an exasperated breath.

"I don't like sarcastic women." He frets. "Be quiet and I'll tell you my theory, only so you'll appreciate how profound I am."

Straightening my posture, my ears perk in anticipation of his theory.

"Any insight you offer can always best my ignorance. Please, go on."

Chapter 25 – 4

"Prepare to be amazed by insights you wished you had!" Kang Lang's proud declarations are followed by a short pause to steady his excitement. Leisurely, he begins. "What happens when a woman is slighted by the man she loves and her child is this despicable man's precise image, from his face to his voice to his name?"

"Do you mean to say Jin's mother hated him?"

"No, not hate. Imagine that Jin was the constant reminder of her unhappiness, the embodiment of her shame for having given herself to someone who won't see her as more than a toy which he's grown bored. And, this symbol of love and disgust constantly flaunted in front of her and begged for attention as any child would, yet unlike his father, he's small and frail."

"What is that supposed to mean? Are you saying Jin was abused by his mother for resembling his father?!"

"Maybe not physically. Surely, he was reminded of his cad of a father's sins daily. Again, this is all purely supposition based on my experiences with women from Circles. This resentment is not uncommon. Some women will project their anger against the father onto the child. Jin is fragile. Naturally, he clung to his mother despite the abuse, and probably took her words to heart. Maybe... she only meant to teach him not to become his father by having him suffered his father's guilt—or lack thereof. That's not to say his mother didn't love him. I just doubt that love was constant. He experienced acceptance and rejection in tandem; hence, it's the only way he knows how to love."

"That's some analysis, Kang Lang. You might as well write a book."

Honestly, I can't refute the possibly of Kang Lang's opinion even though I don't want to believe it. The notion of Jin, still forlorn and tortured after all these years, sends a deep, rippling ache throughout my heart. How I long to hold him in my arms to ease what little of his troubles I can! I thought I could come to understand him and still, I don't know a thing about the man I love!

In Xiong, when we were in front of his mother's home, Jin appeared very nostalgic, though I do recall certain pain that welled in his eyes. And, when I mistakenly mentioned children, he removed me from the scene; fretful and fearful of the thought. He's afraid of the past and so he wants to deny himself a future, is that it?

As my mind sways on the verge of descending into darker thoughts, Kang Lang's sweet, chirrupy voice seeks to lighten the mood. "Oh, you think so, too? I would call it, '*Mu Dan's Makeshift Manual of Madams!*'"

"I gamble the rate of marriage will decrease drastically by your wonderful insights," I scoff. "What should I do to free Jin? He despises himself so much. How can I make him see it's senseless?"

Kang Lang shrugs. "I'm well versed with women. Jin is a frightened little boy. I wouldn't know anything about that."

"You were a little boy, too."

"So? I assassinated at least twenty people before the age of ten. Don't compare me to your boyfriend. Jin couldn't even hurt a fly."

"No, he wouldn't."

Jin is too softhearted. It's not in his nature to be cruel. When he projected his mother's faults and all the faults of the other women from court onto me, he must have followed Consort En's example. He showed me affections by overexerting his desire for my company and then immediately pushed me away with charges for which I did not have fault. Even so, I clung to him because I love Jin. He unknowingly repeated the abuse against me. Yet, one thought resonates. As Kang Lang mentioned, this is the only way he knows how to love and so he does in fact, love me. As sad as it is, the acknowledgment forces a smile to my face.

"Hmm? What's happening? Are you suddenly happy?" Kang Lang throws back a quick glance but can't see my downturned face.

"It's nothing. Thank you, Kang Lang."

"For what? For stating the obvious? Why exactly did you choose such a troubled man to offer your affections when you know he'll only come to hurt you? You must be a masochist."

"You think so? In some ways, I believe Jin chose me because he needed me, and that makes me happy. You've shown me a sliver of hope, a single impression of Jin's hidden heart which I couldn't before perceive. If I matter even a little to him, I'll take my chances."

"I should have known! Women like you are so bothersome. Instead of aspiring for a white knight, you'd rather aspire to *be* the white knight. But... I suppose feeling needed is not a bad thing."

"No, it's not. What about you, Kang Lang? Is He Pi your champion or are you his?"

"Jealous are you?" He giggles. "His Highness is a force to be reckoned with while I am a wrecking force. Together, we're dangerous. Apart, I'm destructive. Neither of us needs a champion."

"Then, are you someone's white knight?"

"Yes, the troublesome woman is sitting behind me."

I know he's grinning. Though I frown, there is no denying the fact. At the moment, Kang Lang *is* my white knight. He's risking his life for my sake and he doesn't even love me. Since I am Jin's champion, there's nothing that should stop me from doing the same, if not more, for his sake.

Suddenly, I understand the reason He Pi is close to Mu Dan. A friend as selfless and brave as Kang Lang is difficult to find; however crazy, manipulative, and sadistic he may appear on occasions. I hope someday I can return the favor.

As we continued the ride east, Kang Lang and I became closer. He told me stories from his past and of his time in the Circles. There were slight reminiscence and hidden repentance conveyed through his usual cheerful tone. Some tales were vividly frightening; others sad enough to wrench my heart in twain.

Through his sorrows, his pain, and sometimes his childlike eagerness, I was able to glimpse another side of him. It's unlike Kang Lang to divulge anything about himself. I wonder if he's worried we may fail and these stories are truly his confessions, a final effort toward absolution. Although I cannot absolve anything he's done, it became apparent my bias against Kang Lang was sorely misplaced.

Chapter 26: Ning

We slipped by the outer borders with ease through Kang Lang's secret route. When the eastern gates came into view, paused to change into our disguises. Since I never learned to ride a horse, approaching the guards would seem suspicious on foot. Moreover, should things go awry, Kang Lang needs his hands free. Thus, it was decided for me to dress in Kang Lang's black and silver armors while he adorned a blue set. We're both covered from head to toe.

With my hands bounded, I march in front of Kang Lang toward the gates while he rides behind. In his gauntlets are the reins of our steed and the other end of my rope bondage. As we approach the gates, Ning's watchers from atop the towers ready their bows. A man in silver armor, who I surmise is the captain of the group, leans over the parapet. Peering cautiously, he calls for our halt.

"My name is Bian Chan," Kang Lang responds in a heavy, deep-toned voice. He sounds so calm and collected. There lacks any hesitant notion of deception.

"What do you want?" The guard captain snaps.

"I've brought the traitor, Zhao Kang Lang. Let me through so I can collect the bounty from the capital."

The incredible declaration merely brings the guard captain to laugh and sneer. "You expect me to believe a boy like you was able to capture Lord Kang Lang? Have you any proof?"

"Proof? That's his suit, isn't it?" Kang Lang points at me. "Aside from Lord Zhao of Han Xing, only two men in Ning dare carry that crest on their armors. The other is Lord Han Bei. If you don't believe me, come inspect it for yourself."

I look straight ahead, as Kang Lang had instructed, and attempt to control my breathing. The full helmet on my head likely provides enough cover, though should I show any fear, no one will believe my act. The guard captain looks over every part of me that can be distinguished from above. Eventually, he orders for the gates to open while climbing down from one of the towers.

Once we pass through, Kang Lang dismounts. The captain continues to inspect me from different angles. How strange. Though my hands are bounded, he is seemingly too apprehensive to come close.

Following a drawn moment, the captain, agitated by his own cowardice, finally musters enough courage to come nearer in order to save face with his increasingly restless men. Through the gaps of the full helmet, his eyes fall on mine. Immediately, a deep frown crosses his heavy lips.

"The Zhao brothers are known for their fearsome, emerald eyes. Your prisoner is a fake!"

Accompanying his thunderous declaration, the guard captain draws his sword and the remaining sentinels move into position. However, before anyone has a chance to retaliate, Kang Lang interjects in his real voice, "You haven't changed a bit, Jie! Still looking at the decoy when the threat is right in front of you!"

The captain, whose face turns as pallid as though having seen a ghost, rapidly directs attention to the real Kang Lang. The frightening atmosphere that suddenly erupts like wildfire causes panic over everyone's brows.

For a long, dreaded moment, silence falls over the scene while tensions mount. My heart is beating out of my chest. I hold my breath, terrified that should I even make a slight noise, a hail of arrows will rain upon us.

The captain's grip tautens around the hilt of his wide blade. Just when I thought a melee is inevitable, Jie smirks and then the two men bursts into unified laughter.

"Where the hell have you been, Kang Lang?" Jie pats the younger man on the shoulders. "And what's with the ugly armor? I almost didn't recognize you."

"None of your damn business, Jie." Kang Lang's harsh words are too friendly. "Are you going to let us through or do I have to kill everyone here? It's been a while since we sparred. I'd love to pick up where we left off."

Jie winces and then runs a nervous hand over the back of his head. "Bastard! You nearly killed me during our last *friendly* match. I still have the scars! They want your head in the capital, you know. Why did you come back?"

"You calling me a coward? The capital is full of weaklings just like you. They're just better paid."

"Oh, yeah? Is that why you've been in hiding for the past six years?" Another soldier descends from the tower while putting an arrow back into his quiver. He seems young, maybe Kang Lang's age, and rather distinguished. Turning to me, the newcomer winks playfully.

"Quit flirting with my prisoner, you idiot!" Kang Lang roars. "What can I say? Nan Rong had such lovely women. It took more time than I thought to bed them all. The ones in the Circle are always best. They're willing to give everything and take anything for a chance to escape from nothing."

"Ah, you lucky bastard!" Jie chuckles. "I wish I had your job!"

"With your face? You'd either make such an ugly woman that the royals would disband the Circle or an uglier nobleman, all the women would leave."

"*Bastard!*" Jie growls again. His gauntlet slams good-humoredly into Kang Lang's arm.

"Why are you really going to the capital, *traitor*?" The guard who winked at me poses sarcastically.

Kang Lang shrugs. "My dear brother must miss me terribly. He was the one who put out the bounty on my head, wasn't he? I brought him this woman as a peace offering."

"Woman?" Swinging on his heels, Jie's eyes run up and down my concealed body. "Her?! That's insulting. She's less of a woman than you!"

He couldn't have seen a thing and still, he managed to realize that I'm inferior to Mu Dan. I suddenly feel more of a failure.

"Han Bei likes strange women. She's the strangest one I've ever met. Enough talk, though. It's getting late, so I'll ask again. Will you let us through or must I kill everyone?"

"Go on, go on!" Jie frets. "If they let you keep your pretty head, we should go for a drink sometimes and maybe stop by the house. My sister misses you."

"Besides you, there's not a man here your sister doesn't miss."

The two men and the remaining soldiers burst into boisterous laughter.

How disgusting! Being around men is not new to me, but the men whose company I grew up with were for the most part, not vulgar. We had the occasional foulmouthed warrior monk, though nothing sordid was used in conversation when implying the fairer gender. I don't know how to respond to the boorishness; my eyes simply drift to the ground.

In time, Kang Lang remounts the steed and then gallops forward, pulling me along by the rope. Once the towers' view becomes an insignificant speck, we pause to change back into our old clothes.

"Sorry about earlier," he murmurs bashfully.

I was prepared to mount the steed when he said that. The unexpected apology sends my attention upward. Kang Lang, slightly flustered, is blushing from ear-to-ear.

"You did what you had to do. I understand."

"Yes, well, you didn't need to hear any of *that*. If I knew Jie was at the borders—"

"You didn't. I'm not offended. If anything, I appreciate everything you're doing for me."

Still glowing bright red, he nods a short acknowledgement.

Is it just me or has Kang Lang changed? He usually doesn't mind offending anyone, especially me. Now, somehow, he seems sweet. My guess is that he's more afraid of what awaits in the capital than I had suspected.

Chapter 26 – 2

In a secluded alley, Kang Lang changes into his true armor, which carries the crest of the Zhao family, and I adorn the blue set. When we approach palace gates, guards instantly recognize him and send for Lord Han Bei while we're ushered into the courtyard.

Shortly after, more soldiers than I thought necessary arrive from every corner and surround us. Kang Lang is bounded and unarmed while I'm far from threatening. Either they are overly cautious or I've yet to grasp Kang Lang's might.

In time, one of the men steps forward and attempts to retrieve the rope binding Kang Lang's hands. I refuse.

"You shall have your reward. No one here denies that you've brought the traitor."

"I won't relinquish him to anyone except Lord Han Bei. Are you he?"

"No. I am Captain Xian. The idiot in that rope is my wife's cousin. You should surrender him to family."

I don't doubt his claims but I promised Kang Lang's safety. Who can say what will happen once I let him out of my sight; not that I'm capable of defeating all the guards here myself. Still, I decline.

For my insolence, Xian draws the blade latched to his hip. His expression was very lethargic when he stepped forward; the face I peer into now is ruthless and piercing. My entire body turns ice-cold.

"I won't ask a second time. You can leave here with your reward or you can simply not leave at all. Those are your two choices. Will you hand him over?"

Dread is crushing my lungs. Intuition tells me that he's not joking. Unlike Nan Rong's soldiers, the surrounding men carry strange shadows over their expressions; heavy airs of order and repression, hard and stern, that can't fully be described. Maybe soulless is a harsh word but it's the closest word I can find.

If I agree, Captain Xian will take Kang Lang and if I oppose, then he'll certainly kill me and take the rope anyway. The choice seems obvious and yet, it's not. Conscience won't permit me to relinquish him and neither can I ask for Kang Lang's advice without giving away our ruse. What do I do?

__Keep holding onto the rope (Continue to page 343)__

__Hand over Kang Lang (Continue to page 344)__

Chapter 26 – 3

I won't betray Kang Lang! My grip on the rope tightens. A scowl runs rampant across my face as I challenge Xian. In exchange, the Captain's eyes narrow into slits. Without another word, the sword in his hand is raised to the air. I suddenly recall Kang Lang's warning. If I fail, we'll both die and as it stands, I am on the verge of failure. Immediately, my feet whip around and I pull the loose rope from the prisoner's hands.

Barely do my lips part to urge Kang Lang's retreat, something solid slams against my shoulder at a force so great that the world around fades away.

Continue to page 348

Chapter 26 – 4

The logical thing to do is to hand him over. I must believe that Han Bei is sensible enough to spare his own brother, at least until I can make my claims to the bloodline and pardon Kang Lang. However, guilt keeps me from being too eager.

"Captain Xian. I will do as you ask, but could you tell me where you'll take him?"

"Ning's affair has nothing to do with you."

"Surely until Lord Han Bei has a chance to meet him, he will be held somewhere safe?"

"Why do you care? If you didn't want him to die, then why drag him here?"

"For the reward of course."

I feel terrible for saying the words, however untrue they may be. Xian's lips purse while staring directly into my eyes. The surrounding air suddenly turns severe and then the sword in his hand is raised.

"The traitor should have taught you to lie better. It's obvious you're both plotting against my lord!"

Deny it (Continue to page 345)

Admit the ruse (Continue to page 346)

Chapter 26 – 5

"You're wrong! I'm not plotting anything!"

Xian ignores my protest and brings down the blade. I close my eyes for the impact. Instantly, someone cradles me from behind while a loud clang reverberates throughout the courtyard.

Kang Lang threw off the rope, rushed forward, and pulled the blade latched to my hip to parry Xian's attack. How he managed to do that in fractions of a second is unimaginable.

The surrounding soldiers immediately retaliate. Kang Lang strikes down man after man but the number of soldiers rushing forth is endless. I pick a sword off the ground and defend him as best I could. However, not long after, the world fades away as my eyes catch glimpse of red hair fluttering in the wind.

The End.

Chapter 26 – 6

"Wait! I admit it! I plotted everything to meet Lord Han Bei. It's vital that I speak to him. The prisoner had no idea. I really did capture him!"

Xian lowers the blade. I hold my breath to keep from wavering, though it's not possible to fool him. Throughout the agonizing silence that passes, his sharp eyes burrow into my face. Once I thought he's calmed, a tremulous sigh squeezes out from my lungs. However, the moment my guard comes undone, Xian's sword is raised again.

"Since you captured Kang Lang, then it shouldn't be too difficult to defeat me."

Xian brings down the glistening blade. Something in his words triggered my mind to retreat from fear. Without thinking, my hand draws the blade latched to my hip and somehow manages to block his swing. The echo reverberates throughout the courtyard, followed by the low hum of Xian's weapon. He wasn't using full force and still, I felt the grave impact in my bones. Just how strong are these men?!

A small smile creeps over his lips as though he had hoped for this open clash. Xian follows with another strike, faster and more powerful than the first. There's no way I can keep blocking his attacks and hope to win, especially when each strike tremendously saps the strength from my arm. Instead, I evade his strikes as best as I can and continue in the same fashion throughout the third and fourth bouts.

"How long can you keep that up? Unless you defeat me, I will kill you."

A direct thrust follows Xian's taunt. The screeching sound of his blade sliding across my metal chest plate prompts a wave of heat to surge over my being. Something deep inside pulsates, turning my body light as air. I can't hear anything except the sound of my heartbeat thumping in my ears. Everything else is drowned out in hollow echoes. At that moment, for whatever reason, his attacks suddenly appear slow.

Taking advantage of this bizarre change in state, I rush forward, parry his swing with ease, and then tackle Xian to the ground. To my disappointment, the effects vanish just as we both slam into the pavement. Dumbstruck by the remarkable event, Xian and I stare at each other; our eyes are as round as the midday sun beating down from above. Scarcely do I move off him, the crowd in front of us parts.

"Enough of this ruckus!"

The hard voice erupting from the back of the lines sends a shockwave over the courtyard. All the men fall silent as if their lives could end with a single sound. I look up to see flowing red hair in the wind. This is all I remember before something solid slams against my shoulder at a force so great that the world around fades away.

Chapter 27: The Edict

Someone's gentle hand is stroking my hair, almost lovingly. The sensation somehow lightens my heavy heart, unburdening this ache that dwells inside. Just as my body twitches closer to the source, excruciating sharp pains erupt throughout my right shoulder and arm. I jolt up and clutch tightly at the injury; the abrupt movement exacerbates the throbbing pain.

"Calm yourself or it will worsen."

What a melodious voice! The tone—slightly deep, mature, and smooth—brings forth the image of an alluring harp whose strings are made of fine silk. I've never heard a voice so tantalizing; so unique. Foreign and yet, also familiar to the ears.

Curiosity wishes to find the answer but I can't turn my neck. The pain is too much and it's penetrated ever deeper since I've sat up. My breathing becomes ragged and then I involuntarily wince.

"Drink this."

Following the same melodious tone, a marble hand presents in front of me, a wooden bowl filled with dark brew. Without thinking, I down the absurdly bitter concoction in one gulp. Whatever it was, my tongue turned slightly numb. I toss the bowl onto the grey blanket and then resume holding my right shoulder, rocking back and forth as though lulling a crying child to slumber.

The same hesitant hand begins stroking my arm. As before, the soft touch is so soothing, the pain eventually dissipates. Releasing a heavy sigh, my entire body slowly turns to the right side of the bed.

Soft, fiery red flowing hair drapes down his body. And what a body it is! His physique is so beautiful, perfectly formed, fit and tall, that I can't help feel somewhat jealous. From silky hair dangling over the fine marble skin of his arms, my eyes trace upward toward his chiseled jaw, curved lips, and other handsome features that seem sinful for one person alone to have. His nose, prominent and well defined. His lashes, curly and long. The moment I catch sight of his emerald irises, my breathing stalls and I jump off the bed.

"Where is Kang Lang?!"

The stranger, agitated by my brusqueness, casts out a disappointed sigh. "Haven't you learned by now that foolishness will only cause you more pain? Lie down."

"Are you... Lord Han Bei?"

"I am," he smirks. "Who are you? Kang Lang's lover?"

"No. I am Bao Lai. I've come to—"

I reach for the edict hidden beneath my armor, only to realize I'm no longer wearing my clothes. Terror takes hold. I spin wildly about the room in search of the missing suit but it's nowhere to be found. Amused by my distress, a light chuckle escapes from the Grand General. "Are you looking for this?"

Han Bei raises the missing edict into the air as one would tempt a starving dog with a bone. A condescending sneer trickles from his expression. More than likely, he doesn't believe it; in other words, he doesn't believe me.

"Lord Han Bei, please allow me the chance to explain!"

"Have I not been paying full attention since you woke? If you had anything important to say, you would have said it. So far, I've gathered your name is Bao Lai and that my brother's welfare is important to you. Neither of these facts interests me."

Han Bei starts up from the chair. The smirk he carries seems to be taunting me or maybe, even baiting me into something more frightening. However, it's not me that he nears. My chest turns colder with each step he takes toward the door. Without recourse, I fall to my knees and then bow low to the ground, stretching out my arms and aggravating my injury. Then, through labored breaths, I attempt to explain.

"Lord Han Bei, I am Bao Lai from Nan Rong! Recently, that edict was found at Tian Mao Yi, a temple to the south of the capital, where I grew up. I've come to find my family. His Highness is my nephew!"

"How audacious! You have some nerve claiming ties to Ning's royal bloodline based on this forgery that anyone could have written. What did you promise my gullible brother in exchange for taking part in this charade?"

My head rises to meet his piercing gaze. "It's not forgery! My mother wrote that. That's her seal, isn't it, the seal of Ning's Empress Piao?"

"Anyone could have made this seal, just as anyone could claim to be Ning's princess. You may have enlisted Kang Lang's help but a traitor's words are baseless and useless, no different from yours!"

Han Bei rips the edict to shreds, making a point to carelessly strew the pieces to the floor. The wider my eyes grow, so does his smirk, until a grin fully covers his face, clearly conveying the pleasure he feels from my misery. I can't believe this! How could he? It was the only thing of my mother that I had and he callously destroyed it without a thought!

I rush forward to collect the pieces. Han Bei tersely grabs my injured arm and pushes back.

"What's there to cry about? Your document is fake. If you will feign being a princess, at least know better than to collect trash off the ground!"

Damn him and his supercilious condescension! I can't stand it! The more I force my way to the torn edict, the farther he pushes me away.

"You arrogant *bastard!*" Unable to control the torrent of overwhelming resentment, I inadvertently scream at the top of my lungs. "Don't touch me! Even if you don't believe me, how could you do it?! That was the only thing she left me! It was all I had!"

"And I told you, it's fake! Enough is enough! Tell me who forged the edict!"

His firm grip is crushing my bone. His long fingers, searching for the most painful points of my injury, tighten by the second as though seeking for me to cry out in pain. Compared to this man, Kang Lang is a saint!

How can I keep being so careless? He never answered me. "Where is Kang Lang?!"

"Where? The traitor is dead. Unless you wish to share his fate, I will have the truth! Who forged this document?"

"What?" The breathless whisper squeezes out as a whimper.

This can't be. I promised to protect Kang Lang and he trusted me with his life. He did everything for someone who didn't deserve his friendship and I let him die! Unimaginable grief and torment bear down on my soul while rage consumes every inch of me. Blood is coursing so rapidly, my entire body is throbbing.

With one swift movement, my left fist flies across Han Bei's face. His grip loosens. Once I manage to pull free, run toward the door, screeching for Kang Lang even if that, too, won't resolve anything.

During my madness, a firm hand jerks my body around and then slams me ferociously against the door. The more I retaliate, the more force he exerts to subdue my rage. Even with the flood of adrenaline pulsing through me, I'm no match for Han Bei.

"You bastard! He's your brother! How could you?!"

"Traitors and deceivers deserve death and nothing less. The loss of one brother is nothing compared to the grief of losing a country. Do you understand? I'll ask once more and if the answer isn't favorable, I'll gladly reunite you to my brother. Who forged the document?"

"No one forged it! Master Tai Hung kept it for me all these years! It's mine! Let me go! I must see Kang Lang! Give him back to me!"

"Tai Hung?" The soft words barely escaped Han Bei's lips when a young man steps forth from behind the dressing screen to end the hectic scene.

"Han Bei. That's enough. Our curiosity is satisfied."

Stunned silent by the confusing ordeal, I slump against the door whilst running my eyes from one to the other. The young man smiles ardently while coming close and then, pulling up a sleeve, gently wipes the tears from my face. He's rather handsome and his eyes are kind. Something about this person is familiar to me though I know we've never met.

"As you wish." Han Bei's grips finally loosen along with the indolent reply.

In the next moment, I attempt to fly out the door but the young man seizes my arm.

"Please, don't be alarmed. Kang Lang is well. We promise. Han Bei was only teasing you."

"T-T-Teasing? You call that *teasing*?! That was cruelty beyond a doubt!"

Han Bei, still unaffected, shrugs at my livid stare. There are no words to describe the fury I feel or the relief that soon come after. My tired gaze falls to the ground, catching sight of the torn edict. I make haste to gather every precious bit of my past off the floor. To my surprise, the strips of paper are all blank. He tricked me!

"You! Give back my document!" I stomp toward Han Bei and grab onto his collar. His response to my forwardness is disinterest.

"Shall I, sire?" Han Bei stares at the young man who nods back a confirmation. The Grand General presents the edict from his breast pocket and then proceeds to dangle it teasingly above my head. I jump to take it from him, cradling my treasure closely to my chest once I manage to retrieve it from his grasp. Thank goodness.

"You'll have to accept our apology, Auntie. We didn't intend to upset you but one can never be too certain."

"Auntie?"

The young man grins happily whilst taking my hands in his own. This must be Emperor Yuan, my nephew. I can't believe he's taller than me!

As though having read my mind, Yuan's grin widens while his posture stiffens to further accent our differences in height.

"Is something the matter?"

"N-No, Your Majesty."

"We're family. Please, call us, 'Yuan.' May we call you, 'Aunt Bao Lai?'"

"Bao Lai is just fine, Your Majesty." I mumble nervously.

I really can't believe this kid is my nephew. Jin said he is fourteen years old. I'd imagined a child whose head I could pat without having to extend an arm above my own. Yuan continues to grin happily. His boyish nature is too apparent even if his appearance is mature.

"Your Maj—Yuan, please release Kang Lang. Whatever crimes he's committed, please pardon him. He risked his life to bring me here and I will gladly pay any price for his safety!"

I attempt to accompany the request with a low bow. Yuan stops the effort. "You mustn't. We've cleared Kang Lang's charges and sent him to Nan Rong. He explained your connections to the Southland's court. It's decided. Nan Rong's emissary will soon come east for a peace summit."

"Your Majesty! You must reconsider! Ning should not have to dirty her hands for the sake of this *woman*! She may be our princess but she's a Southlander through and through!" With his former calm pretense dispelled, Han Bei's delicate hands ball into hard fists. He glares wrathfully in my direction.

Jin was right. This man has little opinion of every country except Ning and yet, in order to have the East's alliance, his approval is imperative. What must I do?

Distracted by my aggravation for his senseless contempt of Nan Rong, I didn't realize my eyes were glued to Han Bei's face. When I finally grasp the mistake, redirect my attention to Yuan, but he's noticed my curious, more so, shameless gawking and misconstrued the situation. Much to my dismay, a sudden mischievous smile curls over his face. I'm fairly certain I know what he's plotting. When I try to explain, he intentionally interrupts.

"Han Bei. We are leaving Bao Lai in your care. You were close to the late empress. Auntie surely has questions to which only you hold the answers. Look after her well."

The Grand General protests. Yuan shrugs off his complaints and then leaves the room, all the while his smile breaks into a full playful grin. I'm at a loss for words. On the one hand, I need Han Bei's approval; on the other, forcing him to suffer me can't be good for my cause. I'm better off avoiding him.

The door clicks. Han Bei, who's been staring after Yuan, sighs exasperatedly. The perfectly curved lips twist into a hard frown. Scowling, he turns to me.

"You are Ning's princess. Have you no shame?"

"I don't know what you mean."

"The Eastern bloodline runs through your veins. Your allegiance should remain with Ning. Keep her from war and chaos. Don't drag our land into unnecessary conflicts. Your sister would never have allowed this madness!"

"I am not my sister, Lord Han Bei. I am sorry to say, I've never met her. In any case, the assassin attacked Nan Rong's leadership and then fled east in order to implicate Ning. I can assure you, Nan Rong did not stage the event. If the assailant wants fingers to point both ways, then with great certainty this *madness* will come to the eastern borders sooner or later. To avoid unnecessary conflict, Ning's best option is to form an alliance with Nan Rong."

"Spoken like a true ignorant pet dog of the South! Did they pamper and drug you with their nonsense at the palace before sending you here to spread more of their garbage? Of the five countries, *we* have the largest and the most powerful army! Just the sight of our colors sends terror through enemy ranks. There is no threat we cannot handle alone! This *proposed* alliance is solely for Nan Rong's benefit. If you even know the meaning of loyalty, you'll call off this summit!"

"I will not! Say what you will but I believe in Nan Rong. They have capable men and plentiful resources. There is no reason to deny an alliance that will benefit us both!"

His seething resentment disperses into the air, filling the room with an oppressive air. As irate as he is, I return every ounce of it in full. In some ways, he's right. Ning is my homeland so I should put her first and foremost; even above Nan Rong. However, there isn't a doubt in my mind that this alliance will be more than advantageous for Ning.

It's impossible to recall how long we've been standing here grimacing at one another. Normally, I would not have the gall to speak to someone of his caliber this way and he in turn, would never suffer my insubordination. I came here to claim ties to Emperor Yuan but even now, I can't imagine myself a princess of anything. I know he can't either. Ultimately, Han Bei scoffs angrily and then parts from the room. So much for earning his favor. If he disliked me before, he must despise me now.

Chapter 28: Han Bei's Proposal

Jin's loving arms protect me from every taunting fear on the edges of my mind. The moment I immerse in the sweet embrace, his warmth slowly fades away. I reach out, only to feel emptiness in the swirling void. Why must I keep depending on him? For all the rationalizations of his past and present, one fact remains: I've done nothing of value for Jin except pushed him to regretful temptation. He was afraid of becoming his father and I've made that fear reality.

Why did I come to Ning? Was it to secure his safety or was it, as San An once put it, an attempt to draw Jin's attention? He's confessed several times his lack of affections but I inserted myself to further his misery because at heart, I refused to believe his indifference. Even now, I keep looking for hints and reasons which may point otherwise. Where is the line drawn, from saving someone from loneliness to pushing someone to a life of unhappiness through coercion? Truly, am I doing this for him or for me?

Thunderous roars echo throughout the large room, followed by the beating of lashing rain against the windowpanes. The vociferous clamors wake me from slumber. I sit up in the darkened room and attempt to calm my aching injury but it is no use.

The physical pain coupled with my emotional tempest send tears down my face. Using the unrelenting rain to veil the shameful display from prying ears, I sob unrestrained; though, barely have I begun, a familiar gentle hand strokes my shoulder. I jump and then retreat from the source.

"Lord Han Bei, is that you?!"

It's too dark to see my own hands; somehow, I know he can clearly see me. I hurriedly wipe the tearstains from my eyes.

"Yes," returns he, from the corner of the bed. "Did I not say foolishness will cause you more pain? Your injury won't heal anytime soon if you keep that up. Lie down."

I can't do it. The only man I can take such a leisure pose in front of is in Bei Ling. I miss him so much!

Whilst lost in reminiscence of happier days, Han Bei startles me when I realize he's moved onto the bed and is sitting so close that his silky hair is brushing against my hand. My lips part to question his motive but I've not the chance to begin. With little effort, he pushes me down.

"What are you doing?!"

I raise my uninjured arm to retaliate. Han Bei threads his fingers through mine and then pins down my hand. The warmth of his palm penetrates and then spreads through me. Oddly, the same warmth also sends shivers down my spine.

"His Highness ordered me to guard you. That is to say, he thinks you vie for my attention. Thus, I must suffer the role of babysitter to an oblivious, disobedient princess. Shall I please you? Is this what you had in mind?"

"His Highness is mistaken. I have a boyfriend."

"And? Many women with boyfriends have found themselves in your position, unable to resist my beauty and strength. Who would deny a lethal blade perfectly formed into a rose? Tell me, which part of me would you prefer to experience; the charming beauty who can fulfill your every desire or the forceful brute who takes everything he wants?"

"Neither! I've neither use for lethal blade nor rose!"

Han Bei laughs amusedly, though beautifully; his tone mimicking staccato beats of a harp. "Your palm is sweaty. Your breathing has shifted. Your pulse is racing at my touch. You desire me, yet you struggle to resist the temptation. It's charming but I must ask why."

"The same reactions can be stemmed from anxiety. You startled me."

"I am well accustomed to causing fear and evoking lust. Yours is an expression all too familiar and it is far from anxiety."

"I told you, I have a boyfriend! I love Shu Jin!"

"Yes, I heard you call for him in your sleep. It's evident he doesn't return your misplaced partiality; else, he would be here to comfort your pain. I'm here, so allow me. Unlike this boy of yours, I won't leave before the sun rises."

"How did you—"

My mouth clamps shut before revealing too much. Han Bei chuckles softly at my apprehensions as though he's fully aware of every sordid detail.

"Did you think you are the first foolish woman with eyes for me? Let me guess. You thought giving him everything meant he would be obligated to do the same? Men are simple, my dear, we take what's offered and sometimes, we simply take. If you give with the expectation of receipt, you'll only be disappointed."

"Don't lump Shu Jin with you! He's—"

"Different? Of course he is. How many times have I heard that claim only for disappointment and reality to strip away every confidence from you like-minded, foolish women? There's no point to resist me; you will come to beg for my attention in the end. For your significance, I can't slight you and so, know that for the sake of Ning's future and perhaps, even for your sake, I won't be dishonorable. I will marry you and remain loyal until the day I die. Can your Shu Jin offer the same?"

His long bony fingers caress my cheek gently while his silky hair brushes against my face. I can't see anything in the dark room and still, I can imagine the provocative look that's undoubtedly on his beautiful face. His painfully tantalizing cologne invades my senses. I've never smelled anything so sweet. Uninvited heat rises to my face while my heart is beating dangerously fast. Inevitably, he must notice that my entire body is throbbing. I can't believe I'm attracted to this cad!

Be that as it may, how dare he insult Jin and practically everyone else my gender with his condescending, judgmental presumptions! He's more experienced than me, I will admit that, but that is all I will admit!

In the midst of my fury, I suddenly become aware of his offer. Han Bei just proposed. Jin said we would marry but that prospect is farfetched and with each passing moment, nears impossibility. My confidence in Jin was based on meaningless promises and sweet words he doesn't keep. He left me in obscurity after our whirlwind romance. In the end, I blamed myself. The more I try to deny the horrid thoughts, the more I'm willing to believe Han Bei.

"Has your mind been made?" Han Bei interrupts the ensuing long, dreadful silence. Even his cool breath, which tickles my cheek, is temptingly sweet.

"Lord Han Bei, I... I want—"

"Say no more."

His hand that's pinning mine increases the force of its hold, and then I feel his face descend. Why is this man so rash? Never stall words before Han Bei! Never again!

My injured arm flies over my mouth. "I want you to get off of me!"

"What?" The breathless response carries both astonishment and fright. He stammers incoherently for a fraction of time and then his palm becomes hot.

"Are *you* rejecting *me*?!" The thunderous outburst nearly overtakes the raging storms outside. Though his body is feverish, the airs around him couldn't be any colder.

"I apologize for having inconvenienced you. I love Shu Jin, that will not change! I'm flattered by your offer and I know you only thought to rally my moods but I must refuse. I'll speak to Yuan. You won't have to oversee my welfare anymore. So please, forgive me if I've offended you."

The room falls silent except for his ragged breathing. By his overreaction, I suppose no one has ever denied his advances. If I did not love Jin, it's highly possible I would allow temptation to take me and accept everything he has to offer.

The more I ponder, the more I wonder what there is to gain from loving Jin except for his abandonment.

Troubled or not, how could he have done that? Not a single farewell! He left me with a trail of broken promises and the last words I recall were his confessions of having used me. The forever-echoing taunts of his impartiality are still clear.

Tears begin welling in the corners of my eyes. I can't grasp whether they're for Jin or for my own wavering heart. What am I thinking? I've made up my mind. Why must I keep questioning my choices?

I shake my head, prepared to rebuff Han Bei's brusqueness, when he lets out an aggravated snarl. Maybe I misheard, but before he stormed from the room, I thought he muttered, "You're just like her!"

Chapter 29: Unfaithful Women

As massive as Nan Rong's palace is, Ning's is at least ten times larger. Unbeknownst to me the reason, I am rarely lost in these halls. When I do manage to go astray, intuition eventually points back to familiar grounds. Maybe something in my blood knows the path. At least, I'd like to think so, that I truly belong here.

Currently, my nephew and I are having lunch. The mood is comfortable and somehow, also awkward. Before yesterday, we were complete strangers. I know we are happy to look across the table and see family. He's been telling me about his studies; astronomy being his favorite subject. While speaking of stars, his eyes twinkle delightfully at each mention of wanting to see them from Mount Guo, the highest point in Ning. I grasp that he wants to leave the palace. Unlike the reckless He Pi who goes wherever he pleases, Yuan probably doesn't have that ability with Han Bei watching his every move.

Regarding Han Bei, I keep trying to find a good lead to discuss the matter with Yuan, though there hasn't been a decent opportunity. After he left last night, the Grand General sent medicine and repast to my chamber. His kindness was a critical aspect for my recovery this morning. I want to thank him but I also don't want to see him again anytime soon.

"Bao Lai, are you unwell? You seem distracted."

"No, Your Majesty. I'm fine."

He frowns for the formal way I've addressed him. An apologetic smile creeps over my face and then he forgives me.

"Have your wounds healed? We're surprised at Captain Xian. He's usually more of a gentleman."

"I'm fine. It was ill mannered of me to have come uninvited and forced Kang Lang to assist, no less. The guards were only trying to protect you."

"Speaking of guards, has Han Bei been pleasant company? We know he can be rather coarse and at times, offensive, but he is a good person at heart and a loyal friend."

My eyes fly to his face. *Pleasant company?* The words send a shiver down my spine. I dearly hope Han Bei's performance last night wasn't directed by Yuan. I wonder, what if Yuan intends to leave his post to me, and since in his opinion Han Bei is trustworthy, forced the Grand General's proposal? While I mull over the objectionable thought, Yuan grins sweetly, as if having understood my concern. His effort to banish my suspicions with boyish charm only makes me question the ordeal further.

Just as I muster enough courage to ask, the subject of our conversation leisurely wanders into the room. He throws a quick glance in my direction and then bows to

Yuan. My face is on fire, so I keep my head down lest Yuan misinterprets my reaction again.

Yuan waves a hand to dismiss the Grand General's ceremony. "Han Bei. Bao Lai is Ning's princess. Surely, you can do better for her."

"How do you mean, sire?"

"Why! That robe would shame an imperial servant and she is without headdress. It's unbecoming for royalty to appear so common. You were tasked as Bao Lai's caretaker and this is how you allow your ward to present herself? Are you purposefully insubordinate or have you no eye for finesse?"

"I..." Han Bei's voice trails away from uncertainty.

I was right! Yuan's pushing me into Han Bei's attention and the latter is miserable for it. This uneasy predicament is one I know too well. Jin didn't have a choice but to suffer me, looked after me, and cared for me because San An gave the orders. If Han Bei must fill Jin's shoes because of Yuan... I can't finish the awful thought. All sorts of terrible emotions are welling inside.

"Yuan, please! I prefer to dress this way, it's much more comfortable. Lord Han Bei has been very kind. I don't wish to take any more of his time. I can look after myself, really."

I force a smile to appease the child sovereign. He's far from convinced.

"Han Bei has been cooped up in his study, keeping himself busy with pointless tasks. He needs a blossom to cheer his incessant brooding."

"This girl is hardly a blossom, sire." Han Bei replies indolently. In contrast, his eyes are sharper than knives. "I would be kind to say she is at most, the common weed."

From Han Bei's implications last night, I doubt Yuan's reclusive, brooding theory. If anything, I imagine Han Bei locked in his study with several women to keep him busy. My presence merely serves to distract him. Who needs a blossom in a field of flowers?

"General, control your tongue. Prepare for Auntie decent attire and show her these grounds. That is an order. You should know better than to disobey us." Without another word, Yuan leaves the room, slamming the door behind.

Is it just me or was that very boorish? Han Bei must be at least twice his age. Emperor or otherwise, Yuan should show more respect for his elders. As his aunt, I feel it necessary to scold him; my responsibility even. Well, I say that, but so far, trust seems to be a fleeting idea between us.

Disengaged from happenings in the room, I nearly fall off the chair when Han Bei's heavy sighs are followed by hard tones calling for me to follow. He is visibly disgusted by my lack of grace. I drag my feet in compliance and then together, we take to the halls.

Chapter 29 – 2

Once Han Bei places me in this dressing room, a horde of ladies crowd inside. My deficiencies are critiqued as they dizzyingly tug and pull at my clothes and hair. I feel hands grope all over.

Focusing on the wall ahead, I force myself to become detached and I was nearly successful, until something cool touches my face. I jump. This is powder to be sure, though not the same type that Jin used to cover my flaws. This powder is finer in texture and paler in tone, much like the mask Mu Dan wears. Rouge and lip stains, along with all sorts of other makeup items I never knew existed, are piled onto my face one after the other. I feel no less than a doll prepared for display. To whom it will be displayed brings the most angst.

Besides from the torture of beauty preparation, my ears are throbbing from the ladies' loud, incessant banters. Apparently, they dearly admire Han Bei and I gather that several might have been his lovers at one time or other. The ones who claim to have been in his company are the very same who now tug at my hair and body with greater, noticeably rougher, forces.

How vile! To know that the same hand Han Bei used to touch my cheek last night also caressed these women, and possibly more, fling a shudder down my spine. Apart from men in the world who seek loyalty to one, there are also men like Han Bei and Jin's father who seek loyalty to many, or in other words, loyalty to no one. I hope Jin will come to his senses and realize he can never become so base. My mind, then wholly engulfed by his image, ignore all the happenings in the room and allow me to tolerate the shrill madness.

In time, the women leave in the same manner as they'd arrived—in a loud, shrieking, over-perfumed wave. I don't know why, but they remind me of Kang Lang. I can't believe I miss that crazy person. Just when we've finally become friends, we had to part.

Letting out a sigh, I turn toward the mirror and nearly fall back. That can't possibly be *my* reflection! I am far from one, but a lady I do appear! I wonder what Jin would say. If only I could run to Bei Ling and show him!

Vanity urges me to dote on my own reflection and embarrassment is the result. The door creaks open and Han Bei sluggishly enters. The moment his eyes fall on me, the sour expression turns blank. Once more, I'm in his attention and can't help but conjure unpleasant thoughts of our dilemma from last night.

"You look… decent," he finally mumbles.

"Was that a compliment?"

"I was stating the obvious," he scoffs.

His usual condescending air returns, Han Bei takes my hand and then leaves the room. His palm is rather warm; though, I wonder why it's necessary to hold hands at all. After treading down a long hallway, we exit through a set of large double doors onto a balcony overlooking the beautiful, endless gardens below. There are exotic trees, flowers, and shrubs; the likes of which I've never seen in Nan Rong. Some, I wonder, even exist naturally on this continent.

Ning truly is a different world altogether. It's beautiful but there's somberness in the air, an intrinsic sadness, almost, that seems to shroud everything in grey shadows. The greatest casted shadow seems to be lingering around Han Bei. He's beautiful but cold. A perfect flower encased in ice, or as he'd said, a lethal blade perfectly formed into a rose. While I cautiously peer at him through a sidelong glance, his attention directs below.

Rain from the previous night brings the scent of grass and moist earth into the air. It's refreshing to stand in the cool wind and my face would have stopped flushing if he'd only release my hand. Much to my confusion, when I lean away, in response, his grip tightens.

"Lord Han Bei, I did not have a chance to petition your freedom earlier but I will persuade Yuan. I promise. You've done as he's asked. Please, don't trouble yourself on my behalf."

"His Highness wishes for me to be in your company today and so, I will."

He continues staring at the gardens and does the very least to acknowledge me. What madness is this?

Are we to hold hands and stand out here all day? During the ensuing awkward silence, I shuffle and sway until Han Bei, irritated by my childish manners, swiftly turns to engage.

"Why exactly did you come here? To meet your nephew and secure Ning's alliance for Nan Rong? What comes after?"

"I... don't know. I'll more than likely return to Nan Rong after the threat is vanquished. You won't have to suffer me for long, Lord Han Bei."

"Nonsense! You cannot leave Ning. I know His Highness detests playing prisoner and he's pushed for our union to secure the country's safety. Even if you will dismiss me, you can't dismiss your role as future empress."

"What if I refuse? I don't want the throne."

"You don't have a choice. Ning's order of succession is to the eldest female and only to the female. Empress Dong Xing did not have a daughter. As her sister, you are the rightful heir. Because you are alive, His Highness's authority is no longer valid. He knows that, which is why he's waiting for our nuptial before legitimizing your position."

"*Our union. Our nuptial.* You say these things so causally. You knew Yuan's plans. Were your actions last night to advance things? Lord Han Bei, you don't love me—"

"Of course I don't!"

The quick, brusque retort is accompanied by a bitter scowl. There's very little doubt that this man despises me.

"You don't. So why—"

"Love has no place in politics. You are the last female in your bloodline and I am Ning's champion. My family is influential and powerful. Together, our lines will benefit from the union and secure Ning's stability."

"I disagree. A union without affections will only equate to misery and acrimony; neither of which can form a base for stability. From what I've heard, you were close to my sister. Why weren't you engaged to her?"

Emerald eyes broaden and then quickly narrow. Fright and anguish flow shortly before anger clears his face of every other emotion. The cruel iron grip tautens around my hand. I must have injured him and thus, he's returning the favor. Until I involuntarily wince, he keeps at it. Then, tersely throwing down my hand, Han Bei retreats from the balcony.

I stand still, dumbfounded, unable to grasp the bestial reaction. What did I say that was offensive? Since his union to a female of my line is beneficial, then my sister should have been the candidate. I thought Yuan mentioned that they were close. Were they not? Or... were they too close?

His words from previous night resound in my mind: *You're just like her.* Did he mean Dong Xing? When I recollect the scene, there was a hint of resentment in his tone. My sister, did she reject Han Bei? More importantly, did he love her? If my suppositions are correct, I fear my stay in Ning will be no different from my previous role in Nan Rong. I'm only a replacement, a shadow reminder of someone better.

Chapter 29 – 3

It's rained again. There was little else he could do to pass the time; thus, Yuan summoned me to his quarters and we've been chatting pleasantly for the last hour. While recounting his studies, once more, he hints at Mount Guo.

"Yuan," I shyly begin on the subject which has bothered me severely. "Do you plan to abdicate and leave Ning to Lord Han Bei and me?"

"He's told you, has he?" Yuan smiles mischievously. "Yes, that is our plan."

"I figured as much. Lord Han Bei merely confirmed my suspicions. Nephew, I don't want the throne. In truth, I don't intend to stay. I know next to nothing about court matters, politics, and the like."

"And you do not need to. Han Bei's role is to provide support. Your role is to continue our bloodline and become the symbol for our citizens' allegiance. It is against Eastern laws and traditions for us to continue our post. Surely, the Grand General mentioned it."

"Yes, he did. What is the point of being emperor if you cannot change the law?"

"If every law is changed based on the whims of the sovereign with no regards for tradition, Ning would have disrupted in chaos and our great nation would have ceased to exist. The idealist covets everything but it's the pragmatist who is forced to pay for the exchange."

"When something is wholly wrong, it must be remedied."

His response is to smile teasingly, as one would to an ignorant child when one doesn't want to slight the child's fragile, absolutely impossible, imaginations. He's twelve years my junior and yet, I feel so deficient.

"Yuan, while I appreciate Lord Han Bei's considerations, I can't marry him. I love another."

"Han Bei also loves another but he is willing to place Ning before his temperament. Is that not the actions of someone who deserves to lead and support our great nation? This man you claim to love, where is he?"

"He's... in Bei Ling. Look, I don't doubt Han Bei's love for Ning or that he deserves leadership, but I should not be the one to confer that title through marriage. Since he loves another—"

"You mustn't be jealous, Auntie. The love of his life died when we came into the world. You resemble her portrait, which was the reason we were willing to believe your claims and the edict. We are the symbol of his misery—a product of infidelity—and nevertheless, Han Bei has watched over us all of our life. He is, in a way, no less of a father to us, while you are the image of our mother. It is natural for a child to want happiness for his parents."

"Yuan, what did you mean by infidelity? Did my sister..."

"Empress Dong Xing won the heart of many. Our father, a mere foot soldier of little significance, claimed her favor. Han Bei was her fiancé at the time and according to stories, loved her dearly. For her inability to remain faithful, Heaven punished them both. The foot soldier died during a campaign and Empress Dong Xing followed shortly after.

To think, for the pain he's suffered, Han Bei's loyalty never wavered. After all the misery she's caused, Her Highness had the gall to request, on her deathbed, for him to find her missing sister. He's been searching for you ever since, all the while raising us as his own. Is this not a man worthy of your affections, Auntie? Compared to the other man you claim to love, who had such little concern for your safety that he allowed you to come east guarded by a wanted man, Han Bei is certainly superior."

Shock and dismay hold my tongue. Floods of thoughts rush; I can't focus on any in particular. A long moment passes and then one realization juts above the others. My sister was unfaithful. And, Dong Xing was my half-sister, meaning my mother also had multiple lovers. Last night, during his advances, I was attracted to Han Bei. More shameful than that, I was tempted and aroused. Does infidelity run in the bloodline? Jin's apprehension is now my own. As senseless as it is, I can't deny the fear that is gradually taking hold.

"You've grown pale, Auntie. Is something the matter? Shall we summon Han Bei?"

"N-No. I'm fine. Yuan, I meant to say something earlier during lunch, but did not have the chance. You must show more respect for Lord Han Bei. Since he is a father to you—well, even if he isn't a father to you— don't threaten him through authority. He's your elder."

Yuan stares back blankly. His eyes slightly twitch. Then, holding onto his stomach, the youth bursts into delirious laughter. "You're lecturing us?! We've always pondered the scene, to be lectured for ill manners by our mother! Never did we think it would be so humorous!"

"How is this funny? I mean it!"

"All the more reason it's too hilarious! We've never felt more of a child! Will you discipline us, too? Shall we stand silently in a corner as repentance or be sent to bed without repast?"

His cheeky smile reminds me of another mischievous boy by the name of He Pi and it makes my blood boils. What is with this kid? Why does he know so much about adult matters and why do I feel as though he's teasing me for being oblivious? The answer is too obvious. I don't want to admit it.

Frowning, I stare at the floor. Yuan eventually ceases his taunts; though, a dubious smirk remains.

"We hope you will consider Han Bei, Auntie, not only for Ning but because we are certain he is the best candidate for your loyalty. He may seem unfaithful, though we think it's merely due that he's never received devotion. If he has someone constant, then perhaps he will cease to search for mindless pleasures to fill his tormented void."

"You… you're a kid! You shouldn't talk like that!"

The thought has run through my mind countless times and I finally blurted it out. What should a kid know about pleasure? When I was fourteen, the only *pleasure* I knew was to sleep beneath one of the magnolia trees during a cool day after my chores were finished early. To my displeasure, Yuan continues his boisterous, teasing laughter.

"Between us… who is really the child here?" He manages to respond between giggles.

I don't know how to respond to that. Thus, our conversation ends with depression overtaking me. My mind is still reeling from the revelations. Yuan is partially resentful toward his mother and in fact, does respect Han Bei contrary to his behaviors. At least now I understand the reason for the Grand General's crude response to my prodding earlier. I opened an old wound that never fully healed. While he held my hand, he must have reminisced of Dong Xing. For our resemblance, I imagine Han Bei both tolerates and loathes me.

Chapter 30: A Piece of the Past

An uncomfortable week passed by during which Yuan continued pushing Han Bei into my attention. The Grand General and I feigned small talk; though, I still don't know much about him aside from the facts relayed by my nephew. As for my kin, we've come to realize that there is very little we have in common and by mutual silent agreement, mostly keep to ourselves.

While at Nan Rong's palace, I never felt like a prisoner. Here, in this great fortress where my family resides, I feel trapped and alone. Parts of me empathize with Yuan's desire to leave, while the rest of me don't want to become his replacement.

Since morning, I've been sitting on this balcony watching the never-ending rain. The swaying lush gardens below are hypnotizing while the steady beating of raindrops drowns out all else. Lulled by the wistful scene, my eyelids begin drooping. However, the comfort of slumber is robbed from me when the door nearby draws open. My grudging suitor comes hither, taking the adjacent seat. His marble hand then holds out a wrapped parcel. I hesitate to reach, so he pushes it into my palm.

"You haven't eaten all day, is that right?"

"I'm not hungry," I reply sleepily.

A soft, seemingly displeased sigh escapes from Han Bei. I awkwardly fumble the warm parcel between my hands until the intoxicating aroma urges curiosity to open the wrapper, revealing two peach buns inside. The light pink-yellow hue of the puffy dough and dainty green leaves accents are adorable. I can't imagine these common treats were prepared in the palace. Han Bei must have treaded out into the rain. For someone who's against this proposed nuptial, possibly far more than me, he's trying very hard. I'm in no mood to eat but the least I can do is act civil.

After taking a peach bun, I hold out the remainder. Han Bei quietly takes the treat, leisurely enjoying it while watching the rain falls. The silence that follows is not uncomfortable. If anything, I am glad to have his company. Maybe for his warmth on this cold day, the skies seem less dark.

As usual, I always ruin a nice moment. A sudden violent sneeze disrupts the serenity. I shove a sleeve over my face to hide the inelegance. Against expectations, instead of taking offense, Han Bei removes his coat and attempts to wrap it around my shoulders. I draw back.

"Do you find me that intimidating?"

"I'm... not afraid of you!" The rebuttal is more defensive than intended. He didn't say anything that was rude. Embarrassed for the outburst, I attempt an apology which comes out as incoherent stammers.

Han Bei removes my failed efforts with a short chuckle. "According to the records, you should be twenty-six years old, and I believe that you are, even if your emotional intelligence is that of a child."

"Emotional intelligence of a child? Kang Lang said the same. You two really are brothers."

Han Bei's chuckle becomes a laugh and then for the first time, a genuine smile breaks across his lips. "Speaking of brothers, mine has taken a shine to you. That's no easy task. You must be something special."

"If only. Your brother enjoys tormenting me, Lord Han Bei. Well, maybe his rough way of teasing. My so-called *childish* demeanor must make me an easy target."

"Yes, but youth is an endearing trait."

He smiles again, and then placing the coat in my lap, returns his attention to the rain. It's pointless to refuse the kind gesture, so I wrap the warm coat around my shoulders. It suddenly occurs to me that after all this time of wracking my brain for a suitable topic to fill our small talks, I never considered Kang Lang. As much as he'd told me about himself, I bet there is much more.

Turning to the Grand General, I begin. "Lord Han Bei, Kang Lang is much younger than you, isn't he? Do you both get along?"

"Not particularly. He claimed that I took his chance at life and I don't disagree. I am not sorry for it nor will I ever be."

"What did you do?"

"My family has power and influence; in short, we have large sums of gold. Ning's laws dictate for every boy to enlist in the army. I was one of the few given the opportunity to escape that fate. As you must know, gold can buy almost anything, including freedom. I chose to enter the army and he was obligated to follow my example. My brother was born a man of peace; for my choices, forced to become a tool of destruction. He hates me for having removed his chance at freedom. I despise his pettiness. Live for your country and not for yourself, that is what I believe."

I knew Han Bei was as patriotic as they come, so why am I shocked? Maybe that's not it. I'm not shocked by his loyalty to Ning, but for my lack of loyalty to the East. In my mind, this isn't home. I belong in the South. However, this *is* my land. This is where I was born and where my blood now resides. The people I've met are my people. Whether I like it or not, Yuan will abdicate and everything will fall to me. I don't want my lack of commitment to cause suffering for others. In my heart, I know the best thing I can do for Ning is to make Han Bei emperor. Yet, my heart also cherishes Jin. Desire and duty tear at conscience. I can't even begin to consider a path.

An indeterminable span of time passes. Han Bei slowly glances over. "Why are you troubled?"

"I'm... I'm not. Lord Han Bei, how old are you?"

Chapter 30: A Piece of the Past

"This is the subject to which you chose to transition? You're bad at conversations," he laughs. "I will humor you. I am thirty-one."

"Was my sister your age? I can't imagine her dying so young, even becoming a mother..."

What am I doing? How could I bring up Dong Xing knowing how he feels!

Realizing my folly, I quickly turn to Han Bei, only to find a blank expression on his face. Before I can apologize, he returns an answer.

"Yes, we were born in the same year; the same month, even. From the moment she first drew breath, we were engaged. If you wish to satisfy curiosity by forcing me to bare my soul, then I expect the same from you."

He's suffered enough. And maybe, the past shouldn't be dredged up, but as Yuan said, there are questions I have which Han Bei solely holds the answer. I need a past before seeking a future.

"That is fair. May I ask anything?"

"As long as you, too, will be fair."

I nod in compliance. Which topic should I ask?

My parents (Continue to page 386)

My sister (Continue to page 393)

Chapter 30 – 2

"My mother, Empress Piao, what type of woman was she?"

"Beautiful and respectable. More than a woman of her words, she was a woman of action. Her only fault was having spoiled and doted on Dong Xing to no end. I'm sorry you couldn't experience the same." Han Bei sighs pitiably while surveying my face.

"Then why couldn't have I? Why was I sent away?"

"He really never told you a thing? Just as well, the truth might have been confusing in the midst of lies. Thanks to our liaisons, rumors that did manage to escape Ning's borders weren't entirely accurate. Half of them were baseless by design. The truth is there were conflicts at court. Your father was a nobleman from Bei Ling. He and Empress Piao had a short affair which ended with his demise by the hands of the North's Emperor, Tung."

"Why? What could my father have possibly done?"

"At the time, Bei Ling and Ning were not on the best of terms. Emperor Tung sought to annex the East through marriage. Empress Piao rejected his proposal; in short, she wounded his pride. For her to then bear the child of his subject—he ordered the execution out of spite."

That bastard! My father didn't deserve to die for having loved my mother!

Unrelenting anger shakes my very core. Tears may stream down my face but rage is the single emotion I feel. My vision grows hazy. I was on the verge of despair when warmth draws composure back from the abyss. Why is Han Bei holding me? I struggle to retreat only to feel his strong arms tauten. His steady heat pierces deeper, spreading through me, calming my nerves. A gentle hand suddenly strokes my head.

"The injustice! Tung needs to suffer for his crimes!"

"Revenge is pointless," he breathes deeply. His chest rises and lowers in gentle rocking waves. "Tung died shortly after you were taken from Ning. Whether through Heaven's punishment or coincidence, a peasant uprising occurred years later and his line was removed from the throne. The current emperor, Cai Pai, doesn't have any tie to Tung's bloodline."

"Did you mention Cai Pai because you're afraid I'll seek retribution against Bei Ling?"

"Yes, and so it seems my warning was not lost. You aren't as hotheaded as I expected." Han Bei scoffs, and at the same time, chuckles softly.

"So that's how you really think of me."

Han Bei truly has a natural quality to raise the spirits, much similar to Kang Lang. Although I will never forget my poor father's fate, for now, I won't do anything foolish either.

Taking another deep breath, I continue. "Tell me. Why did my mother send me away?"

"Your father was Tung's subject. Some at court feared Tung might have used the connection to retrieve you, whereby, if Empress Piao refused, Bei Ling would have marched to our borders. To avoid war, her choices were to hand you over or agree to marry Tung, essentially surrendering Ning to Bei Ling."

"I never knew my mother but I doubt she would have capitulated no matter the threat."

"I agree. Regretfully, only a handful of others thought the same. The popular idea was that your death would remove Tung's motivation and also Empress Piao's reservations; thus, guaranteeing Ning's independence. Your then enraged mother sought to prove them wrong. She knew you would never be safe until Ning was secured. Through her decrees, our army grew tenfold and then, to exceed all expectations. The fact is she never intended to send you away.

I remember... in the midst of one stormy night, your grandfather risked his life, nearly lost it actually, when he crossed the heavily guarded northern borders. They argued for several hours before she conceded. He wasn't convinced you were safe in Ning until matters settled. Dong Xing cried her eyes out. For the rest of her days, she never forgot her sister. And Yuan, he's been hoping to meet you all his life; the faint remnant of his mother. You were loved and despite Yuan's indifference, you *are* loved."

All these years, I'd always thought no one cared. The shame of prejudice and prejudgment! How could I have thought so poorly of my family who has suffered for my sake!

"What reasons have you for tears? Wasn't that everything you wished to learn? That your life has meaning here?"

"I... don't know how to feel. Should I feel happy or miserable because I am loved? Because I lived, my father had to die?"

"If you wish to generalize it, then yes. By that logic, your mother also worked herself to death for your protection. Your grandfather lost his only son. Your sister lost a lover, who was recruited into the army through Empress Piao's decrees. Your nephew lost a mother who surrendered the will to live the day her lover died. And I lost my beloved, who was weakened by grief, and perished the night she gave birth."

His quick, blunt, and decisive blows throw me into a void. No wonder Han Bei despises me. I ruined his life. More than his life, I ruined everyone else's life. Despise is the least I could hope to accrue. This palace, now cold as ice and rigid as stone, is my doing. Everyone in Ning has been robbed of freedom, all so my mother could protect me.

As though having read my mind, Han Bei sighs. "Empress Piao worked tirelessly to amass a grand army for your protection. Ironic. *You* are the reason for Ning's strong military, an assurance of our independence, and yet your loyalty remains with the South. And for what, the love of a simple boy who can't keep his promises?"

"Jin is..."

My stagnant silence incites his resentment. The Grand General scoffs, seemingly reading my misery like an open book. "*Why does my existence only serve to cause suffering for others? Things would be better for everyone if I'd never lived. Maybe I should just die.* Is that what you're thinking? What will that solve?"

"I didn't ask for this!" The excuse blurts out in a fury while I pull away from his embrace.

Guilt makes me defensive and my weak heart is laid bare. With my nerves shaken, I withdraw further. Han Bei's jaw clenches. His hand reaches out. If he aims to strike me, I won't refuse him. I deserve it. The foundation of my life was built on too many sacrifices. If only someone would take retribution against me, then maybe I can disband a fraction of this shame.

My eyes shut tight, prepared for his assault. Moments pass and then instead of pain, warmth draws back awareness. I'm lodged in his arms again. What an insult it must be for patriotic Han Bei to suffer me, Ning's heir apparent who can't turn my back on the

South! And still, he continues stroking my head. He's crude but he's not callous. Regardless of his words, Han Bei was attempting to comfort me all along.

"Lord Han Bei, I'm-I'm sorry."

"Do you think their lives meant nothing?" The strong, passionate whisper somehow shakes away my dejection.

"Of course I don't!"

"Then don't generalize their efforts. You can sit here and wallow in your misery, accomplishing nothing in the process, or you can believe that those who have loved you and do love you paved the way. Because of past predicament, we became strong and no one, not even Bei Ling, dares threaten our land now. You will become Ning's empress. However you choose to continue her legacy is up to you. As for me, I am here for you. I am your sword and shield. You may use me however you wish."

"What if I won't do the right thing? What if I can't break away from Nan Rong?"

"I can only support your life's ambitions. It's not up to me how you live with yourself."

Continuous thumping rain is the single residual sound between us. He must be disappointed and I've nothing to say. My face is pressed against his chest while we're drifting worlds apart.

By luck, a servant opens the door to disrupt the moment. The caravan from Nan Rong has just arrived.

Continue to page 398

Chapter 30 – 3

"My sister, what type of person was she?"

"A rare blossom capable of winning anyone over; witty, fashionable, charming, fun, and full of life. She could make anyone feel as though they were the only person in the room and she was undoubtedly great at conversations. She shined brighter than any star and was lovelier than any jewel." A wistful twinkle appears in his eyes and a heartfelt smile spreads across his mouth. Pausing, Han Bei turns to me. His brows furrow. "In other words, she was your complete opposite. Physically, you are Dong Xing robbed of every allure and charisma."

It's one thing to gush about my sister, but was it necessary to insult me in the process? I don't need him to remind me of my failure as a woman. If I were more like Dong Xing, maybe Jin would have stayed. With my pride wounded, reservations are cast aside.

"What really happened between you and my sister?"

Han Bei grits his jaw. I knew asking was nothing less than sending a hard fist across his face. In truth, the question stemmed more from curiosity than vindictiveness.

"What don't you already know?" His hard tone snaps back.

"I was told... many unpleasant things, which were difficult for me to believe. You loved her, so I can't imagine that she was a bad person."

"Because only good girls are loved? Don't be so naïve. We were meant to wed; a fate we accepted with open arms. For a time, we were happy. That is, until she met the other soldiers who bested me. Then, she wanted *their* attention. Then, I wasn't good enough!" He spits out the bitter memories when resentment become too much to bury under his former adulation. The pain spreading over his countenance is so severe that I think his wounds are as open today as they were over a decade ago.

Still, I thought Han Bei is the strongest of them all. Ning's champion, wasn't that what he said? It took a moment for me to perceive Dong Xing's rejection of his deficiency in strength must be the same reason he's a force to be reckoned with, now. He changed drastically for the one he loved. Considering the multitudes of lovers he's had, I never took him for a romantic.

Despite his efforts, Dong Xing bore another man's child. No wonder Han Bei's angry. I would be furious in his position. Furthermore, as Yuan mentioned, he cared for her son—the symbol of his misery—and brought the child up well. At the time, Han Bei couldn't have been much more than a child himself.

Jin's image abruptly surfaces in my mind. I sought to change myself for him—that is to say, I tried—and for my endeavor, he absconded. Will I, too, become like Han Bei?

"Don't look at me that way. I don't need your pity."

"I-I wasn't. I am sorry my sister hurt you. But, Lord Han Bei, that was a long time ago. Can't you find another? Maybe, she didn't make you happy because she couldn't."

"You do not need to concern yourself over my affairs. I have enough lovers to keep me company."

"Lovers are not beloveds. You don't seem happy to me."

"You have a beloved and you don't seem happy to me." He smirks derisively. The smirk slowly turns into a frown. "I have many lovers. None assumes loyalty from me and neither do I from them. We never disappoint each other."

"But..."

How do I contend with that? What he said isn't wrong even if I can't agree that it's right either. While I rummage for a decent reply, Han Bei moves in front and then proceeds to push my shoulders against the wall. Before I can grasp what's transpired, his utterly soft lips cover mine. Frozen in place, my eyes are as round as saucers. Temptation calls for me to return every stroke of his kiss while my wounded heart expects more. However, conscience prevails. With guilt surging through my chest, my arms push away Han Bei.

"Why must you continue rejecting me? If you care about my happiness, then make me happy."

His usual sharp eyes are glazed over. Hidden distress surfaces in waves. I know he despises me. It's obvious whom he sees when he looks at my face.

"I am not my sister!"

"No, you clearly know the meaning of loyalty. You are not your sister. Relinquish Shu Jin and give yourself over to me. I will fully appreciate your delicate gender."

"You don't mean that, Lord Han Bei. If I relinquish my loyalty for Shu Jin, then I am no different from the woman you love."

His bitter expression quickly turns bewildered. Emerald eyes won't leave my face. I hope he'll come to his senses and realize I can't replace Dong Xing.

Steadily, Han Bei moves back. I thought the awkward ordeal over until his arms pull me forward into a hard embrace. My first reaction is to withdraw, until I notice his body trembling ever so lightly. I'm used to his steeled temperament under façades of derision; this fragile display is unnatural. For him to allow me into his secret torment is no small feat.

I don't know what to make of it and so I remain still and allow his arms to envelop me in their warmth. For some reason, falling deeper into his embrace also calms my nerves. Then, little by little, Han Bei releases me.

It's terrible to admit but I wanted to be held a while longer. I miss the affections from happier days.

Following a short pause, he chuckles shyly. "I didn't know this heart of mine could still beat so..."

His voice trails away. The last words become lost in the heavy pounding rain. I couldn't grasp his intention and the moment I begin asking, the door creaks open. A servant announces that the caravan from Nan Rong has just arrived.

Chapter 31: Emissary from Nan Rong

"San An!"

My arms fly around the emissary's neck the moment I rush into the audience chamber. San An, surprised by the assault, stumbles backward. Despite our recent strained relationship, the Minister is still a friend to me and I'm elated to see a familiar face at last.

"Your Highness. You seem well." He replies calmly.

"Yes. I've missed you and Kang Lang. How is he?"

"As vexing as ever, Your Highness."

"I bet! Please tell him I send my regards. How are things in Nan Rong? Have you... heard from Shu Jin?"

"I'm afraid not. To be honest, I did not know he left until Kang Lang returned. Your Highness was brash. Why didn't you announce your endeavors before treading to the East unprotected?"

"I was protected. I had Kang Lang. I didn't mean to worry you. I'm sorry, San An!"

His kind eyes gently lower as if they could smile. I was entranced by their sweet temperament when Han Bei brusquely enters the room.

"Your Highness should not apologize to a Southern dog come to beg for scraps."

Contrary to his warm nature only moments ago, Han Bei's condescending tone overflows to match his haughty glare of disdain.

"Lord Han Bei. Please don't insult our guest."

"Insults imply what isn't true. I was merely making an observation."

The Grand General stands abreast. With arms folded, Han Bei's sharp glare burrows intently at the Minister. The latter bows courteously whilst returning an amiable smile. A long pause follows, during which San An continues smiling while his eyes pierce my face.

I was too much of a dolt to realize they were both waiting for me to proceed until Han Bei forcibly cleared his throat.

"Oh! Shall-Shall we have some tea? Right! Lord Han Bei, could you send for tea? San An, will you come with me?"

Shortly after San An and I enter the sitting room adjacent to the azalea garden, tea is brought and Han Bei takes the third chair. I look around the table and wonder whether I can stay in the middle of this conversation. To my right is the Minister, who seems more polite than usual, and to my left, the Grand General is scowling threateningly. Maybe small talk is expected, but I don't feel it necessary since San An and I are far from strangers. Thus, I jump to the point.

"Has there been any progress, San An? Did you find Ying?"

"We've not found the assassin. Worse, he's staged another assault, against Bei Ling this time."

"Bei Ling? He Pi thinks the instigator is from Bei Ling, so why would he?"

"Cai Pai, Bei Ling's child emperor, was not injured. The assassin made his way to our Mount Chou after the assault; he meant to implicate the South. Furthermore, Bei Ling's generals have crossed into Nan Rong without discretion in search of the assassin and ours are currently subduing their efforts. I hope this event will not escalate to war."

Han Bei, afraid of my brashness, immediately interjects. "So while your men are defending against Bei Ling, Prime Minister, you came to exploit ties to Her Highness, hoping for reinforcements? I will not have Ning soldiers die in a foreign land for a foreign cause that doesn't impact the East."

His words struck a chord in me. I came to Ning with the single intention of forging an alliance between our two lands. Thus, San An's request should have an easy answer; except now, I'm uncertain. Han Bei has a point. Once I send Ning soldiers south, many if not all, may perish. These are people—my people—not just faceless pawns on a chessboard. These people have families. I can't stand the thought of robbing anyone's happiness.

Conversely, should Ning stand idle, Nan Rong will suffer.

While I hesitate, San An rebuts. "Lord Han Bei, for the sake of your empress, you must consider this fact. Three countries have now been drawn by this conflict and two leaders have been assaulted. If indeed Nan Rong is the target, there isn't a more efficient method to drain our resources than to send the full force of the East upon us. That can easily be accomplished once Her Highness comes to harm."

"I would never allow that." Han Bei's tone is tempered steel. "She is my charge and I will protect her. Unlike the weak southern defenses, entering this palace uninvited is suicide."

An uncomfortable, disquiet pause ensues, during which the two men exchanged defiant glares. My mind is spinning wildly from weighing the costs and benefits. I won't make promises I can't keep and yet, how can I promise to send my people in harm's way?

"San An, I... will do what I can but at the moment, I can't promise anything. Maybe Kang Lang's informant may yet find Ying's handler—"

"Kang Lang revealed that information, Your Highness." San An replies. He's clearly irritated that my answer isn't more favorable. I understand how he feels. If I never came to Ning, I would feel no different.

"Did he? Then why hasn't progress been made?"

"His informant merely knows Ying's handler as Su Jian. At this time, his source is still searching for the details. Once this handler is found, then perhaps war can be avoided. Though, with all that's happened, the expectation may be too optimistic."

The Grand General quickly drops the teacup onto the table, sending a loud clink to resonate in the air. "The simple fact is Bei Ling covets Nan Rong. Any fool can see that. The staged attack against Cai Pai was an excuse to march south. The Southland is ill prepared for war and now that war is on the horizon, wishes to use the lowest form of defensive strategies: diplomacy. History is repeating itself. Once more, these useless users from the South come armed to our doors with smiles on their faces and daggers in their hands. Your Highness must not permit kindness and acquaintanceship to overlook what is blatant coercion."

"Kindness begets kindness, just as friendship begets strength. Ning has military advantage while Nan Rong has ample resources. Our two countries are stronger together." San An's reply carries a slight tone of urgency and is seemingly directed at me instead of Han Bei.

"Well, kindness begets kindness indeed. I suppose karma is just. When Bei Ling last threatened our territory, Nan Rong claimed neutrality and turned a blind eye to our plight. Now that the shoe is on the other foot, naturally, karma should solely play judge and executioner."

This must be what Kang Lang meant when he mentioned that I was oblivious to Ning's history. I had no idea this resentment existed. In Nan Rong, it is rumored that the East is inhabited by single-minded brutes, no less than barbarians, with only goals for conquest and oppression. If that were true, Han Bei wouldn't insist against war. He should be excited to overpower Bei Ling. Regardless of his indifference, when I look into his eyes, I see concern for our people.

San An, still unyielding, continues. "Unless our intelligences were mistaken, the South provided Her Highness safety when her own countrymen sought her demise during Ning's court controversies."

To which Han Bei immediately returns, "Likewise, Ning was refuge to many nobles who fled from the Southland during Empress Pai's court domination escapades."

At the mention of his mother, San An nearly breaks from composure. Han Bei certainly knows how to touch the Minister's nerves without much effort. Still, that was uncalled for. I shyly glance at San An to find an empty smile curved over his mouth. His piercing eyes are of another opinion.

"An apt observation, Lord Han Bei. Our lands have truly proven to be long time friends." San An bows shortly.

With the idea of friendship and alliance yet again thrusts upon the table, Han Bei's smirk becomes a grimace. I can imagine he has more choice words for San An, so I hastily remove his chance.

"Gentlemen, I understand your opinions. You both have made valid points. Ultimately, we must cooperate to find solution. I refuse to let Nan Rong fall but I also don't want our soldiers in peril."

"Are you really that naïve? You cannot have both!"

The Grand General emphasizes those chiding words through an aggravated glare. I stare back defiantly, though his grimace is so severe that a chill runs through me, forcing my withdrawal.

Why must we keep fighting? Obviously, we'll never agree if obstinacy is our single shared trait. Exasperated, I turn to San An for support. To my surprise, he wholly agrees with Han Bei. I cannot have it both ways.

Thus, conversations ended, for now. San An retired to the guest quarters while Han Bei simply left. I never know where he goes. Bias may cloud both men's convictions but at least, unlike me, they aren't without resolve. Still undecided, I remain in silent contemplation while the rain outside increases to deafening fervor.

Chapter 32: A Promise to San An

When dinner came around, Han Bei declined the invitation and Yuan didn't even bother to respond. What an insult to our guest. The table is set for four and two are present. Nervously, I look across the massive spread to find a disappointed San An. From his perspective, I must appear an absolute traitor. In response to my indecision, he's kept conversations to a minimal; though, the Minister remains as civil as ever.

"How's the weather in Nan Rong?" I've exhausted things to ask and the weather seemed as good as any topic.

He looks up and feigns a short smile. "It's been warm."

Another awkward silence drives me to fill the void with obnoxious clinking noises by tapping my index finger against the crystal cup. His upturned eyes are silently chiding. Eventually, San An's temper submits to cordiality. "Is there something else you wish to ask me, Your Highness?"

"Well, I—yes, but... one subject I cannot ask because I know your stance and the other, I'm afraid to ask because... it's about Jin."

San An momentarily glances away in order to hide discomfiture. Jin was right, I am tactless. It's one thing to have wounded the Minister's pride through my blatant rejection, it's insult to injury to constantly show concern for his rival.

"I-I'm sorry, San An. Tell me more about—"

"I don't claim to know my brother as well as I should. However, if there's anything I can share with Your Highness, then it would be my pleasure."

He turns back and smiles genuinely to urge me to continue.

"Ah, well. I won't impose, but if you really don't mind, San An... How much do you know about Jin's past, his experiences at court as a child, and his relationship with his parents?"

The Minister sips from the crystal cup slowly and after placing it down, sighs. "I see. Was that the reason for his departure? Back then, I did not know Jin very well. We spoke a few times before the chaos erupted. He was the quiet sort; kept to himself and had little to say. During the conflict, rumors were as good as fact, and based on rumors, I will tell you all that I know. Jin is my father's precise image. There's no refutation that he is Emperor Jin's son. While everyone else pointed fingers, claimed that his other children were illegitimate, no one could charge Jin. For this reason, he became a target; an even more prominent target than His Highness and me, I'm afraid."

"What do you mean by, '*target*?' Assassinations?"

"Yes, well, we were all in danger of that. Everyone thought he would ultimately claim the throne. Hence, the women who only bore sons sought his death, while the women who bore daughters sought his consummation with their progenies."

I spit out the juice I'd just drink, staining the white tablecloth red. What did he just say?!

"Were they *insane*?! Weren't those girls his half-sisters?!"

"The majority of them, yes." Staring at the table, San An's brows furrow into a knot; disgusted by the recount. "Power is everything and nothing is too arduous for its achievement. While this is also rumor, some say few women sought his attention for themselves, not just their daughters. He is my father's image—the image of their lust."

"B-B-But did anything happen?"

"I don't know. He was abducted on several occasions, I heard. At the time, I was too self-absorbed to care if that were true. I was the crown prince and only thought of securing my authority. I'm sorry, Your Highness."

San An stares grievously as though begging for my forgiveness. It wasn't his fault. It wasn't any child's fault. These women of the court... how I loathe them! It makes my blood boil to even consider the pain he must have endured for simply being his father's son. He distrusts women. I wonder why he doesn't just hate them all! Wait, what am I saying? I'm a woman. Still, I can't shake off this rage that is building in torrents! I need to hit something!

Unknowingly, my fist moves in tandem with my thought, slamming heftily against the table, sending the flower vase to the ground. Ashamed for my brutish behavior, I start from the chair to retrieve the broken pieces. As I kneel down, San An's in front of me, doing the same.

"I'm sorry, I shouldn't have—"

"No," the Minister interjects. "I'm glad your reaction is passion and not retreat. That means you must sincerely love my brother."

"I do. There's no doubt that I do! San An, I'm sorry for prying but Kang Lang thought perhaps Jin was emotionally abused by his mother for resembling Emperor Jin. I know that Shu Jin is also afraid of becoming his father. Is that true? What must I do?"

"I apologize for my ignorance. I truly don't know. As to your last question, the answer is within you. There are parts of a man's heart only a woman can reach, which is why even His Highness cannot free Jin when their trust in one another is indisputable. For this reason, I'm asking you, Bao Lai, please save my brother. Love him for all his shortcomings and make him whole. I failed as the eldest to protect my siblings. I regret placing this burden on another but as you are his best hope, I must ask."

"I understand. It is not a burden when it's for Jin. To have your blessing San An, I'm grateful."

The Minister smiles charmingly and upon reaching for my hands, squeezes gently. His demeanor softens. We pass dinner quietly though the silence is no longer awkward. At the moment, I'm still undecided between Ning and Nan Rong, but there's nothing in me that is undecided about Jin.

Chapter 33: Bei Ling's Interference

After leaving San An, Nan Rong's troubles once more begin to plague me. I should discuss matters further with Han Bei even though it's apparent what he'll say. Well, at least I don't have to look far. Upon entering my chamber, Han Bei's looming figure comes forth from the shadows.

"We have to talk," he tersely remarks.

"Yes, I know. I was just thinking the same. Please, let me say that I understand your opinion—"

"But?"

"But you have to understand my dilemma."

"Oh right, your *dilemma*. Are you so gullible and trusting that you can't see how the Minister is using his own brother to manipulate you? Your sister would have had the common sense to end this farce before it began. You would do well to learn from your predecessor."

So, he was eavesdropping. How nice.

Moving toward the bed, I collapse in a heavy thud. "I am sorry that I cannot meet your standards for Ning royalty."

"Yes, my hopes were too high. Were our coffers to spare no expenses for your fine silks and headdresses, you will still never have Dong Xing's refinement and acumen. It seems what they say is true: the accumulation of talent, wisdom, and beauty are divided amongst siblings. After Dong Xing, you had nothing left to inherit."

There he goes comparing me to my sister again. I have half a mind to dispute, except he may be right.

"If that is all you have to say about the alliance, then you'll have your answer soon enough, Lord Han Bei. I would like to rest now."

"You've not fully heard my contention. The Minister had his chance. With all due respect, I deserve mine."

"Fine. I'm listening." Sighing, I reach for the marble from my pocket and fumble it between my fingers. He's going to lecture me, isn't he? I was never one for paying attention during lectures. At the old temple, I used to skip studies whenever possible. Master Tai Hung scolded me constantly. On the rare occasions I did attend, always yawned so excessively that the monks became infuriated.

I await his chiding, though none comes. A minute passes by and the only sound between us is the thumping rain. When I glance up, Han Bei's eyes are glued to the marble. Slowly, his hand reaches inside his own pocket to produce the other half of the pair.

"Master Tai Hung gave me this. How is it you have one, too?"

Han Bei takes the seat adjacent. A short, yet soft, smile curls over his lips. "Your mother fashioned the Huang Jia Feng Huang eyes the day after you were born. The phoenix, the symbol of the empress, is carved into obsidian. Black is the color of Ning's pride and power. The star your phoenix flies toward is Bao Lai, or Polaris, your name; also serving as a reminder that your father is from Bei Ling. Dong Xing's phoenix flies toward the eastern star, also her name."

"Oh, Dong Xing gave you the marble."

"Yes. On her deathbed, she wished for the stars to be reunited. Now that you're here, this belongs to you."

The instant Han Bei places the other marble in my palm, emotions well and a single tear can't be contained. I've never met her and yet, I suddenly feel a part of me complete. My sister and I are finally together.

Against my volition, more tears career down my cheeks. Han Bei's sudden touch to brush them away causes my body to jolt. I look over to find his handsome face smiling sadly. My heart is aching for his unrequited affections, his genuine loyalty, and enduring suffering. My sister gave her star to Han Bei. For fourteen years, he kept the marble—his promise to Dong Xing. I gave Jin my star and he couldn't wait to return it. If only Jin could give me a fraction of the love and devotion Han Bei has for Dong Xing!

"Lord Han Bei—"

"Just, Han Bei, Your Highness."

"Han Bei, how did my family know Master Tai Hung?"

"During the court conflict, Tai Hung, your grandfather, escaped with you to Nan Rong."

"Master Tai Hung was my grandfather?!" A flood of memories overtakes composure, nearly sending me to the floor. "Why didn't he tell me? I was such an ungrateful child! I caused him so much trouble!"

"Would you really have caused him less trouble had you knew?" Han Bei chuckles. "I have some experiences raising a child. Albeit I'm not his father, he was often purposefully a handful. Children often seek attention through disobedience, don't they?"

"You mean Yuan? I would have thought he was well-behaved."

"More than others, I imagine. Still, no child is perfectly well-behaved. They all retaliate in their own ways."

"Did he? I never would have guessed considering how mature he is now. All thanks to your guidance. From everything he said, I can see that Yuan holds a great deal of respect for you."

"And you must have a great deal of respect for Tai Hung, despite the troubles."

"Yes, I do. I must admit, I am impressed. Master Tai Hung was an adult. It must have been difficult for you, being as young as you were. I could barely care for myself at that age. I can't imagine what you must have endured."

"Under different circumstances, he would have been my son. Age and inexperience were factors; though, I was glad for His Highness altogether. Because of him, the bloodline, and Ning's stability, continued. As the true heir, that responsibility now lies with you."

"In other words, you want me to send San An away."

"I wouldn't dare dream," Han Bei replies airily. "You're as willful as another princess I knew long ago. The choice is yours. Not San An's and not mine."

"You make it sound so simple but I can't be responsible for others' lives."

"Then you shouldn't have returned." Han Bei's friendly countenance suddenly hardens. "In battle, indecisiveness can lead to more deaths and chaos than a poor decision. While your enemies and allies move, standing still makes you a target for both. Nothing is easier to conquer than a still target."

"I didn't know Ning had any ally."

"Your only ally, Your Highness, is the people of Ning. Under Empress Piao, we became a warring country. She led with conviction and fortitude. Our people respected, still respect, her standard. If you send our men to their deaths, or worse, exhaust our resources by being irresolute, it's highly possible a civil war is imminent. That means more deaths; more chaos. Doubt is potent and makes for a potent weapon. Either prove yourself a capable leader or another will prove how easily you'll fall."

"Are you implying that... the people question my legitimacy?"

"Yes. Everyone is aware you returned from Nan Rong. The moment you side with the South, that doubt will grow. Unless there is a reason to drag our country to war, I don't know how many will stand beside you. The law dictates death to deserters and traitors. Should it come to it, I will refuse to enact that edict. While I respect your authority, I am against punishing any man who absconds from defending a cause which he doesn't believe. You may do whatever you wish against me, then."

"Han Bei, I... no, you're right. No soldier should risk his life for a cause he doesn't believe in. The fact remains, whoever is staging this plot against Nan Rong brought Ning into the equation. Even if we abstain from an alliance, that doesn't mean Ning will be spared. Shouldn't we act first, before our enemies are standing outside palace walls?"

"And who is our enemy, Your Highness? Bei Ling or another party who wishes to remove their obstacles by using our strength?"

"He Pi left because he thought the instigators were located north and now Bei Ling is involved."

"Are you confident He Pi's interference in Bei Ling isn't the reason for their involvement?"

Han Bei gauges my reaction cautiously. I can't blame his skepticism. He Pi presented the edict I knew nothing about and tasked me with gaining Ning's alliance while he left for Bei Ling to join an underground faction, following which, Bei Ling attacked Nan Rong and now Ning is expected to join the fray. It's conceivable that something is awry. I wonder whether Han Bei also questions my claims.

"Whatever may come, I will stand with you." He declares succinctly as though having read my reservations.

"What if I'm not her? What if I'm not your Bao Lai? This could have all been a mistake."

"Are you confessing?" He chuckles mirthfully. "He Pi must be a genius. How else could he have put this elaborate ruse together concerning matters he can't possibly know and regarding events which passed long before his birth? The edict is meaningless in contrast to the name Tai Hung and that marble in your hand. It's the little obscure things, not the grand declarations, that prove who you are. Besides that, if you were He Pi's pawn, half of our soldiers would already be in Nan Rong."

"I could be a pawn with a conscience."

Another pretty laugh escapes his rose lips at my shrug. Han Bei's left arm swings around my shoulders, pulling our bodies close. I turn to question his brashness when a warm kiss lands on my mouth. The shock from unexpected tenderness renders me immobile. The touch of his hands caressing my back sends a pulse thumping in my ears. His sweet cologne seeks to seduce my senses while his lips send coursing heat throughout my body.

My eyes gradually close. All I can do is think of Jin and his last words to me before he left. The unbearable thought continues to resonate in a repetitive loop: Jin was only using me. In the midst of my loathsome rationalizations, intuition tells me that my current predicament isn't any different. The moment Han Bei playfully bites down on my lower lip, my eyes fly open to his sensuous smirk.

"Are you... seducing me so I'll send San An away empty-handed?!"

"How childish. You accepted my advances. Don't bother using anger to diminish guilt when it's apparent my touch excites you."

"I-I-I did not accept anything!"

"No? Your body was giving that impression when you leaned onto me."

"Well, I—you—but—you started it! Keep your hands to yourself! I refuse to fall prey to your practiced charms!"

"Believe whatever you will. Just know that if I were seducing you, then I'm still not any worse than the Minister who emotionally blackmailed a fragile woman through coercing absurd promises."

In exchange for my silence, his thumb brushes over my lower lip. Just one simple touch and my heart is racing again, confirming his accusations. For having proven his point, the sultry smile widens.

Enraged or possibly confused, I bat his hand away. Then, stomping toward the door, reach for the handle and then immediately stop in my tracks.

"Wait. This is my room. You, get out!"

"As you wish, Your Highness." He returns sarcastically. Han Bei starts for the door, smiling suggestively during the retreat. With one last look over his shoulder, he casually makes a final declaration. "Don't protest too much. My offer remains. I'm still willing to give you everything Jin promised and much more. Loyalty, partnership, and pleasure without question. Just say the word."

Chapter 33 - 2

What is wrong with me? My face won't stop burning and my heart is racing furiously. For the past several hours, I've been lying in bed recounting everything that's happened since coming to Ning. I haven't accomplished much and I still can't form a resolve. Disturbingly, my mind continues trailing back to the one face I fear to see. He irritates me and against better judgment, a part of me desires his company. How despicable! After everything I'd promised San An, how can I ever consider it? And yet, I do. As he'd said, I'm childish. Pretending to be ignorant of my faults won't solve anything. I'm clearly attracted to Han Bei for indefinitely reasons beyond his charming rose looks and sharp tongue.

Every attempt to push him from my mind only makes overbearing guilt and uncertainty grow stronger. Aggravated, I jump out of bed and take the coat he'd given me earlier. I'll return it and use the excuse for another conversation, during which he'll continue to chastise my shortcomings with his condescension, and ultimately remind my temper that I want nothing to do with him. Maybe then, I can vanquish these unsettling thoughts and obsessive images from my mind.

Conscience rebukes my plan but intuition pushes me to advance. I was still fighting with myself when I realize I'm standing in front of his door. My heart is racing again and my hands are sweaty. Once I ready to call out his name, another muffled voice trickles past the door. A female voice to be sure.

Typical! Why do I even bother? This is the same man who moments ago promised loyalty and partnership? I would never suffer an unfaithful man!

Then, why am I still standing here? I should leave but my feet won't move. Whatever is happening in there doesn't concern me! I tell myself that while vile images are emerging from darker parts of my mind. What should I do?

Open the door (Continue to page 421)

Force myself to leave (Continue to page 425)

Chapter 33 – 3

He had the nerve to promise loyalty when he can't even forgo mindless pleasures this one night. Maybe I don't have a right to complain but I don't care. I've endured his lectures. He will suffer my reprisal!

The door swings open. The unexpected sight rips every ounce of air from my lungs. My trembling hands drop his heavy coat, causing a short echo inside the room. A beautiful woman, no less a courtesan, is standing over Han Bei with a dagger in hand. The two become exceeding alarmed by my intrusion, though perceivably for different reasons. Han Bei, more distressed than I ever thought him capable, mouths something to me which I can't distinguish.

"Stay away from him!" I start to move forward when the stranger raises the dagger to warn against further advancement.

Her amethyst eyes narrow. "The last thing I need is a meddler. Leave. Come any closer and I'll kill him, after which, I'll kill you."

The sweet smile is menacing. Her deceptive fragile figure is the perfect vessel to hide merciless cruelty and possibly, immense talent. If she is anywhere close to Mu Dan's league, I can't hope to best her; at least, not through strength alone.

I glance at Han Bei for ideas. Judging from his distraught, he wishes to retaliate but cannot. All he can do is mouth those same words which I've finally grasp to be, "Run away."

For a moment, I'm back in the peach garden that day San An was injured. Another good man is in danger and my safety is his concern. I couldn't do anything for San An. I refuse to let Han Bei get hurt.

"Don't be stupid." My tremulous reply forces her attention back toward the door. "Once I scream for the guards, your life will end in mere seconds."

"If you scream for the guards, I'll kill him." She replies coolly.

"You're going to kill him anyway. Unless you kill me before I open my big mouth, you'll die with him."

Her eyes waver. She knows better than to challenge Ning's soldiers; her death can only be the result. I don't know by whose orders she staged this but apparently, the cause is not enough to risk life and limb. By her expression, it's apparent our deadlock is causing her anxiety to rise. I best think of something quick before fear causes her brashness.

"Let's make a deal!" I throw out the first idea that comes to mind. "To see... who the better woman is!"

"I don't have time for stupid games!" She turns back to Han Bei; her trembling hands are stalled by indecision.

"Wait! It's simple. Allow me to be your opponent. If you can kill me, then I can't call for the guards, which means you can then kill Han Bei at your leisure. Should I win, you know the consequence. Ultimately, if you think your skills are better, then there's very little risk. At this point, either agree to face me or a horde of Ning soldiers. Should you choose the latter, I hope you are prepared to die because if you are caught alive, I will make you suffer!"

My hands clench tightly to keep from shaking but each time attention trails back to Han Bei, my heart sinks. He's screaming for my retreat, though his voice fails him. He's still mouthing empty sounds. Ignoring his pleas, focus returns to the courtesan whose eyes are also on me. I just hope she's not smart enough to realize the other risky strategy is to chance throwing the dagger at my throat and silence me for good.

Steadily, her hands lower and then she takes a charging stance. Good. She's accepted my challenge. I mimic her pose. I can't move well in this tight dress and it has felt ages since I sparred with others from the temple. Unlike this woman, the monks had no desire to end me and the weapon in her hand is very real compared to the wooden sticks we used at Tian Mao Yi. However, I don't intend to win. Weapon or not, it doesn't matter.

"I'm ready whenever you are!"

The assassin, enraged by the forced cocky grin across my face, dashes forward. I wait for her to gain as much distance away from Han Bei as possible and then begin my charge. Her blade thrusts forward and I evade by sliding to the floor. As I do so, scream for the guards at the top of my lungs.

Shrieking deliriously, I rush to Han Bei and throw my body atop while spreading my hands over the vitals of his neck. Realizing her folly, the assassin makes one last attempt.

Resounding footsteps of thumping armors in the halls cause her panic to mount. I hear her cursing through ragged breaths and then the world around begins spinning when cold steel penetrates through my back. The last image I see before everything turns dark is Han Bei's troubled green eyes. If only I could apologize for having thought so poorly of him.

Continue to page 426

Chapter 33 – 4

It's unladylike and outright grotesque to eavesdrop the happenings in that room. Frankly, I don't want to hear it. Turning on my heels, I walk down the hall.

After about five steps, a woman's shout clearly escapes from the room. Whether jealousy or suspicion caused my feet to pause, I turn around and then rush inside.

Terror sends me reeling to my knees. A woman is standing over Han Bei holding a blood-drenched dagger and Han Bei is... I can't even think it!

Blinding anger and sorrow send me flying forward to exact vengeance. Everything before my eyes then turns blinding white as I step into the next world.

The End.

Chapter 34: Ning's Alliance

This pain is immeasurable. I can't tell whether I'm still in one piece. All of my nerves are on fire. Floods of groans and whimpers escape the moment my lips part. Once I manage to cry out, a gentle hand strokes my forehead. A bowl of medicine is then held toward my lips. Tilting my head to sip the bitter liquid, stiff movements suddenly worsen the pain.

After every bit is drained, my body slumps and heavy breaths discharge in ragged gasps. Each one sends sharp, deep rippling waves of pain throughout.

"You're always so reckless, Your Highness."

I know this voice, except it doesn't belong to the person I was expecting. Dazed eyes whirl about the room until his face comes into view. Once it does, I can hardly keep focus. What was in that medicine? Why do I feel intoxicated?

San An holds my hand and smiles encouragingly. "It'll help you sleep so you can heal. Don't fight it. I'll be right here."

I mumble incoherently until Han Bei's name finally emerges. San An quickly gives confirmation that the Grand General is well. That's all I need to hear. The medicine lulls me under and I allow it to consume consciousness.

Chapter 34 – 2

Whatever was in that medicine must have been magic, I don't feel pain at all. At least I thought so, until I sit up and then massive, razor-sharp, crippling pains spread throughout my back! A piercing groan wakes San An, who was resting quietly on the side table.

Jumping to his feet, the Minister wraps a helping arm around my shoulder. "Your Highness, don't overexert yourself. Did you need anything?"

"N-No, I'm fine." A sharp exhale escapes the moment my back touches the bed; the silk sheets feel no less than pins and needles. He strokes my head gently as if to coax me back to sleep, but that's impossible. I'm too embarrassed for having made strange faces and writhed every which way.

Glancing away, the Minister forces back a smile. "I don't relish your pain but I am glad to have seen this vulnerable side of you."

Teasing me in this state? I didn't know he could be so cruel! Moreover, how does everyone keep reading my mind? Am I that transparent? I would ask if I weren't afraid of the answer.

"San An, don't sleep there. Your shoulders will cramp. There are plenty of guest chambers nearby."

"Your Highness certainly jokes. Shoulder cramps are the least of my worries right now. You nearly died."

"Not the first time," I throw a withered smile. "I don't understand, San An. Why did this happen? Who was that woman? Where is Han Bei? Why target him? Is he okay?"

My array of questions sends his brows to arches. San An chuckles in the same manner an adult would to a curious child full of overzealous wonder; the way Yuan laughed at me. I look away to conceal embarrassment, believing he'd snub the request.

Instead, San An pats my head encouragingly. "It was unfortunate that you were injured. I am grieved for your suffering even though the event resulted in Nan Rong's favor."

"What do you mean by that? What happened?"

"The woman who attacked Your Highness and Lord Han Bei was an assassin from Bei Ling. She's lived in Ning's Circle for several years. I assume the recent attack against Cai Pai, coupled with my visit, brought about this incident. Bei Ling, in their effort to thwart our alliance, sought Lord Han Bei's life."

"That doesn't make sense. While I'm glad he wasn't targeted, Yuan is emperor. Han Bei is merely his council."

"Your authority has not been conferred. Lord Han Bei is Ning, for now. His Highness left everything to him."

So, that's where he's been! That little so-and-so! He left already and didn't tell me! I was offended my own dear nephew didn't bother to visit, if only for a few minutes. This news is more than mere offense. He might as well have spit in my wounds! Wait, does that mean, I'm now empress? The thought is chilling. What am I supposed to do? I need Han Bei! Where is he?

"Your Highness, you're mouthing a lot of words but I can't understand them."

If my eyes bulge any wider, they may just pop. Do I mouth my thoughts? How long have I been unknowingly doing that?!

"I-I uh, um... wh... but... well."

How eloquent! San An's silently laughing at me. He's holding back chortles behind the wide grin spread across his face.

"Allow me, Your Highness." San An kindly continues. "Since your injury, Lord Han Bei has agreed to send Nan Rong reinforcements should a campaign against Bei Ling become inevitable. Our caravan is making preparations. I will return south to gauge our generals' progress."

"He did?! That's impossible! What I mean is... *why* would he? Han Bei was against any form of alliance. I would have thought he'd descend Ning on Bei Ling alone."

"In truth, so did I. He may yet take his own route to Bei Ling. At least for now, Nan Rong has a bit more leverage."

"I thought I understood him. He said this was my decision. Why then choose for me?"

"You've very well answered that question, Your Highness. I assume had it not been for guilt, you wouldn't have hesitated to aid Nan Rong. Lord Han Bei made the choice for you, bearing the burden of your wish through substitution."

"He's shouldering my guilt?"

"So it would seem."

"No one loves Ning as much as Han Bei. He's the last person who should have our soldiers' blood on his hands! San An... I want to help you. You know I do. This is just too much! I can't have this on Han Bei's conscience but I also don't know whether I'm capable of giving the orders. For most of my life, Nan Rong was my home. If I could solely take up arms and defend the Southland, I would. When it comes to others' lives, how can I decree who live and who die? What would you do in my place?"

"I would do no different," he admits shyly after a thoughtful pause. The Minister reaches over to brush a loose hair from my eye, all the while staring down lamentably. "It appears the single-minded party this time, is me. I came here expecting the world from you, when more than just Ning's empress, you are my most precious treasure. I'd forgotten that. Forgive me. I won't ask you to go against your principles. Nan Rong will not submit without first retaliating. I will protect the Southland through all my capabilities."

The Minister bows. An apology is on the tip of my tongue though I know it's not enough.

San An returns my grieved stare with a short smile. "Please, don't be distraught. There is still plenty of time to reconsider. Our soldiers are at the very least, on par to Bei Ling's. For now, your health is more important. Should Nan Rong earn the East's assistance, I will be grateful; all the same, I won't depend solely upon an alliance for victory. Ah, it seems my time is up. Just as well. Should I stay any longer, I won't be able to tear away. Until next time, I wish Your Highness a speedy recovery."

As though on cue, Han Bei enters the room the instant San An stands up. The Minister bows low and then turning to Han Bei, repeats the gesture. The two exchange a short pleasantry before the Minister parts from the room.

Chapter 34 – 3

Frowning deeply, Han Bei resumes the Minister's post beside the bed. His brows are a wrinkled knot. My cheeks are suddenly ablaze. After learning the extent of self-sacrifice he's willing to suffer for my sake, I feel even guiltier.

His frigid stare continues burrowing into my face. Embarrassed, I turn toward the windows just as slivers of apricot light glide inside the room. The never-ending rain outside has ceased.

"Don't lecture me," I fret.

"What made you think I would?" Han Bei returns airily.

"I... Where were you?"

"You wish to change the subject already? How particular! I will answer Your Highness if you will answer me. What were you thinking?"

"I thought you weren't going to lecture me."

"When did I say that?" He asks innocently.

For whatever reason, the blithe response sets my heart into overdrive. "W-Well, why are you agitated? I thought you needed help, so I helped."

"And I told you to run away or didn't you understand me? You could have died."

"So could have you. We're both alive. In the end, everything's fine."

"Don't diminish the detriment. How could you risk it? How could you risk endangering everything on a reckless gamble?"

"This country needs you more than it needs me, Han Bei. I wasn't putting Ning in danger because *you* are Ning."

"That is not what I meant! How could you risk your life, yielding every precious thing you have? Yuan's fraught with the silent burden of having caused his mother's death. Your death would devastate him! And what about your *dear* Shu Jin? You have family and loved ones. Do they mean that little to you?"

"Of course not!"

"No? I clearly saw resignation in your eyes. You weren't planning to escape unscathed, if at all. What could have possibly driven you to such foolishness?"

"Are you expecting an apology? I am not sorry for what I did and I'd do it again if I have to!"

"I couldn't care less for an apology. We are practically strangers! Why did you save me?"

"What should I have done? Let you die?"

"Yes! That would have been best!"

The bitter echo sends everything to silence. His tone, more than chiding, resounds of dejection. Slowly, my full attention shifts toward Han Bei. The perceived despair and loneliness pouring from his eyes wrench my heart. In truth, last night's event still has me in disbelief. Han Bei's a careful man; not to mention powerful. It's inconceivable for him to have been in that helpless predicament unless...

"Han Bei... did you want to die?"

His eyes grow wide. Han Bei glances away and refuses to answer. He's always given off a confident impression. I never thought he was fallible to much, let alone suicide. My quivering hand overlays his cold fingers, squeezing them tightly to give what comfort I can.

"Why? How could you ever consider that? Han Bei, your family needs you. Yuan needs you. Ning—"

"Yes, everyone needs me because I'm integral; because I'm useful." He scoffs harshly. "The Grand General, Ning's champion and protector, is just another man. He's nothing special and once his usefulness is spent, another will take his place. The people will mourn and then life will go on. What difference does it make? Your life matters, Your Highness. You are irreplaceable."

"Because of the blood flowing through my veins? Just the same, once my bloodline ends, another dynasty will establish anew. I wasn't reckless because I wanted to die. I just couldn't accept the thought of you hurt or worse, and it wasn't for your usefulness. If you weren't here, Yuan wouldn't have his father. Kang Lang wouldn't have anyone to blame for his irritation. And I... I'd miss you."

"For how long? Until Shu Jin returns?"

"Is that what this is about? Have you lost interest in living because of my sister?"

"Are you lecturing me?" He scoffs. "Did you come to my chamber last night seeking comfort? You were lonely. Wasn't that the same reason for your willful recklessness?"

"Even if Shu Jin had never left me, I wouldn't have done any differently! I've been miserable during the past month while you've been carrying a deeper pain for over fifteen years. Therefore, I won't presume to know how you feel because our sorrows are not comparable. I'm glad that you loved my sister and as she was my sister, I don't wish to think ill of her, but if you ask me, Dong Xing didn't deserve you, Han Bei!

I can understand the heart wants what it wants. I also don't honestly know everything that's happened between you both; however, I know someone with your loyalty and devotion deserves those qualities returned in full. You've a great deal of admirers. I've heard more praises about you than I can recall. They were for Han Bei, the man, not the Grand General. Once I'm better and if you'll let me, I'll find that person worthy of—"

435

"You must be joking!"

I scantly glance into his eyes, which are much softer than his snappish tone implies. For a moment, I grow entranced. Perhaps it's due to the light streaming in from outside, he seems more beautiful than usual. The dark shadows that casted a heavy air about him has dissipated. His long fingers, which were cold as ice, are now warm. They lace around my own, sending uninvited warmth to my face. My heart is pounding again and I know he's noticed.

A sliver of color enters his cheeks. Han Bei gives a complicated smile while muttering quietly, "What am I to do with you?"

"Hmm?"

"You don't believe Dong Xing deserved me?" His usual scoff is escorted by a half smile.

"No, I don't. Recently, I've spent a great deal of time in the record halls searching for my past. I saw your name still linked to Dong Xing's. To this day, you're engaged to my sister. The moment she decided on Qi Lu, she should have ended your engagement."

"What makes you think it wasn't my doing? Maybe I solicited for our engagement to continue."

"It was her choice to abandon the commitment. It was her duty to set you free, even against your will."

"That thought is too fastidious; I assume you're speaking from experience."

A heavy thump inside my chest causes my shoulders to tremble. There's no denying it, I really am transparent. Han Bei chuckles and then his hand that's holding mine gives a few light squeezes. His soft, friendly smile aims to imply a hidden message I can't grasp. While I look away nervously, he stands up from the chair and releases my hand.

"Hey! Where do you think you're going? You didn't answer my question yet. Where were you earlier?"

"Always so full of wonder, Your Highness. There will be plenty of time for that later. Rest now. I will return tonight."

"You're awfully unfair."

His lips purse and then a short laugh breaks from them. "Well now, if Your Highness continues pouting, I'll be sure to bring candy as appeasement."

"I am not pouting! And stop calling me that! My name is Bao Lai!"

"I might as well call you, Yuan; except, His Highness hasn't been this childish for eight years."

He continues smiling on the way toward the door. At least his sarcasm hasn't been dampened. I can't say I'm not irritated but I am glad to see him smile. I hope in time, those green eyes will burn livelier and that smile will become a permanent fixture upon his face.

Chapter 35: Sweets for my Sweet

"Are you insane?!"

I can't believe the indecency! I was having a nice dream until someone woke me. The offender pulled back my shirt's collar, exposing what lies beneath. My arms fly over my chest and I swat his hands away.

"What are you going on about?" Han Bei sighs exasperatedly.

"What do you think *you're* doing attacking me in my sleep?!"

His eyebrows rise. Han Bei scans my flustered face and then breaks into boisterous laughter.

"What's so funny?"

"You haven't realized I've been the one changing your bandages and tending to your wounds while you sleep? Not to mention, I removed your armor that first day. Didn't you wonder how the edict was retrieved from under your suit?"

"You've done what?!" Oh, my gracious! How much did he see?

"Everything," Han Bei replies derisively to my mental thought. "I must say, you're more well-endowed than I would have guessed at first glance."

I don't know what to say to that. Resetting my collar, I pull the grey sheets over my shoulders and then crouch into a ball. Had I known this whole time... I don't think I could have looked him in the eyes.

"Would things be less embarrassing if I send a woman to look after you?"

"M-Maybe."

"So while a stranger, you would feel less embarrassed to exhibit your intimate parts to her compared to the man who is far from unfamiliar? That is troubling."

"That's... that's beside the point! I'd rather no one sees at all!"

"You'd rather your wounds fester from infections?"

"You are twisting my words around!"

"Am I? The choices are very simple. I can continue changing your bandages or if you'd prefer, send for Dr. Mai and have her look after you. She *adores* the female body. I'm sure she won't mind." Han Bei's smirk is suggestive; though, he won't elaborate. "Lastly, bandage yourself. I would be very impressed if you could in your condition."

I don't like any of those choices. My range of motion is limited in this state and I don't need a stranger learning my *intimates*. That leaves the last option. Grudgingly, I turn my back to Han Bei and slowly lower my collar. He removes the bandages and with an index finger, applies medicine over the wounds. The cold sensation makes me jump and then I hear him chuckle. Sudden nostalgia is unbearable. This is the very scene from the day I became Jin's charge; when I first showed him my shame by accident.

"I'm sorry. I'll try to be gentler."

"It's not you," I blink away the tears. "I'm feeling sentimental."

"I see. My shoulder is here if you wish to cry."

"No, I'm fine."

Han Bei pauses. A moment later, a parcel lands in my lap. Inside are handfuls of colorful candy pieces shaped into various miniature fruits. They're almost too perfect.

"These are adorable! Where did you find them?"

"I made them. Surprised? Did you think the only thing I'm good for is battle and chaos?"

"Not at all. I'm surprised you found the time."

"I promised candy and I delivered, as with anything else I may promise. You won't ever be heartbroken over unfulfilled vows with me."

His insinuation rings clear. I feel his hands slightly shake when replacing new bandages over the wounds. It's hard to imagine him nervous but of course, I am, too.

My face grows warm while increasingly, I become more aware of his hands on me. Unintentionally, my body trembles from his heated touch. The next instant, his arms are around my shoulders as his lips bury into my cheek.

"H-Han Bei!"

"If you ask me, Shu Jin doesn't deserve you either." He continues running soft lips over my cheek. The sensation tickles. I jump, scattering the parcel of candy onto the bed. Before I have a chance to gather them, he's forced a piece inside my mouth; his fingers trace across my lower lip. The light, sensuous touch coupled with the fragranced flavor on my tongue and the seductive warmth of his embrace send my whole body throbbing in ways I've never before felt. I can barely breathe.

"You... you're not being fair."

"On the contrary, it is you who is unfair," he replies. "Do you have any idea what you've done to me?"

"I merely expressed my thought. I did not mean to imply that I was more worthy of you than Dong Xing—"

"I don't care about that. I met San An in the courtyard before the Southern caravan left. Why did you break the alliance?"

"I wasn't ready to promise our soldiers' lives."

"Which was the reason I agreed in your stead."

"You also said the choice was mine to make. You shouldn't have agreed when I know you're against it."

"So, he wasn't embellishing. You were worried for me." Han Bei sighs deeply; his embrace growing stronger.

"Han Bei, I think you might have misconstrued my intentions. I couldn't stand the guilt of having you—or anyone—bear my burden."

"A pure intention to protect me is worth more than a forced attempt to win my favor. I allowed you to use me and you didn't. That is a rarity."

"Don't you think maybe you're reading too much into it?"

"I am giving you a compliment. Accept it."

"O-Oh, I see. Thank you."

Soft, melodious chuckles flow into my ear, sending shivers down my spine. Han Bei plants another kiss on my cheek and then moves away. While his warmth leaves my body, I can't help feel somewhat cheated. As wrong as it was, being in his arms felt right. He evoked these confusing and conflicting emotions in me, only to then become detached when my heart stirs. Teasing, teasing man!

Still trembling, I gather the candy pieces back into the paper wrapping. "Han Bei, thank you for treating my wounds and also for taking my best interest into consideration."

"I am fond of grateful people. With that said, I must admit I've overstepped my bounds and superseded your wishes earlier."

"Meaning what exactly?" I turn about to place the candy parcel atop the side table and then give him my full attention.

"With His Highness absent from court and your coronation a ways off, I am still officially in command, and I've resumed the alliance."

"W-Why? You hate Nan Rong!"

Han Bei's complicated smirk puts my uncalled for accusation to silence.

"Hate implies I care for Nan Rong, while I couldn't feel more indifferent. Bei Ling antagonized Ning. We can't overlook the offense."

"Antagonized? They nearly killed us! That's aggression without a doubt!"

"True, and for their aggression, my first consideration was to lead a direct march into Bei Ling. However, it's senseless for our soldiers and theirs to die when perceptibly, Bei Ling's leadership is ignorant of the instigator amongst them. At the moment, we don't know anything about this Su Jian or to which faction he belongs; though, I feel the Prime Minister is more aware than he lets on."

The East has a strong army, undoubtedly, and could very well conquer Bei Ling with ease; yet, war means death and Han Bei is carefully considering every life involved, including the lives of enemy soldiers. I really thought with his temper and intolerance of... most things, he wouldn't have wasted any time marching north.

"We'll see how Nan Rong moves while our forces ready. Our scouts are gathering intelligence near Ying Ling's borders. Should things go awry, at least the Southern defenses will cover us from one side."

"That's... a bit calculating. San An came for reinforcements and you're using Nan Rong to play defense?"

"Nan Rong will have our support. It is an alliance which benefits both sides."

"Wasn't that what I said?"

"Yes, but at the time, Ning didn't have a reason to join the fray. Now, we do. I won't ever let harm come to you again. You have my word."

Han Bei bows low. His gallantry makes me blush. I still despise the idea of being protected but somehow, also flattered. With the medicine's effects dissipating, my sore back begins to cramp. I lie down and shyly look toward the window when another thought comes to mind.

"Oh, that's right. You never answered my question. What happened earlier? Did you find the assassin?"

"She was captured. After she and the other courtesans were interrogated, I disbanded the Circle. Who knew the North was bold enough to have inserted a mole into our midst and more importantly, she was able to bypass our security."

"You didn't... kill her, did you?"

"You really do think me a brute!" He laughs. "She's in the dungeon for now. I may have more questions for our *source* later."

"I see. What was she doing in your chamber?"

The tone came out more accusing than I intended. A bout of awkward silence lapses and then his cool hand begins stroking my head. I glance up. My cheeks grow hotter from finding feverish emerald eyes gazing down.

"You're jealous," he chuckles. "How adorable."

"You wish! I just want to know what happened."

"Excuses, excuses." He sighs. "She drugged my meal and I was careless enough to have eaten it. What else? I should have been more cautious when my usual servant didn't come."

Han Bei seemingly chides himself when muttering the last part. Our earlier conversation suddenly comes back to me. Maybe he was purposefully careless. I dearly hope his bout of melancholy is over. I would ask but I can't imagine bringing up the sore subject to be beneficial.

"Why drug you? I'm glad she didn't use any, but poison would have been more effective. That's the route I would have gone... if I were to assassinate someone, that is."

"Women!" He scoffs. "It wasn't enough to aspire for my life, she had to talk my ears off, too! I made things clear between us from the beginning, and as usual, she didn't heed my warnings. Taking advantage of Bei Ling's orders, she decided to release all the *resentment*."

"What exactly did you do? Spent the night with her and didn't stay until sunrise?"

Han Bei frowns. Shrugging, he casually replies, "I always stay until sunrise. I've told you this."

Why am I surprised? On the one hand, I'm glad he slighted her; otherwise, she would have used poison. On the other hand, inexplicable anger is building inside, rendering me speechless.

With conversation suddenly reaching an impasse, Han Bei, annoyed by the deafening silence, declares, "From the day His Highness designed our union, I have not been unfaithful. You don't need to worry."

I'd forgotten about Yuan's impulsive plan. Is this why Han Bei's been so sweet? I was afraid he's grown attached but maybe, he's actually been following orders. I'm not certain whether to feel relieved or wounded.

"Yuan was mistaken. After my coronation, I'll relieve you from this duty. Our union won't come to fruition. Feel free to do as you please."

I thought he'd be happy; instead, his bright eyes grow dull and distant. His hand that was stroking my head, gently withdraws. Moments pass by before a heart-wrenching, dejected smile slowly forms across his curved lips, sending a deep pain to resonate in my heart. My breathing stalls and I don't know else to say.

"I hope Shu Jin appreciates your devotion. Not that you care for my opinion, but men like him, who have experienced trauma, sometimes seek comfort from women who remind them of the torture. He doesn't want your gentle affection. He'd prefer the abuse. What I mean is... you will be disappointed."

"Your concern is appreciated but Jin would never—"

"Does he run away every time he's too happy? When you dote on him, how long does it last before he provokes you into another senseless argument? Does he constantly compare you to his abuser because he secretly wishes you were more like her?"

"What are you basing this on? Your eavesdropping?"

"I didn't intend to eavesdrop. I approached the dining hall believing I could dissuade you from being too eager. You surprised me. By then, I thought you'd have agreed to San An's demands. Instead, your loyalty for Shu Jin caused my ambivalence and ultimately, my retreat. He will never fully commit to your relationship, I hope you know that. He'll always have one foot out the door. He can't accept perfection but he also refuses to tolerate your flaws. Am I right? Jin's possessive until one wrong word falls from your mouth and then he won't even look at you."

"Just stop! You don't know what you're talking about!" The accusations are too precise, too close to home, that I couldn't hold back resentment. I shouted at Han Bei; though in truth, I was actually shouting at myself.

"No? Then why are you crying?" Han Bei's hard voice pushes further.

Am I crying? I didn't notice the streams of tears falling down my face until he mentioned it. How weak of me! He'd seen my foolishness and still, I pointlessly rub my eyes to hide the disgrace.

The General, sighing, falls to his knees beside the bed. Without delay, he leans over me. Soft red hair brushes against my face while piercing green eyes render me immobile. I barely have the chance to formulate half a word when a soft kiss presses against my lips. His upper body gently pushes down. Pain from my injury keeps me from wriggling free and my

449

arms lack the strength to budge him. If he's only trying to cheer me up, he's certainly going overboard!

In time, Han Bei steadily moves back. Though he smiles charmingly, rage surges in my heart.

"Stop that! I don't need your pity! Even if you're right, that Jin wants me to replicate his misery, aren't you doing the same? I'm not my sister!"

"Of course you're not," he scoffs. "She never would have risked everything for me, as you had. *We* are the same, Your Highness. Two wounded souls who deserve better. Let me love you."

"You're mistaken. I did what I had to do. You would have done the same for me. Besides, you can't just fall for every random person who helps you!"

"You're not just any random person."

He repeats the previous display of affection. The rush of his cologne sends my mind swimming; I can't make heads or tails of our predicament. The more I try to protest, the more passionate his kiss becomes, until my contentions are rendered muffles drowning under our heaving breaths. With our palms clasped together, his fingers thread through mine. To my horror, against my will, my fingers are returning his hold. He takes the response as acceptance. His kiss grows more fervent until my body trembles from lack of air and overflowing excitement.

Why can't I resist this temptation! The thought of Jin is eating at my core while my body is seeking more of Han Bei's touch. My chest is on the verge of bursting. Frustration and guilt lash out against desire while desire fights back with rationalizations both conceivable and fantastic.

In a state of distress, the remainder of my strength is summoned in order to tear away from Han Bei. As I roll away, a trail of blood stains the bed sheets. Once I tumble down the other side of the bed, all my senses then succumb to darkness.

Chapter 36: An Agreement

During the following weeks, the court physician, Lady Mai, treated my wounds. I must have offended Han Bei. He didn't return and when I summoned him, snubbed me with obvious false excuses.

While the skies outside became more pleasant, I lie in bed growing ever somber. It hasn't rained again and yet, I don't have the strength to venture out. For some reason, I really miss Kang Lang. If he were here, I could look to him for reasonable advice; particularly advice about matters of the heart. I've been confused, not only for Han Bei's recent advances, but for this feeling that won't abandon me. Was Han Bei right? Is it impossible for Jin to love me? Will we constantly fight over nothing the entire course of our relationship, assuming he will even entertain the idea of a relationship after our ambiguous parting? Then again, why must I keep thinking of love and affection when more important matters are at hand!

San An hasn't sent any news and without a method to contact He Pi for information, I'm left in obscurity. Has Kang Lang's source found Su Jian? Why would Bei Ling cause this ruckus now? The more questions come to mind, the more it's apparent that I'm as ignorant as they come.

Groaning from frustration, I slowly start off the bed. The nagging pain deepens. I down another bowl of medicine left atop the side table. Then, with one foot in front of the other, make my way from the room.

Once I'm in the halls, the draught I thoughtlessly took to void the pain is causing lethargy to set in. At this rate, venturing outside carries a high risk of falling down the massive stone steps. I refuse to return inside that room. Thus, I make for the balcony area overlooking the gardens where lush flora sways in the whistling wind. I could watch that wistful scene forever.

The door slides open. Reflexively, I slump to my usual seat to the left of the doorway. Instead of the ground, something softer cushions my fall.

"I-I-I'm sorry!" Flustering like an idiot, I crawl away from Han Bei's lap toward the right side of the door and then press my back against the wall. My heart won't stop racing and I can't seem to catch my breath.

His single response is a blank stare. I'm glad he didn't make a fuss but he's ignored me for weeks and this continuing silence is infuriating. I decide to bombard him with questions just to be insolent.

"Where have you been, Han Bei? Have you been well? Why didn't you come when I called for you? I heard the Grand General was as dutiful and punctual as they come, much different from his rebellious brother. Is that true? Or, were you hiding from Bei Ling? Speaking of which, have you heard any news from San An or Yuan? By the way, that candy you gave me was delicious, could you make more? Could you teach me how to make them? Oh, and do you think it might rain again soon?"

In exchange for my grin, Han Bei awkwardly directs his attention to the gardens below. Well, that was embarrassing.

My fingers nervously tap together until boredom sets in. The whistling wind, which I once found comforting, suddenly aggravates me. In an attempt to shirk the awkward moment, my attention begins travelling and eventually lands on Han Bei. There's something excruciatingly beautiful about his stern demeanor. Once past the cold, stunning shell, the air around him is always dignified, masculine, and strong. He naturally commands respect through his prince-like impression. Something about him reminds me of San An. In fact, there are many similarities between the Minister and the Grand General even though they'd take offense to that opinion.

Unable to look away, a shameless gaze studies Han Bei's handsome features. The closer his face is examined, the more I realize he's not severe but somewhat depressed. I don't like seeing him this way.

Another round of pointless questions is attempted only to end with the same result. Since words won't provoke him from silence, then I should try a more direct method.

Crawling next to Han Bei, I reach for his silky red locks and begin to make small braids. His eyebrows immediately rise.

"You have my attention, Your Highness." He mutters wearily.

"Do I? Then tell me what you put in your hair because mine is nowhere as soft."

"Mountain goats' milk and rose oil."

"Seriously?"

"No," he frowns. "I'm naturally beautiful and you're too gullible."

"So? Stop ignoring me. I hate it."

"You don't want my attention but you don't want me to ignore you. Are you replicating Shu Jin's mistreatment against me?"

"I want your friendship. Why does attention have to allude to intimacy?"

Han Bei scoffs whilst unbraiding his hair. "So you want my unconditional attention while you find ways to vex me. What I hear then, is that you wish for me to see you as a younger sister. I'm sorry to say this, Your Highness, but what I fantasize doing to you, no man should ever do to his sister."

How can he say something like that so casually? My confused flustering and broadening eyes turn Han Bei's smirk into boisterous laughter. I never thought I'd miss his coarseness.

"You're just as vulgar as Kang Lang! You really are brothers!"

"Of course, we are. Do you still have doubts? Why are you here? You should be resting in your chamber."

"How can I? What's happened since San An left?"

"I haven't heard any news. The men are ready to march south any day now. I've been busy with our preparations so I haven't had time to visit. Did you think my replies to your summons were false?"

"Oh, so while you were busy, I was moping like a child because you didn't come to make small talk. I really am useless."

Depression takes me. I wrap my arms around my knees and sigh. Han Bei, glaring momentarily, begins braiding my loose hair. Who knew the Grand General was capable of something so trivial?

"Surprised, Your Highness? Who did you think taught Kang Lang so he could infiltrate Circles?" His soft smile then suddenly fades to a frown. "In my experience, there are two types of self-deprecating people. Either one, by being modest, you wish for me to inflate your ego through disagreement; or two, you wish for me to agree so you can become more pitiable. If the first, I find your tactics insipid. If the second, the same result can be achieved if I simply avoid to comment."

"Maybe I just wanted to state the obvious."

"Then you openly admit to being a simpleton. But perhaps, that too, was an obvious statement." He smiles meanly, or possibly, teasingly. "In the end, you saved me, so if you're useless, then my life must not mean very much."

"I didn't mean that! And about me saving you, I hardly did anything. It wasn't as though I slew her! You shouldn't fall for me because of *that*!"

"When did I say I fell for you?" He returns incredulously.

"But..."

"I said to let me love you. I never said I was *in love* with you."

"S-So, you *don't* love me?"

"Why? Do you want me to?" With a provocative smile, his face leans down to my level.

The more my face burns, the brighter his smile becomes. He's as teasing as his brother, and for his sensuous charms, a hundred times more dangerous. I begin to inch farther away; however, his right arm wraps around my shoulders to keep me in place.

"I won't tell your boyfriend," he chuckles mirthfully. "Sit still and relax."

A long awkward silence ensues; at least, it was awkward for me. He's as unfazed as though we hadn't spoken a word to each other since I came outside.

"Han Bei, is Yuan doing well?"

"Yes, he's also very happy. You don't have to worry. I sent several guides and plenty of guards for his protection. The last report states that he's halfway to Mount Guo's peaks."

"I won't forgive that inconsiderate boy any time soon, but I am glad he's happy. As for us, what do we do about Bei Ling?"

"What indeed. I once told you that stagnation makes you a target for both allies and enemies. While I doubt San An's blatant worship would ever permit his ambitions to cause you harm, I was able to find more information about our enemy and his past ties to the Prime Minister. Our ally and enemy both originate from Nan Rong."

"How so? Does San An know Su Jian?"

"I should hope he didn't forget his own brother."

"B-Brother?!" I whip toward Han Bei too quickly, my back cramps from the shooting pain.

"Exert some control, Your Highness." Han Bei runs a hand up and down the length of my back to dull the pain. "San An presented the name for your benefit. Had it only been me, he would have feigned complete ignorance. Nevertheless, I didn't understand his reason for withholding information unless Su Jian's identity would have us point fingers at the South. After searching the archives extensively, the name was discovered under a pile of forgotten records. He is Emperor Jin's second son, born a day after the Prime Minister; else, he would have been crown prince. Rumors had him perished during Nan Rong's court conflict. Apparently, that was a lie."

"Jin made it clear only three children remain. If Su Jian has been alive this entire time, I doubt his brothers were aware. At least, Jin wasn't. You don't think he's vengeful about the crown, do you? San An was crown prince but he's not emperor either."

"I haven't postulated a motive nor am I certain the Nan Rong princes were in fact, ignorant. I merely wonder what else they've been hiding from us."

"Does this mean you will rescind the alliance?"

"I don't envy the Minister for having to choose between brother and country. What worries me is the role Ning must play in this family feud." He casts down a prying glance. "You needn't look so anxious. I keep my promises. Besides, my brother is impulsive. He'll throw away his life for the grandiose notion of playing hero if I don't intervene."

"So... you really do care for Kang Lang?"

"He's my brother." Han Bei states factually.

"Kang Lang doesn't think you do."

"He can think whatever he wishes. That doesn't concern me."

I should have known. Han Bei is a kind soul behind the derision. He cares deeply for every Ning citizen. In turn, the soldiers respect and entrust their lives to him and the people revere him as the Grand General. Considering his position, it's understandable why he puts on a front regardless of sentiment. I could stand to learn a great deal from him. I'm always wearing my emotions, which is usually the cause for my troubles. By birthright, I may be destined to lead, but if anyone deserves the throne, it's Han Bei.

"Why are you smiling?"

"I just realized how much I respect you, Han Bei, and I'm sorry for my past insolence."

"If it weren't for your insolence, I doubt I'd like you half as much."

"Is that right? I think you and Kang Lang are very much alike in that regard. One aspect still bothers me though. Kang Lang is Ning's assassin. Why is he living in Nan Rong's Circle?"

"The lout didn't tell you? I sent him to assassinate He Pi."

"W-Why? How could you?"

"So he thinks." Han Bei's head lightly shakes. "Six years ago, our intelligence gathered movements between Bei Ling and Nan Rong, specifically, He Pi's involvement with a discreet party to the north. I wondered whether Bei Ling sought to advance upon Ning again; this time, with Nan Rong's aid. As precaution, I sent Kang Lang to infiltrate the Southern Circle in order to gather information. Somewhere in the chain, my orders were replaced and he received notice to slay He Pi. The next thing I know, our intelligence officer asserted my brother's desertion and even more troubling, his engagement to He Pi."

"You knew where he was all along? Why didn't you tell him the truth?"

"Ning's law is clear. Deserters and traitors are dealt capital punishment. There was no point to bring my brother back only to watch him die."

"I heard you placed the bounty on his head."

"Yes, in case he ever thought to return."

"That's dangerous logic. What if someone were to capture him or worse?"

"I would commend the person capable of that feat. Anyway, I hope He Pi isn't heartless enough to abandon his fiancé."

"Then, what about the false orders? Did you find the culprit?"

"Yes, the assassin with heterochromia eyes, the same one Nan Rong is searching for, altered the orders. By the time the guards came to fetch him, he was long gone." Pausing, Han Bei lets out a disappointed sigh. "And so it seems the traitor is pushing his luck a second time."

"Why would Ying betray Ning for Su Jian?"

"Your guess is as good as mine. He was adopted into the prestigious Yang family and given a privileged upbringing. He stood to marry into nobility. In fact, his adopted mother pushed the idea of engagement to Empress Piao the day you were born. Your mother, after having endured Emperor Tung's repeated coercion for an advantageous matrimony, was against arranged marriages. I'd wager if you weren't sent to Nan Rong, the overzealous Madame Yang would have ensured you couldn't marry anyone else."

"That's... scary."

Leaning back, Han Bei bursts into laughter. "An understatement! Before you were removed from court, she came daily to fill these halls with her shrill voice, barked orders at the servants, and criticized everyone else. One never knew whether she thought herself empress, but her concert was amusing to the adults, so they watched on with smiling, contemptuous eyes. Whenever her carriage arrived in the courtyard, Dong Xing and I always fled to the one *unfashionable* place she refused to enter: the barracks."

His eyes lower gently from the fond recollection. He's always sad and happy whenever he mentions my sister. I hate seeing him this way. My heart is twisted into a knot for his misery; though perceptibly, another stranger emotion is surging inside. It's becoming hard to breathe. This strangled sensation; I haven't felt this agitated since... I thought Jin loved Mu Dan.

The mortifying thought sends composure into panic. I try moving away from Han Bei whose strong arms won't permit my retreat. I imagine he's thinking about Dong Xing and finding solace in my company; another folly that shouldn't be entertained. Still, if my companionship can temporarily ease his troubles, then this much I can do.

To calm my own racing heart, I look down at my feet and push an additional question. "He Pi was convinced the instigator is in Bei Ling's capital. Do you know anything about his source, Zhang Tang, the White Crane owner?"

"You must be mistaken. The White Crane Order was exterminated under Emperor Tung."

"Order? He said the White Crane was an inn."

"Yes, well, many rebellions have begun inside inns and taverns. The White Cranes were a misfit lot comprised of exceptional men and women of their trades; from scholars, apothecaries, to assassins and former military men. They formed as a result of persecution for having denied their skills from

463

exploitation by those in power. Tung felt threatened by their growing influence over the commoners he alienated. It was rumored he commissioned the murder of their entire order at Lam Soi Citadel. There's not been any trace of them for decades."

"Are you certain White Crane Inn doesn't exist?"

"Unlikely. That is a symbol associated with rebellion. Tung's dynasty ended through a peasant uprising which marched under banners of white cranes. If the Order was formally reestablished, they are either bold or stupid to taunt the nobles in the capital through that moniker."

"I see. Then He Pi has found them or maybe, they were never gone. Since they were exceptional people, perhaps some escaped Lam Soi."

"A fine thing to reason. You may be right. Anyhow, I assume He Pi knew you wouldn't grasp the meaning, and his message was to the other person in your company. Who was it?"

"He directed Shu Jin. Jin left to join He Pi in Bei Ling." The memories from our last night together are dredged up. My chest tightens and my eyes begin misting over. I couldn't hide the pathetic reaction quickly enough from Han Bei.

"Did he leave because the relationship ended or did he leave to help his brother?"

I glance up to find Han Bei staring down thoughtfully. This isn't a comfortable subject to discuss with anyone; especially not with the man who's advanced on me several times. I can't find the courage to respond. In exchange for my silence, Han Bei continues.

"A man should always hold the person he loves in the highest esteem. However, if he merely left to protect his country, you should forgive him."

The unexpected recommendation is startling. It's the first genuine, unbiased encouragement anyone's given my relationship with Jin and yet, my heart feels stung by those words. Maybe, underneath it all, I don't want to forgive Jin.

In a rush, confessions spill from my lips outlining the confounded way Jin left. From his sweet promises and kind words to his sordid assertions and truths mixed with lies. He said I stirred his every passion and then admitted to using me. He promised to be my protector and then returned my treasure. He loved me and then left without a single notion of his honest feelings. That was the worst thing to have done, leaving me in obscurity. Had he expressed our night together was nothing but a poignant way to prove his point, I might have cried my eyes out and then trudged on. In this way, I'll never know his expectation.

Once my pitiful admissions finish, I realize Han Bei's no longer holding me. He must be disgusted by my weak insecurity and irrational obsession for a man who changed partiality for me as often as he changed shirts. There are more important things at stake than my love life. Even so, I am glad to have released this burdened feeling off my chest.

"I'm sorry, I didn't mean to rant."

"Not at all. I've gone on about Dong Xing while you've kept silent about Shu Jin. We are even as far as things go. I understand your frustration. Sometimes not knowing is worse. Be that as it may, you always have a choice. You can let his indecision dominate you body and soul or you can make the choice to end the routine."

"It's just... I promised to stay with Jin despite his indifference and I also love him. How then, can I just cast that aside when I don't know exactly how he feels? How can I break that promise?"

"Coming from someone who has succumbed to love's folly, my advice must sound hypocritical. For the same reason, I implore you, don't permit the seeming virtuous notion of loyalty to rob you a lifetime of happiness, especially when loyalty is not returned. Don't become me."

I'm the hypocrite for giving advice I don't follow. Even I thought he should have abandoned his engagement to Dong Xing and found another. When it's my turn, I can't find the resolve.

"I'm sorry," the words fall through a soft mutter. "You're very kind to me and I appreciate your counsel but I'm also very stubborn. Until finding my path, I'll keep focus on the important task at hand."

"Which task is that? I fear your impulsiveness. If you intend to do anything reckless, tell me at once."

"My recklessness is never intentional. Besides, that which you consider recklessness, I consider the most logical solution with the highest chance of success."

"That's *frightening*."

"Hmph! I don't need your sarcasm, Han Bei!"

His eyebrows rise. Han Bei's lips purse. "The resemblance is uncanny. You sound just like Kang Lang."

Now that he's mentioned it, I hear it, too. How did that happen? Purposefully copying Kang Lang's pouting tone, I return, "So?"

Han Bei breaks into boyish laughter, petting my head gently all the while. In this moment, his brotherly side is exposed. I can imagine him and Kang Lang this way, with the latter sulking.

"Han Bei, please permit me to follow your leadership. When I am well again, under your guidance, allow me to train with the soldiers."

"I can't say I don't find a capable woman attractive, but why the sudden military interest?"

"The reason I have a place here is due the Eastern blood flowing through my veins. What kind of a leader would I be if I couldn't live and die with my people?"

"While that's a noble thought, your role is to remain the symbol of stability. The most useless thing you can do is die a senseless death."

"It's not senseless when I believe in it."

"It's at the very least, irresponsible. There are more useful things to study. For one, how to build trust with our people. Otherwise, how to present yourself in an effective manner. Ning's strength is derived from our military and your strength as a leader must derive from the ability to command our military superiors."

"Wasn't my mother a warrior in her own rights? What better ways to convince our military leaders that I am not a boastful fool who commands others to do what I can't than to become part of the army?"

That thought wasn't a lie but it was hardly the whole truth. Until Yuan forces the throne in my lap, I don't want to be recognized in any leadership position. In my heart, I still hope that he'll change his mind so I can shirk the responsibility. The only thing which I've ever excelled in my entire life was basic martial training at Tian Mao Yi. Even that, apparently, wasn't enough to defend Han Bei.

"Anyway, that's not the only reason. I thought myself capable until coming face-to-face with that assassin. One look at her and I knew I couldn't win in fair combat. I just... wanted desperately to protect you and I was so afraid of the consequences if I couldn't. I never felt so weak!"

"I won't permit my failure to cause you another injury. I will protect you from now on."

"That's hardly the point! You can't spend every waking moment by my side. What happens when another assassin bypasses security? Shouldn't I be able to protect Yuan and myself?"

"If you wish to learn self-defense, I will train you."

"No. I don't want special treatment. I want to train with the soldiers."

His former good nature diminishes but seriousness in my defiant stare remains. I'm sick of being weak and only good for protecting those important to me through, as he'd said, *reckless* self-endangerment. It's pathetic but it's all I know how to do.

After a time, I notice my own reflection in those deep eyes of his and somehow, I feel that he can see himself in me.

"Stubborn women have no place in my heart," he finally concedes. "Let me rid the stubbornness from you. In one week, you'll attend my trials. If by the end you can still walk, I'll consider it."

"That was nothing short of a threat."

"Rather a promise. Healed or not, don't expect any kindness from me. Should you falter before the day ends, I'll hear no more of this, understood?"

"I understand."

Finally! I will have a chance to be useful! That is, if Han Bei doesn't put me in my place next week. Suddenly, anxiety is suppressing my excitement.

Han Bei smirks as though having read my mind. Behind that sweet face, I know he's deviously plotting the route to my surrender. Between his austerity and my stubbornness, I wonder which of us will have our way.

Chapter 37: Secret Bridge

"Well, aren't you greedy? One injury's not enough; you're aspiring for an even number?"

His half-chiding, half-teasing tone floats up from the base of the ladder. We're in Ning's archive, which is thrice the size of Nan Rong's Peony Palace, lined with shelves and bookcases stacked from floor to roof with history texts, maps, gathered intelligence, poetries, novels, star charts, and all else in between. I've seen sketches of ancient tribal queens and learned of wars when there were seven countries instead of five. Never did I think history could be so fascinating.

For the past three days, despite his busy schedule, he's made time to visit for small talk. I've told him much about my life at temple and he in turn recounted the numerous trips taken to Nan Rong in search of me. I wonder how different life would be if we had met sooner. It's strange. In the short while since we've known each other, I feel as though we've been friends all of our lives. Despite his openly judgmental act, he's more accepting and tolerant of my foolishness than most people I've met. He is an interesting man to say the least.

"Hi, Han Bei!" I wave down from atop the fifty-foot ladder.

"Don't, 'Hi, Han Bei,' from up there! Come down. Slowly! And be careful!"

"I'm not *that* clumsy!"

He's glowering. I might as well concede. With the document I was searching for in hand, I begin descending the extensive ladder. Ten steps from the ground, I turn to Han Bei with a cheeky grin. "And you were wor—"

Oh, geez! How did that happen?! My shoe is caught on the hem of the long robe. Following a short gasp, I find myself cradled in Han Bei's arms, staring at the ceiling. So much for my gloating!

"D-D-Don't say anything! Put me down!"

Smirking, Han Bei casually moves toward the closest round table in the room with me still lodged in his arms, as though this awkward pose is the most natural thing in the world.

"You're full of energy for someone who could barely sit yesterday."

"That medicine you brought last night did wonders. Thank you and... thank you for catching me."

"Oh, don't beguile me with pretense innocence. You planned the direct fall into my arms."

"What?! I did not! Put me down!"

The more I thrash about, the louder his chuckles grow into boisterous laughter. There's something charmingly sweet about that laugh. My heart suddenly skips a beat. If he can't see my reddened face, I'm more than certain he can feel my throbbing pulse.

"Do you take everything I say at face value? You really do have the emotional intelligence of a child."

"I am not a child!"

"There you go again, contradicting yourself. It was good judgment on His Highness's part to keep you from court until further preparations. As you are now, it would be difficult to hold my tongue."

"You're not inconsiderate enough to openly insult me in front of the court... are you?"

"Suddenly, you've become less superficial? Now I do wonder if you have beguiled me. Hmm? Did I say something funny? Why the insinuating smile?"

"That line is from one of your poems, isn't it? Spring Sparrow's Love Song? *Sweet songbird serenading from the mulberry tree; I do wonder if you have beguiled me.*"

His marble face turns pale and then a light pink hue. I've never seen him so embarrassed. My hands fly over my mouth to keep a chortle from escaping but it is too late. Unable to contain my pleasure from viewing his perceived flustering, muffled chortles burst into uncontrolled giggles.

Han Bei's pace ceases and then a fierce glare is sent down. "Where is it?"

"Where is what?"

"Don't mock me. I poured my heart into those pieces and your sister hid them so she could torment me. Is it also your plan to become my misery?"

"I am not my sister!" The strident declaration was so defensive that I froze from surprise; my counterpart, equally perplexed.

"I-I'm sor—"

My apology couldn't complete. In the next moment, our noses are touching. His soft breaths tickle and when he speaks, our lips brush ever so slightly.

"If you won't return my shame, I'll take from you something of equal value here and now."

The seductive and yet, threatening throaty whisper confounds my senses. Even more unsettling, I know we aren't alone in the archives. At any moment's notice, our precarious positions could be discovered. My hands shake and involuntarily drop the document. Smiling victoriously, Han Bei gently plants me on my feet and then manages to scoop up the document before I have the chance.

"Hey! Give that back!"

Han Bei scans the record, only to be disappointed by presumption. A frown quickly settles over his mouth. "If you're planning to escape, studying an outdated map is not to your favor."

Snatching back the map, I start for the table where my other documents are scattered. "I wasn't. At the temple, Master Tai Hung had a single nonreligious book. I've read it over a thousand times. I thought this library might contain other works by Mian Shi Fen. It took all morning but I finally found him. I just never thought... Mian Shi Fen was my father."

My poor father, who was executed by Emperor Tung for having loved my mother, wrote those beautiful pieces I've memorized by heart. The words were so pure and genuine that I often secretly cried when reciting those lines. In the end, their happiness was cut short. The injustice! I would end Tung's reign if Heaven hadn't punished him first.

Without warning, Han Bei's hand gently strokes my back, relinquishing resentment boiling inside. I can always count on him to guess my mood even when I've not said a thing. I smile appreciatively and receive one of encouragement in return.

"Here, I found this copy of his book with a message to my mother. On this page, he referenced a *secret bridge between two lands, covered by stars that need no night... shine brighter in light...* and then he goes on to describe the linkage to beauty and time; wordplays on their names. In the version Master Tai Hung kept, he used the words *starred tunnel dark as night where true lovers flee during their plight.* That made me wondered how my parents could have carried on an affair during the Bei Ling – Ning conflict; or, how my grandfather could have bypassed guards from both sides when he came for me. If we can find their secret, it can be to our advantage."

While the older maps are worn, landscapes were more prominently recorded compared to the newer ones, which focus more on trade routes and roads. The ink on the map I'd just retrieved is somewhat faded and difficult to guess the details. As I lean closer for a better view, cascading heat envelops my back and then red silk hangs past my shoulder. He's purposefully inducing my heart attack. I won't give him the satisfaction.

Feigning indifference, I casually move to the other side of the table and then settle onto a chair; my eyes still glued to the map. He follows thereafter, resting his chin on my shoulder while long fingers run along the lengths of my waist. The sensation sends my body writhing; my forehead nearly slams against the table.

"Han Bei! S-Stop!"

His busy fingers refuse to yield. I can't tell whether I'm laughing or crying from his mean sport. Eventually, my body manages to writhe out of the chair and into his waiting arms, along with several documents strewn to the floor.

"W-What are you doing?"

"That serious, scholarly expression was contrary to your usual easily-amused self. I was afraid you were an imposter. Your clumsiness proved me wrong."

"You...! At least insult me behind my back!"

"What would be the point in that? Besides, it's hardly an insult if it's true."

"Don't distract me! I have to find that secret tunnel!"

"Why? This is all speculations."

"Speculations are better than nothing. What if we come to face Bei Ling? We can't afford to spare any advantage."

"Our army is not so weak that we'd resort to cheap tricks. What's the real reason?"

The blunt question shatters my masked intention. How does he always see through me? And yet, he has in fact, seen all my weakness and still hasn't quit my side. His constancy is more than I can ever expect from Jin. It's a horrid thought but it's one that can't be suppressed.

Timidly glancing up, the truth is admitted to Han Bei: I want to know more about my parents. "After all, we're not often far from our blood. I hear yours are very loving and devoted and I see that in you. Jin's were complicated; I see that in him. And mine... I don't know much about either of my parents."

"Which are you afraid of becoming?"

"W-What do you mean?"

"Don't play coy. You're not oblivious to their temperament. If they weren't passionate romantics, the attachment would have ended the moment danger became apparent. I'll ask again, what's the real reason?"

His hand lands on my cheek. Han Bei reverts my nervous, wavering attention back toward his piercing eyes. My heart won't stop pounding while he's seemingly enjoying my apprehension. He then purposefully tightens his embrace in order to worsen my irrepressible reaction. I can't believe he's so cruel!

"Did you know, Your Highness," he continues. "There is an old Ning tradition where if the eldest is unable to marry his or her betrothed, the younger sibling of the same gender is inclined to substitute."

"W-Well, that would make quite a surprise for the betrothed."

He laughs at my forced composure; his cool breath feathers against my forehead. I can't help but return his amusement. There's something about Han Bei. Near him, I'm all nerves but I also feel calm.

Once he releases me, Han Bei urges again. His attentive smile, kind eyes, and understanding nature coax from me my anxieties. He listens without interruptions and without judgment. Until I compel his opinion, he remains silent.

"So... I-I know you must think I'm crazy—"

"I do," he replies meanly. "Loyalty is a choice. Blood is merely an excuse. Are *you* considering committing infidelity with a certain someone?"

He moves closer, smiling teasingly. I instinctively inch backward. Refusing to yield, his body arches and then he leans over me.

"S-Stop that! What if someone sees?"

"If that is the greatest of your worries, then the answer is clear. You've finally awaken from delusions and realized I am the better man. I will come to you this night and stay until sunrise... longer, if you're still dissatisfied."

"You are aggravatingly arrogant!"

"You are indubitably in denial," he returns coolly. "Look, Dong Xing's father left your mother. I don't know the details. She made a point to wipe his existence from the archives before your sister was born. Your mother wasn't unfaithful, nor was your father."

"But, my mother *was married* to Dong Xing's father when she... carried on with Mian Shi Fen."

"Yes. The days she spent by his side were the happiest I ever saw. You were conceived from that happiness. Would have preferred dejection and loneliness for your mother after her husband's abandonment?"

"No, of course not!"

"Then why wish that fate for yourself?"

Without a proper response, I stare absently into his prying eyes. Dong Xing's father deserted his betrothed and she did the same. Maybe Han Bei was right. I am afraid of becoming my mother.

I don't recall how long we sat there until the archivist found our mistreatment of old documents strewn carelessly on the floor and made a fuss. Though I tried to rectify the mistake, in the nicest way possible, he ejected us.

"It's all your fault, Han Bei!"

"And also yours."

"I was so close! You ruined a morning's work!"

"There will be plenty more mornings to rummage through your past. Now, where is my poem booklet?"

"Bring back that map and I'll tell you."

"You're blackmailing me?"

"Yes."

"How honest." He scoffs. "You leave me no choice. After lunch, bring the booklet to Xiao Xiang Hall on the upper level. I'll have your map."

Chapter 37 – 2

He tauntingly waves the document above his head in the same manner as he had the edict that first day we met. Back then, I hated him. Now, a smile can't help but stretch over my face. Picking up the hem of my robe, my pace quickens into a run down the corridor.

"If you were any other woman, I'd have left by now. You must not really care about having this map."

"I'm sorry! I had to change clothes. It was your fault anyway! Why did you tell me that story? I laughed so hard, juice came out of my nose!'

"Everything's always my fault, isn't it?"

He thumps the document on my head when I come up. I make certain it's the correct map before returning his booklet.

"What will you do with those poems, Han Bei?"

"Burn them."

"No! Don't do that! There were many beautiful ones in there! Besides... it won't do you any good. I made copies of each this morning."

He scowls at my grin and tries to snatch back the map. I manage to slip by and into Xiao Xiang Hall, pausing once passing through the doorway.

There are giant paintings of my ancestors and others from dynasties long gone hung from top to bottom of each massive wall. The entrance contains the first queen's portrait, whose tribal clothes resemble those of warring village chieftains. The next is her daughter and then so on, until their dynasty ended five hundred years later. I follow the trail, entranced by the rich history of this land that is my own.

"Impressive, isn't it?" Han Bei comes up to join the incredible view. His tone is surprisingly wistful and nostalgic, as though having walked this hall often. It's then I realize whose painting must be near the end. I can't imagine how many times he's treaded these halls to find his beloved after her death. The painful thought brings me to tears.

"Why are you crying?"

"I-I'm not! There's dust in my eyes." My sleeve forcibly rubs away the pointless lie.

"You cry very easily."

"Only recently. I never cried before Master Tai Hung died. Now I can't seem to stop."

"Is that so? Then, maybe you haven't cried enough."

Without warning, he pulls me into an embrace. Unable to control the rush of emotions welling inside, I rest my head on his chest and then wrap my arms around his broad back, taking in his warmth. I began crying for him, then for me, and then I just cry for no reason at all. He makes no judgment. Han Bei's hands run over my back to soothe the disquiet until tears finally recede to mere sniffles.

For the first time in a long while, my heart is light. No one's ever told me to cry. Most people are disgusted by the loathsome reaction. I've come to realize that Han Bei is far from typical. Once I lift off his chest, his hands land on my cheeks to brush away the remaining stains. What could I have done to deserve such kindness?

"Thank you, Han Bei."

"My shoulder is here for you, always."

I nod to him and then move a short distance away. "Let's go back."

"Don't you wish to see your mother?"

Regardless of my wants, I can't bear to make him walk this path to misery. I shake my head and attempt to leave but Han Bei takes my hand and then gently draws us farther down the hall. From the side, I can see his brows knit tightly. This must kill him and still, he's doing this for me.

Thousands of years pass by in the course of few minutes. We finally reach the room displaying the current dynasty. My mother's portrait hangs tall to the ceiling. I never imagined her so beautiful. The kind eyes and gentle smile are vivid and familiar. I feel as though she is really there gazing back.

This woman changed an entire nation for my sake and made it strong to protect future generations. Ning is flourishing from her efforts. Compared to her, I've not done a thing. The more I gaze upon her, the more I question why I was ever afraid. I should be so lucky to become my mother!

This is the message Han Bei sought to convey. He must have asked to meet in front of Xiao Xiang Hall for this reason. Knowing my mother's face is the best gift I could have received. His thoughtfulness makes me ever more ashamed for my insolence.

When I turn to express my gratitude, Han Bei's absent stare is glued to the portrait of my sister. A thin and frail flower with light hair and lighter skin, spreading a dazzling smile that can command a room. The charm she carries is something I severely lack. Even so, the resemblances in our faces and even in our eyes are apparent. The more I study Dong Xing, the more similarities I can perceive. The style her hair is woven into that lily headdress, the golden embroidered robe, and rosy painted lips; each piece brings about familiarity. During my musing, an index finger reflexively comes up to tap my chin. The gold fabric of my own robe abruptly catches my eye. Oh, dear heavens!

"Am... Am I wearing Dong Xing's clothes?"

His shoulders tense. Han Bei turns to me; eyes broadened.

"I've been wearing her clothes, her jewels, her headdresses, and... even living in her room, haven't I? She's thin! No wonder these clothes are so darn tight but the maids said strict orders were given and I had to dress this way! Have I become a replacement for you? Is that why you've been nice to me?! How many more times must I say it? I am not my sister!"

My right hand jerks from his trembling grasp. Slowly, I move back. The moment I start to retreat from Xiao Xiang, once more, he seizes my hand.

"Let go, damn it!"

"I would never mistake your lackluster etiquette for your sister's refined composure."

"Back to your real self, already? The only time you see me is when you're being insulting!"

"The truth often is. Who gave the orders?"

"Excuse me?"

"Since the maids dressed you based on orders. Who gave it?"

"Y-You...?"

His brows knit. A frown deepens over his curved lips while stern eyes bear the truth into mine. I cease to struggle from his grasp; my face growing hotter by the second.

"If-If you didn't then... who—Yuan! That little punk!"

"Lackluster etiquette aside, please watch your tongue when addressing His Highness."

"I-I-I don't understand, why would Yuan—so you'd fall for me! He wanted you to fall under the delusion that I am Dong Xing!"

"Yes, you keep answering your own questions. And no, I couldn't care less for your fashion. Your childishness and quick temper overshadow any charm beautiful clothes can impart. Were I to lose my hearing, I couldn't confuse you for Dong Xing."

"Why are you so mean?"

"Am I? Do you intend to make a fool of yourself at court? Instead of thanking me for pointing out your shortcomings, which you would do well to mind, you're taking offense."

I've nothing to say, so my head hangs in silence.

"Why were you angry when you thought I was using you as her replacement?"

"What do you mean, why? Who wouldn't be angry to be held and... kissed because of someone else?"

"So you're angry for the thought and not the action?"

"I... that's... did you notice my clothes were hers?"

"Yes. You hardly seemed high maintenance, so I didn't think it mattered. Taxes are currently used for constructions, expansions of trades, and defenses. Shall I empty the coffers for your new wardrobe?"

"No, I... I'm sorry. You're right, fashion has never been my weakness. I don't know why I keep thinking the worst in you."

"Neither do I," he shrugs. "Perhaps as your new caretaker, I've replaced Jin. You can't trust him and so, you can't trust me."

"That's... not true."

"No? You've never once compared me to Shu Jin? I was wrong about you. You're faultless."

The former understanding gentleness disperses. He's looking at me with the same indifference I remember well. Maybe I have been comparing him to Jin, but always with him in a brighter light. I know he's done the same to me; though, in his eyes, I always fell short.

"Don't badger me! I'm sorry for not being as perfect as your *precious* Dong Xing! I may wear her clothes but I can't fill her shoes. I'll refrain from speaking. You won't have to hear another stupid thing from me!"

Storming off, somehow in the next instant, I find myself locked in his embrace. He forces a kiss so fervent, my mind turns hazy and my body falls limp in his arms. Why is he tormenting me? I can't permit this but I don't want him to stop. This infatuation is too much!

Once his lips withdraw, the pain of loneliness is overwhelming. Our bewildered eyes meet. Regardless of whom he sees when he looks at me, I only see him. His gaze stays on my face for a time before scantly casting a glance toward Dong Xing's portrait. There lies regret and shame. His arms leave me and then Han Bei retreats from the hall.

How is it that he was able to rationalize his devotion for Dong Xing and still spent endless nights with numerous women and yet, from kissing me just now, became wracked with guilt? Was it because in this instant she was watching from her portrait or was I mistaken, and he was actually disgusted from perceiving the real me under her disguise?

Whatever is the case, the heavy feeling in my chest is deepening. I stay under the watchful eyes of my matrons until nightfall. By the time I return to my room, a new set of clothes my size are laid neatly atop the pillow.

Chapter 38: A Family Heirloom

A warm sensation slides across my lips and then disappears, leaving a trace of perfumed warmth. My eyelids pry open only to close again, hoping to forever reside in this strange dream which feels ostensibly sincere.

"I might have made a fuss over opening our coffers but we can absolutely afford for you a bed."

His melodious but chiding voice snaps back my full consciousness. I lift off the cold marble floor of Xiao Xiang Hall, panicking from embarrassment.

"H-Han Bei! Wh-What are you doing here?"

"I could ask the same. That must have been some dream. You were making all sorts of faces and saying very lewd things."

"S-Such as?"

"Well, let me see. *'Han Bei, don't stop. Han Bei, no, not there! Han Bei, kiss me again'.* So I did."

"Y-Y-Y-Y-You kissed me?!"

"I try not to leave a woman wanting." Pausing, he chuckles. "Out of everything I mentioned, the kiss was the most embarrassing aspect?"

His teasing smirk sends burning colors to my face. After the way I insulted him yesterday, he's still smiling as though I never fell from his good grace. I keep inciting arguments over nothing and he keeps coming after me. The arrangement is too familiar except this time, I'm Jin. Having perceived both sides, I don't know whom I've offended worse, Jin or Han Bei.

He inches a little closer and on impulse, I move back.

"I-I did not say those things! You're making things up!"

"You were asleep, how would you know? Do you actually remember your dream?"

"Well... no."

"Then there you have it."

"W-Well, even if I did say those things, you should have waked me sooner."

"You seemed so happy, I didn't have the heart."

"Thanks, I think."

Leaning back, Han Bei stares at the large portrait of Dong Xing overhead. His smile turns ambiguous. I wonder whether he came to find her or me.

"Do you always wear your thoughts on your face?"

"Huh?"

Han Bei gazes back meaningfully. "I came to find *you*. I thought you'd enjoy a stroll around the city."

"Yes, I'd love to!"

"Another day. You were sleeping on these cold floors to dull the pain in your back, am I right? Specifically, in this secluded hall so no one would notice."

"I'm fine now, really! I want to see the capital!"

"There will be plenty of time for sightseeing later."

He lies down on the cold floor, upturning his eyes toward Dong Xing. My back is still sore, so I take a similar pose a distance away from Han Bei.

"Is Your Highness genuinely shy after having such pleasant dreams?"

"I still think you made everything up."

"Why would I do that?"

"Because... you're mean."

He chuckles quietly as though admitting to the fault. The smooth tone of his voice suddenly forces unrest in my heart. My eyes close to conceal embarrassment only to open again when his head bumps against mine. He's moved next to me, so close in fact, that I can feel warm heat radiating from his firm body. My anxiety spreads a pleased smile across his face.

"You grew up in a temple but you're still nervous around men?"

"Only around men who see me as a woman. At Tian Mao Yi, I did my best to conceal my gender."

"It's nigh impossible a man can ever fully see a woman as another man."

"Maybe. They did eject me after Master Tai Hung passed because I was viewed a distraction."

"You were alone for awhile?"

"A bit more than a year."

He sighs disappointedly. "I tried locating you but my trackers didn't have any luck. Several times, I even infiltrated Nan Rong and returned empty-handed. I was afraid you would be lost to Ning forever. And now, here you are. How does it feel to be home?"

"Awkward and lonely at first. Not anymore because of you. Thank you for trying to find me. It's conceited on my part but I am happy to know someone, aside Master Tai Hung, cared that I existed all these years."

"If only I'd found you first. Tell me more about this elusive temple. Where is it?"

"To the south of the capital, northwest of Pa Xu Village in Hong Long Province. It's a very tiny area, often overlooked on most maps."

"Tai Hung knew exactly where to hide you. At least you were safe. Was life at temple difficult?"

"It had its ups and downs. For a long time, life was just constant. Unchanging. Boring, I suppose, but comforting. What about you? How has life been in Ning—beside from... you know?"

"Beside from your sister? Most of my early life revolved around her. We were inseparable until we weren't. Ning, likewise, has gone through various transformations before reaching current status. I guess you can say my life has been the opposite of yours. Everything changed when I wanted constancy. Except recently. Recently, things have been constant and I've searched for change."

"What type of change?"

His head tilts in my direction. A gentle smile curls over his mouth. Of late, I've been hoping for constancy after the abrupt changes from my vacillating relationship with Jin. Han Bei and I are in want of what the other can offer. The insinuating thought is too unbearable; heat is seared onto my face due elation and frustration. I seek retreat only to once again be trapped in his arms.

"You don't have to run away."

His embrace grows and against reservations, I accept his comforting warmth. I don't want to keep running away when he's merely suggesting to pull me from dejection. Once my shoulders slump, I hear him let out a soft exhale.

"Here, this is for you." Han Bei reaches for the dagger latched to his ankle and then gently places it atop my chest. The cool metal of the scabbard is engraved with the Zhao family crest. I can't grasp why this wonderful gift is mine.

"In case I'm not near to protect you and Yuan, at least you'll still have my blade."

Men who know my gender don't often see me as being capable and certainly, don't think that I can defend myself. Both Kang Lang and Han Bei seem to have a more lenient view. They tend to judge capabilities based on comparable strength and talent more so than gender. Ning men are a different breed and I am honestly glad to have Han Bei's trust.

"Thank you. I'll keep it with me, always."

"You seem happy."

"I am! This is one of the nicest gifts I've ever received! Second only to the Huang Jia Feng Huang."

Squeezing me playfully, he bursts into abrupt laughter. "You really are strange! We may be a warring country but most women wouldn't be on the verge of tears over a dagger."

"It's fine craftsmanship! Who wouldn't appreciate quality smithwork? When I was a kid, I wanted to join the army and become a general. My fall back plan was to become a swordsmith."

"That's the most adorable thing I've ever heard."

"What is that supposed to mean? You don't think I could?"

"Oh, I know you can. Your stubbornness will permit you to do anything. It doesn't change how adorable you are."

His forehead bumps against my temple and then a short peck lands on my cheek. I don't know why he thinks I'm adorable when he's obviously more charming. If he keeps up this friendliness, I might genuinely have a heart attack.

"W-Well, what did you wanted to be when you grew up, Han Bei?"

"Isn't this conversation more fitting for children? Even then, I knew exactly what I was meant to become. Regrettably, life's path isn't always a straight line."

I asked another obvious question. He expected the daunting task of becoming emperor. However, without Dong Xing, he's taken the burden of leadership without the reward. The horrid latent idea emerges again. I could change everything for the better, not just for him, but also for me. I just don't know if I can.

During the awkward pause, I fumble the dagger between my hands. The weight of the hilt, the balance of the weapon, even the glistening fine metalwork is all too mesmerizing. My fingers run over the raised lines on the scabbard, tracing along the delicate curves of the beautifully crafted Zhao crest until something odd suddenly catches my eye. Beneath the crest are these words inscribed in gold: *for my heart.*

Don't tell me Dong Xing gave him this or worse, this was a gift to her. Most women aren't in tears over a dagger, did that include my sister? My stomach's in a knot. Shyly, I glance over and then raise the scabbard.

"Han Bei, to whom was this message for?"

His brows crease as though noticing those words for the first time. Han Bei jolts up and then runs his fingers over the raised lines.

"My sister gave this to you, didn't she?"

His strained reaction takes me by surprise; as though I'd sent a hand across his face.

"After everything, you still doubt me?"

"N-No. If you didn't know the inscription was there, then she must have—"

"This has been a Zhao family heirloom for over two hundred years. I've entrusted to you my most prized possession, so before you start accusing me of being heartless, at least consider giving me the benefit of the doubt!"

"I-I didn't mean you were!"

"Just inconsiderate, then? No conscience whatsoever? No pride as a gentleman?"

"That's not it at all! Han Bei, I'm sorry! I..."

What is wrong with me? Why do I keep doing this to him? Am I copying Jin or was he right, I'm placing Jin's transgressions on his shoulders and doubting him for every little thing? Either way, I'm too ashamed to look up.

He falls silent and reels back resentment to regain composure. Once he manages to swallow his pride, Han Bei lays the dagger on the floor.

"So am I," is his final response before retreating from Xiao Xiang.

Chapter 39: The Trials

A set of armor was sent to my chamber this morning; heavy armors to be exact. One gauntlet alone weighs as much as two small watermelons. We haven't even started and Han Bei's already attempting to intimidate me; though, even before the suit arrived, I was worried. My wounds are healed for the most part and Lady Mai provided some numbing topical; however, due to recent idleness, my muscles have grown weak. Should he intend for us to engage in combat, besides from the fact that I could never defeat him, a few swings are all it would take to immediately put me at disadvantage.

I've been sitting on the sofa fumbling with the helmet; my heels thumping against the obsidian-colored floors. He sure is taking his time, unless testing my patience is part of his plan. Just as aggravation sends me to my feet, the door swings open and Han Bei leisurely walks in.

"Are you ready?" The taut tone mirrors his stern eyes.

Following my response of a short nod, the Grand General leads the way. I scuttle behind, stuffing the helmet onto my head. It, too, weighs as much as a melon. Little did I understand the armor was truly significant to the trials.

Chapter 39 – 2

"Where are we going?"

Heaving sharp breaths, my pace forcibly quickens to avoid losing sight of him. We leave the palace and walk from the main part of the city toward the west, where a large dirt path eventually leads to an area of farmland. Aside from the beating sun, this heavy suit of armor, which has grown heavier with each step, is making me sweat from lack of ventilation. Han Bei makes no exception and employs his usual speed. By the time we stop, my legs are burning from fatigue.

"Here," he finally replies. "You'll stay here until sunset. If you leave or become idle, the test is over."

I wave my arms to circulate air inside the suit while breathing sharply to replenish my lungs. As I scan the scene, there are numerous other men adorned in the same armor, toiling in the fields alongside farmers and farmhands. He must have sent this suit so I could hide my identity and to emphasize that out here, I'm every soldier's equal.

"What exactly do you want me to do?"

"Work the fields like everyone else."

"But... shouldn't I learn to prepare for battle?"

"When our soldiers train, they don't always beat each other senseless in the barracks. That will come later if you manage to survive the day. Fieldwork—manual labor—builds endurance and strength. At the same time, the soldiers' energies are put to good use. Captain Xian will direct your tasks for today. I will return at sunset to pass judgment. Why so solemn? Do you wish to withdraw?"

"N-No, General. I'll be here when you return."

"Don't disappoint me." That's all he says before returning down the road.

We haven't spoken much since the awkward event from Xiao Xiang. He's come to visit a few times but the growing distance between us is palpable. Some days, while we sit together on the balcony, he just pretends I don't exist. Maybe I should avoid him since I'm a bother, but I can't. I find his company comfortable. Secretly, I love the sound of his voice. Whenever he addresses me, I feel a bit giddy. Whenever he laughs, I can't restrain from smiling along.

Just now when we walked together, I couldn't keep from noticing his lovely red hair, and in this instance of his retreat, I'm still in awe watching him from this angle. While shamelessly staring after Han Bei, someone from behind startles me.

"Ahem!"

A familiar face comes hither. That dark hair of his glows almost faint gold in the sunlight. Hazel irises surround dark, sharp pupils. His skin tone is unusually pale for someone who certainly spends much time outside. I only know him as the man who injured me upon first coming to the palace: Captain Xian. He discerns my bitterness against his previous assault and though his lips are a firm line, his eyes are clearly mocking me.

"Are you the new recruit Lord Han Bei sent?" Xian tilts his head curiously to the side, peering closely at my face in a boyish manner. His taunting stare is now replaced by complete ignorance.

A crooked smile inadvertently creeps over his mouth when my glare turns wrathful. Xian pulls a list from his pocket and then pretends to search for my name.

"Well, let me see. Lord Han Bei's recruit; not tall, not strong or smart, impulsive, reckless, and oblivious. Here you are. Your name is Tui Tui."

"Tui Tui? What kind of a ridiculous name is that?!"

"Isn't that your name?" He asks innocuously. "Or, should I call you Dong Xing since Lord Han Bei would not tolerate this foolishness from any other woman?"

What is his problem? I can understand that he wants to undermine my position, but must he bring my sister into this? Yet, she is my sister. Why am I angry to hear her name, or was it Xian's implication that makes my blood boil?

He tries to hide it; though briefly, I saw the look of victory surfaced. I don't doubt Han Bei's plan to test me in the fields. Xian, on the other hand, is trying to rile me so I'd quit before the trials begin. Obstinacy and temper refuse to let that happen.

"Yes, I am Tui Tui! What should I do first, Captain?"

Xian stares sulkily for a short moment and then pretends to run through his list again.

"Since you're as stubborn as a mule," he sighs, "let's see how you like being one."

Xian points to a section of field on my right. Five soldiers are struggling to move a plow stuck in the wet earth and the poor water buffalo tied to the plow isn't having better luck. I was glad it rained last night since my sleep was peaceful. Who knew the very thing that had put my mind at ease will now cause me grief? If five men twice my size can't move the plow, adding me in won't help much. However, that concern is frivolous when it becomes apparent he never intended for me to help.

"Lei, Kai, Nan, Qi, Jing!" Xian calls out. "Go assist the men in section seven."

"Yes, Captain!" The men call back.

After they leave, the Captain, smirking mischievously, turns to me. "Tui Tui, get in there and move that plow. Once you do, have this entire section plowed before sundown."

"Are you kidding me?!"

"No. Any more out of you besides, 'Yes, Captain!' and I'm failing you. Got it?"

There are no words to describe how much I want to throw my gauntlets at his face! Glowering, I slide down to the muddy field and attempt to move the plow. Figures! Even if it weren't stuck in a foot of mud, there's no way I could move it alone. Xian snickers at my failure. When I turn to confront him, he's disappeared.

It's not as if I didn't expect to do any real work today; after all, I wanted to prove my worth to Han Bei. I just didn't think the task would be impossible and my judge, a man formed from pure evil. What to do!

__Keep pushing the plow until it moves (Continue to page 504)__

__Survey the situation (Continue to page 505)__

Chapter 39 – 3

The more I push at the plow, the more I realize it is futile. Even so, I continue my failed efforts because there's nothing else to be done.

The heavy right boot slips. My footing is lost, sending me to the ground. My face is covered in mud. Then, I hear that irritating snickering of Captain Xian. He's watching, though from where, I don't know.

Chapter 39 – 4

It's pointless to continue. There's striving when a fraction of success is possible and then there's quitting because logic knows better. As much as I want to keep pushing the plow, my body lacks the strength to make any progress.

Aggravated, I walk around the buffalo and the plow to consider the circumstance. Should I manage to free the blade, albeit this section of land is not very large, the wet earth might still be too demanding for the buffalo. I feel bad for the old and thin creature. We're just two weak beings expected to do the impossible while evil finds humor in our predicament.

Sighing heavily, I reach down to brush some mud off my boots. What would even be the point of plowing a field this wet? The soil will just compact. Now, if this dirt becomes as dry as the globules I'm prying off my armor, the task would be more manageable. Then again, why couldn't it? The sun overhead is beating down furiously and there's not a cloud in the sky.

Falling to my knees, I begin scooping wet earth away from the plow using the metal gauntlets. At ten minutes, my arms are pained and at fifteen minutes, my shoulders are sore. But, I can't stop. The moment I do, the dull pain will become something worse and I won't be able to start again.

"To the east, the elder star lies. The younger's name is Bao Lai!" In order to distract from the pain, I hum the song Master Tai Hung once taught me. Until coming here, I never understood the elder star to be my sister Dong Xing, and the younger is Bao Lai, me. He'd meant to hint at my past all these years. I wonder what kept him from telling me before he passed.

At the thought of my master, my eyes are misting again. I miss him. He did so much for me and I'll never have the chance to repay his kindness. Had I known he was actually my grandfather, I could have overlooked the awkwardness of his holy status and told him the truth. I loved my grandfather dearly. I hope he knew.

With my mind occupied, the notion of physical pains is displaced. Finally, after an hour, I stagger to my feet and urge the buffalo to move. The hapless creature drudge forward while I push the blade with what little strength is left. Slowly and painstakingly, the blade budges a small fraction, then an inch, and then a little more. I stumble to the ground as overbearing heat and fatigue consume every inch of me. By some miracle, we were able to free the plow.

Once his harness is undone, the buffalo and I make for the shade of a nearby tree. Along the way, I notice how firmer the earth feels. It's still not ideal but at least my boot doesn't sink as deeply as before. There's no helping it. I'll have to wait this out. If the excruciatingly hot sun keeps up, late afternoon, the buffalo and I may have a chance to plow the field. However, if the sun retreats behind unexpected clouds or if rain comes again, I'll have to admit defeat. I wonder if Xian knows something I don't.

The moment his loathsome face comes to mind, the Captain jumps down from a branch above and scare the life out of me. That's how he's been watching all this time!

"Are you giving up, Tui Tui? Lord Han Bei said you couldn't idle or I'd have to fail you."

"I-I wasn't. I'm not idling! This is part of my plan!"

"What plan?"

Is it just me or did his irises change color? They were hazel earlier, weren't they? Unless something is wrong with *my* eyes, his are now grey and threatening!

"I freed the plow but the field is still too wet. I'm waiting for the earth to firm up before starting."

"You're betting everything on the weather?"

"Yes. I'm not idling. Is there something else you want me to do in the meantime?"

Xian stares back, half-dazed. I'm really afraid he might fail me; more so, I'm afraid to disappoint Han Bei.

"I see. Call it what you will, I call it idle. If you expect to continue, then make yourself useful. Fetch water from the well and bring it around. It's hot out."

"Yes, Captain!" Followed by, *"Obvious,"* which is muttered to myself.

"What was that?"

Ignoring Xian, I run toward the nearby lodgings where the well resides. It's so hot, I can't stand this armor! Even after drowning myself with water from the well, it's still too hot.

Just imagine everything the soldiers must endure day in and day out! This is their livelihood. They're not allowed to fail. In some cases, such as being on the battlefield, failure means death. I may only suffer for today and if I don't pass the test, then simply return to the palace and enjoy living in the lap of luxury. For all my complaints and gripes, I have it pretty good.

Then again, this is not the time to loathe myself. It's a chance to see the adversity Ning citizens must face. If it can't be helped and I must officially take the crown, it's my duties to do right by the people; not just the soldiers, but everyone.

With buckets latched to the carrier, I tread to the fields. It warms my heart to see the men so happy just from a few ladles of water.

"Drink as much as you want. You're no good to anyone if you pass out, right?"

I smile at a young man who shies to take a full drink from the half-empty bucket. Modesty, something else I never expected of soldiers.

"Mr. Liu. You drink first and then I'll take my fill." The young man passes the ladle to an older gentleman nearby. The farmer receives the consideration with happy smiles. Afterwards, the young man drains the remainder.

Ning's army is really something special, beyond the brute force they can employ. I've never seen soldiers and civilians on such friendly, equal terms. I suppose once a soldier knows the faces of the people he must defend, the effort spent is greater.

Sighing from simple satisfaction, he grins. "Are you new? I've never seen you before."

"Who me? I'm... Tui Tui. Nice to meet you."

"I'm Niu. Nice to meet you, too. Do you want some help?"

"No, Captain Xian won't approve. I can manage."

"He wouldn't mind. The Captain is very nice." Niu replies earnestly.

"Nice? *Him*? Captain Obvious?!"

Confused by my outburst, Niu gawks curiously. I chuckle nervously and then, parting from Niu, make my way back to the well. 'Nice,' he said. The only nice thing Xian has done was not failed me for resting fifteen seconds under a tree. Oh well, I need to stop griping. It's not useful to anyone.

Chapter 39 – 5

For the next few hours, I run back and forth from the well and across the massive fields. Strange, the heavy exercise doesn't feel taxing. Conversations along the way and appreciative smiles on everyone's faces make the task easier.

At the temple, I carried water and did chores too, but it was expected of me to earn my stay. Due to my gender, a few monks were always irritated by my presence and a few more pretended I didn't exist at all. I wonder whether this camaraderie will extinguish should anyone here, besides Captain Xian, discover the truth under my disguise. Aside from gender, my title is probably more frightening than anything.

Title, another foreign aspect. I say it with ease, but I don't honestly feel it belongs to me. I'm used to being a nobody from Nan Rong. During my time as He Pi, around San An, I had to be proper; maybe, even put on slight airs. Around the generals, I had to put up my guards. And, around Jin, I had to walk on pins and needles. Jin... just the thought of him crushes my spirit. I still can't understand him and for all my rationalizations of his past and present, his intentions escape me. Did he run away because it was the only method he knows how to love? Or, was I too clingy? I couldn't let him go and maybe, that's why he left.

Should we ever meet again, a few words are all it would take to change his opinions of me; a few more would change them back. Ultimately, whether Jin and I end up together will rely on my choices more so than his. I only wonder if the best thing I can do for Shu Jin is to relinquish our ties.

After the last round is made, I place the buckets next to the well and then return to the section of field where my test remains incomplete. The earth is noticeably firmer now, but it's still not dry enough. If I force the buffalo, the blade might jam again. Should that happen, there isn't enough sunlight left in the day to dislodge it a second time and still hope to complete my task. Speaking of the sun, it's less hot now, meaning this is probably the best I can hope for. I'm going to fail, that is the most plausible outcome considering how late it is. Well, at this point, there's no harm trying. It's better than sitting around and being useless, which was the very thing I'd intended to avoid.

The dull pains in my back and shoulder return the moment I swing down the hoe. I hum a song to drown out the demoralizing thoughts; increasing the volume as the pains deepen. What started out as a soft tune turns into loud, obnoxious bellows.

"Do you want something to eat?"

"Ahh!"

"You're all nerves!" Niu laughs teasingly when I almost keel over from embarrassment. "Maybe you should rest."

I turn to him, pale as a ghost. Please tell me he didn't hear my horrible singing. I must have been mouthing my thoughts again because the young man grins knowingly. Instead of mocking my lack of talent, Niu holds out a handful of coconut steamed rice inside banana leaves.

"N-No. I'm fine. Thanks."

"Are you sure? Captain Xian's wife made this. It's delicious."

"Captain Xian has a wife?!" I'll admit Xian is handsome in his own way, but to marry him, she must be a saint!

"She must be a saint!" A hand flies over my mouth the moment the thought escapes into words. "I-I mean... she must be a lady."

"She is." Niu smiles. "Miss Hua Ye is over there if you'd like to meet her."

Niu points toward a fair-haired lady, dressed so prim and proper that she appears no less than a celestial maiden from a silk scroll. Her hair is long and flowing, the light robe fits her lithe figure perfectly, and her dainty little feet move just so, that she seems to be floating across the ground. In moments, she notices my incessant gawking and turns to acknowledge me with a grand smile across rosy painted lips. There's something very familiar about that face, though I can't put my finger on it.

The more I stare, the more jealous I become of her fine figure. Ever since coming to Ning, except for today, I've dressed as a lady. However, compared to a true lady, I still feel like a brute. Well, even compared to the cross-dressing Mu Dan, I still feel inferior. Oh wait, now I remember.

"She looks just like Kang Lang!" Once more, the words fly out of my mouth without discretion.

"Hmm?" Niu stares at the pretty Miss Hua Ye, rubbing his chin while he ponders.

"I-I'm sorry. I didn't mean she looks manly. It's just that, their faces are very similar."

"Well, I wouldn't see why not? Miss Hua Ye is the only cousin to Lords Kang Lang and Han Bei. Beauty runs in their bloodline."

"I had no idea."

"You really must be new! Everyone knows Miss Hua Ye! Her humility is famous amongst the nobles and common alike."

"How so?"

Niu gives my ignorance a curious once over. Then, putting on a scholarly countenance, he begins matter-of-factly. "Lord and Lady Zhao of Han Xing weren't blessed with female heirs. As you know, our matriarchal laws dictate the next eldest female stands to inherit their fortune. Miss Hua Ye was the only candidate. Both Lords Han Bei and Kang Lang were bound to lose everything. 'The law is unfair,' she said. So she gave up her title and became Miss Hua Ye after marrying a simple foot soldier."

"So... she broke the law?"

"Yes, essentially. Due to her former rank, she escaped punishment and also for her rank, everyone outside of noble circles applauded her courage. Reverence, to nobles, is fashionable. I hear many have married commoners lately to be in fashion, though I doubt they gave up their wealth, too."

"Huh. I've heard in some Nan Rong provinces, those social rules are also true but in favor of male heirs, where a man could inherit his uncle's estate given that his uncle has no son, and leave nothing to his female cousins. Although I'm glad Ning highly respects women, there remains an inherent disadvantage to the opposite gender."

"Some would call Ning progressive," Niu chuckles.

"From what I've seen, I would say the same. In terms of parents stripped of their rights to provide for their children only because of the child's gender, that is wholly unfair. I'm still unfamiliar with all of Ning's laws but I will definitely change that law to be more just."

He returns my words with an incredulous stare and then shortly after, an amused smile. The reason escapes me until I look down and spot my black gauntlets. I'm supposed to be in disguise. He must think I'm crazy for sounding so confident.

With my cheeks burning, I look about for a change of subject and manage to catch sight of Hua Ye in happy conversation with Captain Xian under the shade of a willow tree. When they're together, he seems less evil somehow.

"Ahem. So... does Miss Hua Ye cook for the soldiers often?"

"Fairly often. Some days, Captain Xian cooks for us too. We all agreed not to tell him how terrible his cooking is; if he does bring one of his dishes, just nod and play along." The last part Niu whispers before breaking to a hearty laugh.

"I'll keep that in mind. Well, I have to finish plowing this area before sunset. Thanks for talking with me, I really do appreciate it."

"You're doing this by hand? Why don't you have the buffalo plow the field?"

"Do you think he'd manage? This earth is still wet."

"I think it's plenty dry." Niu stomps the ground with his left foot a few times and then nods again reassuringly.

The water buffalo I'd left by a copse is sleeping soundly. His tail swats a few flies away and then he seems to let out a contented sigh. He reminds me of an old man—Master Tai Hung to be exact, during afternoon naps he sometimes took at the Lotus Pavilion.

"The poor thing could use the rest. I'll be fine."

I resume the field. After lingering for a short while, Niu retreats. Moments later, to my surprise, several echoes of metal striking earth are propping up around me. I turn about to find a group of men nearby, including Niu, working the ground to upturn the earth.

"Hey wait! You can't help me!"

"Why?" Niu stares innocently. "You brought water when we were thirsty, why can't we help you?"

"Because..." I can't mention anything about the trials or things will become awkward. "Captain Xian assigned this lot to me."

"Did he say you can't ask for help?"

"Well, no. Not specifically."

"Then, don't worry about it."

The others give similar encouraging smiles. They must be so tired and still, they're willing to break their backs a while longer for someone they hardly know. I choke back a few tears and then clamp down quivering lips to hide the weak reaction. I'm so touched by their camaraderie!

For what it's worth, I am really glad Xian is such a jerk; otherwise, I would not have met these fine people.

Chapter 39 – 6

The section was finished in record time and after much urging, I took a handful of steamed rice from Niu. It's not that I was too proud to take Miss Hua Ye's treats at first; I just felt guilty. I eat well at the palace. It's wrong to take others' meager portions, too. That was until I saw their disappointed faces. I see now that refusing their goodwill is no less than an insult.

While enjoying the sweet rice with my new comrades under the shades, I could sense the care and thought put into its preparation. Everything about the simple snack is sublime; from the perfect wrapping to the rice fragranced with a hint of jasmine and coconut shavings. She must be some woman, this Hua Ye, to have won Xian's heart. A man like that requires someone gentle to smooth out his rough edges and turn him into the tamed creature I saw under that willow tree. In some ways, Han Bei is similar. He can be offensive and vicious but I know he's also kind at heart and charmingly sweet.

Soon after his sarcastic smirk comes to mind, Han Bei wanders hither.

"Come with me," he calls out.

All I can do is give an unassuming smile to the curious soldiers and then do as the Grand General requests. He takes little notice of me before starting down a dirt path.

We walk a fair distance away from the fields to an area void of people. The land here is flat and stable with very little grass. Above, the stars have come out in a light net of sparkling jewels. Han Bei, upon halting, pitches a sheathed sword toward me, which I barely catch.

"Eh? What's this for?" Ignorance is feigned out of anxiety.

"You freed the plow and then manually plowed the field with others' help. Xian disagrees with your approach."

"He didn't say I *had* to use the plow and he never forbade me from asking for help."

"You understood his intentions and still discovered technicalities to counter his instructions. I haven't seen Xian this agitated since he mistook Kang Lang for Hua Ye." Han Bei pauses, chuckling softly from the triggered memory which I can only imagine to be fantastic. "Since the result was conflicted, this will be your last test. Don't expect any mercy from me."

Han Bei unsheathes his frightening blade. The metal glistens a shade of crimson resembling his fiery hair. The moment the tip is pointed in my direction, my breathing grows shallow. Is he serious? I thought he might, though I was really hoping he wouldn't. There's no way I can defeat him! Not in this state of exhaustion I'm in. Not ever!

"B-B-But! The sun's already set! Xian didn't outright failed me and you said if I made it to the end of the day—"

"The day's not over. Not until midnight. You want to play war? Then let's play. As weary as you are, imagine the sensation ten times worse. Little nourishment, no sleep, and constant marches. Add to that, the fear of battle and ambush. It's not enough to know how to swing a sword but to hold a weapon knowing your life and the lives of your comrades depend on it. Beyond all that, the steeled nerves to take a life. Can you do it?"

A lump forms in my throat. My response of enduring silence turns Han Bei's expression severe. This trial was a waste of his time. Nevertheless, he's determined to give me the chance.

"Let's just see what you're capable of." Though his words are seemingly encouraging, a sarcastic smile curls over his lips. "Don't make that face. Do you think this is unfair? In battle, you won't just meet people in your league. You may find yourself surrounded by men of my standard who will not hesitate to end you. As I've said, don't expect any mercy from me. Do you wish to continue?"

I understand everything he's trying to convey. At the moment, I'm not certain whether I can take a life. However, the people I met today have made me realized how important Ning is and how important Ning should be to me. I refuse to cower in the palace while they risk their lives for my protection.

"I do."

"Then draw the blade or die!"

The Grand General dashes forward at lightning speed. I don't have enough time to draw out the blade so I lift the entire sword, sheathe and all, to block the strike. He can say whatever he wants, I know he's holding back, and his strength, as reserved as it was, made my whole body quake. My arms are numb! I can't even imagine how he's capable of doing that. It's inhuman!

With a sharp kick, Han Bei knocks me to the ground and follows with another strike. He barely misses me. I roll away and then stagger to my feet. Giving no quarter, another strike is brought down and then another, along with kick after kick from his large boot. My body is bruised. I can barely stand while he's unrelenting. Obstinacy is the only thing keeping me from capitulating.

After several more bouts, he moves back to allow a short moment of rest. My lungs are burning and my chest, heaving. I can't keep this up! The thought has entered my mind but I can't stall this match until midnight; my body just doesn't have the strength to constantly evade his attacks. I must defeat him, somehow.

Once my stance is resumed, Han Bei lunges forward, nearly piercing me with his blade. I stagger aside, after which, his elbow sends me reeling to the ground.

A sudden sharp cry disrupts the calm night air. Han Bei freezes in place.

"My arm! I think you broke my arm!"

Han Bei turns pale. Flustering, he drops the crimson blade and then runs to my side.

"Don't touch it! You'll make it worse!"

"Let me see!"

He reaches for my arm but I draw back. Agitated, he leans over me to inspect the injury. Sucker! With a sharp jerk of my knee—metal knee guard and all—into his sensitive area, Han Bei keels over in tormented agony. Immediately reaching for my sword, I straddle on top and hold it over him. After what feels like an eternity, he regains composure and then looks up. First, there's pain, followed by fury, and then something else entirely different I can't describe enters his expression.

"You fight dirty," he frets.

"So? You never said I couldn't. I win, right?"

He frowns at my grin. His hand knocks away my sword. Han Bei grabs the straps of my breastplate and rolls over, taking the top position.

"You can't cheat, Han Bei! That's my privilege! I've won! Just admit it!"

Instead of rebuffing my protest, he silences me. With his hands clutching mine, Han Bei presses a deep kiss so excruciatingly thrilling, I can't find the will to fight him. I've never experienced such ardent, burning passion formed perfectly into one sweet, tempting kiss. This is how it must feel to truly be desired, even when the person he desires isn't me. Once he's stolen my last ounce of air, supple lips travel to my cheek and then down toward my neck, sending unbridled shivers of excitement and expectation down my spine.

"S-Stop... no, Han Bei, stop."

The unconvincing words choke their way out in a breathless whisper. He yields. Emerald eyes then bear into mine.

"Why? Your lips tell me to stop while everything else is begging for more. If your only obstacle is your wavering boyfriend, the same man who's probably found enjoyment with another by now, then keep crying your pretense objections. It'll make you feel better. That way, you'll still be faithful."

"You—What is your problem?! How can you keep kissing me so freely when you don't feel anything? Is it that easy?! Or, do you see her every time you look at me? For the last time, I'm not my sister!"

"And for the last time, I know you're not Dong Xing!" He shouts back, more pained than angry.

To hear him say her name feels nothing short of a knife to my chest. Every time I think of his love for her and his lust for other women, it infuriates me to no end. And, lately, whenever I'm apart from him for too long, an indescribable ache torments me. I've spent my days thinking of him and nights dreaming of his touch. I know what this is, but I don't want to admit the awful truth. Even just now, when I've told him to stop, my body is trembling from anticipation and I wish he hadn't ceased.

Piercing green eyes beholding me are lovelier than all the stars above. His marble skin puts the pale moon to shame. Amidst the veil of darkened skies, his red hair, which drapes over broad shoulders, is too enchanting; I can't look away. While I'm tempted to accept every passion he has to offer in this perfect scene, other tumults serve to force away desires.

"Han Bei, I appreciate your effort to comfort me but this is not appropriate. You love someone else and so do I. Us being together won't change anything. We'll still be miserable, lonely souls in the morning."

"I have not been miserable or lonely since you've been by my side." He replies faintly.

"Speak honestly, whom are you staring at so lovingly? Bao Lai or Dong Xing?" My lips involuntarily quiver, fearful of the response.

"If you expect my honesty, then be honest with me."

His glance averts for a time into the distance. Before long, they return to me and then hesitantly, he carefully begins sating my reservations.

"At first... At first, I don't know whom I saw. You can't imagine the torment your face has brought me. I loved her, so I despised you, and then I admired you, so I resented her. Now, I only see Bao Lai. It's been so long, the faded memories of my youthful adoration for Dong Xing are barely present in the back of my mind. More than that, when I recall her cruel rejection of my worship, I don't understand why I loved her at all. She was, for the most part, conceited, spoiled, and weak. That's why she wanted someone strong; I wasn't that person. I changed everything for her, but even now, I'm still weak in other ways. What I mean is... I need *you*."

"I'm not strong." The bitter reply falls in a soft whisper. Though his confession makes me happy, I'm ashamed for feeling the elation. Why couldn't I have met Han Bei first, before Jin? The latter will make me wait my whole life for a possibility and I'll be chasing after him until either I give up or he gives in. How is that love? Jin blatantly said he doesn't love me. Wasn't that painfully clear enough? Perhaps... I should just accept Han Bei.

What am I saying? That's a terrible thought! Jin needs me!

"I need you!" Han Bei repeats the declaration as if reading my mind. His pale cheeks are flushed red and though I must have imagined it, saw his lips trembled.

I've shamelessly flaunted in front of him and persistently vied for his attention. He's tried to avoid me but I've kept pushing. Now that we're in this predicament, why am I surprised? Guilt was mine the moment I made him abided me to distract the dejection I felt from Jin's dismissal.

I stare at him, begging for forgiveness, and he stares back, as though begging to be spared.

Time stands still until the heated moment is disrupted by a strong breeze that sweeps over the scene. Given the opportunity, a crooked smile appears on my face. "We're friends and you're my council. Naturally, we'll always be there for each other."

His dulcet expression is suddenly buried under rage. Han Bei grips my hands harder. "I gave you my honesty and you would return it with more excuses?! I will be here for you but neither as friend nor council! Tell me once and for all, do you love me?"

Confronted with the disgrace I tried to hide, my chest begins heaving as blood storms through my veins. My heart is twisted into a knot. Unknowingly, his rage triggers my rage.

"You have some nerve asking me that when you don't love me! You said so yourself!"

"I lied!" He spits the words and then immediately withdraws as though the act was a mistake.

Bewildered, I silently beckon for a reason. I dearly hope it's not because I protected him.

Whether he could construe my unspoken request, aside from anguish that discharges as an aggravated sigh, Han Bei says nothing more. His darkened eyes waver under the pale moonlight like two lost woeful stars. In time, he lifts off from me and then takes to the road at a slow enough pace so I can follow. As angry as he is, Han Bei still puts my safety before his pride.

Chapter 40: Put Him Out of His Misery

Although Captain Xian was adamant that I failed the trials, in the end, Han Bei judged otherwise. True to his words, the Grand General permitted me to train with the soldiers. At first, I wanted to prove my strength and earned my stay at the palace. Now that I've actually spent time with my people, I've come to understand that one soldier can only do so much while a sovereign can revolutionize an entire nation, the way my mother had during Ning's court conflicts.

However, Yuan also pointed out that if every law is changed based on the whims of the sovereign with no regards for tradition, our great nation may cease to exist. At the time, I thought him a difficult boy. Now, I understand the reason he laughed at me. It's always easy to recommend to others what I don't have to worry doing myself. I still believe that change is necessary but caution is best utilized else idealism falls in the same lot as naiveté.

Once I was admitted to Captain Xian's unit, my time in the barracks and civil services in the cities were secretly spent gathering information, opinions, and recommendations. It's my goal to keep Ning powerful without resorting to control every aspect of the people's lives.

For the time being, Yuan is still sovereign despite his illegitimacy due to succession rules. I can't ascend to the title until he abdicates in my favor. He hasn't returned from Mount Guo. I don't blame him for stalling. This must be the first time in fourteen years he's had so much freedom. Still, I hope for a speedy return. I'm afraid to lead Ning but a part of me is also determined. With Han Bei's support and guidance, I'm willing to accept my role.

As for Han Bei, the only time we see one another nowadays is in the barracks. He's engrossed in the units' preparations so we rarely have time to converse. When we do have the chance, he remains friendly though his eyes are always distant. I've become to him as I'd requested: just another random person. Except now, I can't lie and say that this is what I truly want. In fact, I know that I would not spend so much of my leisure time in the barracks if he weren't there.

After having injured Han Bei through my insincerity, I'm still too selfish to look away and yet, too afraid to chase after desires for fear of having to admit treachery. The irony of egotism! I promised to love only Jin as my first and last. The crime of emotional infidelity is no less a betrayal.

"If you keep staring, he might lose composure."

The silky voice that gently flows into my ear suddenly throws breathing into variations. Flustered, I turn toward my right to find her pretty smile playfully teasing me in the subtlest manner. Her grey eyes smile with her, accentuating the charming flower face which carries that same natural beauty I've seen in Mu Dan.

528

"H-How's that?" I pointlessly try to deny. "I wasn't staring at anyone."

"No? Well! I certainly thought Han Bei seemed nervous for your attention. After all, aside from me, you're the only other woman here, Your Highness."

She whispers the last part into my ear, followed by a soft giggle. I start to ask how she knew; stopping once I decide Xian must have told her.

"I know what you're thinking. Xian didn't have to say a word. A woman knows."

"O-Oh. It's nice to meet you. I'm... Tui Tui."

The lady giggles again, in a much more elegant fashion than the girlish style Mu Dan usually employs. "Dear me! You share our cat's name? No wonder Xian is fond of you! He may complain but he secretly dotes on the naughty creature."

I don't have the chance to tell her how wrong she is when Hua Ye casually tugs at my sleeve and then signals for me to follow while retreating from the barracks, leaving me stranded mid-conversation. I feel like a fool for staring awkwardly into the distance, so I follow her.

Chapter 40 – 2

Past the azalea gardens, the waiting pond, and Ning's prized Phoenix Bridge, we then reach the Dream Pavilion. The dark-shingled canopy of the gazebo juts out on four corners, rising high into the air as though mimicking a phoenix taking flight. Surrounding the structure on three sides is a clear water lake carrying lovely round lotuses. Not far away, large willow trees growing near the water's edge extend their elongated arms into the pond, shifting along with the wind as if waving at us. Hua Ye sits daintily on the railings.

"Um... did you want to tell me something?" I begin.

Her dangling jeweled hairpins bobble whimsically in the swaying breeze. Her loose robe flutters gently like ripples in a pond. She gives a teasing grin and then taps the seat adjacent as to invite me over. It's strange, I'm usually nervous around women. For standing here dressed in Ning heavy armor next to a woman no less beautiful than the moon maiden, Chang'e, the discomfiture should be tenfold. Yet, I'm rather complacent. I wonder whether it's because she reminds me of Mu Dan or that I overcame my fear through finally seeing myself as a true woman, just as I've come to see myself as a citizen of Ning.

"Your Highness is too shy." She insists.

"Not at all. I can't swim. If I fall into the lake in this armor, I'll sink like a rock. You'll have to excuse my caution, Miss."

"Miss? Did I forget to introduce myself? Dear me! My name is Hua Ye. Captain Xian is my husband and my dear cousins are Lords Han Bei and Kang Lang."

"It's nice to meet you. I'm Bao Lai."

"Oh, I know all about you, dear." She responds in an almost motherly fashion. "When I heard from Xian that Han Bei was ill, I had to come see for myself."

"W-What are you talking about? Is Han Bei ill?!"

"How did Xian put it? *The Grand General has been suffering a rare case of infatuation. Just the sight of his pining makes me sick to my stomach. There's no saving him from wretchedness. Someone needs to put him out of his misery.*"

She conceals soft giggles, taunting and sweet in tandem, behind her long sleeves. "Oh, don't make that face. I can keep a secret, even if it's hardly a secret. Some women would kill to have Han Bei's attention and others would kill for not having it. My beloved cousin hasn't been the same since your return to Ning, Your Highness. And, neither have you. The skies were full of rainclouds when you came and have since cleared to a lovely hue, much like the colors of your cheeks whenever you steal a glance at Han Bei. Since the feeling is mutual, why not welcome happiness?"

"Are you... asking me to put him out of his misery?"

"In a sense, yes!" She laughs. Hua Ye lifts off the banister and then moves closer. "I understand your reservations. If I were you, I wouldn't feel any differently. In truth, although he loved Dong Xing, I never once thought he was in love with her. If anything, he worshipped her, placed her on a pedestal because she was a fine glass figure meant to be displayed. You are far from her, and I say that with the utmost respect. You are a flower he admires and a sharp blade only a warrior can appreciate. Whomever you both have loved in the past, those affections should remain in their times. Don't forfeit present happiness and future felicity solely to live in past misery."

I want to tell her that she's mistaken but I don't know how. During the trials, Han Bei bore to me his heart. There's not a part of me that still believes he confuses me for Dong Xing. I am the only one at fault.

The thought of Han Bei alone and in pain stings my heart. Ashamed, I look out into the lake and try to avoid her prying gaze, all the while, clearing my throat and furiously blinking to brush away the tears before Hua Ye can notice. I shouldn't cry when I'm the one who's hurt him.

"Why are you telling me this?"

"Because when I look at you, I see my cousin. Even after Dong Xing's death, he spent fourteen miserable years holding onto a love that was never meant to be;

hoping for unrequited love to be returned when it was impossible. I see that same listless look of despair in your eyes now. Whoever this man is who once loved you, if he wasn't willing to do everything to keep you, then he didn't deserve you."

"Then... if I'm not willing to give Han Bei everything, then I don't deserve him."

"Yes, that is also true." Hua Ye nods sharply. "That is why I truly am asking you to put him out of his misery. Break his heart and never look back or love him and be happy. This limbo where you've placed him is the same prison your former lover placed you. What has Han Bei done to warrant the punishment?"

"Nothing!" My heart thumps in my chest. I look down at the ground, ever more ashamed. I knew what I had been doing to Han Bei and now that my cruelty is exposed, I can't stand being seen.

To my surprise, the woman who had charged me for the crimes, draws a sleeve to wipe my eyes. I look up to see her soft smile so full of compassion that tears rain in torrents.

"Now, now. Don't cry. Love is always difficult at first."

"E-Even for you?"

"Gracious!" She laughs. "Xian is a dear but he didn't spare me any difficulties! Upon our introduction, I thought he was the most disagreeable person I'd ever met. Overtime, he became even more insufferable! I'd despised the man to the very core until Kang Lang made the conjecture that Xian was shy. So, I tested that theory. Every time he said a cruel thing, I'd returned it with kind words. And then, one day, he returned my kind words with unexpected ones... words of love."

She sighs wistfully. Faint blushes rise to her cheeks as though recollecting every moment of the scene. "Ning men only know war, so they tend to retaliate against their hearts when they lose control. He was such a dear! Fumbled about as if he thought up was down; trembled terribly. His face was a tomato!"

"I can't imagine that." The frown on my face sinks deeper.

"I know Xian's been particularly harsh, but he actually—"

"That's enough, Hua Ye." The Captain comes hither, irritated and faintly embarrassed for the more human picture his wife painted of him. He stands a distance away and frowns. However, the moment his eyes land on Hua Ye, something sweet surfaces and then overflows. He nearly smiled until taking notice of my gawking. Then, a frown returns and he lets out a sigh. "So, Tui Tui, will you put the poor beast out of his misery? He's no good to anyone with his head in the clouds; especially with conflict on the horizon, a clouded mind will cost him his head. You may always fall back to Nan Rong for safety. Ning doesn't have another

Grand General. Why did you come back just to be the death of us all?"

"Xian! That's a horrible thing to say!" Hua Ye snaps both hands to her hips.

Xian shrugs and then continues glowering in my direction. He obviously respects Han Bei. While I understand his anger, badgering me won't evoke any false promise.

"I will discuss the matter with Han Bei on my own terms, Captain."

"What you mean to say is you'll bait him farther along for your own amusement, no different from your sister. I wonder what Lord Han Bei could have done in his past lives to deserve the retribution of having to fall for the fickle women in your line. Maybe you'll leave him another ungrateful bastard to raise—"

"Xian!" Hua Ye shouts nervously. "I've lost my ruby hairpin! Maybe it fell in the water. Help me look."

Although she had addressed Xian, Hua Ye tugs me along toward the water's edge. I don't know why she bothers. The more Xian proves to be insufferable, the more I see how much he cares for his friend. I'm not offended because based on my shameless behaviors, he's probably right.

"Ah, there it is!" She suddenly shouts.

I look into the clear lake where she's pointed and can't find anything resembling a hairpin. Still, she insists, so I lean over farther until my chest is parallel to the pristine water.

"I don't see it."

Soon as the words leave my mouth, I'm staring at the sky from beneath the lake's surface. My hands reach upward while I continue sinking in the heavy armor. Muffled shouts echo from afar. My lungs are filling with water and the more I struggle, the shorter my breathing grows, allowing more to enter. Moments pass without any sign of relief. No one above will thrust down a helping hand. Is this the grave I dug for myself—my punishment for selfishness?

With the end in sight, my mind grows hazy with reminders of regret. An entire lifetime passes by in the blink of an eye. Too much of it was spent contemplating actions which never took form.

A familiar figure flashes before my eyes and the only thing I regret more than having wasted my life was having wasted his. I feel him there, so close to me, and yet I can't grasp his image. If my subconscious is finally able to form a resolve, I fear it is too late.

Chapter 40 – 3

I can die and leave my shame and worries. I won't have to face Han Bei for the pain I've caused him or confess to Jin that I've broken my promise. It's the coward's way out, fitting for me. Once my eyes close, all my transgressions will be cleansed to purity.

What a selfish thought! Dying is easy. Those left behind are the ones to suffer. I won't leave things to obscurity!

Mustering the last of my strength for a final effort, my arm flies upward. This time, a sturdy hand reaches out to yank me from beneath the lake's surface. Air quickly fills my lungs and I cough out half the lake. I'd barely resume steady breaths when his strong arms then embrace tightly. The water draining off my armor and hair stains his shirt while he pays no heed. With strength robbed from me, I collapse onto him. My face presses against his broad chest.

"H-Han Bei."

"Just hush!"

Though his gentle hand strokes my head, I can't stop trembling. He's being sweet again and I feel guilty for yearning more of his touch. I stagger away from Han Bei only to have him pull me back into his arms. The more I struggle, the stronger his embrace grows.

"Han Bei, don't."

"Why?"

"I'm fine. Thank you for saving me. I guess this means we're even now."

He returns my anxious chuckles with silence. Using the pause as diversion, escape was nearly successful until he snatches me into his arms.

"What did those two say to you?"

"N-Nothing. Where are they, anyway?" I scan the area and they're nowhere to be found.

"Xian asked me to meet him here. When she saw me, Hua Ye pushed you into the lake and then they both left. You shouldn't let your guard down near that woman. Xian may have a sharp tongue but she's deadlier than any poison."

"*She* pushed me?! What was the point of this, to kill me?"

"Unlikely. Since we were baited, my guess is to prove a point. I'll ask again, what did they tell you?"

And I had thought she was such a saint! I had to swallow half the lake for her to prove a point? What point could she have tried to prove? That Han Bei is here for me unlike Shu Jin? That despite my insults and injuries, Han Bei is still kind and forgiving? Or maybe, she meant for the incident to break this wall between us so we can overlook the awkwardness and finally end the charade.

"They told me things I already knew. Excuse me, I need to change out of these wet clothes."

The moment I start up, he seizes my hand.

"Why can't you be honest? You leave me with parts of truths and fragments of lies. You expect my honesty—my loyalty—when you aren't capable of either. Are you purposefully tormenting me? Why give me longing looks only to flee the moment I come close?"

"Because I'm too selfish to put you out of your misery."

For a long while, the air between us stagnates. Once it becomes apparent he understands my admission, I begin to move away. However, his arms tighten around me while his body bears down. In the next instant, his hands pin down mine. His lips rain sweet tempting kisses on my own, growing ever deeper, to take my breath away. When his lips finally withdraw, my body quakes and my chest heaves for air. His kisses travel over my cheek and neck, leaving every inch he touches to burning inferno.

"Han Bei..."

"Don't tell me to stop. I've had enough of your insincerity. This is your last chance. Accept me here and now or never again expect from me love and loyalty."

"You can't be serious! This is—"

"An ultimatum. You've been toying with me but I do have faults in this. I put the idea in your head and maybe, also in mine. That doesn't change the fact that I love you. I love everything about you but your vacillating desires. If you deny me, I will respect your wishes and keep my distance from now on."

Han Bei plants another kiss on my lips and then his face buries in my neck, sending unrestrained shivers over me. My body, throbbing from excitement, desperately craves more of him. My eyes close while a part of me yields.

Despite how tempting he is, the moment his fingers reach to undo my armor, I scurry back on impulse. We stare at one another, dumbfounded; his countenance growing bitter by the second. Alas, he withdraws.

"W-Wait, I..." but I can't finish the thought because there isn't a right thing to say. I can't accept him when a part of me still belongs to Jin. Neither can I ask to prolong his suffering. It's cruel.

Han Bei silently retreats, leaving me in the gentle serenity of a scene in which I can't find peace. This is the end. We were never lovers and yet, my heart is in a million pieces. He said he needed me. In truth, I need him more. His companionship, his love, his guidance. I took these things for granted and now that his regards have faded, I feel strayed. I've lost a part of me. The overwhelming sadness of which robs from me every tear welling inside. No matter how pained I am, I know he is enduring worse.

I'm so sorry, Han Bei. You're too good of a person to have suffered two unworthy women. If this is your last chance to be free, then my resolve will be to keep you from faltering.

Chapter 41: Wang Liang

In the following week, Bei Ling sent a small group to Mount Chou in order to distract Nan Rong from their larger force, which was sent to Lan Yue Pass by way of Feng Jia. Southern forces were able to route the diversion and pushed back the larger force. With Bei Ling's aggression escalating, a letter arrived from Nan Rong requesting reinforcements. Ning fulfilled her promise. Han Bei and Captain Xian prepared to march south, leaving General Liu in charge. I, after persuading Captain Xian that my ties to Nan Rong's court would be beneficial, was permitted to escort the group.

"Your Highness. Lord Han Bei. Welcome." San An comes to greet our caravan at the front gates along with his party and another familiar face I was hoping to find. Kang Lang throws a wide grin in my direction; sulking heftily when his eyes roll to Han Bei. The latter is little bothered by the indifference.

"You must be tired—"

"Please, spare me your false pleasantries." Han Bei brusquely interrupts San An. "It doesn't take an entire production to cause one man's demise. The sooner he is found, the sooner his life may end."

"I'm afraid it's not that simple, Lord Han Bei. However, if you wish to omit pleasantries, then please follow me to council. Qing Hai will show your men to the guard quarters."

Han Bei signals to Xian, who nods back. Then, the Grand General follows San An while the guards follow Qing Hai. I started to pursue the Minister's party when Kang Lang grabs my wrist and practically drags me toward the lily garden. Once we pass the short bridge outside of the entrance, his arms fly around me with the familiar bone-crushing fervor.

"Hey, girlfriend!" Kang Lang giggles. "Don't you look fancy! What's it like playing empress?"

"You dragged me here just to ask that?"

"I had more naughty things in mind but then I realized you're less attractive as a woman. Did you miss me?" He grins.

"I did, actually. Everyone said you returned to Nan Rong safely; I was still worried. I'm glad you're well and I really am thankful for everything you've done. Can I ask... why the change?"

My eyes run up and down his attire. He's no longer dressed as Mu Dan.

"We had an incident. Long story short, San An disbanded the Circle and I can't be the only pretty girl left alone. With all these dirty old men walking about, it's too dangerous."

"As if any dirty old man could put his hand on you and take it back without a few fingers broken."

"Thank you, you're too kind!" Kang Lang taps an index finger to my nose. "Come, I have news for you. Those pedantic old men and their council; they'll spend more time putting each other to sleep than anything."

Kang Lang saunters inside the lily garden with our arms linked together, after which, we rest on a stone bench under one of the tall dove trees. A mischievous smile suddenly curls over his face.

"I see. What do you want in return for the news?"

"You're so mean, Your Highness! We haven't even started and you're accusing me. Whatever makes you think I expect compensation?"

"A woman doesn't work for free!" I quote Mu Dan with a similar giggle.

His lips pucker and then Kang Lang scoffs. "Since you know me *so well*, before I reveal my secret, tell me yours."

"Why should I tell you anything when Han Bei is bound to relay San An's message?"

"Which message would that be? San An is conflicted. Since he came back, the Minister's been going on about not wanting to forfeit another brother—as if he even knows where Su Jian is—and the only advice the council can provide is where to find good taverns with busty wenches."

"You know where to find Su Jian?"

"That I do. I also know where to find good taverns with busty wenches." He winks. "What do you say?"

"You ask that as if I really have much of a choice."

"I'm giving you an illusion of freewill."

"Through indirect coercion? That is just like you. Fine. Which of my secrets do you want exposed?"

"Good girl. You know the one! I want to know how fickle you are."

"Pardon me?"

"Don't play coy. Here I thought you were a plain little thing and yet, you've managed to drive three men to madness. Four, if I were still interested. Did you know San An had new robes made and cologne brought in from Tiao? Ever since he knew you were returning to Nan Rong, he's planned... what was it Han said... a production."

"You miscounted. Anyway, this is the first time in many years emissaries from Ning have arrived in Nan Rong. I don't blame San An for demonstrating goodwill when our alliance is crucial."

"Tsk. Denial is an ugly mask." He sighs. "And no, I didn't miscount. The illustrious Minister pines after you. It's unfortunate his efforts are wasted. Then there's Jin, obviously. And recently, to my greatest surprise, the stiff, Han Bei, apparently lost his mind. I've said it before and I'll say it again, I thought my charms were deadly but they can only kill. You're able to make them suffer. What's your secret?"

The moment Han Bei's name falls from his lips, Kang Lang's countenance turns severe. Anger and resentment cross him as though he'd been slapped and his ability to keep composure is dwindling. I know he's not been on good terms with his brother but in the end, they are still brothers, and an injury dealt to one is twice inflicted upon the other. With his fury mounting, I inch a little farther away while giving him a cautious look. How does he know about Han Bei and me?

"I am nothing if not a resourceful man. Had I known your affections for Jin were so precarious, I would have taken you myself to spare the dolt. Let me guess, one look at your face and he's under the delusion that she's come back. That bitch ruined his life!"

"Don't talk about my sister that way!"

"Oh, defensive, aren't we? What do you even know about your sister?"

"She... was certain of her desires in life."

"Was she? That must be why she refused to break off their engagement."

"W-What? Didn't Han Bei petition to keep it?"

"She had *lovers* behind his back, or should I say, in front of his face? Like you, she baited him along through pretense indecisiveness, and worse, promises of love. Hua Ye finally talked some sense into him. Han gave Dong Xing the choice to continue their engagement or break it once and for all; a choice between him and the others. She wouldn't choose and instead, turned the burden on his shoulders knowing he couldn't let her go. And yet, the tales he tells put her in a brighter light, to preserve *her* honor. I may hate the bastard but I can't hate his foolish loyalty. It's his best and worst trait."

I don't want to continually think poorly about my sister but how could she? If I had met Han Bei before Jin, there's no doubt what my answer is... but that's just another excuse. I've still hurt him and I am no different from Dong Xing. With shame coursing through me, my head hangs in silence.

Kang Lang grimaces. "Did you come back hoping to find Jin?"

"I don't know."

"How long do you plan to drag out Han's misery?"

"I don't want to."

"Then don't. What exactly are you waiting for?"

"I promised Jin... I need to know whether he still wants a future for us."

"Then you're just as stupid as Han! Jin will never truly let you go because you'll always forgive his abandonment; no different from your sister's treatment of Han. So, Jin had a bad childhood. Didn't we all? You think I liked to cross-dress and let old perverts put their grubby hands on me just so I could jam a dagger in their chests? Well, the dagger part wasn't so bad."

A vicious smile curls over his mouth while relishing the gruesome recollections. "Jin needs to get over his mommy issues. And you need to stop using him as a crutch. If you're only stuck on Jin because of a promise, then you don't really love him. Fickleness is not loving someone new, it's the inability to make a decision, shifting back and forth from one lover to another, dragging them along out of greed."

"Why are you telling me this? Han Bei's given an ultimatum, which I failed. He's back to his sarcastic, condescending self."

"Then why didn't you stay in Ning?"

"I didn't want San An and Han Bei to fight. They're not exactly fond of each other."

"Is that the sole reason? Because the way I see it, if you didn't come to find Jin, then it was to flaunt in front of Han so he'd worship you again. You're worried too much time apart and he might forget. Am I right?"

"Yes, I know you think the worst in me and everything you said is probably true. What then? What am I supposed to do? Jin left and Han Bei's too angry to even acknowledge me. As far as I'm concerned, I've lost both their favors. I can't stay in Nan Rong and once I return to Ning, Han Bei is my council. He is fated to suffer me."

Kang Lang glowers. After a short pause, a faint smirk rises to a corner of his mouth. "So the idiot finally grew up, huh? Took him long enough! What about you? What do you want, Bao Lai?"

"I've sinned against them both. All I want is their happiness. I'd trade anything for that."

"Tsk! Do you hear the contradiction? By doing yourself a disservice, you're not helping anyone! I thought you were brave; now I see how much of a coward you are. It's unattractive. What's with that face? Are you offended?"

"Shouldn't I be?"

"I'm giving you my honesty."

"I know and I appreciate it. You don't ever tell me what I want to hear but you do tell me what I need to. So, thank you."

Gratitude came unexpected. Kang Lang blushes while glancing back and forth, puzzled.

"Y-Yeah. Well, whatever." He grumbles softly. "I've said my peace. I won't regret anything when I leave tomorrow."

"Leave? To go where?"

"Bei Ling gathered support from Ye and Feng Jia. That is to say, those two lands will not participate in battle but through claiming neutrality, they're allowing Bei Ling to enter their territories and gain different access points to the South. San An thinks the next wave will march through Ye's Tian Sheng Mountain Path. I'm leaving to give their emperor a piece of my mind."

"You're planning to intimidate Neng Cao so he'll rescind Ye's neutrality pact with Bei Ling?"

"Seduce, intimidate, torture... whatever works." Kang Lang throws his hands in the air.

"What about Su Jian? Isn't he the primary reason for our troubles? Where is he?"

"Hiding in plain sight. Bei Ling's Prime Minister Wang Liang is Su Jian. He's taken over their court with Emperor Cai Pai under his protection."

"How did San An realize Su Jian is Wang Liang?"

"*Excuse me*?" Kang Lang pouts with both hands on his hips. "I was the genius who trashed Master Yu's rare herb collection until he confessed."

"I hope you had a good reason for tormenting the court physician."

"Did I need one? The old man was responsible for treating the royal children during the mass poisoning by Empress Pai. He would have known whether Su Jian died. Apparently, our prince fled north unscathed with his mother, Consort Wu, and later adopted his grandfather's birth name, Wang Liang. Oh, you'll definitely appreciate this, the original Wang Liang is better known as former Emperor Tung, the man who tried to conquer Ning."

I nearly stumble off the bench. I can't believe this! Once more, his line is causing my grief. Because of Tung, my mother was forced to forfeit me. I was robbed an entire lifetime away from her, Dong Xing, and my poor father, whom he put to death. And now, because of Su Jian, Jin is in Bei Ling while Nan Rong and Ning are drawn into battle. Han Bei will be put in danger. He'll see our people suffer and his soldiers die unless Wang Liang is deposed. Hasn't everyone suffered enough? When will the past cease to rob us of the future? I can't stand this anymore!

"I'll kill him!"

"Oh-ho! Is that right?" Kang Lang jumps to his feet when I start up. "I like this bloodthirsty side of you! I may just have to fall for you all over again, Your Highness."

"Don't bother. I'm not interested in anything at the moment except making Wang Liang pay for his crimes."

"Which Wang Liang?"

"Who else? The one still alive."

"To persecute him for both Wang Liangs' crimes? You're so obvious. Letting vengeance get the best of you; you're just like your mother."

"Don't talk about my mother!"

"So sensitive! I guess Jin's not the only one with mommy issues. Listen, darling, she wasn't the forgive-and-forget type. Anger consumed her until the day she died. I'm not saying Wang Liang shouldn't be punished, just keep in mind that charging blindly won't solve anything."

"Han Bei controls Ning's army. He's not bound to foolishly charge anywhere."

"Perhaps, but if recklessness cost you your life, he's *bound* to give that foolish order. It's not just your life anymore, Your Highness. You must live for Han's sake and Han must live for everyone else."

Han must live for everyone else. Those words bring back the horrid memory from that day the Grand General resigned himself to the assassin's plot. Even Kang Lang, who has little opinion of his brother, can see the weight he tirelessly carries alone. The only one who hasn't fully appreciated the magnitude of the Grand General's burden is me.

While I stare at the ground, disappointed by my own uselessness, Kang Lang tersely pokes my forehead with his index finger.

"Well, I'm off to prepare for my trip. Do look after the buffoon. No one's allowed to kill him except me. Got that?"

"Thank you, Kang Lang. Good Luck! Oh and, I have news for you..."

"Han Bei didn't send you to kill He Pi." (Continue to page 554)

"Han Bei really cares about you." (Continue to page 555)

Chapter 41 – 2

"Han Bei didn't send you to kill He Pi. The orders were intercepted and altered by Ying. He'd meant for you to collect information."

Kang Lang stares back dumbfounded for a brisk moment and then casually shrugs. "Why should I care?"

Though he tries to keep the nonchalant attitude, light colors slowly emerge to his face. He looks away, embarrassed.

"You don't have to care. I just thought since you're a wealth of knowledge, you should have all the facts."

He gives a small nod, saying nothing more. Kang Lang retreats from the garden and I follow a distance behind.

Continue to page 556

Chapter 41 – 3

"Han Bei really cares about you."

"I think I'm going to cry!" Mu Dan's melodramatic voice ejects playfully.

"Be serious! He knew you were in Nan Rong's Circle all along. The bounty was put on your head hoping to deter you from returning. If you had, the law would have called for your execution."

"How kind of Han! I never intended to return and because of his bounty, I couldn't leave the Circle! Do you know how troublesome it is to constantly look over my shoulders? He's made me a prisoner and now, there aren't any cute women left in this prison because San An disbanded the Circle!"

"How would he have known you were a prisoner when you're engaged to He Pi?"

"He knows damn well I like women! Anyway, it's none of your business what happens between my brother and me. Until you've solved your dilemma with Han, don't bother lecturing me about our lack of *brotherly love.*"

Kang Lang quickly retreats from the garden and I, disappointed by my failure to reconcile the Zhao brothers, follow a distance behind.

Chapter 42: Bei Ling's Plan

The council meeting continued until after sundown. Xian barred my proposed interruption; hence, I spent most of the day as Tui Tui in the barracks.

Come nightfall, while wandering aimlessly in contemplation of Kang Lang's news, San An comes into view once I round a corner of the balcony's walkway. He's leaning sluggishly against one of the large vermillion posts as though lacking the strength to stand. His breathing is noticeably strained. The bags under his eyes have grown heavier since this morning.

"There you are, Your Highness." He staggers away from the post to make a short obeisance. "Are you unwell? I sent repast to your chamber but the servants informed me that you weren't there."

"I'm more worried for you, San An. You're overworked. This isn't good for your health. Come. Let me escort you to your chamber."

"Knowing my welfare matters to Your Highness is enough to restore my vigor." He smiles kindly.

"You're very stubborn, Minister, but so am I. In this instance, I won't yield. You can hardly stand straight. I won't risk you falling off the balcony."

Taking his loose sleeve tightly in hand, I pull San An inside. The Minister started to protest and then realizes that he doesn't have the strength to stop me. Once he's safely rested his sore back on the bedspread, I pull over a chair and then sit with my arms folded.

"How does Your Highness expect me to sleep under such vigilant eyes?"

"You'll just have to try, San An. I don't trust you to rest once I leave. Oh! Have you eaten? Let me fetch dinner."

The moment I start up, he seizes my hand.

"Stay with me a while longer." His hoarse voice is almost pleading. There lies a deeper meaning behind those words which I fear to acknowledge. Here is another who loves me and whom I must injure in turn. The coward in me seeks to withdraw while the part of me which respects and treasures our friendship won't permit the retreat. He stayed by my side when I was injured; of course, I'd do the same for him.

Resuming his side, my hand tightly squeezes his to ease the trembles. "Don't overexert yourself, San An. I know this ordeal must be difficult for you, but you must take better care of yourself."

He gives a small nod and then closes his eyes. "As difficult as it may be to slay one brother, the sacrifice is less than losing two. I never thought Su Jian was capable of this ambition. When we were children, he was always gentle and kind. His character wouldn't permit him to harm any living creature. It is unfortunate how time can change a man."

"Maybe that's why he took that tyrant's name, Wang Liang. He's no longer Su Jian."

His eyelids fling wide open. San An suddenly sits up. Excitement wholly takes over fatigue. "How did you come by this information?"

"Kang Lang, of course. Why are you shocked? Didn't he tell you?"

"He mentioned nothing of the sort. Su Jian is Bei Ling's Prime Minister... Yes, I see now."

"San An, since you didn't know, then neither does Han Bei. I have to tell him!" I start off the chair when Kang Lang's conniving plot is made clear. He purposefully planned this bit of secret so I'd run to Han Bei and we'd have a reason to speak. He really is Hua Ye's male counterpart!

"Who is Hua Ye?" San An poses curiously.

"How did you... I was mouthing my thoughts again?!" My symptoms are growing worse. What if I can never have another secret?

San An chuckles amusedly. His grip around my hand grows more prominent as though to bar my leave. As I resume the chair, the Minister lies back down.

"You've made many new friends in Ning, I surmise."

"Yes, and I've also met my nephew! He's mature but also mischievous. In some ways, he reminds me of you and He Pi."

"Nothing is quite like family; both comforting and vexing. In my case, inherently dangerous. I keep hoping to put the past behind and now I see that's not possible."

"It's not your fault, San An. Su Jian's grandfather attempted to annex Ning. He must have taken Tung's birth name, Wang Liang, because he can't let go of the past. I only wonder if his grudge isn't also against Ning."

"That would explain the reason Ying attacked us and then fled to Mount Fei Yang. Naturally, our countries were expected to point fingers at one another, exhaust our resources through pointless warfare, and then fall prey to Bei Ling."

"We didn't, so now he's solely targeting Nan Rong. He must know our two lands have a pact. Why is he casually ignoring the East when we're the bigger threat? Does he really think avoiding Ning will keep us from battle?"

"On the contrary, his main forces are hidden. Bei Ling is attacking the South through several vantage points by way of Ye and Feng Jia. With Nan Rong's generals divided to repel the scuttles, our forces are dwindling. I understand your reservation in risking Ning soldiers' lives; thus, I wouldn't have called for reinforcements if I didn't fear the worst. The council is single-minded in their desire to charge directly into the northern territory. I feel that the moment a direct attack begins, the only thing it will accomplish is to have

Nan Rong's main forces surrounded. Our small army will scatter in an instant."

"Then should Ning lead the direct charge? Our army heavily outnumbers Bei Ling's."

"That may expedite Nan Rong's destruction." The Minister sighs heavily; ostensibly chastising himself for lack of solution. "Nan Rong has greatly weakened from the endless scuttles. Once Lord Han Bei's troops pass Ying Ling's borders, Wang Liang will most likely shift his main forces south. As we are now, I can't see the odds in our favor."

"But you have Ning's reinforcements."

"A handful of soldiers spread thin won't make any difference. Should half your army join Nan Rong, I can only hope the remainder has the speed and fortitude to conquer Bei Ling before both our countries' resources expire."

"I doubt Han Bei will be keen on that idea. Besides, Wang Liang could continue deploying decoys south while pulling back his main forces to repel a weakened Ning."

"That is a valid premise. Under Wang Liang's leadership, their forces have become strong and numerous. With only half an army, Ning could lose more than just the battle. Once Ning is taken, Nan Rong will fall in succession."

His chilling words send my heart to my throat. I nearly leap off the chair. "San An! Isn't that what he's doing now? He's been avoiding the East and focusing South with decoys in order to deteriorate your forces. He knew we were bound to shift our resources here. In turn, Ning would become exposed to certain weaknesses that Wang Liang can exploit. As you've said, if Ning falls, so will Nan Rong!"

The Minister's eyes grow bright from the sudden revelation and then darken from uncertainty. Nan Rong needs reinforcements while Ning's forces should be focusing north. However, doing so risks Nan Rong falling into Bei Ling's hands. I can't permit that but I also can't place Ning at a disadvantage by weakening our defenses.

The longer silence between us grows, the more concern overshadows San An's tired brows. With He Pi in Bei Ling, the burden of Nan Rong's safety falls on his shoulders, just as Han Bei solely carries Ning. They really are very much alike, despite their natural aversion. At the moment, the Minister needs to maintain his health.

"No worries, San An. All is not lost. Kang Lang might succeed in Ye and at least now, Wang Liang's plan is becoming clear. There isn't anything left to do. The day is almost over, you should rest."

Too fatigued to contest, San An gives my hand one last squeeze and then closes his eyes. I stay by his side until he's sound asleep.

Chapter 42 – 2

I can't do it. I shouldn't! And yet, in spite of myself, here I am outside of his chamber door ready to intrude. Why must I keep being his misery? He's tried his best to avoid me; I can't keep pushing myself into his attention.

The next thing I know, my feet are running down the long corridor. Ironically, the person I was absconding from is the very same I slam into once rounding the corner.

"I-I'm sorry!" This is the first I've apologized to him since the incident and it's not even for my primary offense. "General, I need a moment of your time."

He stares back with a hint of disgust. "Why have you come in search of my *services?* Was your secret tryst with the Minister not satisfying enough?"

Ever since I failed his ultimatum, he's been distant but never belligerent. Han Bei must have seen me entering San An's quarters earlier. Though I know he's only acting this way due jealousy, to hear him accuse me of such things is unbearable. Still, if disdain for me will wipe away his pain, then I won't contend his ill presumptions. When I don't respond, he walks past me. Instinctively, I scuttle after him toward the chamber.

"Han Bei—"

The door behind us slams shut with such a reverberating force that I nearly topple. He marches toward the bed and then collapses in a heavy thud.

"You're very bold, coming into a man's chamber uninvited this time of night. Were I any other man less deceived, your unabashed audacity might put you in danger's temptation."

Averting from his icy glare, Kang Lang's findings and San An's conjectures are hastily blurted out. Regardless of the Minister's and my opinions, the only person who fully appreciates Ning's capabilities is Han Bei. I am sorry for forcing him to suffer me but it had to be done. By the time I finish, his sour expression has faded.

"What should we do, Han Bei?"

He stares back thoughtfully with lips thinned into a line. "Upon what proofs are you and the Minister basing these *theories*? Our scouts near Ying Ling haven't reported any movements."

"Isn't that the mystery? Why have they ignored us?"

"The easy answer is fear. You've been training with the greenhorns; you've yet to witness our elites. The single useful insight you've brought was Su Jian's identity. The North isn't ignorant and there never was a third-party instigator. Now that our enemies have been distinguished, we've no reason to sit idle. They will pay for their aggressions."

"What if their main army shifts south? Or, what if, during their defense against Ning, Bei Ling manages to take Nan Rong through their current tactics? Once Nan Rong is captured, they'll either flank us or easily employ a pincer approach."

"And where would a sheltered girl like you have learned basic military strategies?"

"I didn't mean to imply I knew better. At the old temple, former military men often came to share stories and I often listened."

"My opinion of temple girls has drastically changed because of you," he chuckles sardonically. "I delivered reinforcements as promised. One of our soldiers is worth five of theirs. That is sufficient for the South's defense until we've decimated Wang Liang's forces. Besides, what would be the point of taking Nan Rong just to give up Bei Ling? Without their entire army, they don't stand a chance against Ning."

"Then... his strategies make even less sense."

"I don't pretend to know the logic of madmen."

Han Bei lies down and, upon closing his eyes, signals for no further conversation. Seeing him so unhappy, I can't bring myself to leave. In time, his hard voice brings back my senses as I linger by the door.

"Was there something else?"

"N-No. Well, I... I just... wanted to apologize for... everything."

"Everything? I didn't know your ego was so considerable."

The melodious voice filled with derision is one he employed often when we first met. The difference now is the sorrow I see buried behind that false smirk. He might have ended our amity, but he's not been put out of his misery. Likewise, I thought once his choice was made, the answer should be simple. However, undeniably, there are parts of me which want to cradle him in my arms and love him in every way possible until the wounds both Dong Xing and I have dealt can mend.

Kang Lang was right. I am a coward. I could have relayed the message to Captain Xian but I chose to come here so we could have this moment together because I can't let him forget me. I miss him. I miss his friendship, his assurance, his attention, and his acceptance, which were wholly mine before I marred his pride. I rejected his constancy and companionship and yet, I won't set him free. What a despicable person I've become!

Pangs of guilt tear at my heart. He peers back with listless eyes, while I turn to hide distasteful tears.

"You have every right to chastise me. I deserve it. I am sorry for hurting you. I never meant to and there aren't any excuses for my shameful behaviors. You are a good man who deserves better than me. In time, I know you'll find someone worthy. Please, don't shut out the world and if you can, please forgive me."

During the long pause that follows, Han Bei's enduring silence is the response to my apology. With nothing more to say, I quietly part from his company.

Chapter 43: My Frustration

This morning, loneliness consumed me yet again. Han Bei left for Ning sometime during the night after assigning leadership to Captain Xian. Unlike Jin's departure, Han Bei's reasons are clear. Still, that acknowledgment doesn't dull this pain in my chest.

More than my petty feeling of abandonment, I'm really worried for Han Bei. Last night, he sounded confident, but intuition tells me this ordeal won't end so easily. He's going to the frontline against Bei Ling and there's nothing I can do to help. I'm not a warrior and I'm an even weaker leader. All I have accomplished so far is watch the conflict from behind high walls.

"Your Highness, there you are."

"Are you feeling better, San An?"

Shortly after morning practice in the courtyard, San An called me to his quarters. I'm happy to see his countenance livelier. He's startled to see my uniform.

"Yes, thanks to your company. I can't recall when I last slept so soundly. I'd hoped to join you for breakfast earlier but Captain Xian mentioned you were training with the regiment. I did not think he was serious. Has the size of Ning's military grown... diminutive?"

"Not at all. I'd asked to join. It took no small effort to convince Han Bei."

At the mention of his name, my lips involuntarily quiver. What is wrong with me? Why can't I exert more self-control?! The more my lips clamp down, the more they tremble. As a last resort, I raise a gauntlet to cover my mouth.

The Minister stares awkwardly for a time and then his trailing gaze slowly pace across the ground. Before I can change subjects, the cautious peer resumes.

"Pardon my intrusion. I know it isn't my place to pry. Are you and Lord Han Bei... more than mere acquaintances?"

"I guess so. He is my council." A soft mutter flows from behind the gauntlet.

San An smiles wryly and says nothing more; though, his expression turns complicated. It takes a moment to realize I really am a dolt.

"O-Oh, you meant... n-not really."

"I'm afraid I don't understand the ambiguity."

"No, we aren't more than acquaintances."

Despite my best, firm answer, San An remains in disbelief.

"Yesterday, his demeanor distorted when I mentioned your name. Now, I understand. His rancor wasn't stemmed from indifference, which means the root must be the opposite. He is another in want of your attention and one who you've placed before me and possibly, Jin."

"Please, not you too, San An! Everyone has an opinion of my love life except me! I won't love anyone anymore if that will suit everyone!"

"My apologies, I just thought—"

"What? That I betrayed Jin? That I'm not capable of loyalty? That I broke our promise because I faltered before the face of temptation and the assurance of constancy? Or, that I'm the same as my sister for leading on others? Neither Han Bei nor Jin wants anything further to do with me, and that's just as well, because the last thing anyone needs right now is distraction and that's all I am!"

His kind eyes grow wide from surprise. I've never raised my voice to him this way. Why am I lashing out against San An when he's done nothing wrong? He's been the only one to have kept me in any regard despite my repeated offenses. If anyone has ever shown me true constancy, it is San An.

Ashamed for the outburst, I hang my head. The welfare of our countries is at stake and yet, everything keeps coming back to this. I can't move forward until this impasse is solved. Inside, another force is mounting; my chest won't stop heaving. I'm angry. More than angry, I'm infuriated! I hate myself for causing their misery but at the same time, I'm angry because of him. The muddled image which flashed before my eyes when I nearly drowned in the lake—the one whose face won't stop tormenting me—is finally made clear. He had no small part in my misery or his and I want him to answer for it. I'm angry at

Han Bei (Continue to page 571)

Jin (Continue to page 582)

Chapter 43 – 2

How dare he resent me when, as he'd said, he placed the idea in my head and his! He's toyed with me from the very beginning to execute Yuan's agenda even after learning about Jin. Casually put his hands on me whenever it suited him, attempted to seduce me so I wouldn't ally with Nan Rong, ignored me when I turned away his advances, and insulted me for falling short of his standard for the perfect Dong Xing! I never knew which of his affections were true and which were false; or when he actually saw me instead of my sister.

Then he demanded the most ridiculous ultimatum! Had I chosen him then and there, how could I have ever considered doing *that* in the open? What did *that* have to do with loyalty anyway! I can't stand the jerk! And despite everything, I can't stop thinking of him!

I knew, but I was conflicted; more so, afraid to have expressed my feelings. For my indecision, he's grown so distant. I may never again earn his favor. Be that as it may, I'd rather love Han Bei from afar than be in Jin's arms with my mind elsewhere. That wouldn't be fair to anyone.

"Your Highness... Bao Lai! Are you all right?"

San An shakes my shoulders more forcefully; finally waking me from my irate daydream. The sight of his worried eyes forms knots in my stomach. Here is another kind person who foolishly loves me; who must continually bear my offenses.

Staggering back, I fall to my knees and then bow low to the ground. "I'm sorry, San An! Please forgive me!"

Startled, the Minister kneels down to raise me up. Drawing my head toward his chest, San An's arms swing around my shoulders. "Whatever for? And there's no need for that!"

"San An, I'm sorry! I'm sorry for having been your misery! I'm sorry that I can't keep our promise! I can't be the woman to save Jin! I am not the loyal person he needs!"

Choked-back tears keep surging forth, staining the Minister's red silk robe. He hesitates for a time and then, a gentle hand slowly strokes my head. I tremble in his arms, as a sinner before the Divine, and in turn, his embrace grows more fervent as though to burn away my faults.

Sighing softly, his lips caress my forehead. "Far from my misery, you have shown me a happiness I've never known. Having your regards is more than I expected. I do not think any less of you and you should never apologize for following your heart. I was thoughtless to have asked the arduous task."

"No, you weren't! I promised wholeheartedly and I still love Jin but I... recently, I can't turn away from Han Bei. There are no excuses for my fickleness. Through my own volition, I've learned the sin of a traitor; all the more reason I can't be the one Jin needs. I'm sorry, San An!"

"You mustn't think yourself disloyal. Shu Jin is hardly immaculate. A devoted man should never leave his lover to tears and you've shed far more than enough. Jin made his choice and you have every right to make yours. Regardless of faults, your life belongs solely to you. I wish to see you happy."

"How can I? My heart is taken. My inattentive company won't make him happy, but in the small chance that Jin still loves me, I don't want him to be sad."

"Do not dwell on what ifs. My life at court has been fraught with war and conflict. I've come to learn that tomorrow is without certainty and the most anyone can accomplish is to live life without regrets. In order for Jin to be spared, another Nan Rong prince who holds you in higher regards must still concede his single joy. You cannot make everyone happy."

The Minister's words wake conscience from desolation. He may have also voiced Kang Lang's opinion, but there's something in San An's dignified and steady temperament that solidifies my confidence. I've come to respect the Minister and depend upon his advice far more than I've realized. Perhaps, under my own delusions, I feel that through their blood ties, San An's vicariously absolved my trespasses in Jin's stead. Either way, a heavy weight feels lifted off my soul.

Once nerves calm, I raise off his chest. "Thank you, San An."

Smiling kindly, his warm hand wipes away the last of my tears and then a light kiss presses against my forehead.

"No need to thank me. All that matters is your smile. I'm glad to see your spirit restored. Now then, how do you intend to proceed?"

"The path for me is clear. I will return to Ning and my people. After this conflict is over, I hope you will join me. There's a lovely garden I wasn't able to show you last time."

"I look forward to seeing you again in happier days. Be safe, Your Highness."

"You, too, San An. Han Bei is planning a march to Bei Ling. He's confident in victory. Still, who knows how Wang Liang's forces will react against Nan Rong? Please, be careful."

The Minister bows graciously and gives one last reassuring pledge. "I will do everything in my capabilities."

Chapter 43 – 3

Captain Xian was not pleased to spare Niu as my escort but he was content to know the reason for my retreat. I plan to put Han Bei out of his misery.

To my surprise, upon entering Ning's courtyard, a familiar face is waving cheerfully from the base of the stone steps leading to the main palace. He seems more grownup than I remember.

"Yuan! You're back!"

"Still stating the obvious, huh, Auntie?" He grins teasingly in an innocent manner resembling Han Bei's smirk. I've just now realized he takes after his father's derisions.

"I wasn't expecting you so soon."

"We'd hoped to enjoy Mount Guo extensively but news of Bei Ling's aggression couldn't be ignored. We've just arrived. Where have you been?"

"Nan Rong. Captain Xian is leading the South's reinforcements and Han Bei is preparing to march north. I'm going to assist him."

Yuan stares curiously as if questioning my use with a sword; ultimately, holding his tongue before chastising me. After all this time, our conversations are still filled with awkward silent skepticism. Experiences may have altered us over the course of the previous months but I guess some things will never change. Such is family, I'm glad to learn.

Yuan, observing my anxiety, does the favor of relieving me from conversation. I run toward the barracks where General Liu redirects me to the Grand General's chamber. Though Han Bei permits my intrusion, the scowl on his face clearly conveys displeasure.

"Han Bei, I'm going with you."

Han Bei continues tightening the black gauntlet around his left wrist, looking so charmingly dashing in the heavy armor, even with that frown over his mouth. "You'd asked to join the regiment without receiving special treatments and yet, failed to stay with your unit. Did you forget Ning's desertion laws?"

"No matter the consequences, I want to remain by your side. I'll do everything I can to help."

"Then stay here where it's safe. Your reckless tendencies won't make things easy for me."

The tone is more anxious than annoyed. He's worried, which means it isn't too late. My heart jumps from overwhelming elation and thereafter, indescribable relief.

His downcast eyes, furrowed brows, and hard frown are too much to bear. I want nothing more than for his happiness, wipe away every unfair misery he's ever been dealt, and return his passion tenfold to make him whole.

Once the helmet is stuffed onto his head, Han Bei nears the door. The escalating emotion is beyond my control. I've been withholding love and desire these many longing months. Composure loses to passion and in a rush, my arms swing around his broad shoulders. A daring kiss presses onto his mouth, burning his lips with my own. He flusters and then freezes while I continue conveying raging ardor against his quivering lips.

Pressing my body firmly against his armor, I pray that my heat will pierce through the cold shell. When his arms move, my heart flutters in anticipation of the embrace I'd come to desperately yearn. Instead, his heavy gloves squeeze my arms to pry me away.

"I love you." Casting the sweetest smile I could summon to express my ardent affections, I hope for the best. Just being near him makes me so happy. I never want us to part again.

In an instant, hopes which dashed high in my chest are casted down and burnt to cinders when his sour expression turns to pure hatred. "It was not enough to reject me; you wish to torment me as well?"

"I'm not! I love you, Han Bei! I have for some time but I was afraid—I'm not anymore. You're practically part of my family. No, you are my family. By your side is where I was always meant to be. Fate brought me back to Ning. To you. I love you so much! There aren't words to fully convey how much you mean to me!"

His eyes narrow. Han Bei releases me and then traces back a step. "Another Ning princess once told me the same, and this promise will end no differently. Your useless words inspire nothing in me."

"T-That's not fair! I am not my sister!"

"So you keep insisting only to prove yourself wrong." With those cruel words, he moves past me.

My body is trembling violently from his rejection, my chest is heaving from terror, and my heart is twisting into a knot. Is this really the end? I turned my back on Jin and Nan Rong, along with the single part of me I ever thought commendable, only to earn his vicious indifference? I can't accept this! Impertinence surges forth to compensate the pain. I move to bar his path, wrapping my arms tightly around his waist and pressing our bodies as close together as my strength will permit.

"Under your misguided fantasy of Dong Xing, you kissed me. You made me love you. Now that I do, you're running away? I thought myself a loyal person; my only redeeming trait. But, come what may, I will gladly resign any piece of me that keeps us apart. I am sorry if I fell short of your expectations! You said you loved me. Is this the extent of your affections?"

During the ensuing pause, his countenance changed to something frightening. Han Bei sends down such an icy glare, void of any humanity, that my breath is caught in my throat.

"I thought hearing those words would finally make me happy but all I feel is disgust. You turned your back on Shu Jin for a stronger man, the very failing to which your sister was fallible. Now that I see what you are, my irrational infatuation is lost. You're not even close to the standard of women I would be compelled to waste a night's time."

"You don't mean that! Han Bei, I love you! I know you love me. I'm begging you... please don't push me away."

My pathetic pleading serves to increase his frustration. I clung to Jin and he left. Now, I'm desperately clinging to Han Bei when the outcome is clear. It's all I can think to do.

"Can you grasp Ning's predicament? We are headed for war. This is hardly the time for your foolish romance! Your Highness has enough admirers in the Southland to keep steady company, including my brother. Make haste, before they, too, change their minds!"

"I don't want anyone else! Once Bei Ling is subdued, I will make up for my previous indifference. For now, I'm coming with you whether you like it or not. Kang Lang is doing his best in Ye, the least I can do is—"

"What did you say?" The breathless whisper is overflowing with panic. Han Bei's widened eyes are fraught with anxiety. They pace back and forth across the room, narrowing from wrath once landed on my face.

"Where is my brother?!" Accompanying his thunderous roar, both gauntlets reach out around me, slamming heavily against the door with enough force to shatter holes in the pristine hardwood. The shock of his rage sends me tumbling back against the door. In the next moment, his left hand is wrapped tightly around my collar. I can't recognize the person behind those feral eyes.

"H-He's in Ye. Bei Ling is using Tian Sheng to access Nan Rong and Kang Lang is—"

"Why didn't you stop him?!"

"I-I didn't know that I should—"

"Don't lie to me!"

Once more, his free hand smashes against the door, the force of which sends tremors down my spine. Even though he's not hurting me, I have never known this terror, to be fearful of the one I love.

"Didn't I express his insipid obsession with heroism? Didn't I say that was the reason I intervened?! For all your talk of loyalty to the East, you let him go to his death for the chance to protect your precious Nan Rong! After everything I've done for your family, this is the thanks I get? He's my only brother. If anything happens to Kang Lang, I swear I'll burn Nan Rong to the ground!"

His grip on my collar tightens. I can't find the right apology nor does he want any useless excuse. How could I have been so thoughtless? Kang Lang is my friend. I was too caught up in my own troubles to see the danger he'd placed himself.

The more I plead for his forgiveness through my pathetic expression, the more disgusted he grows. Were there ever any trace of love for me in those eyes, they've long been dispelled. He's finally free.

Snarling viciously, Han Bei jerks my collar aside. I stumble to the floor while he leaves the room, slamming the door behind.

Continue to page 587

Chapter 43 – 4

I love Han Bei. It seems redundant to admit when I've known for some time my deep infatuation. Beyond his sarcasm and condescension, he is kind, loyal, and constant. He is everything I could ever want and yet, I must cause his misery because my heart won't permit Jin to abscond.

Jin, the cause of my misery. The man who has no consideration for my regards. The man who refused to love me and then made love to me. The man who, no matter how far apart we are, holds tether to my heart. Despite acknowledging my poor judgment, I can't stop loving Jin. I can't break my promise to love him as my first and last. Mostly, I can't stop being the fool that I am.

"I'm sorry, San An. I didn't mean to shout."

San An's head shakes. With a gentle sweep, the Minister forces an embrace. "Your Highness... Bao Lai. I want nothing more than for your happiness. My life at court has been fraught with war and conflict. I've come to learn that tomorrow is without certainty and the most anyone can accomplish is to live life without regrets. Forgive my arduous request. No promise is worth a lifetime of suffering."

"You didn't ask anything extraneous. I do love Jin. I hate what he's done to me but I can't let him go."

"Then, I shall do everything in my power to return Shu Jin safely to Your Highness. He will answer to the woman he's kept waiting."

The Minister's smile carries a hint of encouragement. San An's dignified and steady temperament can always solidify my confidence. I've come to respect and depend upon his advice far more than I've realized.

"Thank you, San An. You're right. He will answer to me. I'll make sure of that."

This entire time, I've been angry with Jin while accusing Han Bei and blaming myself. As others have pointed out, and as I've come to acknowledge, I am the only person capable of ending this vacillating relationship. If Jin won't come back to me, I'll go to him.

"No need to thank me. All that matters is your smile." San An bows courteously.

The Minister is dear to me and while I don't want to keep secrets, it's senseless to make him worry. I briefly mention returning to Ning and Han Bei's plan to march north. Following which, we confer a promise to see this conflict through.

"I look forward to greeting you again in happier days. Be safe, Your Highness."

"You, too, San An. There's a lovely garden I wasn't able to show you last time. When this is over, I hope you'll join me in Ning. For now, please, be careful."

Chapter 43 – 5

Captain Xian was not pleased to spare Niu as my escort but he was content to be relieved of an encumbrance.

To my surprise, upon entering Ning's courtyard, a familiar face is waving cheerfully from the base of the stone steps leading to the main palace. He seems more grownup than I remember.

"Yuan! You're back!"

"So are you, Auntie!" He grins teasingly.

"I wasn't expecting you so soon."

"We'd hoped to enjoy Mount Guo extensively but news of Bei Ling's aggression couldn't be ignored. We've just arrived. Where have you been?"

"Nan Rong. Captain Xian is leading the South's reinforcements and Han Bei is preparing to march north."

"And... where will you go?"

"W-What makes you think I'm plotting anything?"

"We never said you were. Now that you've mentioned it, what are you plotting?"

"Nothing!"

His eyebrows rise in an all too familiar fashion. They may not be related by blood but he is definitely his father's son.

"Excuse me for cutting conversations short. I have to find Han Bei."

Making a short bow, I leave Yuan and run toward the barracks where General Liu redirects me to the Grand General's chamber. Though Han Bei permits my intrusion, he puts no effort to conceal the scowl on his face.

"Han Bei, I'm going with you."

Han Bei continues tightening the black gauntlet around his left wrist, looking so charmingly dashing in the heavy armor, even with that frown over his mouth. "You'd asked to join the regiment without receiving special treatments and yet, failed to stay with your unit. Did you forget Ning's desertion laws?"

"I am Ning's rightful leader. I want to join the march. I'll do everything I can to help."

"Stay here where it's safe. Your reckless tendencies won't make things easy for me."

Stuffing the helmet onto his head, Han Bei nears the door, stopping once we're abreast. "I am not foreign to your willful nature. There's not a single doubt in my mind the foolish things concocting in yours. Just remember that this conflict is the result of Bei Ling's poor leadership. You won't instill confidence in the

585

people by running away. Stay here and let them rally around you. Yuan can't substitute in your stead forever."

With those parting words, he disappears out the door. I don't know why I bothered. Of course, he'd never let me go. Han Bei would never put me in danger. While I do acknowledge his points were valid, I care for him and Jin too much to continue waiting out this conflict from behind high walls.

In the end, he was right about me. I am willful and the foolish things concocting in my head won't be denied.

Continue to page 670

Chapter 44: Nan Rong's Troubles

Two weeks after Ning's army set out, distressing news came from Nan Rong. The Southern ministers, excluding San An, pushed for a direct march into Bei Ling. Ultimately, their generals had no choice but to obey. As San An expected, the direct assault resulted in Nan Rong's forces scattering and only half of the men returned. Had it not been for Ning's reinforcements and Captain Xian's military prowess, all would have been lost.

While Southern forces regrouped, Han Bei's troops passed into Ying Ling. Scouts then reported the number of scuttles near the southern borders increased tenfold. I fear should they seize the southern vantage points, Ning will suffer the same drawbacks as Nan Rong and our military advantage may not be enough. I trust Han Bei, but intuition tells me strength isn't the primary device for victory.

"Why haven't they met Bei Ling's defenses?"

Yuan poses the question to General Liu and a handful of Ning's other military leaders. We're gathered in the war room around a large map with the markers laid. So far, I see San An's predictions coming true.

"Wang Liang is a coward. He won't take the direct approach." Liu responds confidently. "We'll lay siege if necessary."

I don't know anything about war, so who am I to question our military leaders? However, Su Jian isn't as simple-minded as Liu may believe. Bei Ling's army was comparable to Nan Rong's and their soldiers less trained. Yet, they're now a threat to everyone, including the weaker countries in danger of becoming puppet states.

"With all due respect, I don't think Wang Liang is as much of a coward as he is careful. His army is smaller than ours, that is a given, so it makes sense for him to avoid a direct approach. Prime Minister San An speculated a shift in their forces. If we go north, they'll overtake the south and attempt to flank."

"We severely outnumber Bei Ling!" Liu pushes his premise once more. "Lord Han Bei will quash their forces before they have the chance to flee south!"

I am glad our army's strength instills so much pride in the people, but that foolhardy belief is also our primary weakness. Nan Rong's direct charge almost cost them the war so why is Ning employing the same failed strategy? Suddenly, Kang Lang's warning comes to mind. He cautioned against storming blindly, which was the reason he took the infiltration approach. He Pi is also of the same mindset. Maybe His Highness and Jin are waiting for an opportune moment to strike from within. This makes me think Ning shouldn't advance on Bei Ling. We should instead thin their internal defenses by drawing out the Northern army.

"You don't agree, Bao Lai?" Yuan stares curiously at my furrowed brows.

The moment I turn to give my opinion, a runner bursts through the double doors and then falls to the floor. His frenzied message sends the calm room into panic. Feng Jia withdrew the neutrality pact and outright sided with Bei Ling. Currently, their entire force is marching to Nan Rong.

"The South is requesting reinforcements. With Feng Jia in the fray, Ye won't be far behind. We can't hold against three armies! You must send us more soldiers!"

The trembling messenger kowtows to Yuan as though his life will end immediately upon rejection. Yuan raises the man to his feet but can't give a definite reply. Instead of the others, his eyes land squarely on me. I stare back at the map and state the obvious because nothing else comes to mind.

"Maybe we should call back Han Bei."

"Impossible! That heavy blow to morale won't work to our favor. We need to maintain momentum. Let us send even more men to reinforce Lord Han Bei for a speedy victory."

Liu proposes the careless plan and the other generals agree. Perhaps they're right, but I just can't let the thought go.

"Han Bei once asked me, what would be the point for Wang Liang to gain Nan Rong and in turn, lose Bei Ling?

I'm asking you the same. What would be the point to gain Bei Ling if we lose Ning? We need to fortify our defenses and Nan Rong is the barrier protecting us from Ye, Feng Jia, and even Bei Ling."

"Of course *you* would say anything to protect the Southland!"

Liu's resentment is drawing out latent hatred the others carry. They turn to one another with meaningful stares and then disregard me. Han Bei was right. Most in this room don't believe my legitimacy and the more I seemingly put Nan Rong first, the more their doubts grow. My time would have been better spent learning how to approach our military leaders and building ties instead of practicing with a blade I don't use.

"Please, Your Highness! She speaks the truth. Ning is our ally and we are in desperate need!"

Had Yuan not raised a hand to stop the furious general, Liu's aggravation nearly sent him to blast the pleading messenger.

"Bao Lai, what do you suggest?"

"Your Highness! Why are you taking her guidance over your faithful servant's? She may share your blood but she is *not* one of us! I have served Ning for the past thirty years and led over fifteen campaigns. What does she know about war that I don't?"

"In all honesty, nothing." Yuan's hard reply carries a maturity which demands respect. "We are familiar with your opinion, General, but there isn't any harm to hear the alternative. As far as things go, Wang Liang's methods haven't been conventional. Let another propose a different view. Go on, Bao Lai."

"For our own interest and our ally's, I... I think we should help Nan Rong." Without Han Bei present to shoulder my guilt, the full impact of those words weigh heavily on my heart. Swallowing the hard lump in my throat, I press on. "However, we shouldn't overextend ourselves. Leaving our base weakened is probably Wang Liang's strategy."

"You're contradicting yourself!" General Ming, another veteran who's taken offense by my interference, interjects coldly. "How can we both defend the South and keep from overextending ourselves? Sending an insignificant sum of soldiers implies we lack resources; the alliance's morale will be crushed. In the event the defense against Feng Jia falters, our colors will lose all meaning! Half of every battle can be won through sheer intimidation. In one fell swoop, everything we've tirelessly worked for will be destroyed!"

Our colors... Han Bei once said just the sight of our colors send terror through enemy ranks. The black and silver armors of the eastern barbarians signal merciless slaughter; that is what people in Nan Rong believe. For a time, so did I, and with great certainty, so does Feng Jia.

"General, you're a genius!"

Ming's slightly confused, more so disturbed, by my happy grin.

"Wang Liang is using decoys to sap Nan Rong's forces and using Nan Rong, he hopes to draw Ning's resources. Feng Jia is just another decoy and we should take it. That is, we should let them *think* we have."

"You're as vague as you are oblivious," Liu mutters.

"General, that is enough. Please continue, Auntie."

"No, he's right. I've only a vague suggestion. Our colors, as General Ming pointed out, is sheer intimidation. We don't need to send a hundred thousand soldiers but we do have the armors to spare, don't we?"

Ming's widened eyes direct at Liu; following which, the former questions my sanity. "Intimidation may be half the battle; the other half still requires effort. How can Nan Rong compensate when they lack the soldiers to don our armors?"

"Prime Minister San An is a capable strategist. I trust him to find solution. There is one more scrutiny, though. Feng Jia, we can fool, but Wang Liang won't believe in false numbers when Han Bei and the eight hundred thousand soldiers he's leading are past Ying Ling. I think we need to call back the Grand General for our ruse to look believable. That way, Bei Ling will believe our main forces are in Nan Rong, extend their own forces, and then we can meet them head on."

"Our eight hundred thousand are still four times more than their entire defense. Why should we cower for a superfluous deception merely to prolong this conflict?"

I can't deny that Ming has a point. Out of all the military leaders present, he seems the most levelheaded. If this were simply a math equation, I would have to agree. Nevertheless, an unsettling feeling dawned on me. Where would I meet Han Bei's massive force if I were Bei Ling? Based on this map, once past Ying Ling, the Hui An road leads toward Wei Yi and Si Kao Passes; the shortest path being Si Kao. That pass eventually leads to... Lam Soi Citadel.

"G-Generals, did Lord Han Bei divulge which pass he's taking to Bei Ling?"

"The direct route, Si Kao." Ming replies.

"To Lam Soi?"

Lam Soi Citadel was the place Tung mass murdered the entire White Crane Order. Su Jian thinks himself Tung's successor. The insinuation is ominous.

"We understand your concern, Auntie." Yuan lays a reassuring hand on my arm. "Wei Yi Pass is narrow and bordered by high ridges making our forces susceptible to ambushes. The safer path is Si Kao."

I nod my head and concede to the idea of Lam Soi. At the moment, Nan Rong's defense must be reinforced.

"I will take my unit south, if Your Highness permits." The unexpected recommendation came from Ming. For whatever reason, he seems less aggravated. "Fear is a good strategy but let's ensure our bark comes with a bite and not a nibble. My unit and a hundred thousand sets of armors should be enough to hold back Feng Jia. We'll show those novices what it means to play war."

"That is sensible. You have our blessing, General."

With that matter settled, Nan Rong's messenger heaves a sigh of relief. Ming bows to Yuan and then starts to leave. Barely does he touch the door, Liu's voice halts his pace. "We still have a little over two hundred thousand men. I say, send one hundred thousand to reinforce Lord Han Bei and the remainder to Nan Rong. The faster we put down this nonsense, the better."

All eyes immediately fly to the conflicting general. That's odd. Since this meeting began, Liu implied his dislike for the Southland. Why is he suddenly pushing to deplete the last of our men just to protect Nan Rong?

I might have imagined it; Ming sent a glance of caution in my direction before rejoining the table.

"I disagree. Her Highness was right to say we shouldn't overextend ourselves. Our two hundred thousand should remain in Ning's defense."

Disregarding Ming, Liu turns to Yuan with a respectable, albeit forced, smile. "Your Highness, the sooner we crush Bei Ling and Feng Jia, the sooner our soldiers can return. More than enough Ning lives were lost during Nan Rong's recent blunder. I hate to admit it but the Southlander's point is valid. Nan Rong is pertinent to our defense. Let us finish this quickly by reinforcing that front."

Once more, Yuan asks for my opinion. I agree with General Ming and that signals the end of discussion.

Liu, though conceded, still has determination burning in his unyielding eyes. After giving me another look of caution, Ming leaves with Nan Rong's messenger to prepare an envoy south. The rest of the generals return to their posts.

Chapter 44 – 2

"Yuan!"

"What is it, Auntie?"

After council dismissed, Yuan slipped out into the halls before I had a chance. Running to my nephew, I double over to catch my breath once he's stopped.

"Thank you for including me in council. I'm honored, really, but why did you keep looking to me for advice? I'm far from experienced."

"Han Bei instructed, '*In my absence, Bao Lai's opinions will carry my merit.*'"

"He did?! When?!"

"Right before he left. He said you're hotheaded and emotionally indecisive, but the Grand General seems to think your mind, the ability to reason, is your greatest attribute. He trusts your judgment."

"H-He does?!" I thought Han Bei despises me, as he should after every stupid thing I've said and done. I never would have guessed he entrusted his beloved Ning to my judgment. That is the greatest of compliments and one I'm both happy and fearful to receive.

"You're a bit gloomy, is something else on your mind?"

"Ah... Well, Lam Soi. I know I shouldn't. Still, I'm worried. Su Jian is..."

"Su Jian is no match for Han Bei. Trust in him just as he trust in you."

"I... trust Han Bei."

Yuan nods reassuringly and then continues down the hall.

"Wait! Did Han Bei say anything else before he left?"

"Such as?" Swinging around, a cheeky smile lights across his face. That's never a good sign.

"N-Nothing. Never mind."

"Oh? Now that you mentioned it, what is your favorite flower, one that would induce you to accept a proposal from a longtime admirer?"

"Why?"

Yuan shrugs. "A friend asked us to sleuth the answer for his benefit."

"What does this friend look like?"

"Does his appearance matter? That crude mouth of his is enough to make anyone think him off-putting. Most people who don't know him are often drawn in by the pretty red hair and emerald green eyes. What shall we tell him?"

My heart skips a beat. I thought his partiality for me was lost but if Han Bei aims to propose... My chest tightens. I'm so happy, an unrestrained grin plasters on my face. Yuan smiles meaningfully, urging for a response.

"He can't go wrong with—. You're mocking me, aren't you?"

"What makes you say that?" The mischievous grin he tries to hide surfaces behind the composed stare.

"Please don't coerce Han Bei into my attention anymore. I know you mean well but this is a matter between adults."

"The adult thing to do would be to stop running from one another. However, this is a lecture more fitting for Han Bei. We'll do as you've asked, Auntie."

Yuan bows graciously before leaving. It's still difficult to believe how young he is. His refinement and dignified stature are traits I recall from Dong Xing's portrait. He is the perfect product between my sister's nature and Han Bei's nurture; their son. Yuan thought for me to replace Dong Xing. I can't fit in this picture; not even while dressed in her clothes and wearing her shoes.

Once left alone in the halls, insecurity overtakes me. Why was I stupid enough to have become excited by the prospect of his proposal? There's wanting to believe in the impossible and then there's blatant facts. Han Bei no longer loves me. That is, he never did. He may have said I was Dong Xing but I know his rejection was a result of finally seeing past this disguise and perceiving that I could never hold a candle to his perfect goddess.

I am so sick and tired of being compared to someone better. I may be an indecisive brute who's terrible at conversations without the effortless charms my sister carried, but I still love him wholeheartedly. If he can't accept me and my faults, then I suppose I'm not the woman to make him happy either.

Whatever the future may hold, for now I have to agree with Han Bei, this isn't the time for my foolish romance.

Chapter 45: Coup d'Etat

Ever since General Ming's unit left for Nan Rong, I've been cooped up in Xiao Xiang Hall with various documents from the archive sprawled over the pristine marble floors. There aren't any windows; thus, time is lost to me. Under the watchful eyes of my matrons, I pray for everyone's safety as well as the answer to which I'm desperately searching. While I trust Han Bei's capabilities, intuition won't abolish the idea of Lam Soi.

Going through Wei Yi puts the men at greater risk for ambush and going through Si Kao means reaching Lam Soi Citadel. With Feng Jia distracting Nan Rong, Wang Liang could easily deduce the path of the advancing army and pit his entire force against Han Bei's at Lam Soi. General Ming made the point that Ning's marching eight hundred thousand outnumbers Bei Ling four to one. Han Bei also insisted one Ning soldier is worth five of our adversary's. By all considerations, we should be victorious.

The White Crane Annals noted the now barren Lam Soi once flourished as the most fortified stronghold of the former Sixth Kingdom of Zhou. It should have taken weeks, if not months, for Tung's forces to have seized the sanctuary; yet, all accounts seem to point their Order was annihilated in one night. Furthermore, the annals brushed over *how* the citadel was captured.

"Ah! Where is it?!"

I roll over toward the large map and trace along the path between Ning and Bei Ling for the hundredth time. More important than how Lam Soi was seized, if I can find the secret bridge mentioned in my father's poems, then Wei Yi and Si Kao will be insignificant.

My pounding headache is worsening. Lying flat on the cold floor, my attention is sent toward the large portraits above. If you can hear me, Mother, please show me the way. Dong Xing, please protect Han Bei. You loved him once. If by some miracle he can learn to accept me after this ordeal is over, let me love him forever in your stead.

I must be losing my mind. My sister's smile seemingly broadens. Every time I see her face, I grow more jealous of the charms she was bestowed. We look alike and somehow, I'm dull while her blooming smile is accompanied by eyes brighter than any star.

Star... brighter than any star. Wait a minute. The Huang Jia Feng Huang eyes in my pocket; my mother fashioned these wondrous black stars which Master Tai Hung said can sometimes glow in bright light.

Can it be? *"Secret bridge between two lands, covered by stars that need no night... shine brighter in light..."* and *"Starred tunnel dark as night where true lovers flee during their plight."*

There are several obsidian mines on the outskirts of Ning. Which of these could have produced glowing stars? Barely can I begin drawing markers over the map, screams burst from beyond the halls.

Chapter 45 – 2

Bloodcurdling screams resonate from the adjoining palaces. The moment I rush out of Xiao Xiang Hall, the acrid smell of smoke and blood faintly taint the night air. Footsteps running, boots thumping, horses neighing wildly; I hear them but I don't see anyone. Down the stairs toward the archive and then through the large double doors onto the balcony walkway. Once outside, the horrendous scent of blood and gore is unbearable. This can't be! Bei Ling's forces couldn't possibly have advanced this far.

"Tui Tui!"

I started to make a mad dash toward the main palace when Niu's panic-stricken voice calls out from behind. He's not in the least surprised to see the real me.

"Niu, what's happening?"

"Come with me!"

He draws a second sword latched to his hip and hands it to me. I nearly drop the heavy blade from trembling hands.

"I have to find Yuan!"

"Miss Hua Ye will bring him. You have to come with me, Your Highness!"

"Hua Ye? What about everyone else? We can't just leave them!"

"We have to!" He looks away, disgusted at himself for the horrid admission. Somehow managing to steel his nerves, Niu finally shakes off the unsettling thought and then reaches for my hand.

"My orders were to protect you. That's what I'm going to do."

"N-Niu! Wait!"

Without permitting further contentions, he drags me along while I stumble to keep up. Though still a greenhorn, his prowess proves to be lethal. One after another, soldiers in Ning armors aim to take our heads. He easily cuts them down, all the while still holding onto my hand. All I can do is tremble uncontrollably. Why are our soldiers doing this?

"Tell me what's happening!"

He ignores my cries until the path ahead is clear. Niu stops and then lets out an aggravated grunt. "General Liu and his men are staging a coup."

"Liu?! Why?! How?! Where are our defenses?"

"Several days ago, false orders were given to send Nan Rong our remaining regiments one at a time. Regardless of why he's betrayed Ning, you need to stay alive, Your Highness. Captain Xian's orders were clear.

I have to keep you from harm. As long as you live, our people won't stand under Liu's banner."

Our people, the very ones suffering now. I can hear their screams in the distance and the wailings from those left behind. One life lost makes ten lives mourn. Everything my mother worked for and Han Bei sought to protect is disappearing in an instant. I can't stand by and permit this travesty! I won't! I'll make that bastard pay!

"Niu! Over there!"

The instant Niu turns toward the diversion, I rip away and fly back toward the chaos. His panicking voice, which calls out to me, blend into one with the hectic screams and shouts. I can't stop. I won't ever be able to live with myself or look Han Bei in the eyes if I just walk away and let everyone die. What was the point for all my training?

"Auntie!"

His horrified scream halts my pace. Nearby, Yuan is backed against a wall while Hua Ye's dagger skillfully penetrates armor openings of the assailing soldiers. She's his sole defense between life and death. It's doubtful any man could even lay one finger on her.

I rush toward them while she easily dispatches the last man through her dancelike movements. The lady grins proudly for her achievement but relief came premature. Barely could Hua Ye catch her breath, another familiar, tall figure, suddenly emerges from around the corner in front of me. Her dagger manages to parry his blade but the force was too much. Her footing is lost and she stumbles back. Without time to recover, Hua Ye throws her body over Yuan's.

"Liu!"

With rage building in torrents, I bring down the blade. He turns just in time to defend. One after another, I repeatedly swing the sword to no avail. My attacks are not aimed to kill. I want Liu punished for his treachery but a part of me is afraid to take a life. Han Bei isn't here to shoulder another guilt I can't carry. As usual, I am still just a coward.

Despite my reservations, Liu gives no quarter. Each of his attack seeks to take my head. Whether due the heavy armor or fatigue from having slain our allies, his movements seem slowed which provide small margins for me to evade. That is, until his large boot manages to connect to my stomach, sending me to the ground.

Noticing my hesitation, Hua Ye rejoins the fray. Her short dagger isn't enough to reach his vitals before Liu counters. With each passing moment, her arms grow weary. In desperation, the lady becomes bold. Hua Ye closes in farther, making one daring attempt for his throat. The blade grazes his skin and in the next instant, his blade sweeps across her chest. She falls back and into Yuan's arms.

"Hua Ye!" Dear heavens, please tell me she isn't... this is all my fault! She was only trying to protect Yuan. How could Liu do that without one bit of remorse? How much Ning blood has he spilled this night!

Liu's mocking gaze bear down. Realizing that I lack the courage to take his life, he turns from me and then makes for the cornered Yuan, who's still clutching onto Hua Ye's body. She gave her life to protect a boy with no blood ties. Yuan is my only remaining family and I'm too afraid to lift a finger to help! His teary eyes stare at me with the same disappointment from when we last spoke of the woman who left him behind. I am Dong Xing.

Liu brings up the blade. I...

Rush forward (Continue to page 608)

Call for Han Bei (Continue to page 609)

Chapter 45 – 3

I rush forward, my steps thumping hard against the floors in tune with my heartbeat. In an instant, composure crumbles. Liu ignored my interference and brought down the blade. I was too far away to reach them in time.

His still eyes are robbed the light of life. Yuan falls dead with the disappointed gaze casted on the woman who couldn't give her everything to protect him. I wonder, was I afraid to kill Liu because I feared to take a life or was I too afraid to die because I finally had something to live for? And yet, here I am without anything left. My last family is gone. Han Bei will never forgive me. If I lose my soul for staining my hands red, what difference would that make?

Brandishing the blade, I charge forward swinging wildly without discretion. At some point or other, my chest grows cold and everything turns blinding white.

The End.

Chapter 45 – 4

"Han Bei!" I cry out excitedly.

Liu freezes from dread and then turns around. Using the diversion, I rush forward.

"Get away from my son, you bastard!"

He blocks all my swings and still, I have unrelenting energy to deal out more. How my arms have this much strength or my body the flexibility to continually evade his counterstrikes is unimaginable. During my training, I would have been at my limits forty bouts ago.

Exhaustion grows on Liu's brows. He's eyeing the walkways as if expecting support. Surprisingly, not one man has come to his defense and even stranger, the bedlam around has noticeably decreased.

"Surrender, Liu! Your men aren't coming! Surrender and accept punishment for your crimes against Ning!"

He knocks back my blade, the force of which sends the weapon flying from my hand and over the railings of the balcony. I reach for Han Bei's prized dagger latched to my ankle and then resume a defiant stance. For a short moment, we retreat to catch our breaths.

"Everything I do is for Ning! The day the East bows to a Southern dog is the day this country descends into hell!"

"You sent Nan Rong our remaining soldiers because no one else agrees with your insanity!"

"I sent them away for their own safety! They will return to a land cleansed of you and everyone else who follows your leadership! You've corrupted our Grand General and sent our men to their deaths! If it weren't for your influence, he would have taken my advice and ended this nonsense before it began. The frivolous alliance. The indecisive leadership! Here we are risking our lives for a war against the North while half of you is Bei Ling. The other half is Nan Rong. There's not one part of you that is Ning. And now I hear you've a Southern mutt for a lover, waiting to ascend our throne. I will never permit that!"

"You killed all those innocent people... because of me? Why didn't you target me directly?!"

"Why should I make you a martyr when you're more valuable as a saint? The people will believe what they are told: Nan Rong staged the attack under Ning disguises and slew our valiant princess who tried to stop them. Once Bei Ling is vanquished, we'll take Nan Rong and the remaining two territories. Ning will be rid of war permanently. All that's necessary is for you to die!"

The madness in his eyes signals Liu's determination. He won't surrender. He was a loyal Ning servant and for the rest of history, will be branded a traitor because of me. Maybe this ordeal is my fault but, I can't let his crimes go unpunished nor will I die until I've paid for mine.

Anger inside is overshadowed by grief. I can't cry because there aren't enough tears to wash away what can't be undone. There's only one thing I can do.

Liu brandishes his sword and then charges forward. A wave of heat surges over me. I can't hear anything except the sound of my heartbeat thumping in my ears. All else are drowned out in hollow echoes. Everything around gradually slows. I move past his striking blade as easily as though he were a motionless stone statue. The dagger in my hand is stained red. I blink once and then time seemingly resumes.

Chapter 45 – 5

Until his body succumbed to every mortal's weakness, it didn't dawn on me that I'd taken a life. My conscience should be wracked with guilt and yet, I feel complacent. To save my family, I'd do it again.

"Your Highness!"

Niu startles me when he comes up from behind. His anxious voice brings back my senses. Heavy bloodstains cover his armor while the pain of guilt for having slain former comrades casts shadows over his wavering eyes. This is the truth every soldier must endure: war means death and in order to save one soul requires a trade of another, often the protector's.

"Dear me, what a noisy man."

None is more startled than Yuan to see Hua Ye leisurely rise up from his arms, rubbing her forehead absently as if woken from a nap.

"You're alive?!"

"Don't sound so disappointed," Hua Ye smiles. The lady dusts off her clothes and when her arms stretch toward the air, the light chainmail under the tear of her shirt reflects the pale moonlight. Just who is this woman?

While I stare at her hidden armor, she stares back at my bloodied dagger. Her skeptical glance falls on Liu. A half smile curls over petal lips and she says nothing more.

"I'm going back."

Soon as the declaration leaves my mouth, Niu reaches for my collar.

"Tui Tui—Your Highness. Seems the moment fire broke out, many veterans took up arms. They're still subduing the insurgents in the other palaces but most have surrendered. I don't think the men's hearts were in this."

"That doesn't change the fact innocent lives were lost! They can't go unpunished!"

"Auntie, once the head is severed, the body crumbles. Liu is gone. Rule our people with your left hand, not your right."

Rule the people with my left hand; my less dominant, less forceful hand. Those unexpected words from a true sovereign silence my resentment. I've already taken one life tonight. No one else needs this senseless suffering.

Ultimately, I conceded to Niu's plans. Together, Hua Ye, Yuan, and I escaped the city. Niu trailed behind to ensure we weren't followed.

Chapter 45 – 6

Around a small campfire, Yuan and I sit in quiet contemplation. Hua Ye left to inspect our surroundings. I can't pay attention to else except my guilt. I don't regret having stained my hands red but I am responsible for the lives lost.

"It's not your fault, Auntie."

Thin arms sweep me into an embrace, comforting me and so, comforting himself. Under his calm demeanor, Yuan is trembling. He's taller than me, so I keep forgetting how young he really is.

"Thank you, Yuan. It was my fault but it also wasn't. Same as my birth, my existence is built on others' sacrifices. I vow when this is over, I will make Ning stronger than ever."

"Does that mean you've accepted your role?"

"Yes. I thought I did, but a part of me was still unsure. Now, I'm certain. I want to do this just as my sister and my mother before me."

Following an awkward pause, he shuffles uncomfortably. "Auntie, why did you call us your son earlier?"

"I did? When?"

"When you charged at Liu. Don't you remember? 'Get away from my son,' is what you said."

"I don't remember. To be honest, everything that happened is a bit hazy. Time was slowed and then it wasn't. I saw that you were in danger, I thought about Dong Xing, and then somehow unimaginable strength welled inside. If I had to describe it, I'd say I felt... possessed."

"Possessed? By who?"

"I don't know."

He falls silent. The sadness on his face yearns for a confirmation of love from the mother he never knew. Perhaps Dong Xing did guide my hand to protect her only son or maybe, it was all in my head.

"Yuan, despite whom your mother loved in her personal life, I don't doubt for a second that she loved you."

His downcast eyes glisten from unshed tears. Yuan puts on the usual composure while his lips tremble. In a rush, the embrace grows stronger while his face buries in my shoulder. What a stubborn boy. He's withheld his tears all these years under that sturdy mask. I'll do for him as Han Bei did for me. My arms lock around his back. Yuan continues sobbing for a long while until his breathing finally calms.

"Hey, I know I can't replace her, but I wouldn't mind if you thought of me as your mother."

Once the reassuring message reaches him, Yuan lifts off my shoulder. Flushed cheeks and puffy eyes stare back in bewilderment. Slowly, a smile forms and then sardonic laughter fills the air.

"Y-You? We may call you, 'Auntie,' but we think of you as our little sister!"

"Little sister?! You got some nerve, kid! I'm twelve years your senior!"

"No one believes that except Han Bei. The servants all think you're fifteen years old."

"T-They do?"

The ambiguous cheeky grin makes me feel even more unnerved. Is that why he's always making fun of me?

"My! What a lovely portrait! If one didn't know better, one would perceive a young couple in love."

Hua Ye's amused chuckle strikes terror. Yuan and I are still latched to one another and in a flash, separate.

"That's not funny!"

"Her Highness has no sense of humor. An adult wouldn't have taken offense."

"You were eavesdropping, too?"

"I am your eyes and ears," is her quick response.

"I suppose. Thank you for saving Yuan and me."

"Not at all, Your Highness. You played no small part in our safety. I am surprised. More experienced warriors have fallen to Liu's blade."

"I cheated, somehow. What about you?"

"Dear me, didn't I introduce myself properly? My family has always guarded yours. I was Empress Dong Xing's bodyguard. For now, I am yours. Come, you both should rest. Tomorrow we'll ride to Da Lu Village for refuge until matters in the capital settles."

Too tired to contend, Yuan sighs wearily. He curls a distance away from the fire and permit slumber to send him somewhere happier.

Chapter 45 – 7

"Is something troubling you? We've a full day ahead tomorrow, you might as well rest."

Hua Ye tucks a few more dry sticks into the fire and then takes the seat adjacent.

"No, I'm fine."

"You're a terrible liar. Our families are so intertwined, I'd like to think of myself as your big sister. So, tell Big Sis what's on your mind."

"Would that make Kang Lang my little sis?"

She giggles in a girlish fashion as though mimicking Mu Dan. "We look alike, don't we, Kang Lang and I? He fancies himself prettier and I think he's right. Let us three become sisters then. So, what's on your mind? Liu?"

"Yes. I knew he didn't approve of me but I still can't believe Liu went to such lengths. He loved Ning so much that he was willing to destroy her. It's lunacy! And the men who blindly followed him, how can they live with themselves?"

"Soldiers do as they're told. Not everyone is as insolent as we are, Your Highness." Hua Ye, smiling gently, nudges my arm. "That is to say, not everyone is allowed to be as insolent. Sometimes we forget to thank our lucky stars to be born who we are and for the freedom we are permitted. Simple things we take for granted."

"Yes, I'll try not to forget that. What about everyone who's suffering? What could I possibly do to amend this stain of anguish that's marred their lives?"

"Suffering is the cost of war and death is the unavoidable cost of living. No one who died tonight could have escaped death forever. Those who lived would do well to remember that."

"Simplifying suffering is..."

Albeit her tone was cold, Hua Ye's expression is mournful. I'd forgotten under that flower face is a warrior. She must have seen her fair share of war and death. Maybe this rationalization is the only method to help her move forward. At the moment, I should follow her example. Once this is over, I'll try to become the leader Ning deserves. I'll keep her from war, just as Liu sought to do in his own misguided way.

Above, the heavens suddenly grow frenzied. An array of stars shoots down from the skies reminiscent of celestial tears lamenting for the departed; both beautiful and heart wrenching. Are these tears for my beloved people in the capital or those fighting abroad? I reach for the Huang Jia Feng Huang and pray that Han Bei's star could be safe here in my hands.

"What beautiful black tourmaline!"

The abrupt chirrupy outburst reverts my attention back to Hua Ye, whose eyes are sparkling from delight.

"Hmm? Where?"

"Where else? In your hands, silly."

"These are obsidian not black... tour-na-ment?"

"Tourmaline, dear!" She laughs. "A common protection stone also said to bring luck."

"Han Bei said these are obsidian."

"Gracious, you'd take his words over mine? Han Bei can't tell olivine from serpentine! I fancy myself an expert. Against my wishes, Xian has showered me with almost every gemstone imaginable! He is such a dear!"

There she goes gloating about her romantic Xian again. The Captain's ears must be burning.

"I thought Ning is known for black obsidian. Why would my mother have fashioned black tourmaline?"

"They're rare stones in Ning. I have been searching for high quality black tourmaline to fit for Xian a protection charm, but recent imports were disappointing. I may just have to steal those from you!"

"Are they truly that rare?"

"Quality always is and Bei Ling by far has the best. It's a shame we haven't been on good terms with their merchants."

"These stones are from Bei Ling?"

"Who knows? Ning once had a small mine. Empress Piao closed it permanently after some structural mishap. Entry was forbidden under the penalty of death and then rumors sparked that the mine was haunted by jiangshi. No one's bothered with it for decades."

The possibility is too fantastic. I'm immediately on my feet. Hua Ye questions my stupid smile and I divulge my father's secret bridge, Master Tai Hung's mention of stars, and the Huang Jia Feng Huang. She listens intently, delighted by my farfetched suppositions. Once my ramblings finish, the familiar giggle returns.

"You have quite the imagination!"

"Where is this mine, Hua Ye?"

"As stubborn as Han Bei, aren't you? Fine. Once he gets an idea in his head, he doesn't quit and neither will you. We'll ride together at dawn."

"What about Yuan?"

"Niu should arrive soon. Let the boys go to safety. Leave danger to the girls."

"Won't Niu disapprove?"

"Very few men have denied me anything, dear. If you must worry over permission, then you haven't fully appreciated your power as a woman."

"That sounds very much like Kang Lang's sentiment. You are indeed a dangerous woman, Hua Ye."

"Flatterer! You're only saying that because I nearly drowned you."

"Yes, I'll be sure to pay you back for that someday."

"*Scary!* There are few hours left in the night. Tomorrow, we'll have to traverse a haunted mine and battle hordes of jiangshi no less. Get some sleep while you can."

I nod and then lie down beside Yuan. He's smiling innocently in his sleep. Whether for a brief moment I was her conduit or whether it was all coincidence, I hope Dong Xing's love for her son finally reached him.

Chapter 46: A Starlit Cavern

"They're not real."

"I know that!"

Yuan and Niu are safe in Da Lu while my escort and I are traversing through the abandoned mine. She persists to tell me ghost stories about jiangshi and then at intervals, scare the life out of me by making strange sounds and poking her long fingers at my neck.

"You say that but you've gone pale."

"You're as mean as Kang Lang!"

"He's as mean as me, you meant to say. I'm older. The original."

"You're proud of that?"

"So, what's happened between you and Han Bei?"

"Don't change the subject!"

"If you won't tell me, I'm turning back."

"Ugh. Why is my love life the topic of everyone's interest?"

"Such as it is these days. Nothing is more amusing than reality drama. Naturally, I've been rooting for Han Bei in this love triangle. Has he won?"

"You might as well have been rooting for me. If you really must know, I've put Han Bei out of his misery. Once I gave up my first love, he realized I am my sister; his infatuation is lost."

Her pace halts. Yuan Wei turns about. A knot crinkles across the perfect brows. "After everything she put him through, he still can't let her go? I will give Han Bei a lecture he won't forget!"

"To what end? To coerce him into loving me? Despite what everyone says, she was my sister. She had her reasons and Han Bei has his."

"You're obligated to defend your sister. Just don't forget to defend yourself."

"I'm not defending anyone. Everyone I've spoken to, from nobles to farmers alike, thinks Han Bei deserves the throne, as did I, long before love fueled my bias. Maybe Dong Xing didn't relinquish their engagement because Han Bei is best for Ning, and maybe she tasked him to find me so I could take her place. Sometimes, the best-laid plan doesn't succeed and because it doesn't, the intentions are misunderstood."

"By that presumption, Her Highness designed your union to Han Bei. Since he would never go against her wishes, doesn't that just mean he should love you?"

"He shouldn't love me to make *her* happy. I appreciate your concern but please, don't meddle in our affairs anymore. I'm content with loving him from afar."

"Oh, fine! You aren't any fun—"

A deep gasp fills the damp air. Hua Ye brings a hand over her mouth; her eyes are as wide as saucers. I sweep around and draw the blade latched to my hip, only to flinch when a long finger jabs at my neck. Her boisterous giggles return.

"Stop that!"

Shrugging innocently, Hua Ye smiles and then resumes leading the way. Jiangshi or not, this woman might just be the death of me.

Chapter 46 – 2

"Hua Ye, is this tunnel a straight path?"

"Afraid to take a wrong turn, Your Highness? We might, because I've no idea."

"M-Maybe we should find some way to mark the path. Y-You know, just in case."

"Oh, I see! Claustrophobic? Or, are you afraid of the dark?"

"N-Neither!"

"Liar! Wasn't that something to have considered before storming inside a cave?"

Embarrassed, I turn back toward the entrance for comfort. I can still see the horse out front. We've barely gotten anywhere!

"I—"

"Shh!"

The torch in her hand is buried into the moist earth; extinguishing the flame. We stand still, holding our breaths for an excruciatingly long time. It began as a ringing hum and then a thump. The ground slightly rumbles from distant echoes.

Seizing my hand, Hua Ye rushes from the cave. I nearly fall from the steed when she takes off at full gallop.

"I guess you weren't the only one looking for secret passages!"

"Were those Bei Ling's men?"

"Whether they were or weren't Bei Ling, I won't stay to find out! The soldiers Liu sent to Nan Rong haven't returned and the rest are still reeling from the coup. We're defenseless and worse, unprepared. If that was a small scouting unit, then the larger force isn't far behind!"

"How many? Could we thwart their advance?"

"You mean kill them? Bloodlust is not suited for you, Your Highness. Anyhow, should we kill their scouts, the main force will be on guard. We don't have the men to outright challenge them. So long as they think we're ignorant, we can use that to our advantage. Let's regroup and think this over."

Chapter 46 – 3

She rode like the wind and soon enough, the capital's walls appear. Under the afternoon sun, tolls from last night's coup are made clear. Many beautiful palaces were damaged or burnt to ashes. Dried blood splatters covering the ground serve as grim reminders of innocent lives lost. Mostly, shock and grief from the uproar still looms over the tepid air.

"Lord Zhao!"

Red hair sways in the wind. He turns to meet Hua Ye's cries, rendering me breathless the moment I catch sight of those sharp eyes, curved lips, and prominent nose. I know that face; only, there's a hint of age.

"Hua Ye. Your Highness." He bows graciously with the dignified air befitting his son.

"Uncle, there's no time for pleasantries!"

"Indeed. This isn't the place to dawdle. Resentment is still present and thus, danger. I hope you had good reasons for leaving Da Lu."

Her panic mounts. Hua Ye explains the bleak situation to Lord Zhao whose composure never once wavers. His gaze casts off into the distance in thoughtful contemplation during her recapitulation; as though for each difficulty, he's formulated a resolve. Despite the troubles, somehow being near him instills confidence.

"There must be something we can do, Uncle!"

"Her Highness, Empress Piao, blocked the route shortly before her death. Bypassing the obstruction couldn't have been easy. I doubt they'll be keen to repeat the difficult task. Let us follow her example and collapse the mine, preferably before Bei Ling's main group arrives."

"How? By now, they should have made it through." I turn back toward the gates and wonder how far off our enemies could possibly be.

"Wang Liang wouldn't have sent his entire army through a rat hole. As long as his advancing team is put down, we can create another barrier."

"Our remaining defense is in Nan Rong. We don't stand a chance."

"Is that right?" He replies in that same airy, partially amused manner Han Bei tends to employ. "Who was it but old men who subdued the coup? Don't take our presence too lightly."

"I-I didn't mean to offend you, sir, or any old man! I-I mean, you're not old, y-you're just—"

His wry chuckle seeks to cut off my rambling. The smooth tone painfully reminds me of Han Bei. My head hangs in disgrace in front of the man who, under different circumstances, could have been my father-in-law.

"The other old geezers and I will make preparations to collapse the mine. Liu's men are grieving over their mistake. They're aching to redeem themselves. Prove to them your authority, Your Highness. Show them your capable leadership. Hua Ye, your task is to scout the advancing team. Let us make certain they are Bei Ling before taking serious measures."

"Who else could have taken that path, sir? Does it really connect to Bei Ling? If so, where does it lead and could we use it to our advantage?"

"Han Bei didn't jest. Her Highness is devastatingly curious." The cheeky smile is now reminiscent of Kang Lang. "I know why you sought the cavern. Your father and his White Crane colleagues often used the passage to bring intelligence here during Tung's oppression. It was useful. However, sometimes the past should remain buried."

"My father belonged to the Order? I thought they were against nobles."

"That is a dangerous generalization. The Order does have friends in high places and likewise, enemies in low places. As for your father, he was first and foremost, an excellent scholar."

My father was a scholar; I feel proud to finally learn that. So, my mother, the warrior, fell for a man who favored the pen over the sword. In this instance, I see that I take after my father.

"Sir, what about Lam Soi? Tung has returned as Wang Liang and Han Bei is following the path to Lam Soi."

"You children are such handfuls. Your mother was also a worrywart. I said this to her then and I'll say this to you now: permit the Zhaos to be your right hand and focus on ruling with your left. If Han Bei's listened to a word I've said, he'll know better."

I'm not entirely sure what he means; though, there isn't much time to dig further into the past. I bow to him and then part with Hua Ye to gather Liu's men. The downtrodden soldiers are clearly miserable for last night's treachery. It's still hard for me to grasp Hua Ye's assertions but I know she was right; they were only following orders. Under my new authority, they'll have the chance to redeem their mistake and I'll have the chance to redeem my former lackluster leadership; even if that will result in destroying the very thing which I was searching.

Chapter 46 – 4

"Are you ready? Out of their five hundred, let's kill half and the others will surrender."

"You're a little... bloodthirsty, aren't you, Hua Ye?"

"Ha! No more than you, Your Highness. Well, we'll have to make do with our two hundred."

"One Ning soldier is worth five of theirs. I won't forget that. They're still outnumbered."

She smiles reassuringly. I return the gesture though my heart is thumping. If it weren't for the heavy armors keeping my body grounded, I fear the soldiers behind would notice my jitters. As for the men who grudgingly followed me, I can see in their eyes the determination to protect Ning, and that's all that truly matters.

We're waiting on the southwestern end of the narrow Ke Yi Road, whose path winds around the Bai Ma Gorge. Bei Ling purposefully came this way to avoid our watchers on the main Sui Yu Road, which leads to the capital. Under different circumstances, I'd say they made the right choice. In this instance, their cautious tactics will prove to be their downfall.

The scout atop the lookout gives the signal. I call for the foot soldiers to ready their weapons. In the next instant, cries erupt from enemy lines. Bei Ling thought they had the advantage of surprise; thus, our sentinels' volley came unexpected and they are the ones to stagger. Guard Captain Jie gives the next order and another volley rains arrows upon Bei Ling.

Deafening cries, heavy pounding footsteps, and stench of blood fill the air. Shortly after, the scout from atop signals again. In their state of panic, Bei Ling's soldiers are unable to grasp the greater danger awaiting at the other end of the winding path. I raise my sword and give the only words that mean anything to our soldiers.

"For Ning!"

At once, bellowing echoes project pride and the enduring desire to protect our beloved land. We march forward to meet the North's remaining troops that managed to escape the hail of arrows. The sight of our intimidating black armors turns even the bravest men to stone. Some sought retreat but their escape is barred by the wall of arrows that waits behind. With their fates sealed, those who refuse to surrender storm forward.

The first to draw blood between the two charging units is Hua Ye. Her small daggers prove swift and accurate, flying forth like rains of petals. Once weapons from both sides clashed, everything that followed was hazy. I swung my weapon, men fell, a blade slid against my chest plate but couldn't penetrate, and then the battleground stained red. By the time it was over, I still couldn't remember when it started.

"Are you all right?"

Hua Ye's hand lands on my cheek, wiping away the last of my tears. When did I cry?

"I-I'm sorry. The men don't need to see a weak leader."

"On the contrary, a good leader takes every life seriously. Look around. They've never been more proud of their warrior princess."

Their rallying cries bring back my senses. The calm expressions on their faces signal that they've been absolved. For me, this is only the beginning.

After the skirmish ended, Lord Zhao and the other *old geezers* re-collapsed the mine. Those captured during battle were interrogated, giving new worries to our already troubled predicament.

Lam Soi's main water supply from the River Xuan was poisoned and for the time, Han Bei's troops are stranded and dying. Half of his eight hundred thousand were lost; the other half is on the verge of annihilation. Han Bei's whereabouts are unknown. Rumor in the North is that he perished.

Chapter 47: A Suitable Leader

"Let me go! Damn it! I will avenge Han Bei if it's the last thing I do!"

"They're just rumors! Calm down!"

The more she pulls back, the more I forcefully move forward until our stalemate ends with Hua Ye and I tumbling to the floor. I start to crawl out the door while she plops atop my heavy armor.

"Get off, Hua Ye! I can't accept this! I have to find Han Bei!"

"What if they're all lies? You'll only get in the way!"

"I don't care! Get off of me!"

"I've never been more turned on in my life!"

"W-What?"

Hua Ye returns my puzzled glance with a blank stare. We both twist about to find our *younger sister* grinning mischievously by the side door of the throne room.

"K-Kang Lang! You're safe!" By now, he is like family to me. I'm so relieved that I nearly burst into tears.

"Oh, don't mind me," he replies airily. "Continue. I want to see where this is going."

"Get this crazy woman off me! I have to find Han Bei!"

Kang Lang saunters over and then tugs me to my feet from beneath Hua Ye. "Why'd you have to go and ruin the mood by mentioning him? I'm much better than Han!"

Drawing me into his arms, Kang Lang slips a hand underneath my armor through the exposed collar. His fingers trace over my collarbone. I jump from the ticklish sensation, yank his hand away, and then swing a gauntlet at his face. He dodges, laughing loudly during the retreat.

"I love violent women! Whether as He Pi or Bao Lai, I will make you mine!"

"Stop being an idiot, Kang Lang!" My shouts are overlapped by Hua Ye's. He looks from one to the other and then sulks. Against two wrathful women, he surrenders.

"Fine! Anyway, rumors are precisely the reason I came back. So, they say the buffoon got himself killed. I refuse to believe that until I see it for myself."

Usual calmness can't veil the pain and panic spreading across his eyes. I share his sentiment.

"I'm going with you, Kang Lang."

"Dear me!" Hua Ye sighs. "Lord Zhao was right. You children are handfuls. Haven't you learned the danger of inactive leadership? In times of uncertainty, the people need someone to be the pillar of stability. Once you leave, they'll think you've ran away. I'll go in your stead."

"You've placed yourself in danger enough times for my sake. Captain Xian would worry—"

"Xian knew the type of woman I was when we married. He fell in love with my ability to wield a dagger, not a kitchen knife. Now, it's true I was in danger plenty of times for your sake but I haven't been for mine. Big Sis is going whether you girls like it or not."

Kang Lang's pout is followed by a shrug. He doesn't care to be considered our sister. I, on the other hand, concede to her advice. However, just as the two start for the exit, I call them back.

"Wait! Kang Lang, what is the current status for Ye and Nan Rong?"

"You interrupted my valiant undertaking to talk about work? How dull! I'm giving you up, Your Highness."

"Oh, what's this? Are you in love with her, too, cousin?"

"Like I would ever be so desperate!"

"Then why are you blushing?"

Kang Lang turns away and scoffs, fueling Hua Ye's giggles.

"Um... Can we talk about work? What's happened in Nan Rong?"

"What did you think would happen after sending two hundred thousand Ning soldiers south? They mopped the floor with Feng Jia. What I mean is there no longer is a Feng Jia. Xian claimed the territory for Ning and he's fighting San An for the naming rights. Being the boring romantic that he is, San An's contending to rename the territory after you. Xian wants it renamed, Tui Tui, after his cat. By the way, was it your crazy idea to send the remaining defense south? Su Jian never expected your recklessness."

"It wasn't my idea. It was... I'll tell you later. What about Ye?"

"Ye was backed into a corner so they managed to find courage. Their council ejected Bei Ling to keep Ning from invading. Xian's making his march into Bei Ling from the West and San An is leading the charge from the center. If only Han had his head screwed on straight, this nonsense can be over with."

"It's not Han Bei's fault."

"No? He embarrassed the Zhao name. Grand General, my ass! I'll kick that idiot senseless when I find him!"

His jaw grits and then Kang Lang's attention is averted. Under the harsh words is apparent concern and I'm merely worsening his anxiety. Han Bei has to be alive. There are too many who love the Grand General for him to leave us all behind.

"Kick him once for making me worried, too."

I force a crooked smile, to which Kang Lang returns a short, timid nod. The cousins then resume their course while I seek out Lord Zhao's council. There's much to be done and I have to ensure the tragedy Liu caused will never happen again.

Chapter 47 – 2

"Mmm. Han Bei?"

His stern face comes to me in a dream, a dream more lucid than those previous. I'm in his strong arms, being carried down a long hallway. My tired eyes close, to then realize if this were a dream, then I should already be asleep.

"Han Bei! You're alive!"

My eyes pop wide open. Both arms fly around his neck in hopes of tearing him out of my dream in case this isn't real. The jolt causes the Grand General to stumble.

"Calm yourself, Your Highness. I am here. Why were you sleeping in Xiao Xiang Hall?"

My face buries in his chest, staining the silver robe with unrelenting happy tears, while choking through the reply. "I was praying... to Dong Xing... to my mother... for you to be safe. I'm so glad! Han Bei, I've missed you so much!"

He remains as unfeeling as a statue. I don't care if he hates me. I never want to let him go. Once in my chamber, he lays me gently on the bed and attempts to leave. In that instant, we both fall victim to bewilderment. My hands are latched tightly onto his collar and no matter how I command them to release him, brazenness wins over modesty. As shameless as it is, I just want his touch for a moment longer; however brief.

Han Bei's eyes grow wide and so do mine. I've lost the ability to control myself. My trembling arms draw him closer. Despite his indifference, he reluctantly complies. Regrettably, once our lips nearly touch, he jerks away.

"It's late. Get some sleep."

"Wait! Where have you been? Do you have any idea how worried I was?!"

"An explanation can wait until morning."

"No, it can't! I won't sleep until you tell me!"

"How old do you think you are?" Han Bei mutters under a soft, irritated sigh before pulling over the chair from beneath the side table. He lets out another sigh and then begins to explain, seemingly to the wall where his gaze is casted.

It seems that when Han Bei and his men reached the diverging paths to Si Kao and Wei Yi, scouts reported a number of Bei Ling troops stationed at the latter. Knowing he'd take Si Kao, they were waiting to bypass his main forces in hopes of crossing into Ying Ling. They were routed and many of their men were captured. A few prisoners then divulged Wang Liang's plan in exchange for their freedom. He'd plotted to destroy the border cities should Han Bei's troops advance too close to Bei Ling, giving no considerations to the innocent civilians.

At Lam Soi, the medics tested the only viable water source flowing into the citadel and found it poisoned; the same method Tung used to murder the former White Crane Order. None of the texts in the archives mentioned it, but as Lord Zhao and Yuan pointed out, I should have trusted Han Bei. Using Wang Liang's ploy, the camp feigned illness and news were circulated that the Grand General perished. The captured Bei Ling soldiers were purposefully left unguarded so they could return north to spread the rumors. When scouts saw no further movements from Lam Soi, rumors were taken as truth.

While Han Bei's troops slowly receded, Wang Liang's advanced, only to meet the East's elites and suffered a devastating blow. In this way, Han Bei was able to spare the Bei Ling civilians living on the outskirt cities who, after realizing his kindness, then rallied under his banner.

With his plot foiled, Wang Liang sought to rebuild his external defenses against the advancing Ning army. The negligent move weakened his internal lines and allowed He Pi and the White Cranes to storm the palace and claimed Emperor Cai Pai under their protection. The remaining guards who served Wang Liang either surrendered or were put to death. However, Wang Liang was nowhere to be found. Some claimed he perished during the raid, though that supposition is yet confirmed.

"You had troubles here, too, I heard. I apologize for my poor judgment. Liu was a good man and a good soldier. I understood his idealism and he was undoubtedly loyal. I just never thought he'd go so far."

Han Bei pauses, as though to lament for his former friend and comrade. Behind the composure, regret is slowly surfacing. I place a hand on his arm. He remains motionless.

"Through Liu's mistake, Nan Rong was saved and the tides turned in our favor. Han Bei, I can't forgive everything he's done but a part of me understands why he did it. His greatest mistake was not having isolated his resentment toward me."

"The outcome wouldn't have been any different. You're hardly a damsel in distress. Honestly, you surprised me. I never would have guessed you were gifted with Tian Ji Zhong Shi Yan."

"What's... Tian yi-yi sh...?"

"Tian Ji Zhong Shi Yan," Han Bei scoffs. "That's Hua Ye's theory anyway, for how you were able to defeat Liu, even if that only brings up more questions."

The recapitulation suspends while his posture turns rigid. He's suddenly in a worse mood than when I last confessed my affections.

"I'm sorry."

The anger displayed on his countenance apparently isn't against me. I've no idea why he apologized.

"For?"

"For... putting my hands on you so roughly. I'd-I'd never meant to hurt you. I don't know what came over me. I'm sorry. Were you... injured?"

The touch of his hand on my collar, constricting my throat, is a feeling I remember well, before he thoughtlessly threw me aside. At the time and even now, it wasn't the physical pain that marred me. His words cut deeper. I understood his anger. Had Kang Lang perished, I'd have deserved worse.

"Not at all. Compared to your conduct from the first time we met, you were quite gentle."

"Back then, I was merely teasing. There was nothing callous behind my actions."

"So, you're apologizing for the thought and not the action?"

Once, I vaguely remember him saying something like this to me. Usually, he'd shoot my sarcasm back with sarcasm. I can't believe how much I miss his derision! My cheeky grin only serves to distance his already cold eyes. I fear the filter through which he sees me will never again be favorable.

"I don't hold any grudge against you, Han Bei. During the past several months, my fist did fly across your face and I kneed you in your most sensitive area. As far as things go, we're more than even."

"Still, I apologize."

Han Bei bows low and then starts from the chair. That was abrupt. I know he doesn't want my company. Still, panic forces my hand. I can't keep from asserting my foolish petition.

"Don't go. Please, don't go!"

"If you need anything, send for the servants."

"I need you, Han Bei! Stay with me!"

"Those are too brazen of words to bestow a mere soldier, Your Highness. There are fitting Southern princes awaiting those commands."

He makes for the door, each step a knife through my chest. During the past several weeks, I'd imagined the worst. To finally have this moment together after so long, I can't stand to see him leave again. With my heart on the verge of bursting, I lunge forward while even more shameless cries fall from my lips.

"I'm sorry! I'm sorry for my dishonesty! I'm sorry for my indifference! I'm sorry for reminding you of your misery! Please, tell me however you want me to be and I'll become the person you want. I know I'll never replace her but I... Just don't ignore me anymore, I can't take it! I love you, more than anything in this world! More than I'll ever love anyone! Please, forgive me and let me stay by your side!"

His back is to me. I can only see his squared shoulders remain unyielding to my pleas. During the ensuing silence, I hold my breath, fearful of his rejection. The fact that he doesn't have an immediate answer fooled me into believing there was still hope. I should have known better.

"I warned you against becoming me."

He leaves me with those confounding words and then parts from the room.

Chapter 48: Home is where the Heart is

Since his return, the Grand General's been busy with reconstruction from the failed coup, reestablishing the people's trust in our military leaders, and reforming our army now that Feng Jia, officially renamed Hua Lai, is Ning's new territory.

Yuan and I have become closer. The awkwardness between us hasn't changed but at least seeing one another these days is comforting. Often, he treats me as his younger sister, to which I still take offense. Beyond our relationship, another was mended. Many days, I see him visit Xiao Xiang to find his mother. He's come to forgive her and accept his past as a product born from love and not treachery.

After the capital calmed from its previous troubles, Yuan resumed his adventurous tendencies. Last I heard, he was aiming to visit Yuan Zhu in Ke Ren Province, the village where his father originated and where his grandparents still reside. They didn't dare claim relations to the royal bloodline and so, Yuan is adamant to claim them.

Xian and Hua Ye are now stewards in Hua Lai. Kang Lang returned to Nan Rong though it's rumored he's no longer He Pi's fiancée. Instead, he's taken on the role of Ning's ambassador and promised to look after Jin and San An in my place.

As for me, in the past month, my days were spent paying homage to those affected by the recent conflicts. My nights were spent studying Ning's laws and reviewing the people's recommendations and opinions gathered through my secret sleuthing. Ning still needs a formalized council and we've a long way to go. At least for the first time in a long while, I feel as though life is moving forward.

Chapter 48 – 2

Midmorning, a messenger announced that Nan Rong's caravan arrived. Our illustrious guest was directed to the azalea garden but when I arrive to receive San An, instead find another Nan Rong prince under the frilly laced blooms, whose petals are faint reminders of the peonies he once presented to me. He's finally dressed for his proper role and is charmingly dashing, might I add.

"Jin..."

I call out to him as I had in my dreams so many endless nights ago. He turns and smiles sweetly as though we were never apart. Happy tears fall before guilty ones surge to take their place. I stagnate a distance away.

"Well? Are we strangers?"

In saying so, Jin approaches and locks me into an embrace. I'm so happy he's safe that reservations dissolve and in an instant, my arms fly around this person so dear to me. He strokes my head gently while I inhale the faint sandalwood scent from his blue robe. Once I've calmed, he brings a sleeve to wipe the last few tears off my cheeks.

"Jin, I'm happy that you're here but..."

"I know," he whispers tenderly. "San An cautioned me. I came against his wishes because, well, I owe you an apology and an explanation."

"You don't owe me anything! I'm the one who betrayed you!"

He's fully aware of my perfidy; still, I needed to confess. Even now, I despise the idea of keeping secrets from him.

"That's ridiculous. I never should have left without apologizing for all the horrible things I said. What else could you have thought? The truth is I started letters I couldn't finish. The words I sought to say had to be conveyed in person. I knew had I waited, you would have followed me to Bei Ling. I couldn't risk putting you in danger. I thought the sooner the conflict ended, the sooner I could return to explain myself."

"You never intended to quit our relationship? Jin, I... I thought... but then it didn't matter what I thought because I should have, and I didn't... Jin, I'm so sorry! I broke my promise. I never meant to hurt you! Please forgive me!"

My weak, pathetic tears stain his robe. Jin takes no offense, and instead, cradles me against his chest to lull my disquiet. Warm lips press a soft kiss on my forehead, and then descend to kiss the tears away. He rocks back and forth gently, embracing me deeper until my eyes are dried.

"You didn't do anything wrong. It doesn't matter what my rationalizations were. I still ran away. I broke my promise to protect you and I know how much pain I've caused. I'm sorry."

"How was it your fault? I assumed the worst in you!"

"I gave you every reason to. Even if I hadn't, would things have turned out differently?"

The thought kills me but the answer came easier than expected. I'll always love Jin, that won't change. However, my heart belongs in Ning, where it was always meant to be.

My head shakes and then a gaze arches up to convey the honesty he deserves. "No. I love Han Bei. That's why I can't be the woman that you need. Please Jin, don't give up! I faltered but there are loyal women worthy of you!"

"Don't say that. You are loyal. Through your loyalty and friendship, I have learned to trust another, and I look forward to experiencing the wonders in love and life, which I have before denied myself. I will find my happiness while I rejoice in yours. That is my greatest desire, Bao Lai, for you to be happy."

How he can still look upon me without disdain is beyond me. While I don't deserve his kindness, I'm relieved that he traversed the long road to absolve me.

More than that, he's granted the words I've been aching to hear, that he'll be happy.

"Thank you, Jin. I wish that for you, too. I'll pray for your and San An's happiness until dreams become reality! I know you'll find it!"

"Me, too."

His strong embrace grows, wholly enveloping me within the rising warmth. In the end, it seems Jin saved himself. However it was possible, he escaped living in his tormented past and is looking forward to a future, one which I hope will be filled with incomparable happiness and joy.

Once our arms have exhausted all strength, our bodies part. Jin nostalgically taps his fingers to my cheek and we exchange blissful smiles. Whatever awkwardness between us is dissolved and I can finally accept this affection in my heart for him without conflicting with the passionate adoration I have for Han Bei. This love is different; one I don't quite know how to describe but it's one I'll keep with me always.

"You'll stay at least the week, won't you? I want to show you everything Ning has to offer."

"Yes. I spoiled you last time while we were in Xiong, Princess. I believe it's your turn."

Jin playfully holds out his hand and I gladly take it in my own.

"As you wish, Prince Jin."

Together, hand-in-hand, we start for the courtyard leading to the main gate. No matter what happens between us, I'm happy we can still be friends. The same can be said about our two countries. Peace will be maintained between Ning and Nan Rong in my lifetime and I hope for all future generations to come.

Chapter 48 – 3

Once Jin and I part for the night, I'm still drunk on elation and exhilaration of restored hope, that I skip to my chamber. Upon opening the door, my breathing stalls.

"I-I'm sorry! I thought this was my room!"

I rush outside, grasping onto my racing heart. Han Bei was sprawled on the bedspread in his black and silver robe. Red hair draped elegantly over the grey pillows. Green eyes were looking at the ceiling thoughtfully. He was utterly enchanting but I couldn't stay and gawk. I've thrown myself at him enough times. What he must think of me now for invading his private quarters at this time of night!

Once breathing calms, I start for my chamber, only to realize I've nowhere to go.

I poke my head through the doorway nervously. "This is *my* room...?"

"So it is," he leers.

"W-Why are you in my room?"

"Am I not allowed to visit Her Highness?"

He's been avoiding me like the plague; using every ridiculous excuse under the sun to turn me away each time I've asked for a spare moment. And, every time

I've caught sight of him in the barracks, he managed to flee before I could come close. So, why now? Whatever he wishes to discuss must be important.

Moving inside, I take the chair from the side table and place it across from Han Bei, who's moved to the edge of the bed. "Is something the matter, Han Bei?"

"This odd arrangement, perhaps. Why are you sitting over there?"

"Oh, am I too close?"

"No. That is the odd arrangement I meant. Your Highness is suddenly bashful after the earlier brazen display? Rumors in the markets had you spent the entire day publicly doting on Shu Jin."

"I did but... yes, I did."

I won't make excuses. I'm glad for my time with Jin and proud of our friendship. We didn't do anything wrong, not that it should matter when Han Bei couldn't possibly care less.

"I've misjudged Shu Jin. I thought him a coward. He turned out to be a far braver man than me."

"He is a brave man, though why would you say more so than you?"

"It takes mettle to admit faults and selflessness to forgo personal desires. He did what I couldn't do; set the person he loved free to find her happiness."

"Wh—!   You have an undeniable bad habit of eavesdropping!"

"Blame my dutiful curiosity. I was obligated to know to whom the welfare of our country would fall. I heard more than I bargained for."

"How's that? What didn't you already know?"

He shuffles gently.   Distraught enters his widened emerald stars while his breathing shifts. The peculiar flustering, however mild, is suppressed as soon as it surfaces. This may be the first time I've ever seen the Grand General truly embarrassed.   I can't help but shamelessly stare at my adorable advisor.

Han Bei glances up and then immediately averts his eyes. "I never imagined you'd admit to Shu Jin your affections for me."

"I owed Jin the truth. I thought candor was the same as admitting treachery when denial is the greater offense. I learned my lesson after injuring you through dishonesty."

"Am I any different? I called you childish but I am the one still in denial."

"Denial of wh—"

He gives a meaningful stare which somehow, is also slightly seductive.   My face grows hot from the implications, until grasping that the reason he came to me must have been stemmed from jealousy. Once Jin returns to Nan Rong, he will regret this overreaction. I best attempt to brush past this discomfiture.

"Sometimes denial and truth are one and the same. Oh, hey! I forgot. Hua Ye said these are black tourmaline protection stones. I mostly stay at the palace now. Why don't you keep them?"

"Can you endure one conversation without changing subjects in the same breath?"

He chuckles at my poor social skills. Embarrassed, my head is down while I rummage my pockets for the stones. I know I put them in here! Where are they?

"Are you looking for these?" Han Bei produces my treasures from his pocket.

"Wh-how-but-where-when?"

"Eloquent, as usual." He scoffs. "Your Highness was too busy stuffing your face with candy, you didn't notice these fell from your pocket at the waffle stall."

"You were following us?"

"It's my duty to protect Your Highness."

"From Jin?"

"From unwanted hands." Pausing, he chuckles. "I might as well have protected Shu Jin from the *overly* friendly princess. Your Highness couldn't keep your hands off the prince for more than ten minutes."

"I was overly friendly because he is my friend."

"More than friends, I'm certain. You still love him, don't you?"

"Yes. I always will."

"Then why not marry him?"

Han Bei's mood grows somber. He admitted to eavesdropping. Even before that, he knows exactly how I feel. Apparently, he's far from jealous. Every notion of his aim to push me into Jin's arm sends me deeper into misery.

While staring at the floor, I kick my feet against the fine black stone. "Thank you for concerning yourself over my affairs. It's not necessary. I am contented to worship my one true love from afar."

"Who exactly is this lucky person?"

The seriousness in his eyes puts me on the verge of another outburst. He won't accept me, so why force me to admit the answer? How many times must I throw myself at him before he's satisfied?

Then again, he's only doing to me as I've done unto him. I don't have a valid reason to be angry. In fact, I feel that after my multitude of apologies, I still owe him another.

"He is... someone who is too good-hearted and whom I've offended too many times to count. I just hope he'll forgive me and come to find the happiness he deserves."

I start up from the chair and instead, fall into Han Bei's embrace. Tremulous arms sweep me toward his body; heat raging from every inch of him is a billowing inferno. The passion from his supple lips tears my reservations and turns my mind hazy. For the first time, I can fully savor his kiss without guilt. Never has anything tasted sweeter or desire felt more tempting. My body grows limp, yielding to him. Han Bei continues robbing the air from my lungs until I plead for relief.

He cradles me tenderly and through ragged breaths, Han Bei whispers the words I've yearned to hear.

"I love you, Bao Lai."

"Han Bei, I can't replace Dong Xing."

"If that is really all you have to say, then I must be too late."

"N-No! I love you, Han Bei! You know I do! I have never loved anyone as deeply as I love you and I never will. But, what am I supposed to think? Will you still look at me the same once Jin leaves?"

"I deserve that." Following a pause, he shirks off the self-deprecating smile. "I know how dear Shu Jin is to you. You didn't give him up for a stronger man. I am weak and I need you. You resigned your most valued trait for me. It shouldn't have taken me this long to say this. I'm sorry. I'm sorry for every affront and injury

I've dealt. I was insulted you weren't honest when I wasn't any different."

"Then what is the truth? Why did you reject me?"

"You insisted to accompany me to battle."

"I don't mean *then*. Then, you had a reason. My confession was inappropriate in the face of impending war. When you came back, when I felt the other half of me returned after fearing the worst, and each time in succession when I sought your company... I was sure you hated me."

His head shakes. Han Bei looks down as though ashamed. "I was worried and frustrated. On top of that, once you'd relinquished Jin, I felt my devotion for Dong Xing challenged. I thought I could but I wasn't willing to surrender the piece of my heart that was still hers. I was angry at myself for causing your distress that in the end, I couldn't face you, so I kept up my pathetic act of indifference until everything aggravated me. I have never once confessed a love I didn't possess and my affections for you since that first confession has only grown brighter."

"As much as I have been waiting to hear those words, I can't believe them. I don't understand why you'd even love me. I'm nothing like her."

"And that's the reason I adore you. Under the juvenile demeanor and poor social skills is a temperamental, violent woman."

Suddenly, I feel insulted. Han Bei, chuckling, cups my cheek in his hand and then leans in for a short kiss.

"I've been aching to tame those pouting lips. You're not what I expected, Bao Lai, but you're everything I need. I am proud of the woman I love. My own exquisite flower, who slew a traitor to save my son and routed an entire Bei Ling unit to protect our people."

"It was your dagger that protected Yuan and me. Besides, Hua Ye dramatically exaggerated my merits."

"Rightfully so. Any woman who can put up with my stubborn indifference and love me, derisions and all, is worthy of praise. I am sorry for everything. Don't forgive me. From now on, let me spend every waking moment atoning for my transgressions. I'll make you happy, Bao Lai. I promise."

The indescribable elation rioting inside is overwhelming. I don't know whether to laugh or cry. When no words would come, my arms string around Han Bei's neck and emotions pour into a fervent kiss on his rose lips. He returns my passion in full, reinforcing his confession and more so, his promise of our future.

Once our lips part, he lifts me into his arms. Each step he takes toward the bed sends my heart to hammer inside my chest. When we finally lie in each other's embrace, a feeling of completeness settles over me. Our fingers thread together. Han Bei gently traces his lips over the back of my hand.

From there, a loving whisper flutters against my temple, same as his lips. "My dearest Bao Lai, the woman who saved me, my heart, and my life. I thought my fate was punishment but if everything that has happened was meant to prepare me for you, then I am glad that we could have this moment together. I have been waiting for you all my life."

"And I, you. Ning finally feels like home. This is where I belong and you are whom I belong to."

Another short kiss and then I snuggle closer toward my beloved. With a hand stroking my throat gently, his lips descend toward my neck.

"Han Bei! T-That tickles!"

The response is an agonizingly pained stare while he continues touching my neck, conveying his remorse for the previous rough conduct. He lost control from worrying over his brother. I could never blame him for that.

My fingers thread through his red silky hair and then a kiss lands on his forehead. "Stop apologizing. The only thing you should be sorry for is if you answer my next question unfavorably. Han Bei, after my coronation, I want to... that is if you would... we could— should crown you Ning's emperor."

I pause in hopeful expectations. His wrinkled brows slowly smooth, and soon after, rise to arches. The familiar smirk returns. He sighs disappointedly. "You expect me to agree when you propose in this clumsy manner? I can't possibly answer favorably when your rambling was hardly a question."

"Then... why don't you propose to me?" I grin.

"That's a daring thing to say!"

"So you won't do it?"

"A proposal has no value when I won't let another have you."

I nod an agreement. Though, the moment I thought to let the subject subside, he crouches atop; his face ever redder.

"Bao Lai, w-will you... um, m-ma—"

Contrary to the previous composed assertion, he's blushing from ear-to-ear. Apparently, the Grand General is terribly embarrassed.

"You expect me to agree when you propose in this clumsy manner? You never had trouble proposing before. What happened to the forceful, confident Han Bei who gave me the ghastly ultimatum of accepting him in public, midday no less? Allow me to return an ultimatum. During the coronation next week, either take the crown or never again expect to become my lord. What do you think of that?"

He frowns at my cheeky grin. In time, a sweet laugh forms a perfect smile over his mouth. "I hadn't considered embarrassment kept you from accepting my ultimatum."

"That's because you are too popular with the ladies. So, just how many times have you accomplished the daunting task of making love in public?"

"I have never made *love* to anyone. You will be the only woman to receive that privilege."

"Sweet talker. Flattery won't save you. How many women have you bedded, Han Bei?"

"By that I assume you mean only the ones I've taken to an actual, physical bed?"

Curiosity is now regret. I fear to know the answer.

"Don't tell me. I'll hold onto my delusions. You've never made *love* to anyone. From now on, you'll only be mine."

"Is that right? You and Jin made love, so you'll come into this marriage more experienced than me?"

"I... I-I-I-I-I... stop laughing at me!"

"My flower turned out to be a blushing rose. Are you nervous? How will you cope on our wedding night?"

"Well, it's as you've said. I hate to admit it, but I do have the experience."

"Maybe, but you've never experienced me."

"Will the experience... with you... be something different?"

Han Bei breaks into uncontrollable laughter. I have no idea what's so darn funny. The more my obliviousness shows, the harder he laughs. This man is such a bully. I don't think I'll ever win against him.

"Sometimes, I forget how naïve you are." Plopping our foreheads together, a kiss lands on the tip of my nose. "I will never stop craving those pouting lips?"

In saying so, he kisses me in an unsatisfying, joking manner which makes me reach out for more. Pleased by my brazenness, Han Bei's busy hands run over my body while his deep kiss saps more of my will. Once I've yielded entirely, he stops and then moves away. Teasing, teasing man!

"What happened to never leaving a woman wanting?"

"Patience, Your Highness. A woman satisfied might stray farther than a woman dissatisfied."

"It's the other way around."

"Is that right? Shall we test that theory?"

Thin fingers gently stroke my cheeks and then Han Bei starts toward the door. I see his plan but I can't help it. I rush after the man who'd left me dissatisfied. Once past the threshold, he reaches out and lifts me into his arms.

"Your fiancé is a clever man, isn't he?"

"Very clever. Hmm. Fiancé. I like the sound of that. I was engaged once before, when I was He Pi. My *fiancée*, Mu Dan, was... something else."

"I'm aware of Kang Lang's lust. Next time my brother lays one finger on you, there will be a greater bounty on his head and I will be the one to bring him in."

He's grimacing under that stern face. I've induced his jealousy and a part of me wants to see more.

"Did you know, Han Bei, there is an old Ning tradition where if the eldest is unable to marry his or her betrothed, the younger sibling of the same gender is inclined to substitute. Should you decide against me before my coronation, I might just have to accept Kang Lang's offer."

An incensed glare is sent down, following which, Han Bei sets me on the cold floor.

"I thought to be honorable. Since your mind wanders, I'll have to claim you here and now."

"I was joking!"

"That was no mere joke. You've lusted after me long enough. It would be cruel to prolong the agony."

"W-Wait! Not in the hallways!"

"Oh! You're protesting the venue and not the event? I see, I see. Shall we change scenery?"

He moves down the hall with me still in his arms, smiling smugly.

"Where are we going?"

"To the night markets. You spent the day with Shu Jin. Every night from now until the rest of our lives, you will spend with me."

"You were jealous."

"I have been jealous of Shu Jin from the moment your promise to San An was made. I wonder if my carelessness afterwards wasn't a result of envy."

"What happened after—the assassination attempt! Han Bei!"

"Don't lecture me," he frets mockingly in a manner which mimics my tone.

"Han Bei, I was jealous of Dong Xing and maybe... that's why I was reckless, too."

"We really are quite a pair, aren't we?"

"Naturally made for each other."

My dearest Han Bei smirks in the fashion I've come to adore. He plants me on my feet. Once we confer our mutual worship through a longing embrace, the Grand General and I start for the night markets.

To the east, the elder star lies; the younger's name is Bao Lai. I hum the song my master taught me, all the while sending a prayer to everyone who has sacrificed to bring me to this point. In this beautiful land to the east where my family resides, I will build a life with the man I love.

He is not my first love and neither am I his. Through unpredicted paths in life, we have come to find a greater love. True love. A love that has been waiting for us all our lives and one we will cherish beyond eternity.

Home truly is where the heart is. At last, I am home.

Chapter 48: Home is where the Heart is

The End.

Chapter 49: Infiltrating Bei Ling

Han Bei and the eight hundred thousand troops under his command left for Ying Ling's borders a week ago. During this time, I feigned obedience while Yuan sent eyes to guard me. However, I was so terribly dull, sleeping in most days, that Niu begged to be reassigned.

After dinner one quiet evening, the servants were sent away until further notice before I went directly to my chamber. Once the moon was high overhead, long body pillows were set as my replacement while I snuck out to find an accomplice.

"Hey! Wake up!"

Thank goodness Han Bei was gentlemanly; else, this assassin from Bei Ling would have her hands full fending off perverts from the main prison and my plans would have failed before they begin. We're in a secluded part of the dungeon where guards are sparse and lights are dim. The assassin, recognizing her former opponent, darts up.

"Come to gloat did you?" She sneers.

"No, I didn't. I need your help."

"You don't need my help, *Princess*. Some women have all the luck, and if that weren't enough, demand the world of me, too!"

"What are you griping about? You're in there for attacking Han Bei."

"I don't mean this pointless detention. Better women have failed to earn Han Bei's love. I gave everything and he returned nothing. Who knew all he wanted was a princess? How tragic!"

"Tragic, indeed. Because you drugged Han Bei, I was forced to his defense, which led his favor to fall toward me. You are the reason he loves me and I don't feel bad one bit for saying so. I won't forgive anyone who hurts Han Bei."

Her pretty face scrunches into a scowl. More than hatred, jealousy runs rampant across those amethyst eyes. Besides me, I wonder just how many women also love Han Bei.

"I have nothing to say, *Your Highness*." She plops on the straw mat and then, placing a hand over her forehead, stares at the ceiling dramatically.

"Fine, then listen. I need to find passage into the northern capital. Since you're from Bei Ling, you should help me. Once we're in Sai Mi, you're free to go."

"Hmph. The moment I leave this cell, there's a good chance I'll take my revenge against the woman who stole my freedom."

"The moment you leave that cell, there's a good chance I'll take my revenge against the woman who nearly killed Han Bei."

Her eyes roll and then she scoffs. What is wrong with this woman? She speaks as though her infatuation for Han Bei is deep and still somehow manages to blatantly overlook the fact that she held a knife to his throat. Can she not grasp the reason she was placed in gaol?

Here I thought this plan was certain and as usual, nothing is ever simple.

"Look here! Talk about luck; you're lucky to have escaped the gallows for your crimes. I'm offering a chance to go free in exchange for taking me to Bei Ling. Wouldn't you have returned there anyway?"

"What for? Before you came along, I was as pampered as a princess. The Circle was disbanded and the only thing waiting for me in the North is an angry lord who won't tolerate my failure. So, I'd rather stay in this cell. At least it's safe."

"Who is your lord?"

"Who else?"

"That's not an answer. I've reasoned it wasn't Wang Liang. You've been in Ning's Circle for many years without trouble. Someone must have recently given notice for you to attempt Han Bei's life."

"What can I say? I'm loyal to a fault. Nan Rong attacked His Highness, Cai Pai. I couldn't permit that offense to pass unpunished. As if that weren't enough, the South's minister added insult to injury."

"What did San An have to do with your assault?"

"Is that his name? Ah, San An! So handsome and yet, so reserved! I greeted him in the halls and he wouldn't even acknowledge me. A woman can only take so much damage to her pride."

"You're lying. San An is not discourteous. Had you sought retribution for Cai Pai, the Minister would have been targeted, not Han Bei. Who gave you the orders?"

"No one. You had two gorgeous men and I, none. I went after Han Bei out of spite—on my own accord."

She continues to lie. At least it's clear to me one aspect is true: she is loyal to a fault. Whomever she's protecting is still safe.

"We both know that's not true. I think at the very least, you are loyal to Cai Pai. Nan Rong didn't attack your emperor. It was Wang Liang, your prime minister. He's the instigator in this conflict and a traitor to Bei Ling. I aim to depose that despot, so why don't you help me?"

Tilting her head to one side, she slightly squints as if searching me. I stare back to convey my honesty. When I thought she finally grew a conscience; instead, the courtesan turns away and yawns.

"Tell me when you do; then I'll take you to Bei Ling."

Her roundabout logic is giving me a headache. I haven't met anyone this infuriating since Mu Dan. Don't tell me Kang Lang's irksome personality was the result of living in Circles. I guess he wasn't joking. He has studied courtesans extensively. Then, that must mean in order to earn her compliance, I'll have to resort to cheap tricks.

Inching close to the cell bars, I give her a once over. "Have they been feeding you? You're pale and not in a good way."

Dark brows immediately furrow over amethyst eyes. She's clearly incensed, as I'd hoped.

"Is that hair on the floor? What is that white spot on your head?" A hand flies over my mouth and a gasp flows in the girlish manner befitting Mu Dan. "Oh, dear heavens! It's a bald spot!"

"Where?!"

She jumps up and begins fumbling with the hairpins, searching for the elusive flaw every woman fears.

"Lack of sunlight and exercise will wreak havoc on a body. The paleness, the baldness, and wide girth. The awful stench! Not to mention, you're drooping in all the wrong places."

"There's no right place to droop!" She screeches. "Let me out!"

"You're a criminal. Where will you go? Nan Rong is Ning's ally, they won't take you. Feng Jia and Ye are too far away."

"To Bei Ling, obviously! Now let me out!"

"What do you mean?" I pose innocently. "You're safer here, away from your *angry lord who won't tolerate failure.*"

"What's the worst he can do? Take my life? I'd rather die beautiful!"

"Why? Besides me, who comes to visit you anyway? Once you're bald, not even the occasional guard will peep in. No one will remember you, so does it matter if you're hairless and droopy?"

Her fists beat furiously against the cell bars. The lady's screeching rages on like that of a trapped wild beast. For an assassin, I'm surprised she can't do something as mundane as pick a lock, especially with the excessive amount of hairpins on her head.

"All right! All right! I'll let you out, but you have to take me to Sai Mi."

"Fine! Hurry up! I won't survive inside this cell a minute longer!"

"I need two of your small hairpins."

Still flustered, she hands over a bundle of ten. It's been over a decade since I'd last picked a lock. Amazingly, my skills haven't dulled. At the old temple, someone taught this talent to me along with many others which often put me in trouble. Maybe it was that same boy who used to mock me for cross-dressing. We never got along but that didn't stop us from causing mischief together. I still can't remember his name.

"There. That should do it."

The cell door pops open. The prisoner runs past me, nearly falling on her face from slipping on the long hem of the Hanfu dress.

"Hey, wait! We had a deal!"

"That's what you get for making deals with criminals! You're as dumb as you are lucky!"

She disappears out the large metal door into the main dungeon pathway. Just when I start to give chase, her figure recedes into the light, escorted by two armed guards in the midst of making their usual rounds. A long sword gleaming black steel is pressed against her throat. When they recognize me, the two soldiers bow low.

"Your Highness, are you hurt?" The man on the left beckons nervously.

The courtesan's pathetic glance, which seeks my help, is ultimately held back by pride. She clamps down her lips and averts a bitter gaze toward the wall. I honestly feel sorry for her but I also grasp this might be the chance I need.

"Let her go and put that sword away. It's not gentlemanly to treat a woman so roughly."

"But, she's a criminal." The young man on the right stares back wide-eyed.

"And I opened her cell door. Will you detain me as well? She's my charge. Now, kindly escort us ladies to the bathhouse. No woman should be denied a warm bath for this long. Have someone bring a new set of clothes. Hers are covered in straws."

There's much the guards wish to say. However, obedience is one of those values instilled in Ning soldiers. Following a short bow, the men grudgingly set out to fulfill my orders.

Chapter 49 – 2

Enya, the assassin, who quietly noted her name before entering the bathhouse, understood my design for having intervened on her behalf. Still, she was grateful and took the chance to take a much-needed bath. That doesn't mean I trust her wholeheartedly. The two guards are stationed on the other side of the bathhouse in case she attempts an escape.

After a painfully long time, Enya returns, glowing in her dainty lavender robe.

"Well, your plan worked, Princess. I'm not an ingrate. My mother taught me better than that. Take whatever you need and then we'll go."

"R-Really? You're not... going to leave me stranded in the middle of nowhere, are you?"

"I wasn't planning to, but now that you've mentioned it, who knows?" Shrugging, she smiles mischievously.

I suppose I've come as far as releasing a dangerous criminal; I might as well chance it. What other resources do I have? Once preparations are made, on one horse, we set out for Bei Ling.

Chapter 49 – 3

"Unbelievable! You can't even ride a horse. Do you understand how uncomfortable it is having you squeeze me so tightly?"

"I'm sorry! I never had a reason to learn. I like walking." The horse jolts over the rocky road. Inadvertently, I squeeze Enya's waist tighter.

"Excuses, excuses! So, who are you anyway? A con-woman? You must be, because you don't look anything like a princess to me."

"If I were a con-woman, wouldn't I try to look the part? Is there even a standard?"

"Of course! A princess—a true princess—must be dainty, sweet, pretty, personable, and fashionable."

"You mean... like you?"

"Hmph. Exactly! If I didn't know better, I'd have thought you were a lost commoner wandering about the palace in stolen clothes."

"I'll take that as a compliment. I don't want the people to think I'm above them, because I'm not."

Enya quickly throws an irate glare over her shoulder. "*Whatever!* Why the obsession with Bei Ling? You're not fit to assassinate Wang Liang."

"I won't. I want him to answer for his crimes."

"How noble!" She scoffs. "You're a regular knight from an old silk scroll! I'll tell you this, though. Do whatever you wish against Wang Liang. If anything happens to Cai Pai, I'll make you regret it."

"You don't have to worry. I've no intentions to cause Cai Pai harm."

The air between us suddenly stagnates. Enya fidgets for a time; eventually heaving a deep, heavy, disgusted sigh.

"Oh, *my gosh!* You are so terrible at conversation!"

"How so?"

"Aren't you in the least curious *why* I want Cai Pai safe?"

"I assumed because he's your lord."

"He's my half-brother!" She exclaims proudly. "See? I might as well be a princess, too!"

"That's... true. Why aren't you?"

"Our mother was married to Emperor Song. An unfaithful emperor and no one bat an eye, but an unfaithful empress is unheard of. Sinful even! So, her servant raised me and later, I became her personal attendant. She didn't tell me until shortly before she died; worse, didn't leave any proof. I was even jailed by her husband for claiming what's rightfully mine. Then, like a godsend, he took me away and sent me to Ning's Circle."

"And who is *he*? Did *he* give the order to remove Han Bei?"

"None of your business! You're so nosy!"

"Are you kidding me? You're the one bragging about your latent title!"

"I was making small talk because you're a *bore!* My point was, make certain to keep my dear brother safe!"

"Aren't you more suited to protect your own brother, and at the same time, tell him the truth?"

"He wouldn't believe me."

"How do you know until you try? I never thought Ning would accept me either. By some miracle, they have."

"Because you're lucky!"

"So are you. At least you were able to know your parents and sibling. I never met mine."

The boisterous Enya suddenly falls silent and remains so for the duration of our ride until camp is made. I still won't forgive her offense against Han Bei, but I suppose if I were a courtesan in Bei Ling and Yuan was assaulted, I would have raised a sword, too. Two princesses and one is without country. Under different circumstances, we might not be so different. Fate is a curious thing.

Chapter 49 – 4

Once past Ying Ling, the Hui An road leads to Si Kao and Wei Yi. I was afraid we would encounter Han Bei's party until Enya turned west toward Nan Rong's borders and took a path meant for lone riders through the Pengzi Mountains. The rocky route was elevated and narrow. I held onto Enya for dear life and she threatened to take mine if I didn't release my iron grips. Somehow, we managed to survive the precarious peaks and descended Pengzi unscathed. After more than two weeks later, Sai Mi's high walls finally come into view.

"I appreciate your help."

"Yes, well, you should. I hope you find your boyfriend."

"Thanks, I hope you find yours."

She shrugs. "He's not my boyfriend. Not anymore. That's why I'll make him suffer me."

During the past week, I bored Enya with my poor conversation skills. As a last resort, she brought about the topic of men and somehow, that sparked lively discussions. I vaguely mentioned Jin, though not by name, and she mentioned her former boyfriend, also not by name. Who knew banter regarding the opposite gender could be so entertaining!

After bidding Enya farewell, I follow the posted signs pointing to the market. As Han Bei mentioned, white cranes are symbols of rebellion. There isn't an inn by that name on the directory. Thus, I resort to this simple method. Dressed as a man, I walk into every inn along the way and ask if another who resembles me has come by. Finally, after nearly spent from running around the massive marketplace, someone pointed to the Bai He Tavern. Bai He, written as one hundred lotuses, is similar in phonetics to white cranes.

Chapter 49 – 5

"What are you doing here? Skipping work?"

I was looking around the crowded tavern when a small hand playfully slaps my back.

"Are you talking to me?"

The young boy to my right, who gave the slap, looks up with a mischievous grin across his rosy face.

"Duh! Who else? What's wrong with your voice? Why do you sound like a girl?"

"Because I—Oh, you must think I'm He Pi. Say, have you noticed another man who looks just like me? Maybe a bit taller and a complete weirdo?"

I point to my face with a hopeful grin while the child scratches his head and frowns. "You're pretty weird yourself."

"Wh—hey! Respect your elders!"

"What for? You're only two years older than me."

"Where did you come up with *that* assumption? How old are you? Ten?"

"I'm eight!"

"You think I'm ten?!"

"Ahem!"

The hard exclamation from behind turns my body rigid. Dear heavens, what am I doing fighting with an eight-year-old?

"What are you doing fighting with an eight-year-old?"

I slowly turn to meet the chiding tone which projected my thought. An older man glances up and down my disguise; his face too stiff to read. The most noticeable traits on that stern expression are the bushy eyebrows, which are mirrored by this eight-year-old.

"I-I-I was searching for someone who looks like me. He and Shu Jin were said to come here often."

Though it faded as quickly as it came, I saw his eyes grow wide. "Shu Jin?"

"Yes, have you seen him?"

"That depends. Who are you?"

"I'm... a friend. My name is... Tui Tui."

"That's the stupidest name ever!" The child nearly bursts his seams from laughter.

Why do children always pick on me? First, Yuan, and now, this runt.

"Hei." The man's reproachful sigh puts the boy to silence. "Tui Tui, I'm not estranged to secrecy. Your name is safe with me. However, you're free to keep it if you wish. I'm Zhang Tang. Shu Jin isn't here. If Hei is a good boy, he'll take you to him."

"Why do I have to?"

Hei's chubby little fists bounce up and down while he continuously stomps the ground. However, one hard glare from Zhang Tang and his tantrum ceases. Why can't I have that ability to command respect!

"Fine! But if you can't keep up, I'm leaving you behind!"

Hei takes off. At the same moment I turn to thank Zhang Tang, he signals to skip pleasantries. Almost falling on my face, I run out of the tavern after the kid whose tiny feet move as swiftly as those of a housecat.

Chapter 50: Reunion

"Hei! Wait for me!"

His tiny figure slips past the patrons in the crowded street and I, contrarily, slam into almost everyone while trying not to lose sight of him. This is hopeless! He's twenty steps ahead and the distance between us keeps increasing.

"Hei, stop! I'll buy you candy!"

However the thought formed, the words slip out by chance. As Han Bei had bribed me with candy, I bribe Hei, and the result is better than expected. The Grand General does know a thing or two about children... which would imply that I'm a child. How embarrassing.

Hei stops, becomes highly obedient, and once a pouch of candy is in his hand, leisurely leads the way down a narrow street toward a poorer district of the markets.

"Are you really Shu Jin's friend?" Hei's plump face arches up while staring intently with big round eyes.

"Yes. We've been friends for a long while now."

"Good. You better be nice to him."

"Are you close to Jin?"

"Yeah!" Hei giggles cheerfully. "He's fun! He's going to be my big brother!"

"Really? How's that?"

"How else, dummy? Shu Jin loves my sister."

Opposing his happy moods, a cold dread suddenly spreads throughout my chest. What did he just say? Maybe I misunderstood.

"H-How old is your sister? Is she a kid, too?"

"Who are you calling a kid?!" His chubby hands are making fists again. "Mei is twenty-three! Jin said she's the prettiest girl he's ever met. Mei loves him, too. I can't wait for us to become brothers!"

It's as I feared. We've been apart for months. It's no wonder that in this big city, unrestrained by palace rules and etiquettes, Jin was able to find someone worthy of his attention; who could stir his passion and free him from his emotional bondage. I should be glad for him; instead, there's a knife in my chest.

"Almost there."

Hei points to a shabby grey door ahead. Jin and I are so close and yet, once Hei opens the door, I can't find the will to move forward. What am I doing here? I sought to confront Jin's abandonment but if he's happy with another, thinking of marriage even, then the best thing I can do for Jin is leave him be.

One foot steps backward. My body is shaking feverishly. I'm on the verge of turning on my heels when Hei cuts off my retreat with a loud declaration.

Chapter 50: Reunion

"Shu Jin!" He cries, waving his short arms in the air.

My feet are stones encased in ice. I glance toward the direction Hei is waving to find Jin and He Pi. The latter waves back; the former's face is pallid. He must feel guilty for having moved forward and I feel guilty for holding him back.

Shame renders my body immobile. Hei pulls me inside. After closing the door behind, he runs up to He Pi, whose large palm messes his hair.

"What's this then? You brought our friend, did you, Hei? How did you find her?"

"H-H-Her?!" Hei stares back at my disguise, squinting while his bushy brows examine my figure. "You're one ugly girl."

"Oh, yeah? Well you're—!" I can't finish the sentence with Jin watching. Mei is the prettiest girl that he's ever met, isn't that what Hei said? Denying Hei's insult feels like an attempt to redirect partiality toward myself. I can't do that. Intruding in his life was selfish enough.

"Yeah, I'm ugly. Here's the other half of our deal."

I was afraid he'd run off, so this was my security. Hei happily reaches for the sack of remaining candy and then waves to the group while skipping back out the door.

"Bye, Shu Jin! Bye, Bao! Bye, Ugly!"

"Who told you my name?"

The naughty child stuffs his chubby cheeks full of candy and refuses to look back. Embarrassed for losing to an eight-year-old, I glance around at a number of strangers who don't seem to mind my abrupt imposition. Aside from them, I can only look at He Pi. Jin's staring at me but I can't bring myself to acknowledge him. I fear to think the accusing thoughts that must be running through his mind.

"You're awfully daring, Miss Liang, coming all this way alone. I like that in a woman."

He Pi, aiming to break the tension, comes nearer and reaches for my waist. The palm of my hand smacks his forehead to keep him at bay.

"Not at all. I didn't come alone. Someone helped."

"Is this someone who knows too much and must be silenced?" He smiles a bone-chilling smile; sweet and frightening.

"No. We parted at the gates. She doesn't honestly know the reason I came."

"She? Well, why didn't you bring her? I dream to know all the women in the world, at least once!"

He Pi advances again, except this time, Jin seizes his arm and someone else from behind thumps a heavy book on his head. She comes hither, smiling gently. A young woman—more so, a blooming rose with light brown hair and hazel eyes—places a hand on Jin's arm and smiles. Then, turning to He Pi, pinches his cheek.

"You are incorrigible! I'm sorry for his manners. He can't control himself."

"Aww! I can control myself around you just fine, Mei!"

He Pi's last word stops my heart. So, this is she. I can grasp why Jin loves her. She is beautiful, sweet, and a true lady; much like Hua Ye. I can't compete with her... not that I should.

"Hello, I'm Mei. Nice to meet you."

"N-Nice to meet you, too. I'm Tui Tui."

He Pi giggles, much to my chagrin. It's disgusting how naturally the name Tui Tui came out of my mouth. Darn that Captain Xian!

"Is Shu Jin your brother? You look so much alike."

"Ah! No way!" He Pi interjects. "Our brother's taller and he's scary! Tui Tui is a friend."

I'm more than certain I don't look anything like Jin. She really must love him to see the resemblance everywhere. I can't say I'm happy for him, but I am glad. With mixed emotions rising, I become mute from insecurity. The awkward pause is finally dispelled by my host.

"Why don't you show Tui Tui to a spare room?" He Pi poses the task to Jin. "We've a lot to accomplish and we'll need all the help we can find."

Jin nods silently, signaling for me to follow before taking the lead. Once past the rear door of the storage house, a long corridor appears. We're alone and all I can see is his back, five paces ahead of me. My heart is writhing from the torment of having this moment together at last, but neither can I hold him nor confront his abandonment. He's moved on and it's for the best.

"This is your room." Jin declares faintly. He opens the wooden door and then steps inside the small room set with a bed, a single chair, and table.

I give an appreciative nod, believing he'd return to Mei. Instead, Jin lingers by the door, shuffling in place.

"Thank you, Jin. If there's anything I can do—"

"No. You shouldn't have come."

"I see that now. I'm sorry."

Jin heaves a complicated sigh and then moves closer. Fear impulsively sends my feet back a step. I can't tell which of us is more surprised by the retreat.

"I heard you were injured. Have you fully recovered?"

"Yes, I'm fine."

Another long pause follows, during which he stares silently—intently—until I lose the will to resist and return his effort. Why does he look so sad? It can't be for the same reason I want to break down and cry. He has Mei. Or is that why he's riddled with guilt?

"H-Hey Jin, Mei's a nice girl. She seems really sweet." I force a smile which somehow lightens his demeanor.

"Yes, she is. Very sweet."

"G-Good. I'm glad. How have you been?"

"Busy. What about you?"

"Same. I... met my nephew. He's taller than me. Can you believe that?"

Jin smiles shortly, the same sweet comforting smile I remember from what felt a lifetime ago. Back then, when I first discovered I had a nephew, we were in Xiong. Plans were made for the upcoming year to return to his hometown and offer prayers to his mother. Along with that promise is another bittersweet memory of his declaration for us to marry. Every wonderful moment spent by his side surges in waves only to be crushed under the realization that nothing can ever be. It takes all I have to keep back the tears.

"If you don't mind, I'm a little tired." The hoarse whisper manages to escape once I avert from his attention.

I love him. I love him so much, it kills me to think someone else can make him happy! Be that as it may, I also love Han Bei, so I've no right to chastise Jin. I've betrayed one and insulted the other. I don't deserve either of their loyalty. This lingering loneliness, which will never abandon me as long as I live, is my punishment.

Despite my emotional solitude, minutes pass by and Jin still lingers by the door. I quickly glance over to find his jaw grinding furiously. The moment he notices my confusion, he's taken aback by embarrassment. Ultimately, Jin nods and then quietly leaves. Once I was certain he was far off, tears roll down my face in rivers.

Chapter 50 – 2

"I'm sorry about earlier."

Mei sets the dinner tray upon the small desk and then settles comfortably beside me on the bed, as though we've been longtime friends. She gives a dazzling smile, which carries the same natural charms my sister exhibited in her portrait hung in Xiao Xiang. That feminine allure which won over Han Bei is apparently the same necessity to win Jin. While I don't dislike Mei, jealousy inside won't be disbanded. I couldn't save Jin and it wasn't because I didn't love him enough. I was just too much of a brute when he needed a flower. As Enya pointed out, I'm far cry from a princess and somehow, I feel as though I've failed as a woman, all the while, I'm sitting here dressed as a man.

"I didn't mean to compare you to Shu Jin," Mei continues timidly. "He explained you're actually a woman."

"I wasn't offended."

"Oh, good! I was worried. Shu Jin is special to me and you're special to him. I want us to be friends."

"'Special,' might be an exaggeration. He and I are mere acquaintances... now. I'm pleased he's important to you. Could I ask... how long was it after meeting him did you both realize your affections?"

Mei folds petal hands daintily across her lap and then presses her lips together prettily in contemplation. "Hmm. I think the first time we laid eyes on each other, we knew. Love at first sight is cliché, isn't it? I just don't know else to describe it. He is handsome and charming. I've never met anyone like him! I mean, he has his strange, sometimes superficial, moods, but beyond the exterior is a person I dearly love."

"So there weren't any reservation?"

"Not on his part. He's never had a girlfriend. I was surprised how audacious he acted for being so inexperienced."

"Shu Jin said that? He's never had a girlfriend?"

I never once denied our relationship to Han Bei. The moment Jin stepped foot in Bei Ling, our night together and everything prior just never existed? Though I've resigned myself, conflicting rage and sadness bearing down is too much. I can hardly keep still.

"Yes. Can you believe it? I couldn't. Even if he had, I'd forgive him. Well, he did mention a deranged woman who grew obsessed but there was nothing between them. He said she was fixated; always tried to analyze him when she couldn't save herself. All of it brought about by a promise inadvertently made in the spur of the moment. She sounds rather frightening and coarse. Do you happen to know her?"

"That depends... What's her name?"

"He didn't mention it. Why? Were there more than one cross-dressing fanatical woman after my Shu Jin?" Mei raises a hand to her mouth and giggles before reaching over to touch my arm amiably.

"Cross dresser?"

"Yes. Oh! But I knew he didn't mean you! Shu Jin said you're so close to him, he thinks of you as his sister. Apparently, Tui Tui isn't your real name? I very much like it, though."

Her sweet laughter fills the quiet room. I feign a smile while my hands are hard fists. So, he did leave because I was clingy. And here I am, entering into his consideration again, when this pretty creature before me has already earned a true place in his heart. What's more, I feel insulted. Of all the inconsiderate things! How could he claim to see me as a sister after everything we've been through? Who would do *that* to their sister!

As time ticks by, Mei's garrulous love struck confessions become nearly nauseating. I listen closely, merely to grasp that the worship is also mutual on his part.

Chapter 50 – 3

As it turns out, I am in the White Crane Order's base. The handful of members who escaped Tung's mass murder attempt at Lam Soi Citadel, including Zhang Tang, the newly elected leader, reformed the Order. This warehouse holds supplies for the Bai He Tavern in the front and serves as an inn for members in the back. Six years ago, He Pi's investigation led him to formulate the Order was in Bei Ling. He sought to find them. This movement caused Han Bei to send Mu Dan to Nan Rong's Circle as a spy and hence, the existing arrangements.

Currently, Jin and He Pi are in my room recapitulating our predicament and news brought from abroad. Two weeks after Ning's army set out, the Southern ministers, excluding San An, pushed for a direct march into Bei Ling. Ultimately, their generals had no choice but to obey. As San An expected, the direct assault resulted in Nan Rong's forces scattering and only half of the men returned. Had it not been for Ning's reinforcements and Captain Xian's military prowess, all would have been lost.

"This is ridiculous! How could one man cause so much trouble? We have to do something!" I look to He Pi, who's inching closer toward me in his usual lecherous manner. Once he's within arm's reach, His Highness touches my cheek. I smack away his hand.

"I like a woman who plays hard to get," He Pi winks before moving back into a more stoic pose. His lechery is almost impulsive. He can't help but advance on every woman in the room, at least once. "Agree. As it stands, Lord Han Bei is past Ying Ling and is leading the march through Si Kao. Wang Liang sent Feng Jia to subdue Nan Rong while he prepares to confront Ning."

"How? Bei Ling doesn't stand a chance against Ning through sheer force. What does he aim to do?"

"We have two theories. One, he's luring Lord Han Bei north while sending small groups to infiltrate Ning. Should that happen, the advancing army will either divide or retreat to defend. Either way, confusion is a powerful tool against a large herd; morale will take a devastating blow. Our second theory is he's waiting for Ning forces to congregate in one of the outskirt cities and then annihilate the entire area. With the reserves he's been shifting to the southern borders and the men recruited from Feng Jia, he'll have enough to overtake Nan Rong and face Ning's remaining army with greater odds for victory."

"You think he's planning to destroy an entire city? That's a little crazy."

"I thought so, too, until our spies reported the mass amount of explosives he's gathered and the number of transports leaving in troves for the border cities. Wang Liang must be slain before more lives are lost."

"He Pi, Wang Liang is your brother, Su Jian. You know that, don't you?"

"Yes," the young man sighs pitiably. "He is our brother but he'll never see us as such. There's no use convincing him otherwise. Jin and I have chosen to protect Nan Rong and San An at all cost, even if that cost is another brother."

"I see. I wanted you to be aware of facts before actions, so regret won't consume you in the aftermath. Speaking of San An, the Minister thinks Han Bei's march will spur Wang Liang to send additional forces south and flank Ning once Nan Rong falls."

"San An is usually right in these matters. At this moment, his predictions are coming to fruition. If only Lord Han Bei hadn't been so rash, we'd have more time to prepare. As such, I'm afraid our timeline must be moved forward."

"Given the information we had, Han Bei made the logical choice. This timeline you mentioned, what can I do to help?"

He Pi ponders momentarily before shifting to an ambiguous smile. "Well, there is one thing."

"Absolutely not!" Jin, who's been listening quietly for the duration of our conversation, suddenly moves away from the door. "I pledged to you my life and only my life. Should anything happen to Bao Lai, I will never let this trespass go. Leave her out of this!"

"Jin, it's my choice. Everyone is doing their part except me. I want to help."

"The best you can do is remain safe. The East won't stay their hands against Nan Rong should anything happen to you."

"I'm sick of being useless. Han Bei chose to aid Nan Rong. I couldn't. Even after training with the soldiers, they're the ones risking their lives on the battlefield while I ran here to... I won't sit idle. Whatever His Highness asks of me, I will do it."

"I can't permit that."

"I don't need your permission. You don't get to have a say."

"Whether I do or don't, won't change the fact that I refuse to put you in danger."

"You left without giving my welfare any consideration. Why pretend to start now?!"

He's taken aback by my brusque accusation. We haven't been reunited for a full day's time and already, we're at another standoff. I thought we both have changed, but maybe we haven't where it truly counts. I never meant to sound vindictive. That considerate, kind nature of his was giving me false hope. I couldn't control my anger, though I know I was only yelling at myself.

"Maybe you two should take some time to talk." He Pi glances dubiously from me to Shu Jin.

"No, I apologize for my outburst. I came to help. Either let me or I'm marching to the palace and slaying Wang Liang myself."

Jin's lips thin into a line and then he turns away. He Pi shrugs at my indifference. "Funny you said that. We need someone to infiltrate the palace and retrieve Cai Pai. So far, no one's suicidal enough to volunteer."

"I'll do it."

"Then I'm going with you," Jin gallantly declares.

"I don't need your help."

"And I don't need your permission."

"Why? You finally have something to live for."

"Exactly. If you go, so will I."

"You're not making any sense!"

"That's enough, you two." Scratching his head, He Pi groans irritably. "Your lover's spat is boring me."

"I don't have a lover," is my cold reply

Jin's brows furrow from offense. He has some nerve acting that way after leaving me, after telling me that he could stand to live without me, and then declaring to Mei that he's never had a girlfriend. Why then, so quick to put himself in danger?

Now I *am* being vindictive. It's too difficult to push my resentment aside. More than anything, I just want to scream at him those three words I've been bottling up all this time. He'd probably just laugh at my stupidity.

"Oh! I'm so glad!" He Pi suddenly chirps. "Do you remember what I said in Xiong? If in one year's time, Jin hasn't proposed, I'd make you my woman."

His lips come closer. He Pi leans in for a kiss. Out of rage, my hand flies across his face. He moves back and stares on with wounded eyes; though, a teasing smile is definitely surfacing behind the false frown.

"You're mean!"

My throbbing hands are shaking. No words will come. How could He Pi be so inconsiderate as to bring up Xiong in front of Jin? That place held such lovely memories for us; at least, it did for me. During the short time Jin and I were happy there, I'd imagined a future which now, is a fleeting dream. It hurts. Every part of me is aching. What was the point of it all only for things to turn out this way?

Jin's staring awkwardly again. I never should have come back into his life and yet, until this conflict is over, I've nowhere to go. That's not true. There is one place I can go.

"I need some air. Excuse me."

Chapter 50 – 4

Night here is colder than I expected. That doesn't deter the vast amount of patrons from enjoying everything Sai Mi has to offer. Right this minute, the grandest army of all five countries is marching to overtake Bei Ling and there's not the slightest feeling of fear or anxiety in the atmosphere. I wonder whether ignorance or confidence is the root of their bliss.

"Hey!"

"Ahh!" The impact of a sharp slap against my shoulder let slip a small scream. "En-Enya! Where have you been?"

"Here and there. You frighten so easily. How did you ever defeat me?"

"Because you were arrogant."

"Whatever," she frowns. "Why the long face? Did you find your boyfriend?"

"Yeah. Did you find your ex?"

"Decided not to. He doesn't deserve me. What about you?"

"Other way around. I didn't deserve him so he found another, but I can't let go and then... I was snarky."

"God! You're depressing! So what? Is that it?"

"What else is there?"

"Duh! The obvious solution. Take him back!"

"What do you mean? He's taken."

"Yeah? So? You want him, fight for him. He was yours first."

"But he loves her."

"Then make him love you."

"What about her?"

"*What about her*?!"

"Your logic is self-absorbed! They're happy together. It's not right for me to interfere."

"You'll get nowhere in life putting other people's feelings first. Did you make me bring you all the way here just to waste my time? I bet you didn't even tell him what you wanted to say! "

"I can't just—"

"Sure you can! A woman like you, who was able to charm Lord Han Bei, is more dangerous than any pretty little thing. Cross-dressed and all."

Enya smirks during that last comment while scanning me up and down. I'd forgotten I'm still dressed as a man.

"How did you recognize me?"

"Disguises are part of my trade. Anyway, walking about depressed in the middle of the night is a little too dramatic for my taste. Want me to give this boyfriend of yours a good reason to come crawling back?"

She holds up a threatening fist and I can't help but think of Mu Dan. Once this is over, I must introduce them.

"That's not necessary. Beating him senseless will only make him flee farther."

"I know what you mean. Some men are so spineless."

"That's not what I meant. Never mind. So, you're back home. What are you going to do now, Enya?"

"Well, I might ask for my old post at the palace. Who can say no to services from a pretty girl? When the time is right, maybe I'll tell my brother the truth."

"That's great! Things may be difficult at first but I'm sure he'll be happy to find family."

"I think so, too. What about you? What are you going to do?"

"Actually, could I join you?"

"You've a much better job waiting in Ning. I'd kill to have that job. Or, is this part of your plan to depose you-know-who?"

"I have to keep Cai Pai safe."

"Didn't you say that was a task for his sister?"

"I did but I changed my mind. It's too dangerous."

"Outright suicidal! Oh, is that what this is about? I can understand being broken-hearted but wow... this boyfriend must really be something!"

"That's not why!"

"Sure, it's not. I'm the one with the biggest stake in this. My brother is practically held hostage by you-know-who. The wimpy councilmen who are supposed to look after my brother are cowering in their little corners. Worse, according to my informants, most children outside of the capital have been ripped away from families to join training regiments and mass properties were seized, including from those who had next to nothing. As Bei Ling's unofficial princess, I take offense to that. I don't care who you're working for, let me help."

"I can't."

"What? You don't trust me? After everything we've been through, that hurts, you know!"

"You're loyal to a fault, right?"

"Darn right!"

"If you're loyal to me, then tell me who sent you to Ning."

"Nice try. It doesn't work that way. Betraying one for the other is the epitome of disloyalty."

"So is protecting one and letting the other falter."

Enya sighs her usual irritation and then sulks. "Whatever. I still won't tell you."

"Then I'll have to do this alone."

"Fine! Good luck finding your way inside!"

Enya, grinning, runs off. I start to chase after her when someone's hand tersely seizes mine.

"That's enough. You trust people too easily. Come back before she sends trackers after you and find our compound's location."

"You've been following me? H-How much did you hear?"

Jin continues dragging me back toward the Bai He warehouse; glancing around every so often to survey our surroundings. "The part she claimed to be Cai Pai's sister. Cai Pai doesn't have any siblings."

"Because no one will believe her."

"Without proof, neither should you. Let's say she is his sister. Siblings don't always want the best for their kin. Su Jian is a prime example of that."

"If she can help us get inside the palace—"

"Or con you to get inside our base. Where did you find this woman?"

"She um... tried to assassinate Han Bei."

Oh, dear heavens. Why was I chummy with a woman who nearly killed Han Bei and injured me? For all I know, her former lover could be Su Jian.

Jin pauses, unable to find a proper reaction to the stupidity in my confession. The incredulous stare quickly morphs into a bitter scowl. With every step we then take toward the secret base, I can feel his disappointment in me grow.

Once He Pi was relayed the event, under his usual lecherous smile, anger surfaced. The impact of my recklessness couldn't be fathomed. Everyone's safety along with the plot to depose Wang Liang could have been compromised should Enya turn out to be less than trustworthy.

The other members were furious. Though Jin attempted to defend me, from then on, I was kept under lock and key.

Chapter 51: A Chance to be Useful

Two weeks later, the base breaks into uproar. Heavy footsteps stomp up and down the hallways while boisterous, panicked shouts are seeping in from beyond the thin door. The thumping of objects being dragged and dropped all echoes in waves. I pound on the door, yelling for release while praying that this isn't what I think it is.

Finally, after exhausting my voice, the door unlocks and a frantic Jin rushes inside the room.

"Is-Is the base under attack?"

His head quickly shakes to brush away that moot concern in face of direr troubles. "No. There are unsettling rumors spreading across Sai Mi. Half of Ning's army was destroyed at Lam Soi Citadel. Without Lord Han Bei's leadership, the other half is retreating. Nan Rong is losing their position against Feng Jia and Ye is on the verge of falling into this conflict. The alliance is hanging on by a thread. We don't have much time. The Order is making final preparations."

Everything he said after Han Bei is lost to me. I feel numb. Please, dear God, it must be a mistake!

"Jin, when you said without Han Bei's leadership, you don't mean..."

Jin clamps down his lips and nods a confirmation. Dread turns everything to ice. I can't breathe. The more I choke to catch my breath, the more the world around violently quakes from sheer madness of the unimaginable. Life suddenly feels meaningless. No matter which way I turn, this boxed-in reality continues growing smaller while the writing on the wall demands attention.

How could this happen to Han Bei? He is Ning's champion! He is not allowed to falter! I refuse to believe this nonsense! I won't!

"Let go, damn it!"

I never should have allowed Han Bei out of my sight and I never should have come here to burden Jin! Why is everything I do a mistake? For all my foolishness, why won't he let me go?

Jin grabbed my arm when I dashed for the exit. No matter how I fight to tear away, he continues pulling back. In the end, my legs give out and I'm lodged in his embrace. Sobbing. This is all I'm good for: useless tears.

"They could be baseless rumors."

The force of his hold and tender whisper ignite calm warmth to wash over me. Even so, they can't subdue my quivering.

"If they're baseless, then why are the White Cranes rushing?"

"Baseless or otherwise, the East's army should have met with Wang Liang's forces by now. Something is stalling their advance. The latest news from our messengers depicted Nan Rong's sudden retreat. Regardless, the Order is planning to storm the palace and put an end to this."

"I'm going, too. I'll make him pay a thousand times the pain he's caused Han Bei!"

"Stay here where it's safe."

"Who cares about safety? I'd rather die than never be able to live with myself!"

Despite pushing away his protective arms, I can't unlatch from his grasp. With his attention fully upon me, I look down to hide from Jin's awkward stare.

"What's gotten into you? Why are you so defeated?"

"I'm not. Han Bei once said to live for my country and not for myself. He's never steered me wrong. I will do just that."

"You are Ning's empress. We can't put you in danger. Besides, our plans are set. We don't need any more help."

"What about Cai Pai? Without their central figure, Bei Ling will blame the White Cranes and someone else possibly worse than Wang Liang may rise to power."

"Mei's volunteered—"

"Are you insane? You can't let her go!"

"Mei is our best gamble. She can pass for a courtesan and she's thoroughly studied the palace's layout."

"That's not the point! Doesn't she mean anything to you at all?!"

His awkward stare turns perplexed. Is this blatant lack of concern how Jin treats every woman he claims to love? At least now I understand he's only protective of me because of my significance. Should anything happen to me, he's afraid of retribution from the East. Even then, the only person who really needed me in Ning was Han Bei. Without him, I've no reason to return. I never understood just how much I loved him. All he wanted was my honesty, and I couldn't give it. Now that he's gone, I would give anything to bring him back.

The thought of my Grand General brings more surging tears. I love him and I also love Jin. Is this the punishment for unfaithfulness which my sister suffered? She couldn't remain faithful to Han Bei and her lover perished. I couldn't remain faithful to Jin and Han Bei is... the thought is too sad to bear; too horrible to admit. I did this to Han Bei. I won't let the same happen to Jin!

Mustering false composure, I scantly glance up. "Jin, when are they staging the raid?"

"Please, leave this to the Order."

"You don't trust me, Jin? Some things never change."

Grimacing, he slowly releases me. Though he remains silent, those sharpened eyes of his are burning more passionately than ever. Maybe through being loved by the right woman, he has changed after all. He needs Mei. I can't permit her life to be endangered when theirs haven't the chance to begin.

"I'm sorry. You're right. The best I can do is stay out of your way."

He understands my temperament too well to accept my concession. Jin chews on his lip for a moment. Something keeps him from responding. Then, hesitantly, he parts from the room.

Chapter 51 – 2

I don't know why I was remotely offended that Jin didn't trust me. He had good reasons. When Mei came by with dinner, I baited her with vague questions which she inadvertently answered in specifics. Three nights from now, that's when the raid will be staged. It won't be easy considering the substantial number of soldiers stationed inside and out of the palace. Thus, their plan is to detonate the explosives seized from Wang Liang's sources in remote parts of the cities. This will draw out his men and give leeway for White Crane agents to infiltrate.

After vaguely conferring Jin to her care one last time, I asked for two of Mei's small hairpins to keep loose hair from my eyes. Two nights later, the lock hindering my escape becomes inconsequential. With Han Bei's prized dagger strapped to my ankle, I sneak out from the room. Surprisingly, no one is in the corridor.

"You must have the devil's luck."

Barely have I set foot in the front room of the warehouse, He Pi swings an arm around my waist and brings our hips close. Immediately after, he retracts, sighing sharply as if to chastise himself. Lechery really is a bad habit he can't control.

"I won't ask how you escaped, Miss Liang, but I have an idea what you're up to, and a better idea for you to be useful."

"You're... not mad? I plan to interfere."

"I was wondering why you hadn't sooner. Jin said you were stubborn and impulsive. Apparently, capable too. Since you've proven yourself sparsely better than a damsel in distress, I need your help."

"Anything! Actually, He Pi, speaking of Jin, where is everyone?"

"That's what I'd like to know. Mei divulged our plan to you, didn't she? The men sent to the initial detonation site haven't set off the diversion and the reinforced group hasn't returned."

"Wait. I thought the foray was tomorrow."

"Such is conflict, nothing is ever simple. Su Jian was made aware of our proposed insurgency. We had to move tonight, before he can discover the details of our whereabouts. I'm only worried he may already have."

"Someone betrayed the Order? What about Jin and Mei? Where are they?"

"Yes. Unfortunately, loyalty is a rare commodity which often falls to the highest bidder. Thank goodness the traitor was caught before our entire plan's layouts exchanged hands. Jin and Mei are standing by to infiltrate and retrieve Cai Pai as we speak. However, that can't happen without our diversion. I'd have gone to survey the site myself if I weren't needed here to direct the first wave and their runners."

"I understand. I'll go."

"Don't sound so eager. Chances are the first group and their reinforcements were slain. There's a good possibility so will you, if you aren't careful. I'm not sending you to finish their task. Take note of the site and then report back immediately, understood?"

His tone is unexpectedly stern and demanding. Who knew behind the childish façade, He Pi could be so bossy? For a moment, I thought I was speaking to San An.

"Wait. Shouldn't you call off the raid since Su Jian knows your plan?"

"Precisely why I can't. Lately, his main forces have shifted toward the weakened Ning army while his southern group is moving to exploit Nan Rong's sudden retreat. He's overextended himself. This may be our last chance before he realizes the mistake. So long as Cai Pai is taken into our hands, Wang Lang will lose his authority over Bei Ling."

"What about all the lives involved? Does the Order know the danger?"

"Living in fear and subjugation is a fate worse than death. That is the Order's belief. No great change can come about without great risk. They are prepared."

I don't know else to say to that. This sounds reckless to me; though, whether I agree or not, things will go about without my approval. The best I can do is to be useful.

"Where is the first site?"

"Near the Xue Li abandoned warehouse in the Man Chong District; a few steps away from where the Shang Nu and Kuai En roads intersect."

"Where's that?"

His eyebrows rise thoughtfully as though recalling another memory. Jin must have told him that I'm bad at directions. That, coupled with being unfamiliar with Sai Mi, I would run about lost all night searching for Xue Li. So much for being useful!

"Hmm," He Pi taps his chin pensively. "Once Zhang Tang arrives to take my position, I can deal with our obstacles. Sai Mi's massive palace can't be missed from any point in this city. Why don't you head over and look for Jin and Mei near the Long Hu Tavern on the southern end of the gates? The massive gaudy orange sign should be easy to recognize. Tell them to remain patient until the signal is given. If none is received by the hour of the tiger, they should withdraw. We'll find another way."

"No problem. I'll go now."

"I appreciate your willing support. Here's a good luck charm for the road."

His eyelids lower seductively. He Pi's lips pucker as he moves closer. I dodge to avoid the gruesome kiss and then rush out of the door for dear life. From behind, I can hear his sordid, teasing chuckles.

Chapter 52: Bei Ling's Princess

"Please, is she here? Enya. I'm looking for Enya."

These guards have been eying me suspiciously. It's doubtful they'll believe that someone dressed in princess garb would petition to meet a servant. I expected more sympathy appearing as a woman but I should have known these clothes were too fancy. They were all I had.

By the time I'd arrived, Mei was so overzealous to prove herself to He Pi that she didn't wait for the signal. At least, I was told that, though I'm sure she meant to impress her boyfriend. Jin was battling with the notion of running after her. She could pass for a courtesan. There wasn't a good reason for him to request entry. The guards wouldn't be keen to trust a stranger, especially a man, after Wang Liang caught wind of the Order's presence. As such, the number of soldiers stationed outside the palace is ridiculous. I couldn't risk Jin's safety. Not to mention, if he caused commotion, everyone would be in danger, including Mei. Thus, during a momentary distraction, I ran off toward the palace's entrance.

"She has amethyst eyes, fair skin, dark hair, a peppy personality, looks like a... princess?"

The guards stare at one another, puzzled, before becoming annoyed. Had Mei waited, I would have used her ploy and feigned being a courtesan. I just thought following her lead so soon would seem dubious. In all consideration, doing so might have been less suspicious than asking for Enya. For all I know, the assassin never returned to the palace.

"Quite an enchanting description. If such a maiden exists, let's see if we can find her, shall we?"

The guards immediately bow the moment that kind voice resonates from behind me. I swing around to meet familiar traits on a foreign face. Those are San An's eyes to be sure; the smile, possibly Jin's. He's beautiful and the air around him is benign. When this man's identity comes to me, his smile widens as if to acknowledge the fleeting thought.

"I don't wish to intrude." Albeit every fiber of my being is burning from expectation of exacting vengeance for Han Bei, I won't succeed with these guards nearby. Not to mention, I doubt Wang Liang is weak. Once I fail, my connection to the Bai He Tavern could be discovered, Wang Liang's security would increase tenfold, and the White Cranes' efforts would be rendered moot. I've not started and I'm on the verge of failure.

"Nonsense. You've come this way and I would be less than a gentleman to leave a lady disappointed. Likewise, I wish to meet the wonderful maiden you've described; though, I doubt she is anywhere as charming as my lady."

Smiling sincerely, he seizes my wrist and then proceeds inside. I could neither protest in front of so many watchful eyes nor deny the opportunity which I've been hoping.

Chapter 52 – 2

Down several large corridors and then through an antechamber leading to a massive concealed guestroom; Wang Liang finally pauses. Abruptly turning back, a sweet smile spreads across his face.

"Still as adorable as ever, little brother."

"Excuse me?"

"It's been too long. I hope you still remember me. I've never forgotten any of my dear siblings, especially the ones still residing in our old home."

How can he think I'm He Pi? My particular areas are protruding from under Dong Xing's tight robe. Do they look fake? Insults aside, maybe he'll divulge information to his brother which he wouldn't to a stranger.

Stiffening my posture, I return his smile. "I'm glad you're well, Su Jian."

"As am I. Did you truly come to find a beautiful maiden or were you in search of me? I'm guessing the latter. I've caused you and our brothers much trouble, haven't I?"

For someone whose hands are tainted by the blood of thousands, he's standing there smiling as innocently as though his only crime was ignorance. There's not a bit of remorse; not one notion of grief for the lives lost.

And yet, somehow, he seems so pure that I unthinkingly begin doubting his guilt.

"The question remains why, Su Jian. Why are you causing us trouble?"

"I've come to realize a long time ago, destiny is how we choose to make it and fate is reserved for those who stand still. As they say, may the best man win."

"That doesn't explain the reason you wish to slay your own blood. What crimes have San An, Jin, and I committed against you that is worth innocent lives?"

"Don't talk to me about involving innocents! You did nothing! That was your crime!" Pausing, he withdraws from the outburst as though embarrassed. When he continues, the tone is calmer, mimicking San An's composure.

"For a time, I accepted my fate and my place as second born. Your dear ambitious mother broke form and pushed you to the throne. Empress Pai sought to change your fate. Inadvertently, she took mine. I loved my brothers and sisters, which was the reason my mother never raised a hand against any of you. I forbade it. Nevertheless, you all stood idle and hoped for my death; another number marked off the list for your turn. Well, now it's my turn. Feng Jia has been colluding with Bei Ling to invade Ye. Ning, for years, has had eyes for Nan Rong. Despite your ill thoughts, Brother, under my authority, all lands will unite!"

"At what cost?"

"Nothing your mother, the other ladies at court, or the current authority figures wouldn't accomplish given the chance. Even you, Brother, have been coming to Sai Mi for years. Did you think I wouldn't notice? Not once did you come to see me. So much for family."

"I didn't know you were still alive!"

"Don't lie. That day in the market when our eyes linked, I thought family still meant something to the revered Southern Emperor, but you walked away."

I haven't the slightest clue what he's talking about, so I choose the obvious fib. "How could I have been certain it was you? I thought you were dead!"

"You have always been the curious sort. Nothing should peak your interest more than a walking dead man; unless, you had something to hide. Recently, I hear you've been plotting against me—to finish what your mother started. Is that true?"

I might resemble He Pi but I know next to nothing about the true emperor under the superficial lechery. Su Jian's claims might be accurate. Nothing comes to mind that can rebuff his charges. I can't do else but stand still.

"Silence is as good as admittance, Brother." Wang Liang presses again.

"Think whatever you want, Su Jian. At least tell me why you brought Ning into this conflict and why Lord Han Bei had to pay with his life!"

"Don't ask questions to which you fully know the answers. Han Bei's demise wasn't planned because I never thought Ning would lead a direct charge. He was foolhardy; a stupid brute. Such is expected from war. The strong provide shield for the intellectual."

"Don't you dare talk about Han Bei that way! He is ten thousand times the man you'll ever be!" I shouldn't, but I can't help it. My body can't endure this tortuous anger building inside. I can't stop shaking! "How should he have reacted after you goaded Ning by directing your assassin? Do you deny it?!"

The crinkle on his brows deepens. "I did no such thing. You should know me better. That you would put Nan Rong's adversary in a higher position than your own brother tells me a great deal."

He seems pained, offended, and heartbroken. I won't ever forgive him. Just because he didn't direct Enya doesn't change the fact that Han Bei is gone. Be that as it may, a part of me feels sorry for the lonely Su Jian and his misguided ideas for peace. Is there any way to talk sense into this man in order to avoid the loss of more lives? If he merely needs a brother to depend upon, then I... can't believe I fell for it!

Ying injured San An and discovered that I was He Pi's substitute. What makes Su Jian believe I'm the real thing? As he'd said, He Pi is the curious sort. His Highness left the capital to find my identity at Tian Mao Yi. Had he saw his own brother before this conflict, nothing should have stopped him from chasing after Su Jian; which also means, I failed Wang Liang's impromptu test and everything that has come after was merely farce.

"Su Jian. I apologize for everything that's happened between us. Clearly, I've misjudged your character. Since we've both had our say, I won't be a bother any longer. Good-bye, Brother."

I attempt to fly past him. Just when success is in sight, my wrist is seized and my back is forced against the door. He comes closer, altering the friendly smile stagnant upon his face to a mean-spirited one. His free hand cups tightly around my chin.

"So quick to flee, as always. What are you hiding?"

"Nothing."

"No? Well, if that *is* all there is between us, I might as well claim your life. Your mother began this war. Once you die, I promise to end it. It's only fair, isn't it? The rightful order of things. San An will ascend the throne, as he was always meant to, and I will bring peace to this world as I see fit. Tell me, is there any reason I shouldn't kill you here and now?"

"Because we're brothers." (Continue to page 729)

"Because I'm not He Pi." (Continue to page 731)

Chapter 52 – 3

"Because we're brothers."

"So we are, which is the reason you must die. I never personally send any man to hell without first giving him the satisfaction of expressing all his thoughts. Tell me, are there any final words?"

This doesn't make sense. He surely knows I'm not his brother. On the off chance he doesn't, permitting the idea of He Pi's death might give the White Cranes back their opportunity. I failed to find Enya and instead, exposed He Pi. This is the best I can do to correct my mistakes: lower his guard from certainty.

"I forgive you, Brother. You should in turn, forgive ours. In the afterlife, power is nothing but we'll always be family."

He releases my chin. Sharp pains immediately radiate from my chest. I couldn't fathom what's transpired until the numbing touch of his thumb rubs circles on the tip of my right breast, locked tightly in his hand. The beastly stare twisted upon his face must reflect his true nature. I've never been more sickened by beauty in my life!

"Don't touch me!"

My free arm strikes at his face; though, in one swift movement, he easily evades and then both my wrists are pinned under iron grips.

"Brave and suicidal are two facets of the same coin. Not only do you resemble your mother, you also have her spirit. A woman like you is fit to stand by my side."

"How did you—! A man like you is not fit for any woman! Get your hands off me!"

"Or what? Your dear Grand General is no more. Who will protect you? The broken half of your pathetic army? Give yourself over to me, Empress of Ning. I promise to make you scream."

His warm breath wafts into my ear. I imagine he wishes to succeed where his predecessor, Tung, failed. He's right. I am my mother. I won't give Ning over to anyone!

His lips press against my cheek and then slowly move toward my mouth. On impulse, my right clog smashes down on one of his light canvas shoes. Su Jian staggers back, wincing from pain.

Seizing the opportunity, I dash from the room.

Continue to page 732

Chapter 52 – 4

"Because I'm not He Pi."

His expression suddenly turns severe, as though he'd been slapped. "Only a simpleton states the obvious and only a coward states the truth in self-defense. You disappoint me, Empress of Ning."

"How did you—?"

"What kind of a fool did you take me for? Know thy enemy and know thyself. The basics of warfare. You're ignorant to a fault!"

His hand descends from my chin to my throat; his fingers digging deep. My struggling is useless. All the while, my vision is growing hazy from lack of oxygen. This is the end. I failed and the only comfort I can find is to move forward and reunite with Han Bei and my family. Be that as it may, I refuse to go alone.

With one last effort, my right leg shoots up and I reach for the dagger latched to my ankle. Su Jian stumbles back when I bring down the blade. It grazed his arm and a small stream of blood begins to trickle. The madness on his face deepens. The rage in my heart ignites. I will avenge my beloved Han Bei and protect my dearest Jin. For that, I will gladly give everything.

Su Jian and I rush upon one another. Red rivers flow and then everything turns dark. The End.

Chapter 52 – 5

Past the antechamber and then into the corridor; I can't remember all the routes he took when we came in so I merely stumble about. What was I thinking? How could I have been so careless?! For all my good intentions, I've made a mess of things. I have to tell Jin even though I don't know how I could possibly face him.

"Ow!"

She cries out the moment I turn the corner. The collision sends us both reeling to the ground. Amethyst eyes flicker from surprise before matching her acrid frown.

"Enya!"

"What are you doing here, *Princess?*"

"Looking for you! We have to go before he finds us!"

"Who?"

"Wang Liang. He met me at the gates and I—there really isn't time to discuss!"

"You're right, there isn't." Enya stands up, dusts off her robe, and then quickly removes the dagger strapped to my ankle.

"What—hey! Give that back!"

"My lord." Enya looks over me and bows. I turn to find an incensed Wang Liang scowling as he approaches.

"Enya, Wang Liang is your lord?"

"Duh! Who else? You're so stupid, luck must be the only reason you're still alive."

"You're Bei Ling's princess! He tried to kill your brother!"

My senseless protest is met with Enya's downcast eyes. Wang Liang pauses a short distance away and chuckles.

"Spreading more of your lies, Enya? It's a shame the only person who'd believe you is a fool."

Jin was right and so was He Pi. Even Su Jian's accusations are true. I am a fool. What was I thinking being chummy with Enya? This assassin nearly killed Han Bei and me. I wanted to be useful and this is where it's gotten me, stuck between two liars telling tall tales.

Drawing away from Enya, my back is to a wall. "Just who the hell are you?"

My question is posed to Enya; Wang Liang is the one to respond. "A whore I picked off the streets. Pretty little thing. Parentless. She couldn't wait to give Prince Su Jian everything. As if any prince would waste time civilizing a harlot. Lucky for her, she's also a talented liar, thief, and killer. Otherwise, she'd be back on the streets."

"Where do you get off calling her names?!" The nerve! Maybe their relationship isn't my business, but no woman should be insulted that way, especially by the man she loves. "You're the worst of them! The way she gushed about you, I thought you were a saint! All you've done was used a young woman in need. Some man you are! You're not worthy to wipe He Pi's butt! Enya, princess or servant, you deserve better than this filth! He doesn't know what love is!"

Her eyes are to the ground; injured by callous words from the man she's held in regards all these years. Despite her past and even the unforgivable things she's committed for his sake, I know behind it all, she is a woman seeking acceptance. That was the person I came to know during our trip to Sai Mi. As she'd said, some girls are luckier than others. I had Master Tai Hung. Without him, we might not have been much different.

"Your pathetic rant won't save you, Empress. She's loyal, just like you. It's too bad San An found you first; else, Ning would have been mine. It will be soon enough. Enya, kill her."

My blood runs cold. Though her countenance is complicated, the dagger in her hand is raised. Enya comes closer. I can't outrun them, this much I'm certain, and without my dagger, I don't stand a chance against two opponents. One false move and everything will end. However, she's clearly hesitating.

"Stop wasting precious time! Do it!" Wang Liang shouts indignantly, having perceived my observation.

"I-I can't." Enya lowers the blade and then turns to face her beloved. Her teeth sink into the lower lip, staining them crimson. "She has information. She's not here alone. There's a secret group—"

"Enya! Be quiet!" I snap before she says too much, though it seems my effort is moot.

"He Pi is somewhere around, I'm sure." Wang Liang replies coolly. "If we hang her severed head in the markets, the gentleman in him will come to retrieve it."

"I could just as well torture her for information!"

"Assuming she wasn't fed false information. Prove your loyalty, Enya, or die a traitor's death along with this empress."

Loyalty, the only good trait she claims to have. I thought the same about myself. I couldn't truly betray Jin for Han Bei, even when Jin loved another. Enya can't bring herself to betray Wang Liang even though he doesn't deserve her loyalty. Albeit Shu Jin and Wang Liang are nothing alike, the inane idea is the same. I kept holding onto Jin when he sought freedom and in the end, I lost both of those dear to me. It never should have come down to this in order for me to fully realize my folly.

"Enya, loyalty should be bestowed to those loyal to you. Otherwise, you're just being used."

I may be voicing my opinion but I know they're also hers. When those amethyst stars waver, Wang Liang snatches the dagger from the conflicted courtesan. In that instant, a loud explosion shakes the palace. The deafening sounds continue from all directions in succession. Wang Liang stares at me and receives a reflected look of confusion; though, not for the reason he believes. I'm confused because I thought the calculating minister knew the Order's plans.

"Finish this and then come find me!" With those parting words, Wang Liang tosses the blade back to Enya and then runs down the opposite end of the hall toward the commotion.

Immediately as he rounds a corner, a hard fist bops my head.

"Idiot! What the hell were you thinking?!"

"What—you weren't really going to kill me, were you?"

"Who knows?" Enya shrugs. "You're such a pain in the neck; you'd probably come back and haunt me if I did kill you. Tsk! You are one lucky girl! What are the chances?"

Another loud bang reverberates throughout the palace in a deafening crash, shaking the foundation. We both jump.

"Enya, where is Cai Pai? We need to move him to safety!"

"*We?* I spared you, wasn't that enough?"

"This is no time to be blithe!"

"All right! All right! The child is probably in bed by now. Come, I know a shortcut."

She throws the dagger back to me and then takes off down the hall while I stagger to keep up.

"Hey, why did you lie to me?"

"We're turning right at the next corridor. Don't fall behind. This may surprise you but some people don't like admitting their seedy pasts."

"I'm not talking about the princess claims. Why didn't you tell me your lover was Wang Liang?"

"Because he's not. Didn't he say I'm a liar? He never loved me. I just wanted to believe he did. I thought killing Han Bei would make him see me in a better light, but no matter what, to him, I'm just street trash. You're the first gullible person to believe I'm Cai Pai's sister. That was your own fault. Did I mention how stupid you are?"

"What makes you so certain my gullible stupidity isn't pretense to gain others' trusts?"

Frowning, she glances over her shoulder to survey my grin. "You're not that talented."

This entire palace is a maze hidden inside a maze. Had He Pi decided to send me instead of Mei, I would have been lost for days. Whether luck or coincidence, I'm glad for Enya's guidance. In no time, Cai Pai's room comes into view. Along with progress is another impasse. Two heavily armored guards are stationed outside the chamber. With one dagger between both of us, the odds aren't in our favor.

"Our best bet is another diversion. Once I make them chase me, could you take Cai Pai to safety?"

"Don't think me rude," she replies theatrically. "You're not the type of woman these men would chase."

Following her insolence, Enya tersely flicks my forehead and the proceeds forward. Startled, I reach for her arm. She easily shakes off my attempt. Before I can grasp what's happened, the men move away from the door and leisurely follows her. It's frightening because I can't even begin to grasp the idea. There are mightier forces than the blade.

Chapter 53: Brother v. Brother

"Your Highness!"

Once past the door, I call out to Cai Pai only to find him absent. On the table, the ink stone of the calligraphy set is still wet. The parchment is half-finished with the last character smeared mid-word. Paintbrushes are carelessly strewn on the floor. I don't understand. If he's been taken, why were guards stationed out front?

This is just great! Without Enya, I can't even find the exit. It would be impossible to locate Cai Pai. After exposing He Pi and failing to protect Mei, I'm now a liability—a sitting duck in this dangerous labyrinth. In other words: useless, as always.

"Argh! Damn it! Where is that kid?!"

"Tui Tui?"

"Ahh!" Both hands fly over my mouth to keep in the scream. Why is the wall talking to me?

"Tui Tui... is that you?"

Her timid, strained voice leaks from behind the wooden wall. I scuttle over just as a latch clicks open.

"Mei?! What on Earth happened?!"

The lady smiles shyly while heaving ragged breaths. Sweat is beading across her forehead. Around her right leg is a pool of blood seeping from the bandaged thigh.

"She... took him... Cai Pai." Mei labors through the pain, wincing every so often.

"Who's she? Never mind, just relax!"

As I reach to cut a piece of fabric off my robe, Mei's shaking hand holds out a strip already taken from her own dress. It, too, is soaked in blood.

Strips of thin fabric won't make any difference. She probably stopped me from ruining Dong Xing's fine silk robe. Who needs the likes of silk robes at a time like this?

The top outer layer of my robe is removed. I bind the garment tightly around her wound. Mei winces and clamps down her lips to muffle the cry.

"I'm sorry. This is the best I can do."

"Yan Lei... saw her with Wang Liang... she attacked me... ran and escaped through... secret passage. Came here but... he's gone. Warn... Shu Jin."

Having delivered the message, she falls against the back of the hidden passage and closes her eyes from relief.

"Who's Yan Lei? Mei! Mei! Stay awake! Don't fall asleep! What the hell were you thinking, Mei?! Why were you so reckless?!"

She won't respond. Her eyes remain shut. Fearing the worst, tears won't stop coursing down my face. I'm shaking because I don't know else to do except pointlessly shout in the attempt to drown out my own failure.

"You can't leave Jin! You hear me? He loves you! You can't make him sad! I won't forgive you!"

"I wanted... to make... Shu Jin... proud. He was... so worried about... Cai Pai." She mumbles a feeble response as if talking in her sleep. "Why... were you... reckless?"

"To keep you from getting hurt!"

Mei slightly lifts up her right eyelid and smiles.

However heroic are my words, parts of me have been stalling this entire time hoping for Enya to return. I'm a coward. Mei needs help immediately while I'm still struggling to find the courage to walk out that door. As terrible as it is to admit, her injury hinders the chance of us escaping from this unscathed.

"Warn Shu Jin. He doesn't know... about... Yan Lei. I'll... be fine." She casts out the breathless whisper, wincing from pain throughout.

What am I thinking? Why am I being selfish? I've resented Jin for his abandonment. However, I've yet to admit another ugly emotion which has dominated me: jealousy. I'm jealous she took him from me, even though she doesn't know it. I'm jealous of her sweet nature, her pretty face, and beyond that, her courage. Mei has something to live for and yet, she's putting herself last.

I've nothing left and still, I'm clinging onto nothing. The more I look at Mei, the more pathetic I realize I've become. Jin may not be mine but that doesn't diminish his importance to me. Even if I can't do this for her, I have to for Jin. It's clear to me now. The only token of love I can offer that will mean anything is one from which I won't ever benefit.

"You're crazy, Mei. Sit still while I find Cai Pai and then we'll leave together. Do you know where Yan Lei might have taken him?"

"Probably to Wang Liang's quarters... east of here."

"Which way's east?"

"Out the door... and then... left."

"O-Okay. Don't do anything else reckless. Endure things for now. I'll come back. And don't fall asleep!"

She gives a half smile. Maybe I imagined it; I sounded exactly like Han Bei just now. I finally understand his frustration against my recklessness and his sacrifice for the person he loved. For Jin's happiness, I will follow my Grand General's example and do no less.

Chapter 53 – 2

Down the massive hall, passing turn after turn in the seemingly endless path—Wang Liang's quarters are nowhere in sight. Another bout of explosion shakes the foundation. From around, clashing of metal resounds, followed by echoes of blood-curdling shouts and stomping boots. I dearly hope the White Cranes are the ones advancing. Mei can't run in that state, let alone defend herself against Bei Ling's armored guards. Su Jian's perverse manners are coming back to me; I fear for Mei should his men find her.

Quickening into a delirious scramble, my lungs and legs are set on fire. In moments, a tall figure with dark hair comes up to impede the path from one of the adjacent corridors. Though dressed in armor and brandishing a sword much contrary to his usual self, I can recognize him from any angle.

"Jin!"

I can't stop my charging position and inadvertently, slam into him. Jin's outstretched arms draw me into an embrace; binding us so tightly that it's hard to breathe. Through the breastplate, the comforting scent of sandalwood from his shirt floats up my nose.

"Idiot!" He exhales a pained whisper. "Do you have any idea how worried I was?!"

I scantly glance up to find anger surging within his gaze, which then softens to something sweet. My heart skips and I become excited from the insinuation, until realizing the stupidity in my reaction.

"Jin, how—when? Mei's injured! She's in Cai Pai's room at the opposite end of the hall!"

"And where are you running off to *alone?*"

There's accusation in that tone. I can't blame him for thinking the worst in me; except, now isn't the time.

"Yan Lei has Cai Pai. I didn't plan to abandon her. I was going to return for Mei—"

"That's not what I meant! What were you thinking? If Wang Liang had captured you, I don't want to consider the horrible things he'd do."

"You're right. If he had decided to torture me, I might have divulged the White Cranes' plans. Jin, I'm sorry."

"Divulging the Order's plan is the least of my worries! What could have driven you to be so reckless?"

"Does it matter? Feel free to yell at me later. Right now, you have to take Mei out of here."

"He Pi's doing just that. Apparently, I can't trust you to trust me, so come, let's find Yan Lei."

"W-Wait. I thought the traitor was caught. Who is Yan Lei and why are the explosions so close? What happened at the detonation sites?"

"I'll explain on the way."

Chapter 53 – 3

Once we've gone a distance, my questions are posed again. Jin glances over his shoulder and exhales sharply.

"I realized you ran off when I was *preoccupied*. That was a dirty tactic you used at Long Hu. What did you say to those women?"

"Sorry."

"If you were sorry, that smirk wouldn't be so clearly displayed on your face. Anyway, once I understood your intention, I couldn't wait any longer. I thought since the Order failed to set off the diversion, I'd make one myself."

"How?"

"Guards were mostly stationed at the main gates. Only a handful was at the storage house. There were still more than enough explosives inside, so I put them to good use. It seems the other groups around the city took my diversion as their starting signal. Everything that happened after has been sporadic. Wang Liang's men were running every which way—uncertain of how close or far the threat was—and easily fell prey to the Order's agents."

"What are you saying? You... stormed the palace alone? Jin, were you out of your mind?!"

"I could say the same!"

That initial explosion was Jin's doing. If it weren't for his diversion, Wang Liang would have undoubtedly slain me earlier. He doesn't know that he saved my life and I can't tell him without causing Jin further distress. Even though I can't project my gratitude, thank you, Jin, from the bottom of my heart.

Jin glances over. His brows crease and then he lets out an apologetic sigh. "For what it's worth, at least you found Mei. Who knew she was capable of such reckless caprice!"

"She had her reason. Don't be too mad at Mei."

"Why should I be mad? I may not agree with her methods but whatever she chooses to do doesn't really concern me."

"How can you say that? She did it for you. To make *you* proud."

"I can hardly believe that." He mutters meaningful in a manner I can't discern. "Why did you come, Bao Lai?"

"I... didn't want her to get hurt. So much for that optimism. I hope she'll be all right."

"His Highness will see to that. Don't worry."

"When did he come in? I thought he would have gone to the initial detonation site."

"Moments before you arrived at Long Hu, I sent a runner to inform him about Mei. Shortly after I entered the palace, he was at my heels."

"I see. Jin, about Yan Lei. Who is she, exactly? I thought the traitor was caught."

"Zhang Tang's personal scout, from what I gathered. We merely caught her oblivious accomplice; the real traitor was Yan Lei. That would explain the recent change. Our watchers reported that Wang Liang's defenses were fortifying outside palace gates. More were patrolling in the areas we were hoping to set up our decoys. He Pi's been excessively worried lately. He thought your assassin friend had something to do with it. Apparently, the danger was a hair's breadth away. Mei really should have come to me if she was worried about him instead of running off like that."

"About... He Pi? Jin, she was worried about you. Anyway, why didn't Yan Lei expose the base instead of this runaround?"

"The Order's members are numerous and scattered. Only a handful uses the Bai He warehouse from time to time. It wouldn't do him any good to capture three and put three hundred on alert."

"Then the smart thing to do would have been to pretend falling for the Order's bait tomorrow night and then strike with his own ambush party. Increasing patrol merely let the Order know that he's aware."

Another quick glance flies over his shoulder. "I'm glad you're on our side, *Commander*."

"I don't need your sarcasm, Jin."

"I'm n—"

Jin pauses to brandish his steel sword. The path ahead is empty. Though I search all around, no one else is in sight. The agonizingly tense moment suddenly leads to another.

A silver crescent glimmers in the dimly lit corridor, followed by a loud collision into Jin's blade. The assaulter moves back a short distance and then readies his sword again.

"Shu Jin. So, it's you. You've grown, little brother. For a moment, I was fooled into believing our father had returned. I would have enjoyed sending that bastard back to hell."

The derisive smile plastered on his face is no less frightening than his skills. I couldn't perceive from which direction Wang Liang came. How Jin was able to block that lightning-quick attack was impressive.

"Su Jian. Brother. You really are alive." Jin mutters the incredulous thought aloud. His eyes are glazed over as though still uncertain of the phantom standing before us. Though he knew Su Jian was behind this conflict, love for family didn't permit him to tarnish memories of a dear brother. Conversely, Su Jian didn't hesitate to strike at his kin.

"Are you disappointed, Shu Jin?" Wang Liang poses inoffensively.

"Only for what you have become."

"I cannot help what I am. It's true what they say: the fruit doesn't fall far from the tree."

"That's just an excuse. Let go of the past, Su Jian. I am not our father and you are not Tung. We are not bound by our predecessors."

"Bearing in mind your past, you of all people shouldn't say that to me. I know how you suffered; losing your innocence before you could even ascertain the idea. That is the advantage of being a man, isn't it? A woman who bore that shame would have ended her own life."

Jin's hands are shaking from behind the forced composure while I'm trembling from rage. My sister never truly knew me and yet, sought for my safety before she passed. They're brothers, the last of their line, and Su Jian wants to destroy that worldly link. Just when Jin is finally able to move forward, this bastard is dredging up sordid memories for a momentary advantage.

"Hey! Shut up!" Unable to control myself, I dart from behind to stand beside Jin. "He's your brother. Since you didn't lift a finger back then to protect him, then you don't have a right to say anything about it now!"

Su Jian stares back as though he were looking at a ghost. I guess he never expected Enya to spare me, or in other words, disobey him. Instead of exposing his sadistic side, his gaze softens.

"I see. Since Jin is also your weakness, I take it Lord Han Bei wasn't your only lover."

Jin's eyes immediately dart to my face. It's not true. Still, my cheeks are flushed and my eyes are forced wide open from having Jin realize my emotional infidelity. I love Han Bei, there is no shame in that; I just didn't need Jin to hear it from Su Jian. What's more, this is the man who took my beloved from me. I can't let that offense go unpunished.

"Bastard! Don't you dare say his name!"

"Do you see, Shu Jin? This is the loyalty you can expect from women. She'll stab you in the back the moment you turn. Family, on the other hand, is forever. We were the unfortunate ones dealt bad hands. Together, we can change that. Together, we can bring peace to all five countries. No child will ever suffer as we had."

Wang Liang's innocent tone sends chills down my spine. He's finding every chink in Jin's armor to sway and corrode the latter's confidence and resolve. First, his past, and then his distrust in women; even Jin's desire for a reunited family. However, with Mei and He Pi in his heart, I know he'll overcome this. Looking

751

over, I give Jin a reassuring nod and he returns the same.

"Whatever your reasons are, this is wrong, Su Jian."

"Like everything else, peace has its price, Brother. The world doesn't change through poetries and sonnets. All paths lead to the sword. There is always a place for you by my side. All I ask in return is a token of loyalty. Bring the empress to me, Shu Jin."

"I won't let you touch one hair on Bao Lai's head." The younger man replies with great convictions.

The elder momentarily scowls. Then, chuckling smugly, Su Jian's long tongue runs over his lips while a lustful stare falls toward me. "Oh, but I've touched more than just Bao Lai's hair. It's easy to understand your infatuation. Those supple breasts are enough to drive any man to madness."

"Jin!" I furiously grab onto his arm when he lunges forward. "Jin, don't fall for his taunts! Find another route and take Cai Pai to safety. I'll deal with Su Jian!"

At my bold claims, Su Jian smiles mockingly, though for good reasons. I'm nowhere near his league and overestimating my abilities will likely seal my fate. Likewise, Jin is questioning my sanity.

"He won't let us advance and you can't kill him, Jin. He's your blood. It's not right. I have to avenge Han Bei and my fallen people, no matter what it takes. Mei is waiting for you. Please, just go."

A short exhale to steel myself and then the grip around my dagger tightens. The moment I start rushing forward, Jin flies past me. Instantly, loud clashing of steel against steel reverberates in the air. Their blades are flying furiously; my eyes can't keep up. Once again, I'm too useless to help. Despite training with the soldiers, I'm not much stronger than I was before. More so, despite my overconfident assertions, I'm not certain that I can take a life. Jin is going against his strong morals in family in order to protect me; the burden of which will never leave him. After all this time, I still can't do anything for Jin.

Chapter 53 – 4

Another loud explosion echoes. This time, the scent of smoke trickles down the corridor. Jin's diversion was on palace grounds. The others were supposed to be in secluded areas of the city. So far, I've noticed several blasts closer than the first, which means this is someone else's doing.

Afar, more screams erupt from both panic and surprise. A loud rumble echoes similar to that of a collapsing roof and then the scent of smoke intensifies. I can't believe Wang Liang is this crazed.

"Wang Liang!" I would rather distract Su Jian and not Jin, so I cry out the former's name instead. Su Jian pauses momentarily, sending over a scowl.

"You aim to raze the entire palace, don't you, with the White Cranes and your men inside?"

"You're not as stupid as I thought, Empress. Too bad the revelation came late. There's no escaping now!"

"What were you thinking, Su Jian! You can't be that far gone! I know somewhere inside, the old you must see how wrong this is!"

Jin's cries fall on deaf ears. Wang Liang grits his teeth from annoyance. His gaze slide from Jin toward me, and then he shrugs.

"The building is collapsing and you'd rather place faults, Shu Jin? Fine. Since you'll both die here, let me impart a secret I've been too kind to have divulged. You'll realize how wrong *you* are." Staring at me square in the eyes, Su Jian smirks derisively. "Remember what I said? The fruit doesn't fall far from the tree. Your mother also couldn't resist that face."

He glances over at Jin before turning back to me. I can't grasp his hint. Wang Liang frowns at my wide-eyed stare.

"You really don't know? Long before Emperor Jin took the throne, he had an extensive fling with the Eastern Empress. She expected eternity. He left her pregnant and alone. It's no wonder she married so quickly to spare her bastard child from shame and no wonder her husband left when he discovered the child wasn't his. You and He Pi are mirror images of each other, Empress. Doesn't that make you wonder who you are to Jin?"

My breath is caught in my throat. Likewise, I can feel Jin's uneasiness and wavering composure. My mother and Shu Jin's father had an affair and I look just like He Pi. That makes Shu Jin and I...

"No more lies, Su Jian!" Jin bellows from anger and disbelief. His shoulders are trembling as though on the verge of tears.

If I am Jin's half-sister... the thought is too devastating to consider. My hands clench from terror.

Impulsively, I reach for the treasures in my pocket to seek comfort. It's then I realize that I do have a past and that is something he can't take from me. My name is Bao Lai because my father was from Bei Ling. Master Tai Hung was my grandfather. I know who I am. That is the gift Han Bei gave to me.

"My father is Mian Shi Fen!" Resentment I didn't recognize I've been withholding lash at Wang Liang through a strident scream. "Your grandfather killed my father, harassed my mother, threatened my country, and took from me my life! Save your pitiful lies! If you wish to take his place, allow me to take my mother's. I will do no less to you than she would to Tung."

The grip around the dagger in my hand tautens. Jin quickly raises an arm to keep me from charging.

"Bao Lai, let me. He's my brother. My responsibility."

"By all accounts, I, too, am her brother and so are you, Shu Jin." Wang Liang continues to assert his sordid claims. "You can believe whatever you wish. The evidence is right before you. She is He Pi's image."

That is something I cannot deny. He Pi, Dong Xing, and I share the same face. Su Jian's story explains the reason Dong Xing's father wasn't mentioned in the archives and the motive for my mother's husband to have absconded. Everything he said is probable and at the same time, possibly coincidental. I rummage for the right response to calm Jin, only to realize he's found the answer within.

"I believe Bao Lai." Jin replies without any note of doubt.

"Because it's the easy answer? Just like your mother, sweep everything under a rug."

"You don't know my mother and you clearly don't know me, Su Jian. I couldn't care less what Bao Lai is to me; who she is to me won't change. You, Brother, have changed. I will lament for the man you once were."

Jin brandishes the blade. Soon after, rising acrid smoke floats heavily down the corridor. Each passing minute lowers our margin of escape. Without recourse, Jin rushes forward and then the clashing of blades resume.

We don't have much time to flee and certainly, less time for this scuttle. Wang Liang aims to kill everyone inside, so why did he stop the first detonation site from signaling the White Cranes' charge? He doesn't seem the suicidal sort but he is manipulative. I wonder what else he's planning.

Another loud blast is followed by even more flooding screams. What am I doing? Why am I standing around being useless? The White Cranes were forcing their way in to seize Cai Pai. The child emperor is the reason we've all come. While not one part of me wants to leave Jin, I know his expectations.

However, just when I think to make a mad dash past the melee, Su Jian suddenly changes position and charges toward me. While my weapon readies, Jin frantically cries out my name and runs to thwart his brother's dirty tactics. The latter abruptly stops short, swiftly turning on his heels to meet Jin, who can't slow his storming pace. In the next moment, a silver arch flickers, a loud clang, and then Jin's sword lands out of arm's reach halfway down the corridor. Su Jian unyieldingly follows with strike after strike. Jin manages to dodge but the adverse predicament finally gets the best of him. As a last resort to avoid a critical blow, he tumbles to the ground.

My body is trembling so violently, everything appears to be shaking. I'm scared, not of dying for Jin, but to take a life. Despite my previous proud words, I'm afraid to inherit the burden on my soul. After he disarmed Jin, Su Jian's back was right in front of me. I could have attempted to slay him. I was too much of a coward and for my frailty, Jin's demise is imminent.

The petrified look on Jin's pale face is directed toward me. He's worried for my fate once he falls. The heart-wrenching, apologetic stare sends an icy chill over my chest.

What is wrong with me? Jin wouldn't even hurt a fly. Yet, he is willing to stain his hands red for my sake and I can't even do this one small thing. I haven't avenged Han Bei and Su Jian is going to kill Jin. The same fear I faced moments ago is back. When will I stop being selfish? I can claim to love him but words are meaningless without actions. In contrast, Jin's previous harsh words couldn't overshadow the loving way he's continued caring for me since the day we've met. Maybe that's why I never fully believed in his indifference.

Jin loved me and I will always love him; no matter to whom his heart now belongs. They deserve to be happy. I will guarantee that felicity for him. I won't permit another man I love to fall! I have to kill Su Jian! More than obligations, I want to! He needs to pay for all he's done!

"Su Jian!"

The loud bellow escapes in a thunderous roar, overpowering the clamors all around. My entire body feels numb and yet somehow, it's flying forward. I've lost all control. With a heavy pulse thumping in my ears, Jin's voice reaches me in hollow, drowned out echoes. Su Jian's blade thrusts forward, something feels cold, and then red streams cover my hands when Han Bei's dagger is lodged in my opponent's chest. Su Jian falls back, clutches onto his open wound, and then staggers away for support while gasping for air.

Jin dashes to catch me, shouting indiscernible words still muffled to my ears. I can't make heads or tails of everything that happened. Until the touch of Jin's hands pull back awareness, I didn't realize Su Jian's blade in lodged in my belly.

Chapter 54: A Chance to be Free

It's been two weeks since my reckless gamble and as Enya repeatedly stated, I am one lucky girl. Perhaps the Huang Jia Feng Huang are protection stones after all.

As a result of our scuttle, Bei Ling's prime minister disappeared. News of his retreat caused the remaining guards who served Wang Liang to quickly surrender. One miraculous news soon sparked another; one that put me to happy tears. Han Bei is alive! The false rumors were spread to bait Northern forces from behind their fortress and spared Bei Ling's outskirt cities from annihilation. How Han Bei managed to discover Su Jian's merciless ruse is still a mystery to the Order.

Yan Lei's flight was intercepted and Cai Pai was formally placed under the White Cranes' protection. Though casualties from both sides were heavy, in the end, a new council was established with Zhang Tang in line to become Bei Ling's new prime minister. As sordid as his thoughts were, Wang Liang proved to be right. The world doesn't change through poetries and sonnets. All paths lead to the sword. However, a blade can do more than create chaos. It can ensure stability. That is my hope for the White Cranes' influence over Bei Ling.

While the alliance armies are making their ways north, He Pi and Enya have been working endlessly on reconstruction efforts. Enya was proposed to become Cai Pai's bodyguard; though, it's highly possibly with He

Pi's consistent flirting, she aims to follow him south. I tried warning her to no avail.

As for me, my days are filled with awkward silence when Jin and I are alone. He's taken it upon himself to become my sole caretaker, but besides from constantly staring at me from next to the bed, he's been rather quiet. Small talks between us are becoming more tedious with each passing day; the main topic always being the weather.

"It's warm today," Jin remarks cautiously the same comment he's used to greet me for the past week.

"Is it? Why don't you take a stroll with Mei and enjoy the weather? Tell me all about it when you come back?" I force a smile to urge him to relinquish my side. The lovers have been apart for too long. She came by to visit once, gave me an awkward stare, and then removed herself soon after from the room. I suppose she's discovered that Shu Jin and I were more than *friends*. I just hope that hasn't strained their relationship.

"I'll be here, whenever you need me." He replies.

"Why are you such a worrywart? I can't run off and do anything foolish in this state."

"I know. In sickness and in health, I naturally worry over you."

"Why?"

"Must you really ask?" He looks away, seemingly agitated.

"Jin, I'll be fine. Mei's a nice girl but even she can't be kept waiting."

"Why do you keep insisting on her? Scream and yell at me like a normal angry person. Don't pawn me off on someone else."

"What are you talking about? Why would I be angry?"

His jaw clenches. Jin's troubled gaze averts before turning back with his brows in a knot. "Are you complacent because I no longer mean anything to you? Was Su Jian right? Are you Lord Han Bei's lover?"

The accusing tone is one he's employed many times before. I have tried my best to be supportive when knowing how he feels about Mei is killing me inside. I injured Han Bei with my dishonesty in order to keep my love for Jin unsullied. Is insult to injury all I can expect in return? By now, I should know better than to be goaded into another senseless argument. Except, I can't help it.

"I am sorry to say I am not his lover. Even if I were, why should that concern you? According to Mei, you never had a girlfriend before her. I was only a certain *crazy* woman who wouldn't stop clinging to you in Nan Rong. That's why you've been agitated ever since I arrived, isn't it? Believe me, soon as I can walk again, you won't ever have to suffer me for another moment!"

Beneath a grimace, a thousand words are contending to escape from him at once. His lips are parted, though no sounds will project. I start to look away when a frustrated Jin reaches for my hand.

"I wasn't agitated because of you." He whispers. "I'm angry at me. Why aren't you for the way I left?"

"I'm not mad, Jin. Not anymore. It was my fault for being stubborn. Despite what we once were to each other, your current opinions are perfectly clear. Don't let compassionate force you to dote on me. Your future is waiting. A girl like her doesn't come around often."

"Haven't you grasped a thing I said? Mei and I are not together!"

"Y-You're not?"

Frantic footsteps suddenly stomp down the hallway. Jin isn't able to utter another sound before the door flies open and Han Bei rushes in; his red hair a tangled mess.

"Bao Lai!" He cries in that familiar melodious voice I was afraid to never hear again.

"Han Bei! Thank goodness! I was so worried!"

Despite the recent good news, the fear of never seeing him again kept gnawing at my chest. Now that he's here, a flood of relief spreads over me. I feel as though I can finally breathe. However, my happy greeting is met with his scowling stare. He's on the verge of lecturing me again.

"What were you thinking?!"

Disregarding Jin, Han Bei moves in between us. His cool lips brush against my forehead while strong arms pull me into an embrace. He inhales deeply as if taking me in and I embrace him as strongly as the strength in my arms permits.

"Mind yourself, Lord Han Bei! She's injured!"

Han Bei sighs regrettably. After planting a kiss on my cheek, he turns to the younger man.

"She's injured because of you. How could you let this happen?"

"Han Bei, I charged in blindly and Jin tried to save me. It wasn't his fault!"

"You're still defending him after the fact? If he were any sort of man, he'd have died to keep you safe!"

"I agree," Jin responds with the same seething resentment. "*My girlfriend* nearly died saving you from Enya. The scar is still on her back. What were you doing?"

"Jin, I was reckless. Han Bei—"

"I'm taking you home, Your Highness." Grimacing, Han Bei cuts off my defense. "You're safer with family."

"She isn't any safer in your care than in mine. From now on, I will protect her no matter the consequence. You have my word."

"For all your grand promises, you'll leave her to despair again. She's cried herself to sleep too many nights. I won't permit another senseless tear to stain those cheeks. For her own good, I'm taking her back to Ning."

"She's injured. She shouldn't be moved."

"The necessary preparations were made. We're leaving."

"That is not your choice."

"And neither is it yours!" Han Bei rebuffs Jin while leaning down beside the bed and sending a meaningful gaze into my eyes. "Bao Lai, I never stopped loving you. Even if you can't love me, return to Ning—to your family. He doesn't deserve you. You must know the outcome by now. He'll bait you with sweet words, guilt you into devotion he doesn't possess, and then flee. Nothing has changed!"

I can't contend. In truth, Han Bei voiced my hidden view. Jin is not making any effort to defend himself. His eyes are to the floor like those of a repenting sinner. I came to force an answer and now that he wants to explain, I'm not sure if I should stay. How can we both move forward when we can't express our feelings and air our grievances? He left me without an explanation. I don't want to return that favor.

Then again, Han Bei is right, nothing has changed. Sometimes love just isn't enough. With time, Jin and I will be happy and then he'll become miserable when I eventually say the wrong thing. I always do. Each time we repeat the cycle, more resentment is built. If ever I can free him and myself, now is the time.

Han Bei's pleading gaze. Jin's detached expression. I stare from one to the next and realize the right choice to be

Stay with Jin (Continue to page 767)

Leave with Han Bei (Continue to page 782)

Chapter 54 – 2

Jin has more to say. I won't leave until I've given him that chance. After all, there are thoughts I, too, wish to express.

"I'm not in any condition for the long trip. Why don't you return to Ning first and I'll join shortly?"

"I won't leave you."

"Han Bei, I was irresponsible. Yuan doesn't know where I am and Ning must still be in uproar over the rumors of your death. Someone should relieve the people's anxiety and watch over Yuan until things settle. I'm sorry for placing the burden on your shoulders. Please, accomplish this for me."

The Grand General exhales sharply. After scanning my face, his sharpened eyes roll to Shu Jin. The displeasure deepens. For a time, Han Bei fights with himself and then finally, bows in concession.

"I see. Her Highness has made her choice. There is naught your servant would deny you."

Grudgingly pulling back composure, Han Bei stands up and with one final cordial bow, parts from the room. I watch him leave. Both pain and relief surge inside; his words resonating in me. I made my choice. I always had a choice and this time, I chose to stay.

Still, what is the point? Enough time has been wasted through concealing wounded hearts behind false smiles. If I were to stay for the next ten years just to keep up the act, we might as well part now. No matter my choice, I always have another. I choose to confront Jin.

"You're a real bastard, you know that?"

Jin's taken aback by the sudden attack. Soon after, he smiles. "It's about time you're angry."

"I'm furious! First, you accused me of lying. Then, throughout your constant indifference, played the possessive boyfriend. To top it all off, you admitted to using me. You couldn't leave one lousy note? After the way you *loved* me during our night together, I didn't know what to think! Had I known our entire relationship was a joke to you, I would never have denied Han Bei. And yes, I love him, too! I suppose that makes me the same as every woman besides Mei you've ever met in your life! Worst of all, the unrelenting denial! Mei isn't the delusional sort. You told her that you never had a girlfriend. She fell head over heels for you. Now that I'm here, you stand there and say you're not in any relationship with Mei! What is the truth, Jin? What are you after? How many more women must worship you before you're satisfied?!"

He's been standing against the wall staring intently; taking in every word without showing the slightest bit of emotion. I intended to stay and permit Jin the chance to air his thoughts; instead, I was the one to gripe. Well,

I'm not in the least embarrassed. He wanted my anger and I gave without restraint.

Releasing a deep exhale, I beckon for his grievances. Jin's response is to move toward the bed and lean over me. Before I could react, his lips cover my own. His hands reach for my face. Whatever it is he wishes to convey loses all meaning. I can't focus on anything except the ardent, rising passion in his kiss which seeks to take my everything. My anger, my resentment, the strength in my body, and even my will. Recollections from our previous unrepressed intimacy send fires to both our faces. Though it's felt a lifetime ago, we are again on the precipice of falling prey to desire. This isn't right.

"Jin, don't!"

I push against his chest. In turn, his lips travel toward my neck and then it becomes difficult to keep my breathing steady.

"Haven't you heard a word I said?!"

"Yes, every word."

"Then what are you doing?!"

"Explaining myself because *you* haven't heard a word I've said. When have I appeared to love Mei? What exactly do you think is between us?"

"What else? Your affections for Mei, your relationship and soon-to-be engagement, how there was a certain crazy woman who wouldn't stop clinging to you in Nan Rong. This doting is your way of compensating for feeling guilty over our night together, isn't it? You're wasting your time. I'm not happy that you finally learned to love another but I am happy for you."

He lets out a frustrated growl before our lips connect again. The pain from my injury, the intoxication from the medicine, coupled with the inability to deny rising excitement inside permit him to continue. From a simple sweet kiss, he grows more audacious, running his hands gently over parts of me which force sharp gasps to escape, much to his delight. The shock sends back my senses. I turn to escape from his burning lips.

"Jin! Have you gone insane? This is inappropriate!"

"How can you still not understand? I only love one woman."

"I know that! Mei expressed your mutual love!"

"You mean Shu Jin loves her."

"Yes... *you* love her."

"No. Shu Jin, His Highness, does."

"I don't understand."

"He used my name to conceal his identity and directed Zhang Tang to send anyone who mentions that name to his attention. That was the reason His

Highness instructed me to send a letter and sign my name before treading north. I assume you were led to the White Cranes' base without question from having mentioned me. The fact that you are He Pi's image naturally helped."

"Which name were you using?"

"Bao," he answers shyly. "I thought you could deduce that much from Hei's comments."

"Oh!" Maybe I could have but I was too blinded by jealousy to have noticed anything else. "I thought Hei was referring to me. He meant I was, 'Ugly,' and you're, 'Bao.' That makes sense. So, Mei loves He Pi and the crazy woman must be Mu Dan. And that means you—"

My heart jumps inside my chest. Happiness flooding through me is soon after followed by learnt fear. I'm still expecting the impossible and he'll still be miserable.

"Jin, I've fallen for Han Bei. I couldn't keep my promise."

"Are you choosing him over me?"

"No. I love you more than anything but I am not the devoted woman you need."

"That's ridiculous. I never should have left without apologizing for all the horrible things I said. What else could you have thought? The truth is I started letters I couldn't finish. The things I sought to say had to be conveyed in person but I knew had I waited, you would have followed me to Bei Ling. I couldn't risk putting you in danger. I thought the sooner the conflict ended, the sooner I could return to explain myself."

"You never intended to quit our relationship? Jin, I'm-I'm so sorry!"

"Sorry for what? You didn't do anything wrong. It doesn't matter what my rationalizations were. The fact is I still ran away. I broke my promise to protect you and I know how much pain I've caused. I'm sorry."

"How was it your fault? I assumed the worst in you!"

"I gave you every reason to. I'm not proud for leaving but I'm glad I did. It's true that Mei was never in my attention."

However confident he was seconds ago, his demeanor stiffens to uncertainty and anxiety. Jin looks away, embarrassed; more so, ashamed.

"You don't have to tell me."

"No, I want to." He turns back to fully convey his confession. "There were others who sought my company. I was tempted. The pain of desire was too much. I'd considered... I almost... but I didn't. I couldn't bring myself to hurt you, even though you'd never know my betrayal. I learned that I'm not my father. You've told me that before but I had to see it for myself. Bao Lai, I love you."

"You wouldn't say that if you knew the truth. In our time apart, I learned that... I'm not a good person. I've hurt Han Bei. Other women might have approached you but I... flaunted in front of the Grand General because I was—am—attracted to him. I love him and I love you. He's willing to love me despite all my faults. I wonder... maybe a part of me came to Sai Mi for you to say that things are over between us, so I wouldn't feel guilty. Even now, I'm still selfish."

"You're not. You're human and humans make mistakes and falter to temptation. Even in the face of temptation, you chose to remain loyal to a man who couldn't show you one fragment of loyalty. I couldn't blame you had you chosen to leave with Han Bei. What matters is that we're here together. When I thought you'd died, I was ready to follow. I can't perceive any joy in living without you. In other words, I can't live without you, Bao Lai. I love you."

"I love you, too, but I have been by your side for many weeks. Why the sudden confession? Are you jealous of Han Bei or have you learned San An's folly? Don't fall for me because I defended you. If it hadn't been for you, Su Jian would have slain me."

"That's not why." Running a heavy hand over his face, he sighs sharply. "I thought you were upset. The way you refused to look at me. The way you kept distancing yourself and pushing the idea of Mei; I was too much of a coward. I should have just said what was on my mind. You were right about one thing. I am possessive." Pausing, his fingers lightly tap against my cheek in the familiar fashion. A gentle smile curls over his face. "This body is mine. Neither Han Bei nor anyone else will have the pleasure of provoking that lustful expression on your face but me."

Another unrestrained, passionate kiss lands on my mouth. His fingertips skillfully crawl beneath the collar of my shirt toward my heaving chest. I love him so much, this feels like a dream. And maybe for that reason, I can't accept his sweet words to be real.

"Jin, stop! Every time in the past when you've overcompensated with desire, usually led to blaming me for something before you run away. I can't accept waking every morning and wondering if today you'll love or hate me; if you'll leave or stay."

"What else could I possibly say to make you understand that I've changed?"

"Nothing. Words only provide momentary comfort. I will always love you but this is the last straw, Jin. If you leave again, I won't prolong either of our suffering."

"I understand. I promise. No more running away. That goes for you, too. You may grow sick of me, but I won't let you go. You're mine. Now and forever."

He really is possessive. The longing words make me so delighted, happiness is inadvertently voiced through a burst of laughter. He takes my reaction into offense, planting countless more kisses to silence my insolence.

The warmth of his body, the familiar scent, the loving nature; all of him is finally mine. My arms wrap around the man I dearly love—my first and last lover—and I inhale his nostalgic scent forever into memory.

He stays by my side as we recount our time apart. More than joy, Jin shares with me his sorrows; the parts of him buried these many years under shame and silent torment. Once he's able to fully release the burdened pain, a truer version of him emerged.

We are happy—happier than we could ever imagine. For once, we are at ease in each other's company. I don't feel the need to hide my imperfections while Jin makes the effort to show more of his. Each moment feels as comfortable as though we've been together all our lives.

For the months that pass during my recovery, he remains my adoring boyfriend who tends to my every need. I was convinced we could move forward into a more serious relationship. At least, that was my hope.

Chapter 54 – 3

I was having the nicest dream until a barrage of tiny fingers rain down upon my face. My eyes fly wide open to Hei's bushy brows and deep frown, following which, a cheeky grin lights up his chubby cheeks.

"Wake up, Ugly!"

"What is your problem, kid?!"

I swat away his hands. Hei runs to open the window on the other side of the bed. It's chilly out.

"What's my problem? What kind of woman sleeps until noon and drools all over the pillow? Your hair looks like a fuzzy rat. No wonder you don't have a husband."

"Wh—Come over here and say that to my face!"

Accepting my challenge, Hei jumps onto the bed. His swift movements are those of a chubby but nimble housecat.

"You're ugly!" Hei screeches before holding onto his belly and falls over laughing.

Obnoxious brat! I don't know why I bother fighting with a kid. I can't make him eat his words. I have to swallow my pride.

"Fine! I'm ugly. Why are you here? Where's Shu Jin—I mean Bao?"

"He left this morning. Your ugly face must have scared him away."

"H-He did? Did he say why?"

"Nope! Just told me to bring your lunch."

"Really...? Since when are you obedient, Hei?"

"I am always a good boy!" His small fists bump up and down. Hei squirms about in the most theatrical manner.

"Liar."

"You're a liar!"

"I bet Bao gave you candy, didn't he?"

His face freezes from shock and then I realize it *is* possible for me to win against an eight-year-old!

"I'm telling your father! You've been taking bribes and ruining your dinner. What will the illustrious leader of the White Cranes think when his only son can be bought with candy?"

"H-Hey! D-Don't tell him! He'll be mad!"

"Why shouldn't I? You've been mean to me since we met. Bad little boys should be punished."

"Okay, okay! I'm sorry! You're not ugly!" His forehead lands on the bed, bowing in desperation.

The reaction is too adorable. He's afraid of Zhang Tang the way I used to be afraid of Master Tai Hung. That is to say, the fear is stemmed from respect—anxious to remain in our guardians' good opinion—and not truly intimidation. The longer I stare at Hei, the more I grasp that I used to be ten times the brat that he is. Hei is a good boy but I may never have another chance to win over an eight-year-old. Grinning mischievously, I gently pat his head.

"I'm pretty right? I won't tattle if you'll say, '*Miss Bao Lai, you're so pretty and smart and strong! When I grow up, I want to be just like you!*'"

"This is the honor of the East's leadership, blackmailing a mere child?"

"Ahh!"

His hard voice, which carries the same chiding tone as Master Tai Hung's, sends my nerves reeling. For a moment, I thought the Master was standing behind me. A hand flies over my mouth just as I let out a small scream and then I move next to Hei and bow low.

"I'm sorry! I'm sorry!"

Oh, wait. No, I'm not sorry. If Han Bei saw Ning's empress bowing to the prime minister of Bei Ling, he'd have a fit. Taking a deep breath, I muster my composure and sit up in the most dignified manner I could pretend. However, it is too late. My tarnished image is irreparable. Hei pinches my cheek tersely before running off the bed and out the door. That little so and so! If only he were twenty years older, I'd seek vengeance!

However irritating Hei was, without him, the room grows tense. I look around nervously, unsure of the right words to say to this ever-somber man, and so I say the obvious. "Hello?"

"Have your wounds healed?"

"Oh! Yes, they have."

"Then what's keeping you? Do you require assistance for your departure?"

He's kicking me out of Bei Ling? While I don't wish to stay here longer than I must, that's a little rude. Still, the only reason I haven't left is because of Jin.

"Minister Zhang, did J—Bao leave?"

"Prince Shu Jin and His Highness, He Pi, have both returned to Nan Rong." Zhang Tang replies coldly to emphasize the truth, all the while, taking offense to the lies the brothers told.

"Did Jin say why he left or when he would return?"

"No. The Prince's final request was for the Order to watch over you. Since Your Highness is well, our debt is paid."

"I'm sorry for being nosy, but why do you sound resentful? Jin and He Pi precipitated Wang Liang's downfall and placed the Order into Bei Ling's council."

"Is Your Highness that naïve? Our Order was formed to keep ourselves and those innocent from exploitation. In the end, the White Cranes benefited, but we were tools to carry out a mean. I'm not certain whether Yan Lei or I was the fool here. We both fell prey to false pleasantries. My daughter's suffering is proof of that. Your Highness doesn't appear to be callous. Allow me to leave you with this piece of advice: you best be careful whom you invite into Ning. He Pi and Wang Liang are two sides of the same coin."

With his brows in a knot, Zhang Tang parts from the room. I couldn't gather my thoughts fast enough to ask about Mei's *suffering* and false pleasantries but then, the only reason she would suffer is over losing He Pi.

Jin mentioned His Highness's lechery is an act to avoid relationships. Did He Pi use Mei to find entry into the Order? What about Jin? Was he aware? Did he permit He Pi to break a young woman's heart? Where is he? Why did Jin leave? Are things over between us? Is he following He Pi's example?

My aching head falls into trembling hands. A hundred more horrid thoughts run rampant which can neither be extinguished nor subdued. In the end, it doesn't matter why or how. I don't have a reason to stay in Bei Ling and my expectations were fully relayed to Shu Jin. No more pointless rationalizations. This was the last straw.

Continue to page 786

Chapter 54 – 4

By now, there have been enough chances for Jin to express his sentiments and derisions. He's chosen silence. Likewise, I couldn't bring myself to chastise him. Jin is indecisive but he isn't callous. I thought the worst of him to relieve my own shortcomings when, if there were faults, we shared them equally. It's time I do the right thing for us both.

"Han Bei, take me back to Ning."

Smiling gently, the Grand General reaches to support me. Jin brusquely pushes away his arms and then kneels beside the bed. The warm hand that suddenly envelops mine is also shaking.

"Bao Lai, you promised to stay with me no matter how foolish I may become."

"You're using guilt to coerce Her Highness? A real man fights for and protects what he holds dear. Why guilt her into devotion you won't return, only to run away when she imprudently gives in?"

"Han Bei, I appreciate your defense but I am far from faultless. You've experienced my cruelty as well. Since you're both here, please accept my apologies."

"There are ways for Your Highness to experience repentance. A few punishments come to mind." Han Bei chuckles teasingly.

Conversely, Jin is silent. A simple apology won't suffice.

"Jin, I'm sorry for the stupid things I've said and done. I kept pushing myself into your attention every time you sought to be free from me, including recently. I was being selfish."

"I love you."

Jin bears a serious stare into my eyes; conveying a notion of ardent worship that I've only ever experienced from San An. The wonderful words I've been aching to hear from the man I hold dear set my heart aflame. I feel dazed, ecstatic, and lost in a fantastic dream from which I never want to wake.

From a distance away, Han Bei's harsh scoff brings back my senses. As wonderful as Jin's confession may be, I've heard those words before. Now that they are indisputably genuine, I'm afraid of the receipt. The painful outcome of his offer is clear to me. For once in my life, I must find resolve.

Swallowing a lump in my throat, I stare back with equal fervor. "Jin, I love you, too. I just can't accept waking every morning and wondering if today you'll love or hate me; if you'll leave or stay. Every time we walk down this path together, we're both unhappy. I'm not placing faults. I'm just not the understanding woman you need. I can't make you happy."

"Bao Lai, I am a changed man! You are the only one who *can* make me happy! I'll do anything to return that happiness! Please, don't leave!"

The panic in his voice, the overbearing anxiety, and tattered composure coupled with the burning grip of his hand force me to tears. I don't ever want to be apart from him but considering all that has led us to this point, maybe we should never have been together.

Mustering the last of my courage, my hand pulls away from his tight grasp. "And I've changed also. I won't overlook your best interest to sate my own selfishness. I'm sorry, Jin, for everything. I hope you'll forgive me someday. Farewell."

Jin chews on his lips furiously while searching for the right reply. Once he does, as Han Bei mentioned, I'll imprudently give in. This is the end for us. My heart is bursting at the seams. I don't want my tears to encourage him, so I turn away. Everything in me desperately wants to hold Jin in my arms, now and forever. As a final resort, I push off the bed and then walk toward Han Bei; falling into his arms when the pain of my injury becomes unbearable.

"Please take me back to Ning, Han Bei."

His gentle fingers brush away my tears. Han Bei scoops me up and then starts out the door. I can sense Jin's misery and loneliness pouring forth from behind but I can't look back. Right or wrong, I've made the choice for us both. Each step Han Bei takes sends a lightning bolt to scorch all my nerves. Closing my eyes, I pray for Jin's future to be bright and for all the shadows I've casted over his life through my egotism to disappear.

__Continue to page 798__

Chapter 55: My First and Last

It's become chilly recently; chillier than any autumn I've ever experienced in this Southland known for warm weather and abundant flora. Leaves are scattered everywhere on the massive temple grounds while strong winds render the apprentices' efforts at sweeping moot.

I sent Han Bei notice and then came back to the temple where I was unexpectedly welcomed with open arms, even by the seniors who once refused to acknowledge I was alive. Several men who were once like brothers to me were afraid to look me in the eyes. It's disappointing to see holy men fallible to the idea of rank and wealth. Ning's empress or otherwise, I'm still Master Tai Hung's "*bastard child.*"

Master Tai Hung, my grandfather, is resting quietly under his favorite magnolia tree. After he died, I couldn't accept being left behind. I shied from going to his grave, and that was after I refused to attend the funeral. In the past month, I was at least able to clear the weeds from his gravesite and burned incense daily for my master. Most days, I sit for hours to recount our time apart. It might just be my imagination but I feel that he's happy whenever I run my mouth about nothing, the way I used to when he was alive. One day, I will find Mian Shi Fen's grave and reunite father and son.

"And, Grandfather, that boy who used to come by the temple... I still can't remember his name. Well, he and I were the ones who drank your secret wine on New Year. We let Master Po Li take the blame because he was sneaking meat into the temple, you see. So, we didn't feel bad one bit. We paid for it, though, by falling down the stairs in front of the Lotus Pavilion. Actually, he was drunk and fell against me, so we tumbled down the stairs. What a lightweight!"

The face Grandfather made upon discovering his special wine missing was one I'll never forget. I can't help but laugh, toppling back onto the grass while a happy tear rolls down my face.

"I knew you were a naughty child."

A familiar voice remarks from the other side of the thick magnolia tree trunk. My heart, hammering furiously, flies to my throat. I start to my knees and then crawl behind the tree.

"J-Jin! Wh-wha-how-when?!"

"Go on, finish your story. I thought I was your first love but apparently, this boy you keep mentioning won your heart long before me."

"I didn't love him! How long have you been eavesdropping?!"

"I did no such thing. I've been here since morning. You suddenly appeared and started ranting about *this boy* to your master. You didn't mention me even once."

"That's because I ranted about you daily for the first month. What are you doing here?"

"Is that how you greet all your boyfriends?"

I stare back, stunned silent by the casual assertion.

Jin leans against the tree trunk and then cocks his head to one side. "Well, I'm waiting. Where's my apology?"

"Apology for what?"

"What else? I lost a few years of my life when I returned to Bei Ling and found that my girlfriend ran away. I had to chase her all the way to Ning, made an ass of myself by contending with Lord Han Bei because I thought he kept her from me, and then spent a week wandering about this area searching for the elusive Tian Mao Yi temple, only to learn that she loved another man long before confessing to me. So, how will she ever make it up to me?"

"Are you kidding? You're the one who left without saying anything!"

"Your wounds weren't fully healed. I thought you should rest another week in Bei Ling. Besides, you were asleep. That's why I left the note."

"Note? What note?"

"The one that was on the side table which I skillfully doodled your drooling face on. How could you have missed that?"

"There was nothing on the side table... except... my lunch. Hei must have set the tray on the note. S-So that means... Jin, I'm so sorry!"

"I don't believe you. Say it again."

He smiles teasingly while I burst into tears. Jin draws me into his arms, squeezing as tightly as his strength would permit. I'm crushed under the force but also unimaginably happy. He kept his promise and came after me when I doubted him again and again. Apologies fall one after the other until finally silenced by his kiss. The deep, thrilling, and excruciatingly long kiss takes my breath away. When our lips part, I collapse onto his chest. Jin continues gripping tightly as though to validate my existence.

Once our nerves calm, his warm breath brushes against my ear through a seductive whisper. "You're always causing me so much trouble. I deserve recompense from the naughty empress. Nothing would be naughtier than making love on temple grounds."

"Are you nuts?!"

My scorched-red face flies off his chest. He draws us back together, chuckling impishly.

"You're still as gullible as ever, Bao Lai. Well, I hope you learned your lesson. It doesn't matter where you run, I will find you. You're mine forever."

"I'm sorry I doubted you. Why did you leave?"

"His Highness ran into trouble in the capital. He sent for me when he should have relied on San An as I'd instructed prior to his departure from Bei Ling. I gave him a talking to."

"*You* lectured He Pi?"

"That I did. I also told him, '*It's time you learn to take care of yourself. We're so codependent that Bao Lai thinks I'm in love with you.*' He was a bit more than offended by that."

"Well, if you weren't in love with him, you would never have fallen for me, right?"

I grin at his disgusted glare. In retaliation, his hands squarely land on my chest.

"Unless he has these, I'm not remotely interested."

"H-Hey! This is a holy place!"

I slap away the inappropriate touch. My cheeks burn furiously from the recollection of our night together. There wasn't an inch of me that his busy hands spared. Their touches now evoke all sorts of unsettling desires inside. As though having read my very thought, Jin looks away to hide his blushing. How innocent he seems now compared to the dominant, lustful creature who yielded to nothing but his own desirous whims. I love every side of him.

My head presses against his chest to take in the nostalgic scent. After a time, Jin begins shuffling nervously.

"Bao Lai, if I hadn't come... what would you have done?"

"Your real question is if I would choose Han Bei, right? Truth be told, I wasn't sure where I would go after leaving Tian Mao Yi. I thought about returning to the capital so I could yell at you again. Who knows? Had you waited long enough, I might have gone to you."

"I'm glad I came. How else would I have known about your excursions with this other mischievous boy?"

"You're jealous? I don't even remember his name! Speaking of mischievous boys, are He Pi and Mei still together?"

Jin heaves a sharp sigh and then coyly shakes his head. "No. His Highness is heartbroken but there will be others."

"*His* heart is broken? Zhang Tang implied *her* heart was broken. Mei loves him. I know that for certain."

"I'm sure she didn't wish it. Zhang Tang was not pleased with He Pi's method to infiltrate the Order. It would be difficult to have a future with a man her father doesn't approve."

"Who ended their bond?"

"I don't know. They're adults and they can make their own decisions. Things may yet change."

"Oh. You're right. Sorry for being nosy."

"Not at all. I'm glad you worry over my family. Maybe someday soon when he's forgotten the unpleasant scene I made at Ning's palace, you can properly introduce me to your nephew."

"Did you really make a scene?"

"Yes, a complete ass of myself. Until Han Bei showed me your letter, I was running through every room in the palace shouting out your name."

"I can't imagine that." Though as I try to suppress it, a pleased giggle blurts out. "By the way, how is Han Bei? I haven't had the chance to apologize for the foolish things I've done. He's a good man who didn't deserve the wounds he's been dealt, especially by me. I wish all the happiness in the world for Han Bei. I just don't know how to make things up to him."

"I'm not sure if you have anything to be sorry for. Han Bei was arrogant, sarcastic, and yet, also surprisingly cordial. He kindly gave me directions to Tian Mao Yi and conferred your protection to me. He's conceded for the sake of your happiness. Aside from my bias, I have to agree, he is a good man. A better man than me on some level. I wonder if maybe, you should have chosen him instead."

"If you keep leaving without waking me first, I just might!"

I pinch both his cheeks to turn that hard frown upside down. Puffing out his cheeks to loosen my fingers, Jin draws my hands gently into his own while sending a serious gaze into my eyes. "Since I can't trust you to trust me, from now on, His Highness will have to wait. You're my first and only priority. What I mean to say is... Bao Lai, will you marry me?"

The question came so unexpected that I couldn't have heard that correctly. Shock renders me silent until the pause becomes awkward. I look up to find a hopeful smile beam down. I love him so much, my heart is aching from overwhelming elation. Nothing would make me happier than to have our eternities intertwined. I want to stay with him, now and forever.

My lips part to give a response, except the answer isn't one he expected.

"I can't."

Jin winces as though he'd just been struck. Words are stuck in his throat. His mouth is moving but nothing comes out.

"Jin—"

"You can't or you won't? Is this because of Han Bei? Have you finally realized you love him more? Or, don't you trust me? Bao Lai, I am a changed man! I won't leave again, I swear it! What must I d—"

His frantic rant is subdued under my kiss. The quickened pace of his heart and overwhelming anxiety; I would be lying to say that I didn't find it adorable.

"I love you more than anything, Jin."

"But?"

"But we're not ready for marriage; at least, I'm not. I doubted you and that only proves maybe we—I—advanced this relationship too quickly. I wanted forever when I should have enjoyed the present. I should have given you the benefit of the doubt."

"You didn't see the letter. After every stupid thing I've done, who would have thought differently? Bao Lai, I love you! Don't end what we have over a genuine mistake!"

"Jin, calm down! I won't ever let you go either. I'm just not ready to be your wife. We haven't spent enough time together. Could I... stay your girlfriend for a while longer?"

His widened eyes are fixated and afraid. He's holding his breath. Similarly, my heart is on the verge of bursting if he won't answer soon. Following the tense pause, he finally exhales a sigh of relief. Then, threading long fingers into my hair, Jin brings our foreheads together and plants a light kiss.

"You're only denying me because I expect ten children. As punishment, when we do marry, I demand twenty."

"That's fine, so long as you bear eighteen of them."

A sweet laughter bursts into the air. Jin falls onto the grass, taking me with him. Under the shade of the magnolia tree, we lie in each other's arms, mesmerized by the breathtaking view of the clear blue sky. Whatever chill came over me has been shed from my soul, to be replaced by indescribable peace. Cuddling closer to the person I love most in the world, I take in his warmth and return them fully until our hearts beat as one.

"Jin, once we marry, you'll become Ning's emperor. Are you prepared for that title?"

"No, but I won't let fear keep me. I will go wherever you go. Maybe... I'll steal you away to Xiong in your sleep, my bride. At my mother's old house, we'll bring joy and love to make it our home. Would that please you?"

"More than anything. That is, until a grand party from Ning is sent to track us. We'll have to spend the rest of our days running from one province to another. Would that please you?"

"Yes. It's been my dream to travel across all five countries. Knowing we'll have a chance to sightsee together makes me very happy."

Chuckling faintly, Jin leans over and kisses my frown. His fingers thread through my hair, drawing our faces closer for a deeper kiss to convey his affections. I close my eyes to savor this token of love which grows more wondrous to me each time our lips meet.

Though there is much about our future to consider, words feel meaningless in this moment. All that matters is that we are together and will remain inseparable. From now until my last day and beyond, my heart will beat solely for Jin, my first and last love.

The End.

Chapter 56: One Lucky Girl

Lately, things have been excessively quiet. Yuan left for Mount Guo again, determined to fully absorb the wonderful sceneries which he was cheated on his previous trip. Hua Ye comes by from time to time, though conversations between us are usually stale. She's offended by my lack of consideration for her cousin and I don't blame her. After our return, Han Bei realized that leaving Bei Ling didn't mean that I'd chosen him. He's resumed distance between us. In truth, I love him just as much as I love Jin, and for that reason, I don't find it fair to accept his proposal. How can I give Han Bei all of me when half of me belong to Jin?

Surprisingly, the one person who's kept by my side is Captain Xian. We don't actually converse. Some days after regiment training, I sit in the twilight to watch the skies. Those days, my companions are usually long casted shadows from surrounding high walls and the Captain. Once, his hand reached over but stopped in time before petting me. It wasn't until weeks later that I discovered his cat, Tui Tui, passed away.

"Ahem, Captain Xian."

We're enjoying the night sky again. Until he's finished grieving for Tui Tui, I intend to spare as many days sitting with him as I am allowed. The only difference today is that his hand actually landed on my head. Thus, I feel the need to run my mouth.

Xian looks over, initially surprised that his cat could talk, and then annoyed.

Drawing back his hand, Xian's scowl carries daggers. "What is it, *Your Highness?*"

"Don't address me as, 'Your Highness,' if you will be sarcastic about it. Bao Lai is just fine."

"That would be disrespectful, wouldn't it, *Your Majesty?*"

"Not at all. Captain, I... I'm sorry about your cat."

"You've never met her. Why are you sorry?"

"I'm sorry for... you."

"So you pity me?"

"N-No! Well, yes and no. That is, I'm sorry you're sad over your cat."

"It was a cat. Cats die. Unless you killed my cat, stop apologizing."

"It's just... wouldn't you rather spend this time with Hua Ye instead of Tui Tui's replacement?"

"Tui Tui's replacement? That's some ego!"

"I was just trying to be nice!"

"I don't need your niceness. If you had half a brain, you'd realize that I've been acting as your bodyguard until you're safe inside the palace. The reason I've been ignoring my lovely wife is because your head's been in the clouds."

"I'm sorry! I didn't know! Why are you my bodyguard? I'm not in any danger."

"Of course not. I'm your bodyguard."

That kind of roundabout logic irks me to no end. I start up when he suddenly grabs at my sleeve.

"Sit. The stars are not out yet."

"Shouldn't you go home to your wife?"

"She's out tonight with Lord Han Bei. Thanks to your stubbornness, Hua Ye's determined to find him a suitable lover. They're at Madam Ai's."

I've not yet lived in Ning for a full year and even I know Madame Ai as the infamous matchmaker from Si Li District. She's never failed to find a match for any of her customers. Whether any of those marriages turn to domestic felicity is highly debatable.

"I-Is Han Bei looking for a wife?"

After having rejected his honest proposal multiple times, I don't have the right to be jealous. I say that but I can hardly breathe. My chest hurts and everything suddenly feels cold.

"You really are something, you know that!"

Chapter 56: One Lucky Girl

Xian smacks my back with his heavy gauntlet as if to knock back my senses. For whatever reason, it helped.

"You don't want Lord Han Bei. Let him go."

"It's not that I don't—no, you're right. I'm sorry. I'm happy for him."

"I said let him go, not blatantly lie. I don't understand why you're so upset. Your lover's been waiting for you all day."

"My what? Who?"

"J-Jan, Jen, Jun?"

"Jin?!"

"Whatever his name is. I sent him to wait in the azalea garden since this afternoon. He really is your soul mate, dense and stubborn. Let's hope the mosquitoes don't eat him alive."

"He's been here all day? Captain Xian! Why would you do that to Jin?! That's incredibly cruel!"

"Are you going to stand here and lecture me or save your precious Jun from the mosquitoes?"

What happened to watching over me until I go inside? He's such a lying jerk! In response to my trembling fists, Xian shrugs and then starts away. I would chase after and give him a piece of my mind if Jin weren't waiting. As fast as my feet can fly, I rush out of the barracks toward the gardens.

Chapter 56 – 2

"Jin! Jin, where are you? Jin, if you can hear me, say something!"

"The entire palace can hear you."

Smiling teasingly, Jin's head pokes out from under the gazebo. There's not one trace left of his former anxiety. It's as though a completely different Jin is standing before me. A wave of relief rushes over. I nearly collapse from joy.

"Jin, why are you still outside? I can't believe Captain Xian's rudeness! I'm so sorry!"

"What do you mean? I've just arrived. Who is Captain Xian?"

"You've... just arrived?"

"Yes. Unpredicted rain delayed our envoy at Da Lu and then one of the carriages was stuck in the mud. Major Niu directed me here only moments ago. If anything, I apologize for being late."

Jin gives an awkward stare and in turn, I feel rage burning in my chest. Darn that Captain Xian! Why do I keep falling for it!

"W-Well, come inside. Had I known you were due, I would have prepared a welcome party."

"Precisely the reason I asked Lord Han Bei to keep you from the news."

"Han Bei knew? Why didn't he come to greet you? Oh right, he's at Madame Ai's."

The reminder leaves a bitter taste in my mouth. Misery takes me. The air between us grows unnervingly quiet until Jin's forced cough brings back my senses. I look up to find him troubled.

"Sorry. Spaced out again, didn't I? I didn't mean anything by it. I am glad you came, Jin." I say that honestly. After the way I left things, I was afraid he wouldn't move forward from dejection. Seeing him here now, smiling, brings me joy. It may be optimistic on my part but I want us to remain friends. "Shall we go inside for dinner or would you rather eat out at the night markets?"

"Actually, this can't wait."

Unlike prior when he'd shuffle in place before bringing forth an uncomfortable subject, determined eyes and a composed stare are directed at my face. I, on the other hand, begin feeling anxious.

Taking a step forward, his warm hands seize mine in their firm grasps. "You left Bei Ling under false presumptions before I had the chance to explain. Maybe it's too late but I still owe you the truth. Mei and I are not together. We never were. As you know, the Order resents those in power except for the few who have proven themselves. His Highness used my name to protect his identity. I went by the name, 'Bao.'"

"Oh! I thought Hei was referring to *me*. He meant I'm, 'Ugly,' and you're, 'Bao.' That makes sense. So, Mei loves He Pi and the crazy woman he mentioned is Mu Dan. And that means you—"

My heart jumps inside my chest. Unbridled happiness sets my cheeks on fire, same as his burning touch. Smiling gently, his fingers tap playfully against my right cheek.

"You still blush so easily," Jin chuckles. "I never should have left Nan Rong without apologizing for all the horrible things I said. The truth is I started letters I couldn't finish. The things I sought to say had to be conveyed in person. I knew had I waited, you would have followed me to Bei Ling. I couldn't risk putting you in danger. I thought the sooner the conflict ended, the sooner I could return to explain myself."

"You left... to protect me. And, you never intended to end our relationship?"

His head shakes. Jin's gaze carries deep lamentations. "It doesn't matter what my rationalizations were. The fact is I still ran away. I broke my promise to protect you and I know how much pain I've caused. I'm sorry."

"How was it your fault? I assumed the worst in you! I'm the one who's sorry!"

"Don't. I gave you every reason to doubt me. I'm not proud for leaving but I'm glad I did. It's true that Mei was never in my attention."

However confident he was seconds ago, his demeanor stiffens to uncertainty and anxiety. Jin looks away, embarrassed; more so, ashamed.

"You don't have to tell me."

"No, I want to." He turns back to fully convey his confession. "There were others who sought my company. I was tempted. The pain of desire was too much, I'd considered... I almost...but I didn't. I couldn't bring myself to hurt you, even though you'd never know my infidelity. I learned that I'm not my father. You've told me that before but I had to see it for myself. Bao Lai, I love you. If your answer remains the same as it was in Bei Ling, I will never again return to Ning. However, if this news has favorably changed your opinion of me, I wish to make you the happiest bride in the world."

The proposal is pure and genuine. Ardent love conveyed from Jin's tender gaze puts me in shock. That was the last thing I expected to hear. The first answer that comes to mind is that I can't.

"I'm sorry, Jin. I love you, too, but we shouldn't be together. You deserve better."

"Don't give me the excuse you used on San An. I wasn't aware you've chosen Lord Han Bei."

"I haven't. I can't. Jin, the truth is I love Han Bei, too. It's not fair to him when I keep thinking of you. The reverse is also true. It's not fair to you when I can't stop thinking of Han Bei. You both deserve better. I'm sorry. I've already made up my mind."

"To do what? If not Han Bei or me, then who?"

Pulling away from his grasp, my lowered head shake. It will sound unreasonable and he might think I'm irrational, but this was the only method I could conceive that would be fair for all of us.

"If I'd never left temple, seclusion would have been my life. So really, I'm not following any extraneous path. I'm not the right person for either of you. I'll do everything I can to ensure your happiness if you'll permit my meddling."

Looking up, I force a smile, only to find a hard frown over his mouth. In the next instant, Jin's arms encircle me with the same fervor from that day in the peach garden when I foolishly confessed my love and brought him down this painful path. Regret surges and consumes my composure. No matter how I try to force them back, useless tears begin flowing.

"Jin, d—"

"Be quiet. You haven't heard a word I said, so listen. I love you. So long as you love me, I couldn't care less how many other men are on your mind. When you have accepted me, each moment we are together, I will make you forget everyone else. Marry me, Bao Lai!"

"B-B-But that wouldn't be fair to you!"

"And I haven't been fair to you. I never should have left and you don't deserve to feel miserable because of my previous unrelenting doubts. I'll accept any fraction of your partiality. Anything to remain by your side!"

His kindness breaks down everything I've tried to restrain. Tears flood uncontrollably onto his robe. My arms clutch tightly around his back. A weight feels lifted off my chest. I've admitted to Jin the truth and he doesn't hate me. Still, as happy as I feel, Jin may be getting ahead of himself.

As I draw back, his long sleeve brushes the remaining tears from my face. When his lips lean in, my feet retreat a step.

"Jin, I can't begin to describe how happy you've made me. However, my coronation is next week. If we marry, you'll become Ning's emperor. I know how much you despise court, so is that arrangement fitting?"

He tries to hide the surprise from under those widened eyes. It's obvious Jin didn't consider the consequences of our union. He doesn't want authority. In fact, he fears the notion of power. On the other hand, Han Bei has been Ning's leader for many years. In my heart, I know the best thing I can do for my country is to bestow the Grand General the throne.

I wonder if I've been mouthing my thoughts again because Jin's demeanor suddenly softens and he's giving me a knowing look.

"Then marry him."

"W-What are you talking about?"

I look down, embarrassed for my bad habit and also saddened by my own selfishness. It's painful to hear Jin release me again.

"Two men not enough for you, Bao Lai? Why are you disappointed?"

"What is that supposed to mean?"

"It means you keep jumping to conclusions. You're absolutely right. Lord Han Bei is indisputably best for Ning. So, are you. This is your home. This is where you belong. You should make the right choice and marry Lord Han Bei. And, if you'll allow me, I would like to stay and become part of your family."

I don't understand what he's insinuating; or maybe, I do. That's why I'm stuttering incoherently.

Following a short burst of amused laughter, his fingers gently tap against my cheek. "I almost feel terrible for Lord Han Bei. I'll still have my beautiful lover without the political weights on my shoulders. Hopefully, he'll be too busy to hoard you all to himself most nights. And maybe most nights when he isn't busy, I'll still keep you hostage."

Jin reaches out and I instinctively fall back, unnerved by the amorous glance in his eyes. Is he insane?

"Are you insane?! Jin, y-you can't be serious!"

"On the contrary, I'm dead serious. I won't give you up. Not now. Not ever. Since you're stubbornly loyal to both Lord Han Bei and me, this is the only way."

"You're asking to become my consort. Do you hear how crazy that sounds?"

"Why is it crazy? Because my mother was also a consort? I am nothing like my parents, Bao Lai. You've taught me that."

"I'm glad you finally see that b-b-but, let's say that is best, Han Bei won't agree."

I throw out an easy excuse and he tosses one right back.

"If Lord Han Bei's feelings for you are reflective of mine, he will agree."

"For once, a Southerner is capable of sensibility and selflessness."

Oh, dear heavens. Han Bei's intruding airy tone turns my body to ice. My breathing stalls while I clumsily swing around as though my feet were made of lead to find the Grand General with a smirk across his face.

"Shouldn't I be the one in shock? This is how I must gather your secret love for me, through your confessions to another man?" Han Bei's smirk gradually becomes a smile. This is the happiest I've seen him in a long time.

"How long have you been eavesdropping?! I thought you were busy discussing marriage with Hua Ye."

"Are you accusing me of indecency? Hua Ye is my cousin. I thought you knew."

"That's not what I meant. Weren't you at Lady Ai's?"

Taking offense, Han Bei scoffs while moving closer. I furiously turn from one to the next while trying to determine which man is joking. Hopefully, both; and yet, seemingly neither.

"Don't insult me. A man of my quality doesn't require matchmaking from a hack. Besides, I have found the woman I love and only moments ago, learned of her returned affections."

"I am sorry you had to find out this way. In the end, does it matter? You must have heard my dilemma."

"Indeed and I also agree with Shu Jin."

"Are you nuts?! How could you possibly want this?"

"I love you and so does Shu Jin. You love him and also me. At this point, it's painfully obvious either we all become one family or remain alone forever. I can endure that for myself, but not for you. We played no small part in your dilemma. You mustn't be denied a future for our sakes."

"I agree. Ning belongs to you and Lord Han Bei. I am here for you, Bao Lai."

The two men nod in agreement; after which, Han Bei's smile morphs into a scowl. "I heard your plan, by the way, Prince Shu Jin. If you intend to keep her from me, I will respond in kind. I am a gentleman but I am also a man who will not tolerate being cheated."

"I will do no less than you, Lord Han Bei."

In mere moments, the friendly conversation is now a standoff. Sparks of jealousy are flying between the two. They're already asserting claims to territory when nothing has been accomplished.

"Wait a minute, you two. I never agreed!"

"You are stubborn that way and so it appears we have decided in your stead." Han Bei replies factually. "I will never relinquish you either, Bao Lai. Don't look so worried. There will be difficulties and we will quarrel, but at least a lively household will make a happy home for the children."

"Children?!"

"I still want ten," Jin asserts matter-of-factly.

"And I will not lose to him. I expect ten of my own."

"You're both insane!"

Smiling amorously, both of my beloveds slowly approach as I draw back anxiously. I know they are joking; at least, through their pretense advances. As for the rash plan to have one become my husband and the other—my lover, I fear they are serious. At the same time, exhilaration wells in my chest. If I can make both Jin and Han Bei happy through fulfilling my own selfish desires, it would be a dream come true.

"She will become my wife. I always have priority." Han Bei glares at his rival in the midst of their advances, as if to declare rules both must live by from this moment forth.

"Nonsense. She loved me first. I am here to serve in the pleasure of Her Highness. I have priority." Jin rebuffs coldly.

Under their squabble, I sense an understanding; mainly, the desire to tease me. They sure are putting on quite a show. I might as well return the favor. While the two continue engaging in their deadly confrontation, I pull up the hem of my robe and take the opportunity to flee. The two realize their folly, giving chase while I scramble away toward the direction of the Dream Pavilion.

"You're both crazy!" I shout over my shoulder.

Contentions from my suitors begin, lively and in good humor. I wonder who will be the first to catch me and who will be irritated for falling behind this time? Maybe, for the rest of our lives together, this same question will need an answer each night. The thought has crossed my mind and while I don't look forward to causing either of my beloved displeasure, I do look forward to the happiness I can bring to them each day.

I can't force back the smile on my face. While the future may be riddled with obscurity and unforeseen challenges, I vow this promise to myself: I will make Han Bei and Jin happy and always feel loved.

Be it fate or chance, I couldn't ask for more than the love of such wonderful men. I glance back over my shoulder, ecstatic by the acknowledgement that they are *my* wonderful men. The two halves of my heart are united and I finally feel whole, able to love them both unrestrained.

There's no denying it. I am one lucky girl.

The End.

www.ingramcontent.com/pod-product-compliance
Lightning Source LLC
Chambersburg PA
CBHW070531030726
47505CB00001B/7